Searching for

Quillquest Books

USA

Also by Frank Mosco

Fiction_____

The Whitemoon Crisis
Monkey
The Last Ghostrider
Cane's Gate

Nonfiction_____

Adventures in Black & White, Vol 1
People, Places & Things

Adventures in Black & White, Vol 2
Native American Dancers

Cybersafe
What you need to know to safely navigate the Internet

Film Scripts_____

The Last Jazz
Cane's Gate
A Monkey Tale

Visit the author's web site at;
www.frankmosco.com

Quillquest Books

A division of the Quillquest Publishing Co.
Quillquest Books, Quillquest Junior Books, Quillquest Classic Books, and
the sailing quill are the exclusive trademarks of the Quillquest Publishing Co.,
For information or comment regarding this book
contact: Quillquestbooks@msn.com

Trade paperback edition ISBN: 978-0-940075-11-5

First edition hardback published in the US by Quillquest Books,
ISBN-13: 978-0-940075-12-2, ISBN-10: 0-940075-12-1

This book is dedicated to:

My wife Kathy
A devoted Parrothead who would
love to live in a beach house on the moon.

🌴 a note from the author

Usually in most book forwards the author composes a lot of well crafted amiable praises demonstrating his appreciation for all those wonderful people who helped him create his literary masterpiece, giving recognition and thanks to the folks who provided inspiration and encouragement, who corrected his grammar and spelling, and checked for kinks in the story. He thanks them for contributing or helping refine his clever work into an epic piece of classic prose that all are convinced will stand the test of time and become a milestone in the annals of literature, if not civilization itself. Not to mention those who poured the tequila in times of frustration. *Usually*.

It's not that I'm ungrateful, but in the case of this particular book I doubt very much if any of those people would want to be mentioned and if they were they most likely wouldn't admit to any participation or association whatsoever. My guess is they would sooner be involved in a thirty-car pile up on a freeway. Not only that, they would probably sue me for defamation of character. So when I say I'm totally responsible for the contents of this book, I'm not only protecting the innocent but I really mean that I am totally responsible for the contents of this book, warts and all, and that's saying a lot because this book manages to break all the rules.

What rules, you asked? Well, aside from all the violations of accepted literary standards, this book is definitely *politically incorrect,* and these days that encompasses quite a large bank of rules, most of which aren't even written or recorded or legislated. They just kind of hang out there like coconuts in a palm tree 🌴 waiting for you to do or say the wrong thing so they can drop down on your head and ruin your day or your entire life. In this book however, I have attempted to be an *equal opportunity offender,* therefore, if I have somehow missed offending your particular race, religion, physical challenge, sexual preference, and political ideology –

I apologize. I'll try and do better and catch you next time around. But for all those oversensitive ethnocentrics out there without a sense of humor who think the world will come to an end due to a little social satire, and who think they have a right to be deeply offended, traumatized, or aggravated simply because they exist and share the same planet with us kids who have grown into adult size flip flops, well then what can I say? Just try not to drool on the pages. Also please limit the four letter words when you send me your letters of displeasure because I feed them to my dog Fudd and I love my dog Fudd so I certainly don't want him to be... *offended*.

Okay, so if you've read this far you're probably asking yourself, *"Self, I wonder just what the hell this guy is talking about?"* which is a perfectly legitimate question. In fact I asked myself that same question many times while I was writing this book. I said, "Self, just what the hell are you writing about?" Well, self never really came up with an answer other than to say, "Sorry dude, it's out of my control because the characters in the book just kind of magically took over the keyboard." So you see even though I had an idea of where the story was supposed to go, it seems those characters (most all of which are a little *socially askew*) ran away with the entire concept. But then, isn't that the way of things when it comes to *fiction*? (just ask any politician) So for now take this as a warning that you are about to encounter people, places, and events that may not exist in your world. On the other hand if by chance you can actually associate with these characters and their story you may want to seek counseling.

Also challenged will be your ability to read ethnic accents as well as bayou Cajun which I think may qualify as its own language. I know it was certainly a challenge to write. But don't worry, in the end it's not really that difficult to read; just kind of think outside the box as though it's some sort of phonetic 3-D experience, or better yet a juvenile tweet or text message. Regardless, I promise that if you have half a brain you will enjoy every page. (Note I said *half* a brain)

As for thanking anyone in particular for the inspiration and encouragement to write such a novel; except for a lot of impatient fans who hounded me on my web site to *"just hurry up and get the damn thing done,"* I have to credit Jimmy Buffett who is the plot's *MacGuffin* that brought it all together in the first place. Jimmy tends to have that affect on people. I also wish to thank Jimmy for giving us beach bums all those great times at the Trade Winds Lounge in old St. Augustine many years ago. (Oops, did I just give away *our* age?) That's right, I'm a veteran of the Trade Winds, the Milltop Tavern, The Paladin and a few other old haunts of the ancient city. So if I'm a demented author and story teller then Jimmy and those times can take partial credit for contributing to my creative state of mind, albeit not intentionally. A mind influenced by his lyrics and example as he continues *flying* through life with a smile and a song. In doing so JB has become an enduring part of our culture, so much so as to have spawned an entire new race of people known as *Parrotheads*, all of which I'm sure have the *brain half* that will enjoy this book the most. As for what they do with the other half I won't venture to guess.

Just one other note. After completing the book I came to realize that a more fitting title would have been *Fruitcakes* but being that's the name of one of the story's principal characters as well as the title of one of my favorite Jimmy Buffett CDs and song, I thought it best to just keep the title relevant to the story plot. After reading the book however, I'm sure you will have a few names to describe it as well, especially if you're one of those paranoid *Politically Correct* animals who are easily offended.

Mea culpa, mea culpa.

Searching for JIMMY BUFFETT

a novel by
frank mosco

chapter 1

Tropical Trade Winds Vigil

Sister Moonbeam-Goom-jigi was an idiot. And she was damn good at it too.

Sister Moonbeam-Goom-jigi started out as a middle class baby-boomer born in the late forties, who in spite of the distractions of the prosperous cultural evolution of the fifties and the drastic counter culture social revolution of the sixties, and in spite of being naturally beautiful and appealing, she had always managed to keep her feet planted firmly and responsibly on the ground. In doing so she held exceptional promise as a truly amazing academic achiever and a shining beacon and example of the great American dream. All things considered you would have thought Sister Moonbeam-Goom-jigi was bound for success and definitely on the fast track to, well... who the hell knows where? But instead, Sister Moonbeam-Goom-jigi was an idiot. In fact, she had long ago regressed far beyond the stage of idiot to become, in a slow docile hazy kind of way, just plain stupid. An incredible accomplishment indeed considering she was once thought to be near genius.

When in grade school she always sat dutifully in the front of the class, stayed fully focused, always followed directions and achieved straight A's on her report cards. When she was in high school she sat in the front of the class, stayed fully focused, always followed directions and again achieved straight A's, graduating *summa cum laude*. Then again in college Sister Moonbeam-Goom-jigi sat in the front of the class, stayed fully focused, always followed directions, achieved straight A's and graduated *egregia cum laude*. In fact she would have graduated *maxima cum laude* but for the simple reason she refused to have sex with her Applied Logics professor during her freshman year, something she appearently didn't consider to be very logical. Unfortunately for her the man carried a grudge because as a coed predator he had never before failed to conquer his young prey. Still he gave her an A in the course of course; he had no choice because he could not ignore or deny her achievements, but it was an A with an asterisk. This resulted in Sister Moonbeam-Goom-jigi graduating a single asterisk short of *maxima cum laude* and instead graduating with only a respectable *egregia cum laude*. Still it was a feat accomplished by very, very few students anywhere. Most surprisingly however, her entire life of study, including and especially the essence of the course in logic, must not have left much of an impression because in spite of all her efforts and achievements... Sister Moonbeam-Goom-jigi became an idiot.

Sister Moonbeam-Goom-jigi's real name was Frances Camilla Freewater, or at least that was her name until 1969 when she sailed off to Ghana in West Africa to work on her Masters thesis. The scholarly work was to be a complete analytical evaluation of the evolution of Ghana from a fragmented slave-trading territory to a consolidated unstable occasional half-ass republic and how it affected the indigenous population morally, socially, and religiously; an ambitious and impressive undertaking to say the least. In truth however, she wasn't quite sure why she chose that particular course of study or why she chose that particular part of the world to pursue that particular course of study other than the fact she had a schoolgirl crush on Sidney Poitier at the time and somehow managed to connect the two. As implied, logic often escaped her. On the other hand Sister Moonbeam-Goom-jigi's decisions were certainly understandable. Her dutiful attention to detail and all those high marks and academic achievements were indeed perfectly understandable with the realization that Frances Camilla Freewater was a *total recall* who could read, remember, and regurgitate just about anything and everything; quite an enviable talent. Her problem however, was that she was not only a total recall but also a total ditz with all the deductive powers of a plastic flamingo. If she did actually possess any form of original thought or so much as an ounce of common sense it was most likely used up each morning when she managed to tie her shoes... when she wore shoes.

Frances came to change her name two months after her arrival in Ghana while she was researching how she was going to approach the research necessary to achieve her ultimate research. Without guidance she had a way of complicating such things, and having absolutely no ability to conjure up the necessary original thought required for such an endeavor or how to construct her thesis of which she knew nothing, she found herself at a total loss and academic quandary in which she reached an intellectual impasse, or to put it bluntly, a deductive coma. In the field as it were, there were no instruction manuals or written study guides to give her direction. There was no material to memorize, no fellow students to answer occasional questions, and no librarians to provide assistance and guidance and to keep her on track. There was simply no one anywhere to give her any help or advice at all, not even any sex crazed pseudo intellectual statutory rapist Applied Logic professors. No one that is, except Lord Reginald Baxter Framingham III whom it seems was always full of demonstrative counsel.

Lord Framingham was a young Englishman who went by the informal name of Skeeter, or most often Lord Skeeter. But in truth he was not an English Lord at all. In fact he wasn't even British, though everyone assumed he was because of an alluring British accent he had perfected while attending school as a theater major at the University of California in Berkeley. He chose to be a theater major because he thought he was as talented as Gregory Peck, as handsome and dynamic as Errol Flynn, and though he was only five-foot-four and three-quarters inches short, thought he was just as manly as the six-foot-four action hero John Wayne. Lord Skeeter was actually from Cranberry, Pennsylvania, son of a fairly successful immigrant Croatian-Jewish butcher who claimed to be a non-kosher Polish owner of his very own meat and deli shop. Claiming to be Polish made for an impressive uptick in business since they lived in a predominantly Christian Polish neighborhood. Hence the origin of how Lord Skeeter obtained the talent to be who he wasn't. Lord Skeeter's real name was Georgie Souseburger. Georgie Souseburger, in addition to being the beneficiary and heir to the Souseburger Meat & Cheese Emporium, was simply a Jewish pretend Polish-Croatian pretending to be British.

Sent to college to gain a little knowledge, it seems all Georgie, or Lord Skeeter, wanted to do was learn how to score. Capitalizing on his acting talent and the popular British music invasion of the sixties, Georgie's near perfect counterfeit British accent paid off handsomely and got him invited to all the best and coolest parties on and around campus where he could do exactly that, learn how to score... repeatedly. Also his being in such demand saved him tons of money because as the always popular trophy party guest and companion he rarely if ever had to pay for anything. Certanly an appealing state of affairs for a young non-kosher Jewish pretend Polish-Croatian British young man on a college budget. The creative fraudulent handle of *Lord Framingham* also made him a popular fixture at many prestigious social events around town where he often mixed with the rich and famous, again never failing to get him laid, especially when he claimed to be a personal friend of Paul McCartney, one of the world famous Beatles. Georgie Souseburger, alias Lord Skeeter, falsely and happily existed in his idea of heaven on earth, which was far and wide removed from the prospect of packing unkosher pork sausage in Cranberry, Pennsylvania.

It was following one of those extended socialy prestigious psychedelic sixties parties that eventually migrated aboard a private jet, and while Lord Skeeter was getting laid on that same private jet by the prominent well known pineapple heiress who owned it, and because during the exhilaration of sex with said pineapple princess he let his accent slip back to that of a Cranberry, Pennsylvania local yokel, that he suddenly found himself a stranded phony Englishman in Ghana, unceremoniously bounced off the aircraft during a refueling stop. It was there he eventually met and came to mooch off the kindness of the beautiful but naïve and gullible Frances Camilla Freewater. Gullible enough it seems to believe just about everything Lord Skeeter had to say.

"What you need are changes," he told the credulous and confused Frances. "A change of character to loosen the intellectual reins, a change of soul to free up your inhibitions, a change of name to divorce yourself from the bonds and demons of society. Changes," he said, "changes in latitude and changes in attitude. Oh, and by the by, did I mention that I know Paul McCartney?"

Of course Frances had no damn idea what the hell he was talking about, but she concluded that he was after all an English Lord and with his sophisticated attitude and accent anything he said simply had to be true. She knew this because she had watched recycled BBC TV programming on National Education Television for many years and as a result believed, as do most Englishmen, that all things British are proper, correct, and far more superior to most all things American or all things in the world in general. And so the susceptible young Miss Freewater surrendered both her money and her virginity, never once questioning Lord Skeeter's second-hand drug inspired Timothy Leary bullshit sixties wisdom. Nor did she question the consequences of the funny little pills he gave her with the promise they would expand her mind. In that Lord Skeeter certainly was correct. For Frances Camilla Freewater's mind expanded so much that she literally forgot who the hell she was for nearly a month, and in fact began forgetting almost everything most all the time. Then, not knowing who she was but liking who she was becoming, she expanded her mind even further until she decided to be one with the universe and a born again flower child known as Sister Moonbeam. She would later add the African Buli language name of *Goom-jigi*, which translated means *peace.*

The name Goom-jigi came to her while she and Lord Skeeter were on a footbound safari in search of exotic mind altering mushrooms. While squatting and taking a shit inside a very large hollow tree near Ghana's Daka River she had a spiritual experience.

"Peace. Peace. Goom-jigi," she heard a strange voice echo magically all around her inside the cavernous hollow tree.

"Yes. Who's there?" she asked.

"Goom-jigi," came the mysterious voice again.

"I'm here. I hear you," answered Sister Moonbeam. "I'm here. Tell me what you want. I'm listening."

"GOOM-JIGI DAMMIT! GOOM-JIGI!"

When Sister Moonbeam emerged from inside the tree full of inspiration and excited about the spiritual experience that took place during her number two, she discovered her number one companion, Lord Skeeter, was nowhere to be found. Little did she know he had been captured by tribal warriors, hacked up with machetes and his various parts distributed among the tribal chiefs of Ghana. The violent act was an effort on the part of angry tribesmen to demonstrate British vulnerability and mortality so as to bring the rest of the tribes together to rise up against the government and fight the foreign oil men who had come to steal their land.

Lord Skeeter's death was a dreadful incident to be sure but then he had brought about his own demise through his own ignorance of the region's current affairs and his often-practiced counterfeit British demeanor.

"Good day chaps," he had said with his best British flair when he bumped into the small band of native gorilla fighters who had come along while Sister Moonbeam was still occupied inside the hollow tree. "Out for a walk in the bush are we? Allow me to introduce myself. I am Lord Reginald Baxter Framingham the third, current of the great Royal British Empire Oil Conglomerate. God bless the Queen."

Lord Skeeter heard a British oil company was poking around the neighborhood and thought he'd take advantage. He lied of course as he always did when trying to impress anyone and everyone he met. This time however, the English accent and the mention of oil were just enough to raise the gorilla fighters' ire. As a result they quickly encircled him with threatening glares of bad intent and gleaming machetes, leading Lord Skeeter to realize he had pretty much screwed the pooch by offering up the wrong lie at the wrong time and in the wrong place, for it was in fact that very same British company that was attempting to steal their land and drill for oil and as such certainly not the time to pretend to be a tight-ass Brit.

"Gentlemen, please. Can't you see I'm a man of peace? I come to pump black gold from the earth and bring you great fortune and prosperity. I come to deliver a whole new world of opportunity and riches with um… good stuff like, uh… hermetically sealed foods, indoor plumbing, mopeds, Bazooka bubble gum, and Jack Purcell sneakers."

The warrior tribesmen were not impressed, not to mention the fact they hardly understood a damn word he was saying. All they knew was Lord Skeeter's enunciation and demeanor seemed British and that was all they needed to know - plus he said something about oil.

"Peace. Peace." said Lord Skeeter as they backed him against the backside of the large hollow tree in which Sister Moonbeam squatted to relieve herself. "Goom-jigi," he said, drawing from his very limited knowledge of African languages that he had picked up while attending an African/American Cultural Awareness seminar at Berkley that was sponsored jointly by the Berkley Society for Social Enlightenment for World Peace and the Black Panthers. "Goom-jigi. Goom-jigi," he nervously continued as the tribal fighters moved in slowly, threatening, raising their machetes. "GOOM-JIGI," repeated Lord Skeeter, growing ever more concerned and desperate. "GOOM-JIGI DAMMIT! GOOM-JIGI!"

Like an FBI raid on a shack full of Disney ticket counterfeiters, it was all over in a matter of seconds as Lord Reginald Baxter Framingham III, alias Skeeter, alias Lord Skeeter, alias Georgie Souseburger of Cranberry, PA, was lopped, chopped, diced, sliced, bagged, and in the mail, leaving little Sister Moonbeam alone to her inspirational poo poo inside her organically grown port-o-let, and also leaving her to somehow believe Lord Skeeter's last words that had echoed through the hollow tree were some sort of soulful epiphany or spiritual revelation. It was Sister Moonbeam's very own incredible burning bush Moses moment in which she had eagerly absorbed every single pulsating echoing syllable. Eagerly done because Sister Moonbeam, with the aid of Lord Skeeter's magic little pills, had become… an idiot.

Following the loss of Lord Skeeter, Sister Moonbeam, now the divinely self-christened Sister Moonbeam-*Goom-jigi*, wandered the Ghana countryside like a retard in a house of mirrors, harvesting and partaking of strange mushrooms that grew in elephant shit, talking to trees, bees, birds, and animals, and surviving off the kindness of local natives who thought it would be bad mojo to do otherwise simply because they all thought she wasn't all there in the head, which of course she wasn't.

Sister Moonbeam-Goom-jigi did eventually make her way back home to the USA thanks to the kindly good graces of an old French priest and three Portuguese nuns who eagerly shipped her off on the very first available boat. They did so gladly and not caring where the boat was bound because they quickly discovered Sister Moonbeam-Goom-jigi was a stoner, a total flake, and a hopeless idiot, and decided her presence was agonizingly unbearable if not somehow sacrilegious. Also because Sister Moonbeam-Goom-jigi had taken to dancing around their mission boob-free-native-naked wearing only a few flowers in her hair and an artistically woven grass g-string trimmed with a few periwinkle shells and a lion's tooth, which was beginning to adversely affect the old French priest who was beginning to look ravenously upon the middle-aged Portuguese nuns. So the nuns, in desperation, dressed her in a nun's habit and shipped her off.

As she departed the magic of Africa on that slow boat to America, Sister Moonbeam-Goom-jigi reflected on her Dark Continent experience, often thinking of and dearly missing Lord Skeeter who had taught her so much about life and universal bullshit, most of which she had forgotten because she had overly expanded her mind. Sometimes she even missed the three hundred thirty-seven pound Ashanti Chieftain named Floyd who forced her to marry him against her will and was so pleased with her sexual performance the night of the wedding that he rewarded her with a sack of sacred stones. It was a night of magic that was for the most part imagined or fantasized by Chief Floyd just before he had passed out. He had passed out because Sister Moonbeam-Goom-jigi had persuaded him to try some of her funny looking smelly little elephant shit mushrooms. Then, fortunately for Sister Moonbeam-Goom-jigi, Chief Floyd was killed the very next day while participating in a coup to overthrow the government, a coup inspired by the death of a British oil man called Lord Framingham, which is when she had been rescued by the Portuguese Nuns and French priest.

🌴

Years later, Frances Camilla Freewater, alias Sister Moonbeam-Goom-jigi, having evolved into a total airhead with the wherewithal of a hubcap, sat in the Tropical Trade Winds Lounge in the old city of St. Augustine, Florida sipping on a tall cool glass of Boone's Farm apple wine - with a twist. Among other things, she was a misguided creature of the sixties who somehow survived and managed to slide into the seventies, and who favored the natural high of natural herbs, had an insatiable appetite for banana pancakes and Spam, possessed an expanded but fried mind full of useless and irretrievable *egregia cum laude* knowledge, yet somehow still possessed the idiosyncratic ability to identify nearly every kind of sea shell found on nearly every beach on the coast. She was an eccentric yet uncomplicated child of nature who required little, desired little, possessed even less, and quite often willingly rolled over and gave her all to any man who could make her laugh. She had it all, she would often say; "…a small cottage on the beach, the sun in the morning and the moon at night, everything any child of the universe could possible want and everything in the world anyone could possibly need." Not to mention a 1955 Nash Metropolitan convertible. Oh, and a sack of sacred stones courtesy of the late large Ashanti Chief Floyd, although she never could seem to remember where she put them. However, none of that was important now because after all her magnificent academic achievements and all of her forgotten exotic travels and adventures, Sister Moonbeam-Goom-jigi had finally found… *love*.

His name was Jimmy Buffett, a relatively unknown musician who sang and played the guitar at the Tropical Trade Winds Lounge years before. Each night when he played she would sit there at her usual little table near the small stage and watch and listen. She listened first to the entertaining monologue and folksy music of that great troubadour Gamble Rogers, and then would laugh at the antics of the object of her affection Jimmy Buffett as the two men joined together in musical harmony and story telling humor. But she was most drawn to and would listen most intently when her Jimmy performed alone. It was during those special moments that the chattering patrons, the aroma of stale beer and liquor, and the lingering smoky environment of the small dark lounge surrounding her would somehow simply dissipate, leaving only herself and her Jimmy floating through her fluffy cloudy mushroom or hashish or cannabis influenced fuzzy universe. She sat wrapped in the magic of his talented fingers drawing across the strings of his instrument, his voice causing each fiber of her soul and loins to tingle with emotion. She would close her eyes and fix his winning smile, long fair hair and exaggerated mustache in her mind. She would mentally embrace him as he became her Romeo, her Heathcliff, her Lancelot... her Elvis. It was a love like none before and none that would ever be again. And it was all in her damn imagination.

It began one night in Sister Moonbeam-Goom-jigi's newly adopted home of St. Augustine, Florida while she was wandering the waterfront, admiring and tripping on the soothing movement of the reflections on the water's surface of the lights of the old city's landmark Euro style Bridge of Lions. She heard the distant sound of music and laughter and it drew her to the nearby Tropical Trade Winds Lounge where she first discovered and was captured by the man of her dreams. Sister Moonbeam-Goom-jigi was looking especially radiant that evening after having spent the day at the beach skipping through the surf, singing with the shore birds, and feasting on a bowl of fresh strawberries and Spam cubes. Her radiant appeal didn't go unnoticed and he came to her during the break, sat at her table and struck up a conversation. The moment he joined her and smiled she just knew they were soul mates and she would never love another man. "I could feel the magic right away," she would often say as she recalled the occasion, which was impressive and fairly remarkable because having long since expanded her mind she now remembered very little for very long. But she did recall that he asked her name and a few other questions and she thinks she answered. She remembered he made a few polite jokes and she thinks she laughed. And she remembered as he rose to leave her table and return to the stage that he touched her hand and when he did a slow arc of electricity flowed straight to her heart... or some other organ. It was at that moment it all began for Sister Moonbeam-Goom-jigi - and it was at that moment it all ended for Jimmy Buffett, for it wasn't difficult for him to realize that Sister Moonbeam-Goom-jigi was a crazy-ass name, even for a near incoherent burned out nut case of a hippie flower child. And though he was a truly fun loving kind of guy he had no desire to enter into a relationship of any kind with a walking talking vegetable.

Each night she sat at the same table. Each night Jimmy laughed and sang and played his music, politely acknowledging her presence with a wink and a smile. Then one evening there was only Gamble Rogers. Again the next night there was only Gamble, and the next night... until she finally realized her Jimmy had departed.

"Where is my Jimmy?" she asked Joe the bartender.

"Moved on," said Joe. "Gone down to the keys I think. Yeah, think he said something about heading south down to Key West. But I'm sure he'll be back," he said. "Don't you worry, Sister. He'll be back some day."

And so each night Sister Moonbeam-Goom-jigi continued to plop her ass in the same chair at the same table, drinking the same Boone's Farm apple wine - with a twist. She sat alone, waiting for Jimmy Buffett to return. Waiting and waiting… and waiting…

More than three and a half decades later Sister Moonbeam-Goom-jigi continues to plop her now middle-aged-plus chunky ass in the same chair in the same dark corner, except now she's listening to a four-piece band made up of graying semi-bald sixty-something musicians playing sixty-something oldie goldie rock and roll.

Always the first to arrive and the last to leave, forlorned yet hopeful, she waits for her Jimmy. The first to arrive and the last to leave each night, all the while hoping and praying he will return. Three and a half decades later she sits and waits and sips her Boone's Farm apple wine – with a twist.

And Sister Moonbeam-Goom-jigi is still an idiot.

chapter 2
It's a Boy!

"He is soooo hot, but… duh," said the slow strolling brunette as she checked out the young man surfing about forty yards off the beach.

"Oh yuh, but, like, a weird dude. Like… strange, ya know? Surfs alone and stuff, and… yuh, like, he never talks to anybody, ya know?" said the really gorgeous girl wearing a nearly illegal yellow thong bikini as she slowly ambled along the beach in stride with her friend. She was beautiful with perfect long blonde hair, a perfect ass, and perfect perky tits. For teeny-beachers both girls were made of real pin up quality stuff, but possessing a combined minimal amount of talent good for nothing except punching out meaningless text messages and tweets. For the most part they possessed the collective intellect of a perfect kernelless corncob with a vocabulary consisting primarily of two words being, *yeah* (pronounced yuh sounding like duh) and *like* (pronounced, well, like *like*, duh). The words were interchangeably meaningless but somehow meaningful to anyone under the age of about fifteen or people who scored a mere twelve on an IQ test. Their only other talent was cruising and shopping the mall in order to fashionably dress down at high expense. In this day and age it's not cheap or easy trying to look like an under-aged slut.

The girls watched the impressive young surfer catch a not so impressive three foot wave, ride a few yards, cut back when the wave petered out, then settle down on his board and start to paddle in.

"Wul, like, yuh, and... like, most definitely in the weird class, like ya know," stated the blonde.

"And, oh yuh, like, I hear his mom's a crazy woman who, like, walks the beach at night half naked and, like, talks to the moon and stuff and junk," said the other girl as she surveyed the beach for boys to ignore. "And, wul, heard she's, wul, like... into African jungle magic stuff or some kind of shit. I mean, like... wul, duh, what's up with that?"

"Oh yuh. Like... duh. And... like... I wonder if he's crazy too. Like maybe a DNA tard or aut... um, automistic or somethin'?" questioned the blonde.

"Wul, like... can tards surf?"

"Wul, um... like, guess so, huh."

"Wul, yuh."

"Oh my god. That reminds me," said the blonde.

"Oh like, yuh? What?" asked her friend, growing excited with anticipation of an unanticipated change of subject.

Being they were both ADD poster girls, spur of the moment changes in subject weren't the norm although always exciting because they seemed so rare for both of them. Most of the time the only thing they ever talked about was boys, none of whom ever met their pseudo slut standards which was completely based on the rule, *would that boy ever make it on MTV, and if so, would he be accepted and hook up with their queens of slut idols, Madonna and/or Lady Gaga and make the grade according toMadanna's inspirational illustrated book on sex.* Most likely the only book they ever read. The only other occasional subject changes usually involved something about hair or gross body parts.

"Hold on, 'kay? I'll remember and figure it out in a minute cause I forgot, 'kay? But just hold on, 'kay? Cause like... wul... um..."

While the two parading goddesses continued strutting along the beach trying to remember something that would never threaten the existence of mankind, their object of momentary interest, the young surfer, paddled to shore, threw back his long blonde hair, snatched up his board and set off in a trot for a small oddly painted cottage a few hundred yards away.

The little cottage, painted in a Picassolistic arrangement of varied shades of purple, green, and yellow, stood out along the beach like a birth mark on the forehead of a Norwegian albino. It sat smartly in the center of a ten-acre piece of natural dune and palmetto covered beachfront. Next-door on its left rose a new six story condominium complex and on the right a sprawling new resort hotel. On the weedy white sand around the small wooden cottage laid the results of decades of beachcombing in the form of washed up artistically shaped faded driftwood, the empty shell of a large leatherback sea turtle, glass Portuguese fish net balls, Styrofoam lobster trap float markers, and mounds of conch shells, all mixed with pieces of ship's rope and fish net. Depending on your perspective, the stuff lying around the little house comprised either an ocean junkyard or a near forty-year time capsule and treasury of artistic beach combing memories. A sun beaten paint-chipped lattice shaded deck wrapped around the ocean side of the old place until it met a slightly askew carport on the side, under which sat a rusty bicycle with only one wheel and a rusty old moped scooter with two flat ones.

The porch sported no less than 38 wind chimes created from just about anything that could hang from a string and make noise. With each breeze that blew off the sea the chimes sang out in an unharmonious symphony of dings, dongs, clinks, and clanks. Across one corner of the deck stretched a hammock on which rested a few handmade pillows sewn from a combination of the remnants of a paisley velour bean bag, old blue jeans, and a used Wal-mart Navaho print herculon car seat cover. In another corner sat a rickety old papa-san chair in the center of which on a large round faded floral print cushion laid an eight-pound multi-colored scraggly-haired ugly little who-done-it dog with an out of kilter protruding bottom tooth and no left ear. His name was Fruitcake and he was stretched out bottom side up, balls to the sun, which was his preferred and usual position. As dogs go, Fruitcake wasn't much to look at and wasn't very ambitious. He knew the key to life was simply having a steady source of food and the freedom to laze bottom side up, balls to the sun. Next to Fruitcake's throne sat a hashish bong, a champagne glass, an empty Boone's Farm wine bottle, and an anemic aloe plant, none of which were actually his, all resting on top of an antique flower stand covered with five layers of faded crackled paint, mostly pink and yellow.

The young surfer cradled his much seasoned dinged and duck-taped surfboard snugly under his arm as he trotted along the well-worn hot sandy path to his home. As he approached the cottage he heard the all too familiar sound of his mother's favorite singer-songwriter coming through the open windows and screen door and he smiled. It took only a few notes of the song to drift via the salt air and through the tall sea oats to his ear for him to recognize the tune. It was the one about a beach house on the moon, the one she swore was written just for her. He trotted up the steps to the deck, parked his board against the wall in the corner behind Fruitcake's papa-san chair and made a final visual sweep of the beach and the horizon, noting with some concern the dark clouds in the far distance. He then entered the house.

Upon entry there immediately came the recognizable aroma of something cooking in the kitchen. It was another of his mother's original recipes, a spicy mix of rice, pineapple, mango, black-eyed peas, and honey barbecue Spam that would probably come with a side of banana cake, or banana pudding, or banana Jell-O or banana something. Maybe even banana sherbet. She called this main dish

Creola, which is what she called a lot of her original recipe main dishes. In fact, nearly everything Sister Moonbeam-Goom-jigi ever cooked in her little one-butt kitchen was an original recipe simply because she couldn't remember from one meal to the next what the hell she had cooked before. Her cooking decisions were usually based on her desires at the moment, which in turn were based on whatever herb happened to influence her decision process at the time, plus whatever was available in the kitchen. In other words, Sister Moonbeam-Goom-jigi's cooking adventures were as much or more artistically influenced and driven by a false sense of hunger as they were by any sense of nutrition. As to why she called her creations Creola, she wasn't quite sure. It was either because her very first Creola dish was supposed to be Cajun but actually turned out to be an international island mystery, or because it reminded her of something she couldn't remember that she thought had something to do with her long lost love, Jimmy Buffett.

On the other hand there were those days when she forgot to shop, or forgot to cook, or just forgot everything, and so she would at the last minute simply do up a couple TV dinners, or simply give her son the money to trot over to the beachside Beachcomber Restaurant where he could get his favorite food of all time, a cheeseburger. The rest of the time nearly every original recipe that emerged from the little galley in the little green, purple, and yellow beach house was labeled Creola, and more often than not tasted much the same in spite of the varied contents or difference in color. Although it required an acquired taste for consumption it was somehow healthy, as evidenced by the more than healthy constitution of her son. Healthy or not, the boy had no problem in that regard, having eaten her cooking for the past 14 years. He would always dutifully partake of his mother's kitchen creations with a smile and a nod of approval, and a large glass of milk to kill the indigestion sometimes caused by her exotic spices. And of course there was always something baking in the oven. His mother had heard somewhere long ago that all mothers should always have something baking in the oven so through force of habit she always seemed to have something baking in the oven. She wasn't sure why but did it just the same.

Fruitcake picked up on the Creola aroma and as always this motivated him to conclude his sun bathing and trot on in through the hole in the screen door then park his ass in the center of the kitchen. There he sat ready to slide under the table because there he knew he would be the recipient of the more unpalatable but filling portions of Sister Moonbeam-Goom-jigi's Creola creation of the day. But Fruitcake didn't always depend on his nose to determine when it was dinner time. He also possessed other attributes, one of which was the ability to telepathically anticipate what his humans were up to in order to be ready to consume food. His clairvoyant abilities also included participation in their conversations which when it involved Sister Moonbeam-Goom-jigi was sometimes difficult, even for a talented dog like Fruitcake. This ability came about one day when Sister Moonbeam-Goom-jigi mistakenly fed Fruitcake a generous mix of her mood arrangers and mushrooms that sent him on a two day journey through doggy wonderland. When he returned to normal he wasn't quite normal.

"Mom, I'm back," announced the young man as he lifted the lid and peaked into the pot to see what color Creola was on the menu for the day.

"That's nice dear," said his mother from a yoga position in the center of the living room floor. She had been frozen there, her right leg crossed and resting in the bend of her left arm for the last 15 minutes while trying to remember what came next, not that she could achieve it. "Uh... what was that again? Who's here?" she asked.

"It's me, Mom."

"Oh. Okay."

"Fruitcake's in the kitchen, mom," the boy announced as he checked to discover a pan of half-baked cookies in the oven, then shook his finger at the dog. Sister Moonbeam-Goom-jigi had a rule that Fruitcake was never allowed in the kitchen at mealtime, though she never enforced the rule because she never remembered it. The boy always informed on Fruitcake if only to maintain a clear conscience. He was honest to a fault that way. Actually he encouraged the dog's dinner participation just in case the Creola of the day wasn't quite up to par. Fruitcake knew the ritual well. The finger was the signal for him to exit but instead he always took it as an order to hide his scraggy little hairy butt under the kitchen table where he wouldn't be seen.

"You're in the kitchen. Oh, okay. Fix yourself something to eat," she replied, forgetting she had cooked dinner and still contemplating her next yoga move. "Um… is there something on the stove?"

"Yes, Mom."

"Oh, okay. You can eat that too if you want."

"Okay, Mom."

"And is there something in the oven?" she asked.

"Yes, Mom."

"Oh, um you can turn that off."

"Okay."

"Um… is there something in the oven?" she asked again, either forgetting he had answered or forgetting she had already asked.

"Yes, mom."

"Oh, okay."

The boy checked the cookies again, pulled them out of the oven and placed them on the counter. It didn't seem to surprise him that each cookie was a different size and a different shape, nor did it surprise him that the cookies were blue. He was a good boy and unlike his mother he wasn't an idiot, though like his mother, had he been an idiot he probably wouldn't have known, for he was to say the least, a bit naive. He was born at home and home-schooled by a genius idiot mother who managed to teach him to read, write and function in spite of herself, which actually meant he was pretty much self-educated, and somehow successfully. Being home-schooled, or the product of benevolent neglect, a general loner by choice, and preferring the wide open and peaceful spaces of the beach and ocean, he was happily ignorant of most of the rest of the world and its many complications. He readily accepted and never questioned his mother's philosophy of being perfectly happy with only the bare necessities of life and had yet reached a point in his life where curiosity would surpass his instincts of right and wrong. Additionally, unlike his mother, his name wasn't Goom-Jigi or even Freewater. His name was James William Buffett Jr, the name and his birth both being the product of a hallucination had by Sister Moonbeam-Goom-jigi while she was being carnally had by another. She called her son *Bean* for short and she had no idea or memory as to why.

It all happened back in 1995 and began, of course, at the Tropical Trade Winds Lounge. There she sat in the Trade Winds at that same table sipping that same Boone's Farm apple wine – with a twist, and enjoying what she thought was the same high from a newfound avenue of drug induced nirvana, when all of a sudden there came his song. *His song!* Then there came another of his songs! Could it be, she wondered? After all this time, could it be my Jimmy? She donned her glasses and parted the cloud inside her brain just enough to discover the man on stage from which emanated all the Jimmy songs. Happy songs of sun, sand, sailing, sailors, islands, cheeseburgers, and a place called Margaritaville. It was him! It was him at last, she thought in a bubbly spurt of intoxicated joy. She swooned and crooned and just plain melted as the melodies and lyrics flowed from the stage and over her half empty head.

He was back! After all those years, after decades of patient anticipation, he was back. All the while she had been listening to his music, following his travels and career and his rise to become a world famous cultural icon. All those years memorizing and forgetting the thousands of lyrics to hundreds of his songs. Then memorizing and forgetting them again and again… and again. Absorbing all that was Jimmy, his humor, his philosophy, his acceptance of life fantastic and his wonderful ability to spread and share it all with the world. She absorbed it all like a sponge as though it was a religious experience, and in fact it became her religion, her solace, her soul, and the very meaning of life. Then, like the Creola she whipped up each day in her little one-butt kitchen, she would forget it all and start over. For Sister Moonbeam-Goom-jigi regarding the center of her universe Jimmy Buffett, life was a continuous journey of discovery, even though she had no damn clue where it would take her or for that matter where the hell it had already taken her. Much like a small child who discovers something new at each turn on each day, each day Sister Moonbeam-Goom-jigi would rediscover her love and longing for Jimmy Buffett.

On this night at the Tropical Trade Winds lounge her Jimmy had returned. He had returned! He didn't really look like Jimmy but then in the low light of the lounge and considering all the years that had passed; she didn't count that against him. And the voice seemed just a little different than what she remembered, just a little, a difference of which she just couldn't quite place at the moment, even though she listened to Jimmy's music exclusively all day, every day.

But for her on this night those differences were insignificant, just minor concerns, because on this night a determined Sister Moonbeam-Goom-jigi was not going to be denied and let her Jimmy get away. Not this time. And so her fuzzy logic of love ruled the day and at first opportunity she corralled her singing soul mate into an all night marathon of herbal inspired syncopated sex. So engulfed was she at this wonderful coupling that she failed to realize her rapture was the result of a coming together with a low budget lounge singer from Oshkosh, Wisconsin, named Seymour Torborg Svenson who lived and traveled in a rusty 1972 six cylinder Chevy van that ran on only five cylinders, sounded like a percolator coffee pot, and consumed 40 weight oil like it was free government cheese. Seymour was working his way along the east coast crooning Buffett songs for fifty bucks a night plus drinks. He was on his was south to Miami, his final destination where he intended to gain fame and fortune and never again have to shovel snow.

Following their rapturous coupling, Seymour was up and gone with the sunrise, heading for a gig in Daytona Beach after which he would be again on his way south. And so by the time she opened her eyes that morning he was miles away and for a while Sister Moonbeam-Goom-jigi wasn't quite sure if the entire experience was real or a dream until she became pregnant soon after. By then Seymour was crooning Jimmy tunes in a seafood restaurant in Satellite Beach and about to bed yet another middle aged beauty. Seymour wasn't picky.

"Of course he loves me. He just couldn't stay that's all. My Jimmy belongs to the world now, to his fans," she told herself as she wandered along the beach chewing on a Spam sandwich.

Typically Sister Moonbeam-Goom-jigi had no problem at all rationalizing and convincing herself of the reasons and purpose of events that took place and affected her life. It was all in the stars, she would say. Such as the time she fell into the dolphin tank at Marineland or when she got arrested for reckless driving in her Nash Metropolitan at the intersection of Route 3 and A1A while sitting dead still for twenty minutes waiting for the stop sign to change. The

Marineland incident was an unavoidable act of destiny, she reasoned. Necessary for her to discover she could communicate with dolphins, a psychic gift she claimed to have obtained in a big hollow tree somewhere in West Africa. And the traffic incident, she angrily informed Judge Weingarberger, would not have occurred if the stop sign had functioned properly and turned green like it was supposed to. And that it was totally illogical to write her a ticket for a moving violation of reckless driving when she was just sitting still. Judge Weingarberger was hard pressed to argue the point and dismissed the case.

For the longest time after that she would visit the dolphins at Marineland just down the road to console them by informing them their captivity brought joy to little children. And on the way, showing a streak of rebellion, she would always refuse to wait for the stop sign to change. In fact, as for that stubborn Route 3, State Road A1A intersection stop sign; after a hundred and twenty-seven letters of protest from Sister Moonbeam-Goom-jigi, most all of them written because she didn't remember writing the one before, the judge finally ordered a traffic light to be installed. A very large traffic light at the cost to the county of nearly $300,000.

"My Jimmy left me again," she mumbled to a nearby seagull through a mouth full of spamwich. "But," she rationalized, "I know he came back to me for a reason. He came back to show his love and leave me something, the next best thing possible – he left me a baby."

And so it came to pass as the sun rose far out beyond the surf on the horizon, a new being had entered her life. Somehow, in spite of herself and in spite of all the questionable mentally liberating substances of which she partook on a regular basis, and with the assistance of her old burned out friend Joe the bartender who always stocked a well dated supply of Boone's Farm apple wine just for her, and who was acting as a midwife because he once watched

33

a labrador retriever have puppies, there came into existence one James William Buffett Jr., affectionately called Bean.

And so little Bean Buffett's saga began, born right there to Sister Moonbeam-Goom-jigi in her little Picassolistic purple, green, and yellow cottage by the sea. Admittedly, Joe the bartender was a little stumped with the dilemma of that thing connected to the baby's belly and as a result young Bean ended up with an outy. And as far as the circumcision went, well, midwife Joe skipped that procedure altogether on the grounds of gender empathy and a fear of messing it up with dire consequences. And somehow, even after experiencing all the pain and the miracle of birth - Sister Moonbeam-Goom-jigi remained an idiot.

chapter 3

The Waterspout!

Bean sat at the small kitchen table with a bowl of Creola, a slice of buttered bread, a cup of green banana strawberry Jell-O, and some blue cookies. Remembering milk, he rose and crossed the room to the refrigerator. It was then he noticed the extremely darkened sky and increased wind whipping up the surf. On the beach there were two bikini-clad girls who appeared to be in a panic as they half ran, half stumbled around in circles like a couple of confused idiots more concerned with the state of their hair than in what direction they were moving.

"Oh, wul, like damn! My hair is all messed up and stuff!" yelled the blonde, her hair whipping around as though she had just grabbed a live power line.

"Wul, yuh, girlfriend. Like this truly sucks. Like… what's up with all this wind and junk? I mean, wul… like… like… like… wul…" cried the other girl just before a gust of wind snatched the wet foamy top off of a wave and blew it upside her marginal brain. The surprise and force of the slap of water threw her butt-first down on the sand, tripping up her blonde companion who landed flat on her belly next to her. When they looked up they both screamed, holding their hair for dear life because they were too stupid to do anything else. Their screams were continuous and even increased in volume sounding a lot like a diving WWII German Messerschmitt fighter plane, and for good reason. When they looked up from their ungraceful ass-bound place in the sand they discovered a massive waterspout ripping across the surface of the sea. The marine tornado came over the surf and across the beach in the blink of an eye and had no trouble at all snatching up the two girls and swallowing them in its howling dark funnel like a couple of lightweight, life size Barbie dolls.

Bean watched in amazement until he suddenly realized the huge waterspout was bearing down hell bent straight for their little cottage, causing the 38 assorted home made wind chimes to announce its arrival in a symphony of noise that only a tone deaf drunken locomotive driver could appreciate. Bean had no time to get to his mother in the other room, not even time to yell out and warn her. It sounded like a freight train and looked like a huge black twisting cartoonish Tasmanian Devil that had risen from the depths of the sea to collect unwary souls. Just before a wind driven wall of water hit the cottage, Bean caught a quick glimpse of two of those captured souls in the form of the air head teenie-beacher girls as they flew past the window in a ball of screaming, flopping, discombobulated, uncoordinated fear and desperation.

The cottage shuttered and rocked. Bean braced himself against the wall. A moment later the main body of the twisting monster made contact. It took only a few seconds but in his mind it occurred in slow motion, a surreal moment of fear and disbelief when first the porch disjointed itself piece by piece and flew away as though it were defying all the laws of gravity and physics. Then the kitchen bucked and buckled like a wild bronco and along with the rest of the cottage, rose and twisted, breaking apart around him, somehow seeming to both implode and expand at the same time. The last thing Bean was conscious of was Fruitcake's muffled high pitched desperate yelp that sounded a lot like an over anxious bicycle horn, and he wasn't sure but he could have sworn he heard Fruitcake say, "OH SHIT!" Fruitcake's words somehow made their way through the overwhelming roar of the wind and into his mind, along with the terrifying sound of ripping and wrenching wood, breaking glass, and the metallic shredding of the tin roof.

"Wow, man. I ain't never seen anything like that before," said the paramedic who went by the name of Zippy, as he ogled the ass of a passing nurse in the emergency room. "Except maybe that time we untangled that guy on that Harley motorcycle that had an Oldsmobile wrapped around it over there at the intersection of Route 3 and A1A. You remember that one don't ya? It was right after they put in that big-ass traffic light that never works right? That was pretty gross. Remember that one, don't ya, Herbert?"

Zippy's real name was Eisenhower DeMonza but he didn't like the name Eisenhower. His mother was a high school history teacher who liked republican presidents because she believed they usually didn't take any shit from anybody, so she named him Eisenhower after President Dwight Eisenhower. She liked people and presidents who didn't take shit from anybody because she had to take shit from students and parents all the time and couldn't do anything about it. His name Eisenhower had somehow translated to the nickname Izzy instead of Ike so he took it on himself to change it to Zippy. Zippy, thought Zippy, was a cooler name for a surfer and a hell of a lot better than that stupid guy named Izzy on that Laverne and Shirley TV sitcom. That was way back when he was a little kid and couldn't surf. Now he can surf and is known around the beach as Meat Wagon because he's the paramedic who usually drives the rescue truck. His little brother's name was Theodore Nixon DeMonza. Zippy at first thought it was odd that his mother would give his little bother a first name that belonged to a democratic president but his mother always insisted it was a traditional name from her side of the family and that it was okay anyway because President

Teddy didn't take any shit from anybody either and she was certain he was a republican at heart. Zippy avoided and never claimed to know his little brother because it was just too damn embarrassing. He equated his brother's first name with a famous chipmunk and his second name with a famous liar, neither of which was cool if you were a surfer.

"What the hell you lookin' at? That nurse is old enough to be your mother," said Zippy's partner Collin who didn't like his name either and went by his middle name Herbert. Most everyone he knew was in the medical profession and would always call him *Colon* instead of Collin. He didn't think that was funny but had to admit it was better than being called Kidney or Pancreas.

"No. I don't think the Harley crash was the worst," said Herbert. "I think it was those Hodgie dudes. You remember, that time in Sadr City over there in Iraq when all those crazy Hodgie cops started killin' each other. Those dumb bastards were always killin' each other. Dumbasses never could make up their mind who the hell they were fightin' for. Dumbass Hodgies."

Zippy and Herbert had served in the Army together in Iraq after they got out of high school. After being discharged from the Army then recalled to service by the Army and sent back to Iraq, then discharged again then recalled again by the Army and sent to Afganistan, then discharged again and recalled and sent back to Iraq again then discharged, they went on the run, hiding out where they couldn't be found and recalled again. While traveling through Latin America on a continuous party bender using all their accumulated combat pay, they eventually came to find themselves lost and penniless somewhere in Bogotá. It was then they decided to come home and put their broad experience as Army medics to work. As emergency paramedics they had a steady paycheck allowing them to live an uncomplicated life at the beach where they could surf and chase sweet young booty with nice boobs and butts and limited vocabularies.

"Yeah, I remember. Those Hodgies tore each other up so bad we couldn't even connect the body parts. Talk about a meat puzzle," recalled Zippy as he checked out the nurse's ass again, "I think I screwed that nurse once."

"Dude, she's old enough to be your mother. No way."

"Yeah. I mean no. I mean yeah. That's what I mean. I mean maybe ten years ago, dude. I mean, isn't that Roger Gorby's mom? You know, from high school. The kid whose mom always gave parties so Roger Gorby would be popular and all the guys always went because she'd always take one of the guys upstairs and screw his brains out."

"Oh yeah, Gorby's mom. Sweet," remembered Herbert as he looked about the ER, sipped a cup of cold coffee, and remembered his trip up Mrs. Gorby's stairs. "She was pretty hot. But no, that ain't her. She wasn't smart enough to be a nurse. Works in a bank I think."

"So how bout this lady we brought in from the twister? She gonna make it?" asked Zippy. "I never saw anybody all tangled up like that. Not even that dead Harley driver after we peeled that Oldsmobile off him. Don't know how anybody could get all tangled up like that. Hatin' it, man. She's gotta' be hatin' it. Know what I mean?"

"Don't think she'll make it," answered Herbert. "I heard the doc say to that nurse with Mrs. Gorby's ass that they had to break most of her bones to get her untangled and that most of 'em were already broken to start with. A real Gumby deal, ya know? Said she was an internal mess too and she wouldn't last long. He asked me how come we drugged her up so much but I told him we didn't give her anything except an IV cause she was unconscious and zoned out the whole time anyway."

"How bout the kid?"

"He was scratched up pretty bad. But I don't think he was busted up any though. Not as bad as that naked blonde chick they found in that prickly pear cactus patch on the other side of A1A. That girl had a broken arm, a broken leg, and more prickly pear cactus puncture holes than a dartboard. Hell, I don't think we woulda even found her if she hadn't been screamin' so loud. Man, that chick can really scream and holdin' on to her hair the whole time. And she was delirious too. Tried to tell me she had a friend that flew all the way across the river to the mainland. Can you believe that? Yeah, right, all the way across the Intracoastal. Sure. Like anybody is gonna believe that shit."

"So how come we didn't get to bring in the hot naked delirious chic? How come we got stuck with the chunky broken spaghetti lady?"

"Because."

"Oh, okay," accepted Zippy. "That nurse's ass sure looks a lot like Gorby's mom, though."

Down the hall, lying dormant in intensive care bed number 3 was Sister Moonbeam-Goom-jigi. She was completely wrapped in a plaster cast from her toes to the top of her head with all four limbs extended and hanging up in the air from straps and lines that ran through pulleys that were attached to stainless steel frames and connected to counter weights like some Rube Goldberg masterpiece. There was a small opening where her mouth was supposed to be and another slit of an opening that ran across from one eye to the other revealing the upper bridge of her nose that was covered by a Band-Aid. If it weren't for the eye opening, anyone would be hard pressed to conclude there was a person inside. She looked like some weird upside down modern art coffee table or a white plaster version of one of those tacky robots in one of those low budget 1950's science fiction movies, except without the springy wiggly sparking antennas.

Through various outlets in the massive cast the hospital staff and doctors had somehow managed to fit all the essential life support connections such as plumbing lines, oxygen tube, heart monitors, pulse monitor, and IVs. Around her bed was a collection of high tech monitoring machines that beeped, clicked, sucked, gurgled, or oozed in a symphony of sounds and critical care drama that only a TV scriptwriter or medical billing clerk could appreciate. It was a fate most anyone would consider worse than death, anyone except Sister Moonbeam-Goom-jigi that is. Between the morphine and other drugs introduced into her at the hospital plus her daily intake of exotic mood swayers she had taken before the arrival of the waterspout, she was on a super high of which only an astronaut could comprehend and with which only Superman could empathize. Therefore, whether she was lucky or unfortunate was a matter of opinion.

She was most likely still alive because she had been most likely fully loaded with self-induced mind expanders, leaving her body flexible or supple enough to survive the impact of the waterspout and the destruction of her little beach house. On the other hand, at the time of impact she was still tied up in a Yoga knot, having finally managed to get both of her chunky legs above and behind her head, restricting her arms and becoming unable to disengage. While still in the tangled yoga position she was violently thrown around inside the crumbling cottage like a steel ball in a pinball machine, finally coming to rest in the sand dunes with the rest of the debris. When Herbert, Zippy, and members of the local fire department pulled her out from under a big chunk of tin roof they found her out cold, covered in fish net, and balled together like a wad of Chinese noodles.

So now she lay in a full body cast in intensive care bed number 3, stretched out like a WWII Honolulu hooker on a Saturday night waiting for sailor number 167, when in walked her son Bean. Bean was covered with bruises and bandages and sporting a few stitches, but for the most part he was remarkably unharmed, true testament to the benefits of daily sun, surf, exercise, and a lifetime diet of Creola, fruit and exotic cookies. He looked around, impressed if not overwhelmed and even a bit intimidated by the sight of all the noisy high-tech life support life saving death delaying devices.

"Mom? Mom? Is that you?" he asked of the plaster robot while politely leaning to look inside the eye opening in the cast. He noticed that the Band-aid on her nose sported a small picture of Spider Man. It had been borrowed from the childrens ward because Zippy and Herbert had stolen all the emergency room Band-aids to supply their rescue truck and to decorate their faces for amusement during their down time at the Krystal Burger.

Sister Moonbeam-Goom-jigi was now pretty much incoherent and nearly unconscious, which for her was pretty much normal, but recognizing Bean's voice she managed a moan, "Ohmmmg."

"Mom?"

"Ohmmmg."

"Mom?"

"Ohmmg? Be... Bean? Is there... ohmmg, is there sommmm... in the oven? Ohmmg," she managed to say through the little hole in the cast and the tube in her mouth without moving her jaw.

"Mom?"

"Ohmmmg?"

About that time there entered a priest who slinked quietly past Bean to Sister Moonbeam-Goom-jigi's bedside.

"Who are you?" asked Bean.

"I'm Father Sabatino," answered the priest. "I'm here to give the patient his last rights."

"It's not a he. It's my mom," corrected Bean.

"Oh... *her* last rights," corrected Father Sabatino.

Father Sabatino was a real piece of work. He didn't look like you would expect a Catholic priest to look. He looked more like a mafia hit man. This was probably because he actually was a former mafia hit man by the name of Guido Fulgenzi from New Jersey. He had also been known as Five Nose Freddy because he used to cut off and save the noses of his victims as trophies, and the most he got in one day was five. He was about to be convicted of a triple nose homicide in 1979 but was released because he turned State's evidence and testified against his mafia employer who in turn was convicted for operating a chain of shady laundry mats all around New Jersey and New York City known as Fast Eddie's Squeaky Clean Launderettes. They were very lucrative laundry mats because they were used more for laundering money than washing dirty underwear. Of course no one ever robbed Fast Eddie's Squeaky Clean Launderettes because they didn't want to die without a nose. Somehow this all seemed perfectly logical and acceptable to the U.S. Attorney, to let a professional killer free in order to close down a dozen laundry mats.

Now Five Nose Freddy is in the witness protection program in a manner in which his federal case officer thought would be most beneficial to all concerned. He is employed by the Catholic Church under the alias Father Alphonso Sabatino and specializes in comforting horny nuns and the terminally ill. For this the Federal government pays the Catholic Church a million dollars a year to maintain Father Sabatino's cover, a large portion of which is pocketed by Cardinal Fulgenzi, Five Nose Freddy's cousin who brokered the deal and Five Nose Freddy's federal case officer who accepted the deal and a piece of the action.

In spite of the dark suit and distinctive priest's collar, Father Sabatino didn't stray too far from his roots. For the right price he would accommodate relatives and other beneficiaries of wills and insurance who wished to expedite the inevitable with an occasional confidential and convenient act of euthanasia. Of course he had long since forgone the collection of noses because it would have ruined what is a perfect set up in which no one ever suspected him, a priest who had every right to be present at the time of death or near death, even though death wasn't always imminent. The money was very good as well. Usually 20% of the beneficiary's take; more than reasonable considering all the money that the next of kin or beneficiaries saved on hospital bills and doctors' fees had the victim continued lingering for any length of time. His most lucrative cases included coma victims. Sometimes Father Sabatino even performed the service for medical insurance companies. One year he even made more than his cousin, Cardinal Fulgenzi. Father Sabatino had taken the Dr.Kavorkian concept and turned it into a masterful and profitable art.

"Last rights?" asked Bean.

"Yes. She's dying. I got a call from your Uncle Albert."

"Who?" said Bean.

Sister Moonbeam-Goom-jigi's eyes opened wide behind the restraining plaster works where she had been dreaming about a previous conversation she had with a dolphin. In spite of the dream and her current and usual mental state and the drugs, her mind still managed to process Father Sabatino's words.

She was dying, she thought he said. *She was dying? She was dying! What? What the hell? Shit! Nobody told me I was dying,* she thought in a panic. *In fact, nobody told me anything. When did I start dying? What the hell happened and why am I stuck inside this...thing? Why can't I move? Where am I? 'She's dying! He said she's dying!' Am I the she? I'm dying! Who said I'm dying! I never thought of that. Did I ever think of that? What the fuck!*

"Are you a relative?" Father Sabatino asked of Bean.

"I said she's my mom. I'm her son," answered Bean.

44

"Oh, yeah. Right."

"My mom's not Catholic. She's a child of the universe."

"We're all children of the universe," said Father Sabatino. "But we all need a little help getting to the gates of heaven. Don't you agree? Last rights wouldn't hurt any. Don't you agree?"

"Guess so," said Bean. "Do last rights hurt."

"No," replied Father Sabatino.

"Is she really dying?" asked Bean.

"That's what the doctor said," replied Father Sabatino.

"Who is Uncle Albert?" asked Bean.

"Ohmmmg," interrupted Sister Moonbeam-Goom-jigi, meaning, *she had no damn intention of dying.*

Bean and Father Sabatino turned their attention to the big plaster robot in the bed.

"Ohmmmg," she moaned again.

"I think she wants to say something," said Father Sabatino. "Do you want to say something, my child?" He always liked to throw in the words *my child* because it felt saintly and because that's what the priest on TV always say.

"Ohmmmg," moaned Sister Moonbeam-Goom-jigi, meaning, *yes.*

"Perhaps you would like to make a confession, my child?" asked Father Sabatino.

"Ohmmmg," moaned Sister Moonbeam-Goom-jigi, meaning, *no.* Her eyes darted to Bean. "Ohmmmg."

"Oh, perhaps you'd like me to give you your last rights then?"

"Ohmmmmmmg!" moaned Sister Moonbeam-Goom-jigi, meaning, *shut the hell up and get the hell away from me!*

Bean moved close to her side. He wanted to take her hand but he couldn't find it. It was hanging up encased in a big wad of hard plaster the size of a football, so he tenderly touched where he thought her forehead was supposed to be.

"I'm here mom," he said. "I'm here."

She looked at him and blinked her eyes affectionately. She could do that because even though her eyes were black and blue and bruised making her look like a raccoon, they were pretty much the only thing she had left that wasn't broken.

"Ohmmmg."

"Huh?"

"Ohmmmg."

"What?"

"Ohmmmg," she moaned, now accepting the fact that she was dying simply because the priest said so.

"I'm here mom," said Bean again, awkwardly reaching out and stroking the big plaster wad that surrounded her head or at least where he thought her head should be relevant to where he could see her eyes. With his other hand he compassionately patted the big plaster football where he thought her hand was supposed to be. "I'm here."

"Ohmmmg..." she moaned. "You... must... find... ohmmmg... must find Ji... Jimmy," she managed to say with great effort through the little hole and obstructing oxygen tube.

"Find Jimmy?" repeated Bean.

"Ohmmmg," she blinked. "Must find... Jimmy's... ohmmmg... must for... soul... peace... life... find fa... father's... Jimmy... ohmmmg... in heart."

"Delusional. She's going fast," said Father Sabatino as he moved to the side of the bed. "I'd better give the last rights now."

When Father Sabatino moved closer to her side he bumped the IV hanging above the bed, almost knocking it over.

"Oops," he said, catching it and righting it. When he did he covertly adjusted the flow of the attached morphine drip, increasing it to maximum - a lethal dose. The morphine drip being open to full blast sent Sister Moonbeam-Goom-jigi into over dose heaven.

"Bean... mu... must find... ohmmmg... ohmmmg... mmm? MMMM?" moaned Sister Moonbeam-Goom-jigi as the morphine kicked in. "MMMM! Far out man!" was her final garbled words as she closed her eyes and let her body surrender to the drug. A minute later her heart stopped and all the beeping, clicking, sucking, and oozing machines started blinking and whining and whistling and lighting up. The nurse with Mrs. Gorby's ass and a doctor rushed in, looked into the robot eye slot with the Spider-Man Band-Aid and verified she was dead then started turning off all the blinking and whining and whistling machines.

Father Sabatino crossed his heart and mumbled something in Latin, even though he had no idea what the hell he was saying. It was just something cool he heard in the movie *The Exorcist*. While quoting *The Exorcist* he checked out the nurse's ass and gave it an 8 1/2 on a scale of on to ten. Ten years younger, he thought, and it would be a full ten. Still, he thought, I wouldn't kick her out of bed for eating crackers.

Bean just stared. He wasn't sure how to react. The possibility of losing his mother was something that had never occurred to him. There had never been any trials or tribulations or social drama in his life or his home. Now his home was destroyed, his mother gone. In the blink of an eye his life had taken a turn for which he was not prepared. Silent tears ran down his cheeks. "Mom?" he said softly. No *ohmmmg* reply emitted from within the little mouth hole of the big plaster robot. Sister Moonbeam-Goom-jigi... had left the building.

🌴

Herbert and Zippy were walking past intensive care bed number 3 on their way out of the hospital when all the machines were blinking and whining and whistling, and

Father Sabatino was crossing his heart and quoting *The Exorcist.*

"Looks like that spaghetti lady didn't make it," said Herbert.

"Yep, looks like," said Zippy, again eying the nurse with Mrs. Gorby's ass. "Bummer, dude. Hatin' it."

"Yep," agreed Herbert. "Hatin' it."

"Wonder if they'll take all that plaster stuff off before they bury her?" said Zippy. "I mean, she's got this mummy thing goin' on there, ya know. So why not take advantage, know what I mean?"

"Dunno," said Herbert. "That's a lot of plaster, though. Coulda plastered a lot of walls with all that stuff."

"Yeah, spose so."

"Or made a whole bunch of those science project volcanoes with the smoky oozie shit comin' out the top. Remember those… with the smoky oozy shit comin' out the top?"

"Yeah," said Zippy. "But they're made out of paper mache not plaster. Hey, remember that big plaster elephant my mom had and we put a cherry bomb in its ass and blew it all to hell? Remember that? Man was she pissed. I mean really, really pissed. Beat my gluteus maximus big time for that one. I was hatin' it, dude."

"Yeah hatin' it, I bet. Hey, I could go for some Krystal burgers," suggested Herbert. "You up for some Krystal burgers?"

"Yeah cool," said Zippy. "I could do some Krystal burgers."

"Yeah, okay, cool. So let's go do some Krystal burgers."

As they exited the emergency room, in rolled a gurney hastily pushed by two other paramedics.

"Hey guys. Whatcha got there?" asked Zippy.

"Young girl. Found her naked in a tree west side of the intracoastal. Says she flew there in a tornado."

"Wow, tornado. Hatin' it, man," said Herbert.

"Sounds like a head case to me," diagnosed Zippy.

"Yep. Think you're right. So, Krystal burgers?" confirmed Herbert.

"Definitely. Oh, hey looky. I copped some of those Hannah Montana Bandaids."

"Hey, cool. I like the ones with the pictures," said Herbert as he dug into his pocket. "Lookit this. I got the Incredible Hulk. See there, he barely fits on top of the anticeptic gause pad part cause hes a big green bad ass. See there? He's a big dude."

"Yeah, the Hulk, cool. Hey, you sure that ain't Mrs Gorby?"

"Dude, that ain't Mrs Gorby."

chapter 4

Uncle Who?

When Bean came up from the beach and approached the debris strewn vacant spot in the sand among the dunes that was once his home, he came upon the upturned fat butt of a man in a poorly fitting three piece suit rummaging through the wreckage. The man was angrily mumbling to himself at being unable to find whatever it was he was searching for.

"Um, excuse me, sir," said Bean.

"What? What? What the hell…" said the man as he stood upright and turned to discover the boy. "What… Who the hell are you? You shouldn't be here, kid. Get lost. Get the hell away from here."

"I'm Bean Buffett. I live here…um, well, I mean I used to live here two days ago."

"Oh? What? Oh, oh, your…" said the unpleasant plump semi-bald man. His attitude changed dramatically when he realized who the boy was. A forced smile that somehow failed to fit his face quickly appeared and he even tried to suck in his potbelly but failed. "Bean? You're Bean boy? Why of course you are. I can see it in your face. You're Franny Camilla's boy all right. Why of course you are. So glad to finally meet you, Beanie boy. So glad indeed," he said as he extended his hand, then nearly slipped and tripped over an empty Boone's Farm apple wine bottle. "Shit," he exclaimed, slipping out of his phony cordial persona, then catching himself and quickly returning to being the pleasant man of which he obviously wasn't.

Bean backed away. Not so much from caution but because the man smelled not only of whisky but as though he had generously sampled every man's aftershave in the Wal-mart store and maybe even some of the women's. The odor seared Bean's nasal passages being it was a far cry from the natural pleasant open-air odors of the beach and ocean salt air that Bean was used to.

"Oh, sorry. I forgot we've never met," said the sweaty man in the long extinct striped polyester suit. "I'm your uncle. Uncle Albert. Albert Freewater. Your mother's brother. I'm sure your mom told you about me."

"No," said Bean.

"Oh. Um… well, I'm him alright. In the flesh."

"What are you doing?" asked Bean.

"Who me? Oh, uh… just looking for a keepsake… of your dear departed mother. So sorry about your loss," he said with obvious insincerity as he retrieved the Boone's Farm bottle, shook it, looked at it with false affection and tossed it away. "Um… stones. I seem to remember your mom had a collection of stones or crystals. Thought maybe they would be an item of fond remembrance. You know, since she was so into nature and all." He searched Beans eyes with serious curiosity as he posed the question, "You… uh, wouldn't happen to know of any stones or crystals or anything like that that your mom kept around the house would you?"

"Mom never said anything about stones… or an uncle," replied Bean. "Except Uncle Joe the bartender who's not a bartender any more and not really my uncle."

"Well now, wouldn't that be just like our Franny. Absent minded as she was."

Bean just shrugged.

"Welp, I'm your Uncle Albert alrighty. Came all the way down from Baltimore I did. And I want you to know I'm gonna take care of you. You don't worry. You don't worry about anything. I'm gonna take care of everything."

"I didn't know mom had a brother."

"Son, to tell you the truth I don't think your mother even thought she had a brother or any other family. Know what I mean? I mean, after her fateful excursion to Africa and all those years of... well, lets just say your mom wasn't the brightest star in the universe," said the unpleasant man as he approached Bean and laid his hand on his shoulder.

Bean winced, trying to somehow politely close his nostrils without touching his nose.

"You see, I haven't really seen your mom in a long time. 'Bout thirty years actually. But I kind of kept in touch in my own way... for the family's sake."

"You mean I have other relatives?"

"Sure... I mean well, no. Not any more. They're all dead and I'm all you got now, Beanie boy," he lied. "But don't you worry. I'm gonna take care of everything." He leaned to Bean and asked reticently, "Are you sure your mom didn't have any stones around here some place?"

"No sir. I don't know anything about any stones. She collected shells off the beach mostly and used them to make wind chimes and lampshades and stuff. She made a necklace for Fruitcake once."

"Fruitcake? Who the hell's Fruitcake?"

"Our dog. Fruitcake's our dog. I mean, was our dog. I'm afraid he's gone. Lost in the twister."

"Dog? Did you say a dog? Was it a little raggy rat of a dog with one ear? Sounds like a broken bicycle horn when it barks?"

"Yes sir!" said Bean. "Have you seen him?"

"Sure. It came out from under that pile of junk over there and started following me around. Little bastard wouldn't shut the hell up so I tied him to my car."

Bean looked around until he spied Uncle Albert's beat up twenty-four year old Buick parked on the side of A1A. He ran to find Fruitcake tied to the bumper, taking refuge from the heat in the shade under the car. Needless to say

Fruitcake was elated at their reunion. He had been waiting among the wreckage of the cottage for two full days in a doggy state of trauma and without so much as a single bowl of Creola or a sip of cheap Boone's Farm wine to sustain him. *An experience he wouldn't wish on a dog,* thought Fruitcake who, after spending most of his life with Sister Moonbeam-Goom-jigi, failed to realize he actually was a dog. The disastrous experience of the devastating waterspout confirmed this even more. Fruitcake was supposed to be with people instead of being stranded all alone among the debris in a disaster zone like some mongrel.

"Fruitcake you're alive!" Bean cried out as he untied and hugged the mutt.

Of course I am, thought Fruitcake. *And just where the hell have you been, dude?*

Fruitcake could think in human but never could figure out the vocalizing part, though he did come close once after discovering and consuming some of Sister Moonbeam-Goom-jigi's exotic mushrooms and wine. Just the same, it didn't matter that he couldn't actually talk because he always assumed that people, of whom he thought he was one, where all as telepathically gifted as he and could hear everything he thought just as he often heard their thoughts. As for their lack of response to his part of the conversation, he simply assumed he was usually ignored because he was short and ugly.

Where's the house? Where's the food? Where's the house? Where's the food? Where's the house? Where's the food? Fruitcake thought as loud as he could while he wiggled excitedly in Beans arms and slobbered all over his face, managing only a strained broken bicycle horn wine of excitement.

"I bet you're really hungry aren't you boy," said a caring Bean.

Damn right I am, thought Fruitcake. *Creola. Creola. Creola.*

"Interesting dog you got there," said Uncle Albert as he approached the car. "Only got one ear. You know he's only got one ear. Lose it in the twister, did he?"

"He's all I have left," said Bean. "Just Fruitcake and the Celestial Rocket."

"The Celestial Rocket?"

"Yeah. That's what mom called the car. It didn't get destroyed in the twister cause it's in the shop getting painted again."

"Again?"

"Yep. Mom always got it painted for special occasions like when the stars did something special or when she was planning a trip."

"She would take trips?"

"No. She just planned trips but never went because she couldn't remember why she wanted to go in the first place and when she did she wouldn't remember where. This time she wanted to get the car painted in paisley but she couldn't find anybody who would do it. I usually do all the driving now because she would always forget to get gas."

"So what color is it now?" asked Uncle Albert.

"I don't know. They're supposed to deliver it today. That's why I'm here. I'm waiting for the Rocket."

"Say kid, where are you staying now?"

"With Uncle Joe the bartender. He lives in town. He's not really my uncle but I call him Uncle Joe."

Just then a tow truck that said ROY McROY AUTO WORKS on the door came into view, slowed and pulled over in front of them. In tow was Sister Moonbeam-Goom-jigi's little 1955 Nash Metropolitan convertible, the Celestial Rocket, with a shiny new paint job. The body had been painted a bright yellow, the two front quarter panels painted red and the two back were blue. All four with alternating stars of gold, green and pink. Painted on the hood was a poor facsimile of a manatee wearing a backwards baseball cap and sunglasses. Across the continental kit spare tire cover was painted the name Celestial Rocket, except rocket was spelled *rockit* instead of rocket. Mr. McCroy wasn't a very good speller. Before he painted the letters he looked up the word *celestial* in the dictionary but neglected to look up the word *rocket*.

Uncle Albert stared in disbelief, as much at the paint job as the very existence and perfect condition of the 56-year-old car. Bean just seemed to take the oddly painted vehicle in stride.

After Roy McRoy detached the Celestial Rocket he came over to Bean, patted him on the back and said, "Real sorry about your mom, Bean. But remember, anytime you need anything you give me a call. On the house as usual, Okay? Anytime at all. Wasn't for your mom… well, you know. Anytime you need me…"

"Yes sir. Thank you sir," said Bean.

"On the house?" questioned Uncle Albert as Roy McRoy and his tow truck pulled away after disconnecting the Celestial Rocket.

"Mom always paid in advance in case she forgot to afterwards. She did that a lot. That was Mr. McRoy. He does all our car stuff and he never takes any money 'cause mom paid him enough in advance to start his business."

"You don't say. So everything's paid for, huh. And in advance too. Well now just how did she do that I wonder? I don't recall her ever having a job except for a short time in Philly back when she first came home from Africa. She was sellin' roses on the street corner for that Korean guy Moon something or other that started his own religion and used to marry people a thousand at a time. Some kind of Hairy Krishny kind of shit. So now where'd you suppose she got all her money?"

"Don't know," answered Bean, showing more interest in Fruitcake than his newfound uncle. "She said money wasn't important. That the earth always provides what you need when you need it."

"Say Beanie my boy, do you know if your mom had a last will and testament?" asked Uncle Albert as he looked to the impressive new hotel next door then hungrily surveyed Sister Moonbeam-Goom-jigi's undeveloped ten acres of valuable beach-front property.

"Don't know," said Bean, wishing this unpleasant man would stop calling him Beanie. "But she said something before she died. Wanted me to find somebody. Wanted me to find Jimmy."

"Jimmy. Who the hell's Jimmy?"

"My father."

"You mean Franny was married?"

"Well not really. She said it was a coming together of souls in a moment of universal ecstasy," explained Bean. "Well, I have to go now. I need to feed Fruitcake."

Hearing Bean's expressed intentions, Fruitcake started wiggling and licking again. *Where's the food? Where's the house? Where's the food?*

"Hey wait a minute kid. Are you old enough to drive?"

"Yes sir," answered Bean. "I've been old enough ever since I was ten."

With that he set Fruitcake in the passenger seat, hopped in behind the wheel and drove off.

It's true; Bean had been driving ever since he was ten years old. All the local cops knew this but none of them would ever pull him over because he was actually a very good driver and Sister Moonbeam-Goom-jigi was usually in the car with him. All the cops remembered or heard about what the other officers and the Judge had to endure during the famous incident involving Sister Moonbeam-Goom-jigi at the intersection of Rt. 3 and A1A and none of them wanted to go through that again. It was mind-boggling. Besides, Judge Weingarberger had a standing order that Sister Moonbeam-Goom-jigi was not to return to his courtroom again for any reason – ever, and for that reason all the cops greatly respected her.

"Albert old man, seems like you've got some planning to do," Uncle Albert said to himself. *And before little sister's funeral tomorrow,* he thought. Then he turned and again surveyed the ten acres of prime beachfront land. *Yes sir, some serious planning,* he thought with a devious smile.

Albert Freewater was an asshole. And he was damn good at it too. Unlike his sister he wasn't an over-achiever as a young man or even an older man. In fact he could have been classified as an exceptional under-achieving black sheep and major moral disappointment to the family. He made a marginal living as the owner of a grungy little corner bar in Baltimore that he won in a poker game. The bar specialized in beer, cod cakes, pickles and pickled eggs, and advertised questionably fresh Chesapeake Bay raw oysters on the half shell that were actually shipped up from contaminated waters somewhere near south Louisiana. The only reason he made any profit at all was because he encouraged all his regular customers to run a payday to payday tab of which he usually increased on the sly by about 30%, knowing the customers were all usually too damn drunk to remember how much they drank in the first place. In addition he would take over-the-counter bar bets on sports events that were taking place live on the overhead TV that he had rigged with a five-minute delay. The real-time sporting results came in over a small receptor he always had stuck in his left ear that he claimed was a hearing aid. The hearing aid was necessary, he told everyone, to compensate for a hearing loss resulting from an injury he sustained as a Green Beret in Vietnam. It was a lie of course. The only actual uniform Albert Freewater ever wore in his entire life was in the third grade when he had to dress as one of the king's men in a Humpty Dumpty play on parent-teacher's day. And the only reason he did that was to impress a girl named Alicia Claremont so he could get a peak at her yet to be developed boobs.

Albert had shot down from Baltimore in his rusty old Buick to St. Augustine without hesitation as soon as he got word of his sister's imminent death because somewhere in the back of his mind he recalled her mentioning something about being forced to marry a fat African chief who gave her some valuable rocks. This plus the fact he noticed over the years that Sister Moonbeam-Goom-jigi, though never flaunting any real wealth, never found it necessary to take a job or ask the family for money but still always managed to get by; like when she bought her piece of valuable beachfront property with cash. And then there were those times such as when she bailed out the struggling nonprofit bankrupt Southern Society of Unwed Nuns of the Universal Church of Maternity. And, of course, the time she entered a bid to buy the Miami Dolphins football team because she liked the color of their uniforms and was convinced she was the only one who could actually communicate with them.

If my sister had a stash of cash or valuable rocks, thought Albert, *I'm gonna get my hands on 'em. But first I have to deal with this kid.*

chapter 5

Farewell Sister

The procession, consisting of eight sister members of the Southern Society of Unwed Nuns of the Universal Church of Maternity in their long flowing scarlet habits, moved reverently down the long St. Augustine Beach pier carrying before them a bronze urn containing the cremated remains of Sister Moonbeam-Goom-jigi. They strolled along mournfully, step by step, all the while singing an oddly chosen dirge, a slow harmonious angelic version of the sixties song *San Francisco*.

> *If you're going to San Francisco,*
> *Be sure to wear some flowers in your hair.*

At the far end of the pier, high above the ocean waves waited Bean and Fruitcake, along with Joe the bartender and his girlfriend, Uncle Albert, a number of patrons of the Tropical Trade Winds Lounge, and Mr. Roy McCroy and his family. Standing nearby were a handfull of smelly, unshaven, unkempt old local retiree recreational fishermen who were waiting for the service to end so they could cut bait and cast their lines. One of the old fishermen was getting impatient because the blue fish were running and he was losing precious fishing time.

"The way those women are movin' this shit could take all day," mumbled old Ben as he leaned back against the pier rail. He put his foot up on his dirty 20-year-old K-Mart cooler chest that sat next to his other gear, a folded plastic and aluminum drugstore chair, his three cast rods, and his beat up old tackle box. "Ain't got all day. Blue fish are runnin'," he mumbled as he adjusted his fish blood and oil stained faded old ball cap with the Marine Corps emblem on the front and the words *Semper Fi - Fight or Die.* He bought the hat at an interstate truck stop. It led everyone to believe he was a retired Marine when he wore it, of which he never confirmed or denied because it sounded better than the truth. The truth was he had in fact worked for 35 years processing people shit at a sewerage plant in Gineawatchi, Michigan. What the hell, he thought; he would have joined the Marines if they had ever asked him, even though he was missing two toes on his left foot that he lost to a bicycle chain when he was seven years old.

Old Ben pulled a flask from his back pocket and took a swig, then offered some to his buddy Conrad who looked a lot like Floyd the three hundred thirty-seven pound West African Ashanti Chieftain. He always offered Conrad a swig and Conrad always declined. Conrad was a good non-drinking Christian and regularly attending member of the Piney Creek Ebenezer AME Church.

"Put dat away and shows some respect," said Conrad. "Dey is buryin' dat crazy lady what lived down the beach and gots kilt by dat waterspout."

"You mean that woman who used to talk to birds and shit?" asked old Ben.

"Yep, dats the one," said Conrad. "Nice lady she was too. Brung me a Spam sandwich one day back when I remembered dat I forgots my lunch. Always aks me how was da fishin'? Never got my name right though. Always called me Floyd."

"Those are some damn slow women in those funny costumes is all I know," said old Ben.

"You best be respectful. Dem's some kinda church nuns," said Conrad.

"Nuns," said old Ben. "Shit, some them nuns look a little bit pregnant you ask me. Maybe even a lot pregnant."

"That ain't right. You can't be a little bit pregnant," said Conrad.

"Maybe *I* can't be a little bit pregnant but it sure looks like some of *them* can be a little bit pregnant," said old Ben.

"I don't mean *you*, I mean *them*," said Conrad.

"That's what I said, *them*," said old Ben.

"No, a little bit pregnant, I mean. Nobody can be a little bit pregnant. You either is or you ain't pregnant. Can't be a little bit pregnant," said Conrad.

"Okay, so maybe not a little bit, but you can be a lot pregnant," said old Ben. "And some of those church nuns sure look like they might be a *lot* pregnant."

"Maybe," said Conrad. "But they ain't a *little bit* pregnant."

"Shit, religion ain't what it used to be," said old Ben.

"That's fo sho. Dey gots a lady reverend now at the Piney Creek Ebenezer AME Church, preaches all that hell fire and damnation stuff just like a man. No differnt. Just like a man, except sometimes her voice screeches kinda like a pig with a belly ache."

"Really? A woman?" said old Ben.

"Yep, and you won't believe. All da mens is comin' to church every Sunday now," said Conrad.

"Oh, so she's a real looker," said old Ben.

"Nope, not necessarily. But she hugs everybody when dey's comin out the church and she gots these really big titties," explained Conrad.

"Well, maybe she's a *little bit* pregnant," said old Ben. "My ol' lady got big ta-ta's when she was pregnant. Maybe that preacher lady is pregnant. Religion ain't what it used to be you know."

"No, you ol' fool. I told you, you can't be just a little bit pregnant," said Conrad.

"Why not? Maybe nuns and lady preachers got some kind of secret thing goin' on. You know, like all those Catholic priests got goin' with all them little altar boys."

The singing members of the Southern Society of Unwed Nuns of the Universal Church of Maternity progressed closer to the end of the pier.

For those who come to San Francisco,
Summertime will be a love-in there.

Just then the wind picked up, crossed the pier and blew the light silky robes of two of the nuns up past their ass, exposing their panties and unshaven legs. Old Ben got a rise when he noticed that one of the nuns who looked a little pregnant but less pregnant than the others, wore panties with little cartoon Sponge Bobs all over them.

"Hot damn," said old Ben, coming to attention. "You see that?" He was now even more impatient, except he was impatiently waiting for another gust of wind so he could get another glimpse of Sponge Bob and the nun's forbidden zone. "Ain't never seen a nun's pootie before. You ever seen any nun pootie before?" he asked of Conrad. "I wonder if it's different."

"You is one despicable ol' white man," said Conrad. "God's gonna strike you down right chere on dis here pier and you ain't gonna be catchin' no fishes never again."

"What? What'd I say? What you bitchin' about. I just never seen any nun pootie before is all I'm sayin'. But somebody sure as hell has cause some of them nuns look a little bit pregnant you ask me."

"Ain't no little bit kind of pregnant, I told you. And nun pootie ain't no differnt than any other pootie."

"Is that a confession?"

"Confession?"

"That you seen nun pootie before. I bet you seen nun pootie before. I heard all about you black boys. You boys see all kinds of pootie. You seen nun pootie, right? Right?"

"Lord Almighty. You is one twisted ol' peckerhead."

The nuns finally reached the patiently waiting group of mourners at the end of the pier and handed the urn containing Sister Moonbeam-Goom-jigi's cremains to her son Bean. The nuns then came together to sing a final tribute to their benefactor in the form of another harmonious slow version of another familiar song, one of Sister Moonbeam-Goom-jigi's favorites, *Margaritaville*. The song brought those in attendance to tears as they all joined in. All except Uncle Albert that is, who didn't have a clue as to the significance of the song, or who and why any of those people were there, and he seemed to appear about as comfortable as a Navy Seal in a gay bar.

"Hey, they're singing about booze," said old Ben the fisherman. "Ain't that somthin'. Pregnant church nuns singin' a song about booze at a funeral. Well I never. What the hell they gonna do next, sing that hippity hop shit and do the Can Can? Religion sure ain't what it used to be."

Conrad rolled his eyes and shook his head. "You is one uncouth ol' bastard. Almighty gonna strike yo wrinkly bony ol' white ass down fo sho."

Bean turned reverently to the open expanse of the sea, unscrewed and removed the top of the bronze urn and set it on the rail of the pier. Teary-eyed, he extended the urn out over the rail and turned it over. Out pored Sister Moonbeam-Goom-jigi in the form of gray ashes, but instead of descending the near fifty feet to the water below, her ashes were caught up in a swirling gust of wind that twirled into a dusty cloud that somehow managed to circle the entire group, including the nearby waiting fishermen.

Old Ben was about to take another swig from his flask just as the ashes of Sister Moonbeam-Goom-jigi came his way. The wind changed quickly and instead of a gulp of his preferred peach schnapps that he always claimed was Scotch whiskey so he would seem manlier, into his mouth flew a dusty portion of the late departed.

"Ahch! Ahch! Bluhch! Ahch!" was all old Ben could manage as he tried to expel the unexpected dry ashy substance from his mouth. It tasted like how he thought dog food would taste, except shittier, if he ever tasted dog food, which he did once in the middle of the night when he was half drunk and thought he was eating Cocoa Puffs cereal.

Conrad's eyes grew large. "I told you you dumb ol' fart. You see. I told you. You done pissed her off. She done gone and give you the kiss'o death. You in big trouble now you dumb ol' bastard."

The wind driven cloud of cremains then flew off and descended to the sea. Everyone present watched with intense interest. While they did, the sisters changed their tune, smoothly segueing into their version of the Jimmy Buffett song *Beach House on the Moon*. Bean stood at the rail looking out to sea with the urn still upturned in his hands. Uncle Albert leaned over and looked down at the urn to assess its value, thinking he could pawn it later, claiming it was a valuable European antique. When he saw *Made in Taiwan* engraved on the bottom he lost interest and looked back to the now almost fully dissipated remains of his sister, or at least what everyone thought was his sister. In truth it was the cremated remains of a combination of pig snouts and chicken backs, and a fifty pound bag of Kibbles & Bits dog food that he paid some low life sleaze ball he met in a bar $50 to render to ashes. Rather than pay the thousand bucks it would take to cremate his sister, he instead sold her body off for a pretty penny to be used for scientific research or as a cadaver stabber for medical students. For whatever purpose she was purchased he didn't bother to ask and didn't actually care, as long as the check didn't bounce.

When there was nothing more to see, the sisters of the Southern Society of Unwed Nuns of the Universal Church of Maternity, while continuing to sing, turned and led the group in a solemn procession back down the pier.

"Bout damn time. Ahch, bluhch," said Old Ben, taking a swig of his peach schnapps whiskey, swishing out his mouth and spitting it out over the rail. "Thought we'd be standin' here till hell froze over."

"Don't you worry none bout hell freezin' over," said Conrad. "Boss Beelzebub keepin' it nice and hot down there just fo yo nasty ol' white ass. I swear. Lookin' at da nuns panties and shit. You some kinda despicable ol' man, you is."

"But I ain't never seen nun pootie before," said old Ben. "I bet you seen some nun pootie before though, huh. You sneaky ol' bastard. Yeah, I bet you seen nun pootie." Old Ben collected his gear and headed for his usual spot at the end of the pier. "Probably scared all the damn fish away, too," he mumbled.

Bean looked back over his shoulder, offering a final gesture of farewell to his beloved mother. Fruitcake the dog looked back as well and in doing so wandered into Uncle Albert's path. He then had to scurry away to avoid being kicked aside by Albert who mumbled something about him being a pesky little rat dog.

Whoa, that service was beautiful, thought Fruitcake as he trotted alongside Bean for safety. *The old lady woulda loved that. Could swear she smelled like Kibbles & Bits though. Kibbles & Bits? Hey Bean, where's the food? Where's the house? Where's the food? Where's the house?*

chapter 6
Beachcomber Conspiracy

It was hot at the beach but an easy breeze coming off the ocean and through the shaded open-air Beachcomber Bar and Restaurant more than compensated. Fruitcake sat at the base of Bean's stool at the counter, his head jerking back and forth in the direction of every human that moved in and about the establishment. Fruitcake had been on the beach many times but was never before this close to so many people. He usually just surfed with Bean or sniffed around, took a quick crap, then fast tracked it back to the security and comfort of his papa-san chair on the porch. He did this because one day while he was on the beach some mean fat guy said that dogs shouldn't be permitted on the beach near his condo and if the law didn't do something about it soon he was going to "start shooting the damn things" then pointed his finger at Fruitcake and pulled an imaginary trigger. Fruitcake didn't want to get shot by a fat guy so he always avoided the beach if there were any fat guys around, even moderately fat guys who might be just as dangerous, and for good measure even fat ladies. Now that his house and chair were gone, he hadn't left Bean's side for security sake since their reunion a few days earlier. At the moment however he wasn't feeling too secure and was a little apprehensive here at the Beachcomber barefoot bar because there was not just one but two fat guys sitting at a nearby table.

"Beanie boy, I think it's time we discuss your mom's final request," said Uncle Albert, sitting in the stool next to him as the bartender slid his beer across the counter. A cheeseburger with french fries slid in front of Bean. Beer was Uncle Albert's main food group though he sometimes supplemented it with sardines and canned macaroni and cheese. Also an occasional pizza if someone else was buying.

"Mom's final request?" asked Bean.

"Sure, you know. Her final request that you find your father," said Uncle Albert as he took a gulp from the bottle of beer. He surveyed the Beachcomber patrons to discover a very pale creamy white chunky lumpy middle-aged tourist with cottage cheese thighs and a straw hat in an ill-fitting fluorescent orange bikini. By no reasoning known to mankind should that bikini ever have been matched to that body, concluded Uncle Albert. He winced. The sight almost made his beer go flat.

"Oh, I don't know," said Bean. "I'm not sure I can..."

"Of course you can, Beanie boy. I got it all worked out for ya," said Uncle Albert. He pulled an envelope from inside the coat pocket of his only other suit that was just as outdated and ugly as his other suit. Uncle Albert was probably the first person in the history of the world to ever wear a suit in the Beachcomber. "I have the answer right here in this envelope. You see, I told ya I'd take care of everything didn't I?"

"What's that?" asked Bean, just before taking a bite of his cheeseburger. He chewed and looked curiously at the envelope.

"Why, it's your trip ticket, son. So you can go find your old man. You know, to go find that Jimmy guy, your dad from that, uh... universal ecstasy... thing your mom told you about."

"But I don't think..."

"Nope, nope, no way," interrupted Uncle Albert. "I'll not be the uncle who would deny a young boy the opportunity to unite with his father. No sir, not me. Like I said before, you don't worry about a thing cause I'm gonna take care of everything. And that includes uniting you with your old man."

Bean just chewed his cheeseburger and stared, not quite sure what to make of his newfound voluntary guardian. Even though he always saw people on the beach he didn't actually know or interact with them. As a consequence he wasn't quite sure how to deal with people he didn't know. As far as any real social intercourse went, Bean's experience was pretty much limited to Joe the bartender, Roy McCroy, the sisters from the Southern Society of Unwed Nuns of the Universal Church of Maternity, some guy named Gator Bait who delivered herbs and mushrooms to his mother on Tuesdays and who taught him how to surf when he was three years old, and of course Fruitcake who really wasn't a person even though he thought he was.

"You see, Beanie boy," continued Uncle Albert, "the natural bond between a boy and his father is... well, it's a sacred thing that every boy should experience. Believe me I know what I'm talking about."

Bean just stared. Wishing Uncle Albert would stop calling him *Beanie boy*.

"Know what I mean, Beanie boy?" asked Uncle Albert.

"No," said Bean as he flipped a ketchup covered French fry into his mouth.

"Now, I know you missed a lot by never knowing your old man but now you have the chance to find him and make amends, to uh... to... experience the joy of the father-son relationship. You know, take in a ball game, go fishing, talk about, um... guy stuff, you know. All that male bonding shit."

Uncle Albert didn't have a friggin' clue about the relationships between fathers and sons. He always avoided his own father because he was always in trouble and his mother always threatened him with the universal phrase, *"You just wait until your father gets home. Then you'll be sorry."* Albert never waited until his father got home and always avoided his father so he wouldn't be sorry. In fact he managed to avoid his father for years until he ran away from home in the company of an over the hill but well financed intellectually challenged and emotionally insecure hooker named Gloria that he met at a bus stop.

The middle-aged pale creamy lady in the fluorescent orange bikini bent over to pick up some dropped change. Uncle Albert was about to take another swig of beer but the sight made his left eye twitch. It reminded him of Gloria the hooker. He set the beer back on the counter.

"Buh hu ma uhmg mua ga uhg fng and yuhg ba," said Bean through a mouth full of cheeseburger.

"What?" said Uncle Albert, turning his attention away from the atrocious fluorescent clad cottage cheese ass and back to Bean. "Say what?"

Holy crap, thought Fruitcake of Uncle Albert. *This guy doesn't even understand plain English.*

Fruitcake didn't realize that his psychic ability to understand human thoughts preceded the spoken words that got scrambled by a mouth full of chewed up cheeseburger. Fruitcake's doggy sense also told him that something wasn't quite kosher about Uncle Albert, not to mention the fact the asshole tied him to a bumper in the hot sun on the side of A1A.

Bean swallowed then repeated, "But how am I going to find him?"

What neither Bean nor Uncle Albert realized was that Sister Moonbeam-Goom-jigi's last request had nothing at all to do with Bean searching for his father. What she was actually trying to say through the complications of her robot plaster cast and tubes and drugs and all the high tech machines that beeped, clicked, sucked, gurgled, or oozed, was that she wanted Bean to find and discover the joy and comfort of Jimmy Buffett's wonderful philosophy of life, and to embrace all the wisdom to be found in the lyrics of his music just as she had often done… then would forget and rediscover once again… time and time again. As it were, Bean's misinterpretation of his mother's "ohmmgs" and struggling final words turned out to be a convenient answer to Uncle Albert's dilemma, which was how to rid himself of his kid sister's kid and legal heir so he could… take care of business.

"What I have here, Beanie boy, are a means to an end," said Uncle Albert as he opened the heavy envelope and withdrew its contents. In front of Bean he placed five hundred dollars cash and a prepaid credit card good for a thousand, both of which were derived from the benefits of Albert selling his dead sister.

"What's that?" asked Bean as he dove into another good sized bite of his cheeseburger.

"I want you to take this here money and this credit card and that dog Frisbee…"

"*Fruitcake*," Bean corrected through his bite of cheeseburger. He took a french fry and dropped it down to Fruitcake.

Yeah, that's Fruitcake, dumbass, thought Fruitcake as he inhaled the french fry.

"…Fruitcake," corrected Uncle Albert, "and get in that Moon Rocket…"

"Celestial Rocket," Bean corrected through another bite of cheeseburger.

Yeah, Celestial Rocket, dumbass, thought Fruitcake with disdain. *Man, is this guy a…* He failed to complete the thought when he was hit on the head by another french fry.

"…Celestial Rocket," corrected Uncle Albert. "Get in the Celestial Rocket and hit the road. I mean, go find your father."

Bean thought a moment. It kind of made sense since he didn't have his house on the beach any more and he really didn't like staying with Uncle Joe the bartender who wasn't a bartender any more. Mainly because Uncle Joe had a girlfriend who didn't like Fruitcake and always smiled and stared at Bean a lot like she was wanting him to do something, and he didn't know what. The sisters from the Southern Society of Unwed Nuns of the Universal Church of Maternity offered to take him and Fruitcake in and they were all very nice but they were always cleaning or singing or praying, or cursing Father Sabatino, that nice priest he met at the hospital, for not using a condom, whatever that was.

"Well, maybe... Well, I... um... suppose I could maybe..."

"Sure you can, kid. You're a good smart boy. Smart as I ever come across. You can do anything you put your mind to. I could tell that right off the bat the very first time I met you. Ain't no flies on your ass, no sir," declared Uncle Albert.

Bean turned slightly and looked at his ass. Fruitcake looked up at Bean's ass too, then at his own ass, then licked his balls.

"Now the only thing left to do is for you to sign this here paper so I can take care of your mom's unfinished business." Uncle Albert pulled another envelope from another pocket in his ugly suit.

"What's that?" asked Bean.

"Oh, just a bunch of legal mumbo jumbo. Nothing for you to be concerned about. Like I said, Beanie boy, your ol' Uncle Albert's gonna take care of everything. All you have to worry about is finding your father."

"Oh, okay," said Bean. After looking at his ass again for flies and dropping another french fry on Fruitcake.

Uncle Albert whipped out a gold pen he had stolen from the business supply store where he bought the blank generic Power of Attorney legal form. He had already filled in all the blanks on the form, which basically gave him power of attorney to act on Bean's behalf regarding all legal and financial matters, including the matter of the disposition of Sister Moonbeam-Goom-jigi's ten acres of high value beachfront property inherited by Bean. The form had already been signed by Uncle Albert and witnessed by the same low life sleaze ball who cremated the pig's feet, chicken backs and Kibbles & Bits. The sleazeball's signature cost Uncle Albert ten bucks and three Bud Lights. The form had even been notarized with a phony signature and a Notary Public stamp that was actually an embossing tool that Uncle Albert always kept handy for just such occasions as this. He came by the embosser years ago in a Goodwill store while he was shopping for a new suit. The embosser made a round impression the exact same size as that of a real Notary Public stamp except it actually said *1st Place Winner-Girl Scouts of America,* with the same Girl Scout emblem in the center that was on the Girl Scout cookies that nobody ever wanted but everybody always bought anyway because they would feel guilty if they didn't. To most people the embossing was just a pretty bunch of legal looking bumps at the bottom of the page that was never questioned or closely scrutinized. Now the only thing Uncle Albert needed was Bean's signature.

The creamy cottage cheese lady in the fluorescent bikini came over and sat on the stool next to Uncle Albert and smiled. Uncle Albert tried to pretend she wasn't there and forced down a gulp of beer.

Bean accepted the pen, but hesitated. "What legal stuff?" he asked.

"Oh, just anything that might pop up. Never can be too careful, you know," said Uncle Albert, sliding aside Bean's plastic basket of food and replacing it with the document.

"That's for sure," said the creamy cottage cheese fluorescent bikini lady. "Never can be too careful about legal stuff, and I aught to know. Why, after my third husband died…"

"Shut the hell up, lady," said Uncle Albert.

She shut the hell up and moved to an empty table on the patio. Apparently she had been told to shut the hell up before because it didn't seem to surprise her that a complete stranger would tell her to shut the hell up. It wasn't uncommon for Uncle Albert either. He was always telling people to shut the hell up in his bar where people were always saying very stupid things because they were drunk. It's easy to tell drunk people to shut the hell up. It's the sober ones who don't take any crap and punch your lights out when you tell them to shut the hell up. Uncle Albert never tells sober people to shut the hell up but this lady's case was the exception because she was about to offer up a life lesson that could have quite possibly exposed his entire scheme. And besides, she reminded him of Gloria the whore and he didn't want to think about Gloria the whore.

Bean looked down at the document, pen in hand.

"Just sign right there by that X," said Uncle Albert.

Better read it first, thought Fruitcake, looking up to Bean and wagging his tail in order to emphasize his warning. Bean dropped another french fry and Fruitcake quickly lost all interest in any ongoing legal affairs.

"Well, okay," said Bean so he could get back to his cheeseburger. He singed on the line by the X. "Oops," he said. "Got some ketchup on it. Sorry."

"Ketchup? No problem," said Uncle Albert as he snatched up the document. "No problem at all Beanie my boy. Now, how bout another cheeseburger?"

Bean smiled. He never got a second cheeseburger at one setting due to his mom's philosophy. "All things in moderation," his mother used to say, though she wasn't sure why. She thought it was something she learned in college, or maybe Sunday school, something that was supposed to be repeated often to children. She wrote it on a picture of Barbara Bush and stuck it on the refrigerator so she would remember to repeat it often to Bean but she always forgot. She even forgot who Barbara Bush was and usually just assumed the picture was a relative. But then, that was okay because Barbara Bush always remembered to remind him every time he went to the refrigerator.

All things in moderation, remembered Bean. And he wondered if that applied to cheeseburgers.

chapter 7
Bean's Quest

The next day Bean was again at the Beachcomber, this time with Uncle Joe and Uncle Albert, where he was about to launch his quest. He didn't have much, which was probably a good thing because the Celestial Rocket didn't have much room. It was a midget of a car with only two seats, both of which would be needed to accommodate Bean and Fruitcake. The few things he did have, consisted of only one change of clothes and a toothbrush in a small Darth Vader back pack that Uncle Albert picked up at the Goodwill store for seventy five cents, a large box of Kellogg's Sugar Pops that Uncle Albert said was healthier than trail mix as well as cheaper, a six pack of Yoo-hoo chocolate drinks that Uncle Albert said was jam packed with vitamins and was the original energy drink, and some bottled water and Kibbles & Bits for Fruitcake. It was all tossed in the small trunk behind the continental spare tire. Uncle Albert had also given Bean a new three pack of Fruit of the Loom underwear as a farewell gift. Long ago Gloria the whore told Albert he should always wear clean underwear to avoid embarrassment in case he was in an accident and had to go to the hospital or even died. He wasn't quite sure he bought into Gloria's wisdom however, because he figured if you're in an accident you'd be covered with blood and guts anyway and if you died you would probably shit your pants, so what the hell was the point. Just the same, wanting to appear the ever-thoughtful uncle, and also thinking or even hoping Beanie boy might become a fatal statistic on some far off highway; he thought the three pack of grundies was a wise gift and an appropriate gesture as opposed to say, a black jack or a sawed off baseball bat for protection. And besides, the briefs were on a closeout sale at the Dollar General Store, two for the price of one, and he could keep one of the packs for himself.

"Well, guess it's time to hit the road, Beanie boy," said Uncle Albert.

"Um... yes sir. Guess so," agreed Bean looking up from behind the steering wheel.

"Remember, you get on the I-95 and keep goin' south," said Uncle Albert. "Just like Joe said. Follow the I-95 'til it ends then just follow the signs to Key West. You can't miss it. When you hit water and can't go no farther, well then you made it. Good luck and remember to always wear clean underwear. Ya never know. Know what I mean?"

"Um... yes sir," said Bean as he cranked up the Celestial Rocket and checked to see if Fruitcake was set. Bean wasn't quite sure about the philosophy of the underwear though because he pretty much lived in a bathing suit that required no such thing and was reluctant to alter his comfort level.

With the Celestial Rocket's top down, Fruitcake lay in the passenger seat belly up and balls to the sun, his eyes closed in sun-drenched ecstasy. *Let's roll*, thought Fruitcake, *Time to blow this pop stand Mac. I got an itch for a change of scenary.*

Fruitcake once found an old paperback detective novel on the beach titled *Sam Slade Ace Detective* and brought it home to Sister Moonbeam-Goom-jigi who assumed he wanted her to read it to him so she did. Ever since then Fruitcake sometimes utilizes the hokey dramatic jargon contained in the old book as though he were a regular Humphry Bogart.

Joe the bartender was pretty much a seventies burn-out much like Sister Moonbeam-Goom-jigi but not quite as far gone, and of course he wasn't dead yet. He told Bean that to the best of his memory Jimmy Buffett had set out for Key West, but he failed to inform him that that was nearly 40 years ago. "In fact," said Uncle Joe the bartender, "I think he became President of Key West when they declared independence and seceded from the United States and became the Conch Republic."

The Key West secession was a joke that made national headlines decades ago. Joe, like many Americans, didn't really keep up with the news much except for accidental occasional sound bites from TV news promos that aired between commercials, shows full of gratuitous sex and violence, and the more genteel game of football.

President, thought Bean. Wow. Not only was his father a famous singer but he was also the president of a country. The prospect of finding his father was getting more interesting each day and he was eager to be on his way.

The word had gotten out that Bean was going to be leaving town and for some reason this inspired the members of the local police department to form a covert escort that would insure his safe passage west as far as I-95. When Bean drove off he was unaware that there were patrol cars strategically parked all along the route, with another to travel the road in front of him running interference, and yet another one bringing up the rear to make sure no one could catch up with him to change his mind, all of which was coordinated by Sheriff Bubba Boyd Trumain in a police helicopter hovering above.

One would think that with Sister Moonbeam-Goom-jigi gone the cops would take the opportunity to finally apprehend the under-aged unlicensed driver, but the truth was the entire police force had a great deal of respect for Bean's driving and especially respected his mother because she was the only one in 32 years that had ever stood up to crusty old Judge Weingarberger. All the cops hated Judge Weingarberger because all the cops were former young hell raisers and juvenile delinquents who Judge Weingarberger forced to join the Army, Navy, or Marines Corps after he declared them guilty of something, even if they weren't actually guilty. The alternative was becoming the girlfriend of some very large hairy bad man in the county jail or prison. Judge Weingarberger declared everybody guilty all the time, equating expediency with justice, also so he could play more golf and lay on the beach near his condo and watch the girls. So the local cops were always very careful who they arrested. They certainly didn't want to arrest Bean, the son of their local hero, because he was too young to join the Marine Corps but not too young to be some big hairy bad man's girlfriend in a six by nine cell.

The entire St. Johns County police force was geared up and ready to go. Bean was geared up as well, having just consumed a farewell cheeseburger and fries, another fine unselfish farewell gesture by Uncle Albert. So as the morning sun hovered over the Florida coast, he was finally on his way, except he was about to throw a monkey wrench in the works of the intentions of his guardians in uniform. Bean liked being close to the ocean and he had studied the map he'd gotten from Uncle Joe. In fact he had never been far from it, and the map showed that State Road A1A ran south along the coast all the way to Key West. Bean decided he and the Celestial Rocket would travel that route as well.

The word went out via a prearranged call from Porky Fister who worked behind the counter at the Beachcomber. "The Kid's leavin," was all he said over the phone to Sheriff Bubba Boyd.

"I'm from Canada. Have you ever been to Manitoba, Canada?" asked the creamy cottage cheese fluorescent bikini lady sitting at the counter. When she removed her broad rimmed straw hat it revealed a head of streaked permed hair that looked like something only a young freak headbanger would have.

"No," answered Porky Fister. "You ever been to Siberia?"

"No," said the creamy cottage cheese fluorescent bikini lady.

"You should go there," said Porky Fister. "Soon."

Sheriff Bubba Boyd relayed Porky's message over the radio that Bean had hit the road. A few minutes later another radio message informed all the waiting cops that Bean had apparently gone off course, vanished off the grid before he even reached the intercept point. The radio chatter between the cops increased a hundred fold and they all immediately scattered in every direction in a desperate attempt to protect Bean from any incident that would put him in the clutches of miserable Judge Weingarberger.

As Bean drove the A1A bridge across the Matanzas Inlet to Summer Island and points south he looked east to the sea. Just then a white seaplane with a large round logo on the tale crossed low over the horizon heading south. He wondered what it would be like to ride in such a craft, to fly above the waves and into the clouds.

By the time the chopper located the oddly painted Celestial Rocket containing the boy and his dog; they were cruising down A1A well into neighboring Flagler County to the south.

"There's nothing we can do now boys," came the concerned voice of Sheriff Bubba Boyd. "He's out of our jurisdiction and on his own. Good luck kid."

Porky

A quarter mile behind the Celestial Rocket glided a 1958 red convertible Cadillac with a plastic bobbing head figure of Jesus attached to the dashboard. The driver played with the dial on the radio until it landed on a channel playing classic Frank Sinatra songs. He turned up the volume, leaned back and smiled, humming along with the music, his left hand on the wheel and his right mimicking that of an orchestra director. As he drove along, he casually debated whether he should once again begin collecting noses.

chapter 8
Chi Chi de Cocoa

Bean pulled to the side of the road at a spot that overlooked the breaking surf somewhere near Cocoa Beach. It was getting dark and he decided he had driven far enough for one day. It had been a trying journey so far because it seemed that just about everywhere he went people would stare and some would even honk their horns, especially if there were small children in their car. After driving through a number of towns and seeing so many other different cars he finally figured out that the unwanted attention was most likely due to the odd clown like custom paint job of the Celestial Rocket. Once while he was sitting at a red light an elderly woman actually got out of her car to inform him that Rocket was supposed to be spelled with an *E* not an *I,* and that it was kids like him who never paid attention and were the reason she became frustrated and disillusioned and retired from teaching school. There was little or nothing he could do about the state of his car so he put it all out of his mind, although remaining a little confused at the old woman's concerns because he had never attended any kind of school.

He and Fruitcake took a walk on the beach, munched some Sugar Pops and Kibbles & Bits, then settled back in the Celestial Rocket for the night. It was a clear pleasant evening with a warm breeze coming off the ocean. That along with the continuous sound of the surf, a rising moon, and the occasional sound of a few shore birds reminded him of his home and the many nights he would sleep in the hammock on the porch next to Fruitcake on his papa-san chair. Fruitcake was thinking along the same lines. He missed his papa-san chair and actually preferred Sister Moonbeam-Goom-jigi's mystery Creola to Kibbles & Bits, the smell of which somehow reminded him of her funeral on the pier.

Nearby a girl with long flowing dark hair, dressed in brown biker leather and high top jungle boots, was strolling unenthusiastically along A1A when she noticed the oddly painted little car with two heads protruding just above the seats. In the dim light she couldn't see them that well but well enough to think that the one on the passenger side was having a really bad hair day. She reached the conclusion that perhaps it was two young lovers taking in the moon and was about to continue on down the road when she spotted a shadowy figure of a man hovering nearby behind a palm tree. She slowed her pace as she focused more closely on the dark figure in the shadows. The man seemed to be taking a special interest in the couple in the funny little clown car. He moved closer, using the nearby palm trees and shrubs as cover until he paused, reached into his pocket and withdrew something shiny. The girl quickly put two and two together and came up with *danger* and decided to take action.

"Hey!" she yelled across the road with an obvious Cuban accent to the occupants of the funny little car. "Hey, meng, where da hell es chu guys bin?"

The girl's sudden appearance and outburst caused the man to pause and back into the shadows.

"Hey, meng. I bin lookin' for chu all day. Where da hell es chu guys bin?" she said, startling Bean and Fruitcake when she popped up next to the car. "Chu know chu ain sposa bin dissapearin' on me ly dat. Makin' me look all over da friggin' plaze for chu."

Bean stared, not sure what to make of her, so he said nothing.

"Whoa," she said as she looked into the car, surprised to not find a girl but discovering Fruitcake instead. "Das one ugly friggin' dog chu gots dere, meng."

Dog? What Dog? You ain't exactly Miss America yourself there, mango mama, thought Fruitcake. *Could use a little more hair on your face.*

She leaned closer to Bean and half whispered. "Dun chu be lookin' now kid but chu gots some compny in dem bushes dere and he gots him a gun or sumpen."

Bean looked over just in time to catch a quick glimpse of someone backing into the shadows.

She darted around to the passenger side of the car and hopped over the door, nearly sitting on top of Fruitcake when she landed in the seat. "Chu better crank dis leetle munchkin bucket clown car up and get da hell outta here before we gets our asses in some big bad troubles."

Bean did as instructed, though he wasn't sure why. In spite of her atrocious English the girl demonstrated enough authority that he thought he should obey. Fruitcake had been knocked down and wedged between the two seats so the girl picked him up as though he were some kind of diseased carcass she found dead on the road and placed him in a roomier spot between and behind them. As they sped away, the man in the shadows stepped out into the light. In his hand was a very sharp, very impressive pearl handled switchblade knife. He touched the button and the blade retracted with a quick click and he slid it back into his pocket. "Shit," he said as he walked away.

"Whoa, meng. Dat wass a close one," said the strange girl as she leaned back in the seat. "I thin maybe I juss safed chur ass, meng."

Bean just sat silent and drove, catching an occasional glance at her when the road and his driving permitted.

Hey, whass wit all dis meng stuff lady? Chu sung kina chi wawa or sungthin? thought Fruitcake, mocking the accent of their uninvited passenger.

"Whassa matta, meng?" she asked Bean. "Cat got chur tongue?"

"Bean," said Bean in a shy uncertain manner.

"Huh?" said the girl.

"Bean," he repeated.

"Hey, es chu callin' me a beaner? Dun chu be callin' me no beaner. I ain no Mexican. I'n from Kooba, meng," she said, pronouncing her homeland Cuba as *Kooba* as most original Koobans do.

"Um, no ma'am. *I'm* Bean," corrected Bean. "My name is *Bean*. Bean Buffett."

"Bean? Chure nem es Bean?"

"Yes ma'am."

"*Ma'am*? Chu es callin' me *ma'am*," said the girl, surprised. "Ho chi mama. Ain nobody ever calls me ma'am before."

"And Fruitcake," added Bean, taking his hand off the wheel long enough to point to Fruitcake with his thumb. "This is Fruitcake."

"Fruitscakes. Ho chi mama. Yep, he look likes sung kina Fruitscakes. Whassa matta wit his ear?"

"He only has one," said Bean.

"Das what I min. He ain't gots no ear an he gots a funny tooth. How come?" said the girl. "An wha kina nem es Fruitscakes?"

It's my name, and that's my damn seat you're in... Miss ho chi mama, thought Fruitcake.

"I don't know, ma'am. He's just always been like that," said Bean.

"Dun be callin' me no ma'am. Es Corena," she said. "Corena Maria Christina Gertudis de Avellaneda. Das my nem. Buh chu can call me Chi Chi. Cause Chi Chi, das my moofy star nem."

"Your what? You're a moofy star? I mean, movie star?" said Bean.

84

"Hell no. Course I ain no moofy star. Buh I gonna be a moofy star. An when I gonna be a moofy star I gonna be *Chi Chi* the moofy star. I gonna be a bigger moofy star den dat Chay Lo."

"Chay Lo?" questioned Bean.

"Yeah, chu know. Chay Lo. Chees a big Chicano moofy star and a big singer too. But chees got a bubble butt. I ain gonna haff no bubble butt when I'n a big moofy star."

"I've never seen a movie," said Bean.

"Ho chi mama. Chu tellin' me chu neffer seen no moofies? Where chu live at kid, on da moon?"

"No ma'am. St. Augustine Beach."

"Oh, well, das kina like the sane thin."

"That's a pretty name," said Bean. "I mean the other name, your name. But very long."

"Das why chu juss calls me Chi Chi."

"Yes ma'am."

"Bean and Fruitscakes and Chi Chi," she laughed. "Das soun kina like Chreestmas dinner in Kooba."

Corena Maria Christina Gertudis de Avellaneda, alias Chi Chi, was a survivor. As a twelve-year-old refugee she had survived the arduous crossing from Cuba on a raft constructed mainly of a wooden sugar cane wagon kept afloat by a combination of about four hundred inner tubes, Mickey Mouse beach balls, assorted Styrofoam noodles and inflatable Buzz Lightyear blow-up pool toys from Wal-Mart that had been shipped to the island from relatives and Cuban/American liberation groups in Miami. Her parents who were unable to make the trip from Cuba to the Keys so they placed her on the raft. Upon arrival Chi Chi was supposed to search out her aunt and uncle who worked at some tourist attraction up in Miami called the Monkey Jungle, feeding monkeys and cleaning up monkey shit so the monkeys wouldn't throw it on the tourists. A lot of people who live in Miami want to throw shit on tourists but it's illegal because it's bad for the economy. Only the monkeys can do it and get away with it.

The raft missed the Florida Keys altogether and came to rest on South Beach early one morning with the help of a tow by a fellow Cuban charter fisherman who found them in the Gulf Stream heading for Iceland. As soon as they were feet-dry all the newly liberated illegal alien refugee Cubans aboard the raft quickly fled and melted away into South Florida's population of millions of other illegal alien refugee Cubans. Chi Chi was left sitting all alone on the beach until tourists and local beach goers began to arrive asking to buy the beach balls, inner tubes, noodles, and Buzz Lightyear pool toys. Chi Chi, a quick thinker and fast learner, was more than willing to accommodate them. She was alone in a strange country but she had already discovered the benefits of American free enterprise starting her off with a keen knack for survival and a grubstake of nearly six hundred dollars. She never looked back and Chi Chi has been a survivor ever since.

Chi Chi's happenstance encounter with Bean in Cocoa Beach was the result of a fight that took place with her biker boyfriend who went by the name of Pounder. It took place up the coast in Daytona, the Florida destination of choice for bikers from all over America. After the fight she dumped him because she discovered he wasn't actually what he claimed to be, a bad-ass biker and part time actor with connections that could get her a part in an upcoming flick with Ben Afflack. She discovered he was in reality a married GED adult education instructor from Pompano who coached little league soccer and was only on a thrill-seeking summer vacation road trip, and as such not at all interested in a long term relationship or helping Chi Chi become a major movie star. His real name was Clarence Bittle. She left Clarence Bittle painfully prostrated and holding his cajones in a biker bar called Bertha's Wheel House Saloon & Chicken Shack. Bertha was actually a sixty-two year old balding fat guy named Brumo with facial scars and a beard who always wore black T-shirts that sported obscene statements like *Eat Shit and Die,* and studded jeans that showed his butt crack. Brumo's butt crack was showing when he tossed Clarence Bittle out the door just before Chi Chi hit the road hitch-hiking back to Miami.

"I'm going to Key West," said Bean. "Should I pull over so you can get out?"

Yeah, pull over so she can get out, thought Fruitcake. *I want my seat back.*

"No thanks. I'n good, meng" said Chi Chi. "I bin to Key Wess. How come chu gonna go to Key Wess?"

"To find my father," said Bean.

"Oh yeah? To find chur papa? So, who es chur papa? Es him lost or sungthin?"

"Jimmy Buffett," said Bean.

"Wha?" said Chi Chi. "Are chu kidden me?"

"Jimmy Buffett," repeated Bean. "I think he lives in Key West. Uncle Joe told me he lives in Key West."

"Oh yeah? Did Huncle Cho also telt chu da moon es made of grin cheese?"

"No," said Bean.

"Ho chi mama. I choulda know," she said to herself. "A clown car anna Fruitscakes dog. I choulda know, meng. Dis kid es sung kina whack job. How come I'n alwaze gets da whack jobs?"

"You see, my mother was killed by a waterspout and she wanted me to find him. And my Uncle Albert wants me to find him too. He's a singer and Joe says he's the President of Key West," added Bean proudly.

Ho chi mama, thought Chi Chi, *he sung kina whack brain hokay.*

Ho chi mama, thought Fruitcake. *Chu ain zactly no Einstein churself, toots.*

chapter 9
Babes in Dude Land

About twenty miles south of Melbourne the Celestial Rocket and its passengers came to a lone stretch of road they thought would be a good place to pull over for the rest of the night. It was past midnight and Bean and Chi Chi both agreed they needed some sleep. Chi Chi chose to sprawl out across the hood of the car on top of the bad rendition of the manatee with the backward baseball cap and sunglasses, leaving Bean in an uncomfortable partial fetus position across the seats inside. Fruitcake was stretched out on top of the trunk against the continental spare tire, balls to the stars.

Hours later the sun was straining to rise far out over the horizon, presenting a hazy gray orange ray of light over the ocean that eventually gave way to a brighter red and yellow burst that introduced a new day. Shore birds took flight and began their morning feeding rituals in the new light and change of the tide. On a nearby post sat a gray pelican with its wings spread wide to the rising sun in an effort to warm and rid itself of unwanted parasites. Also with the morning sun there came the occasional passing vehicle that our sleeping travelers failed to even notice. Two of those passing vehicles pulled quietly to the side of the road. The sound of opening and closing doors caused Fruitcake to stir and open one eye. His upside down line of sight revealed nothing of interest except a pelican on a post so he closed his eye and went back to dreaming he was Sam Slade Ace Detective about to crack the case of the missing blue searching for jimmy buffett 🌴

cookies. Fruitcake was a better imaginary detective than he was a watchdog.

"Dude."

"Whoa, dude."

"Duuuude, yah yah."

"Oh yeah, dude, whoa."

"Dude, like… check it out dude."

To Bean, the not so intellectual conversation seemed like a fuzzy distant dream that grew closer and seemed to surround him. He stirred uncomfortably until hitting his head on the steering wheel caused him to wake enough to recognize human voices. At least they sounded human.

"Hey dude, check it brah."

"Oh dude. Righteous."

"Whoa, like bitchin' brah."

"Far out, dudes. Like awesome."

Then came a voice he actually recognized.

"Ho chi mama!"

Chi Chi's *ho chi mama* cut into Fruitcake's Sam Slade Ace Detective dream with about as much subtlety as when the vet sticks a cold thermometer up his ass when he goes in for his booster shots. His dream grinded to a rude halt and he was thrown back into reality, opening his eyes and rolling over to discover a group of oddly speaking near naked natives.

"Whoa, truly awesome conveyance, dude."

"Like other worldly, brah."

"Oh yeah… like… a truly enlightening ride, dudes."

The eight odd creatures stood surrounding the Celestial Rocket in awe of its appearance as though it had descended from the heavens onto their small isolated island world. Almost as though it were some chariot of the gods or an alien space ship come back to check on its experimental earthbound inbred children.

"Ho chi mama," said Chi Chi. "Chu gotta be kidden."

Ho chi mama, thought Fruitcake. *What the hell is this?*

"Good morning," said Bean, sitting up in the car and offering an innocent sleepy smile.

"Dude," acknowledged one of the eight natives, the one with the long beaded hair standing next to the driver's side door.

"Brah," greeted another, the dark one with dreadlocks as he shook his head and smiled approvingly of the Celestial Rocket. "Truly enlightening ride, brah. Truly."

"Dude," said one of the other natives to the one with the beaded hair. The single word statement appointed the beaded haired one as spokesman.

"Dude," replied the braided beaded haired one with a nod, acknowledging acceptance of the honored role. He looked down at Bean and just bobbed his head up and down as though he were trying to keep rhythm with some distant jungle drum.

"Um, my name is Bean," said Bean with an uncertain half smile.

"Bean," repeated the braided beaded haired one.

"Bean, dude," said another.

"Whoa, *Bean."*

"Bean, brah."

"Bean. Yuh, *Bean,* awesome."

"Dude Beeeean."

The natives nodded their heads in agreement as they repeated Bean's name in their own limited dialect until it rolled comfortably off their collective tongue. Apparently they approved of Bean's name.

"Ho chi mama," said Chi Chi, sitting up on the hood of the car.

Ho chi mama, thought Fruitcake, sitting up on the trunk of the car.

"Um… who're you?" asked Bean.

"We are…" said the braided beaded one with a very extensive pregnant pause as though he were about to reveal a cure for cancer, "…*the Dawn Patrol,* seekers of waves, harmony, inner peace… and cool chicks. Currently bound for the inlet of Sebastian, the Mecca of Florida surfers everywhere. For a distant storm has brought crankin swells and the surf… is up."

"Oh," said Bean. Looking over his shoulder he noticed their vehicles, a red and white two tone 1964 Volkswagen Micro Bus and a royal blue 1949 Ford Country Squire Woody. On top of each vehicle was racked a pile of classic style long boards.

"They call me…" another long pregnant pause by the braided beaded one, *"Dude Slicer.* But you may call me… *Dude Slicer."*

"And I am called… *Dude 'Cuda,* as in… *barracuda,"* said one of the well tanned chiseled hard body dawn patrol surf natives. He reached out and gallantly took Chi Chi's hand and kissed it.

"Hooo chiii mama," said Chi Chi with a smile. "And I'n called… *Chi Chi."*

Crap, I think I'm gonna puke, thought Fruitcake.

"Like man, we could not help but admire your awesome ride," said Dude Slicer.

"A most eclectic ride indeed, dude," said the native with a straw hat that had a small stuffed alligator mounted on top. "You may call me *Dude Zeus."* He looked down at Fruitcake.

Try and kiss my hand and I'll bite off you nose… duuude, thought Fruitcake.

Their names kept coming as introductions; most all preceded by the titles Dude or Brah. Names like *Dude Banzai* and *Brah Bird, Brah Buster,* and *Dude Hammerhead,* until the eighth and final surf native reluctantly introduced himself.

"Bob," he said.

"Chu es juss a *Bob?"* asked Chi Chi.

"Um… *Dude Kahuna Bob,"* he corrected, seeming a bit embarrassed.

"You will join us," said the Braided Beaded one. "We have food and drink. You will join our *surfary* to Sebastian Inlet. We insist."

"Uh… well, okay," answered Bean, looking to Chi Chi for confirmation.

"Why not. I gots no plazes to be," said Chi Chi. "I'n wit chu, Bean. An sides, wha dose guys got to eats gotta be better den Chugar Pops and Chu-yoos."

"Yoo-hoos," corrected Bean.

"Hokay, whateva."

"Hey Brah Bean, man, like your dog only has one ear," observed Dude Zeus.

Yeah, well, so what? Like, you only got one brain cell… Brah, thought Fruitcake.

Fruitcake might have done better to keep his thoughts to himself because Dude Zeus wasted no time taking over his coveted passenger seat when Chi Chi joined some of the other surf natives in the VW Micro bus.

The now three vehicle surfing surfary convoy cruised down A1A along the beach looking like some kind of nostalgic throwback work of art on the cover of yet another *Best of the Beach Boys* album. The '49 Woody led the way, followed by the Celestial Rocket with the VW Micro bus bringing up the rear. Bean noticed that as traffic increased people were no longer staring at them as though they were freaks in a clown car but instead were honking their horns and offering up the two-finger surfer wave salute of approval. Some even gave the ultimate tribute by dropping their shorts and hanging their ass out the window. Most of the traffic included vehicles carrying young people and surfboards that were heading, as were they, for the State Park at Sebastian Inlet.

Just as Dude Slicer said, there was a big storm named Hurricane Tyamekwa (pronounced *To-oa-mick-az*), about a hundred miles or so off the coast. The storm was named Tyamekwa (pronounced *To-oa-mick-az*) because one day some Congressman in Washington who didn't have anything else to do and needed some television face time to show his constituents at home in Chicago he was actually doing his job, held a press conference complaining and bitching about tropical storms always being named after white people. Not that they had to worry much about tropical storms in Chicago. NBC news was all over it and the issue developed into a major story on the front page of the New York Times because, well, that's the kind of stories they put on the front page of the New York Times.

The government's knee-jerk response to NBC's prominent coverage and its subsequent discussion and commentary programs, and a two-hour special documentary exploring the existence of inexcusable rampant racism in our government's weather and climate bureaucracy, and the New York Times important story and its subsequent editorials about the existence of insensitive rampant and blatant racism in our government's weather and climate bureaucracy, was to hold four months of hearings and investigations by the House of Representatives and Senate to find out why tropical storms were always named after white people, and to find out if that's why tropical storms existed in the first place, and if so, what political party was responsible. Then they held five months of committee meetings to decide who to prosecute, what to do to fix the problem, how much money it will cost, and who to tax in order to raise the money.

Eventually Washington spent two years and two billion dollars and decided to blame George Bush and the Republicans and prosecuted three employees of the National Hurricane Center, one of which was only the janitor who had once helped pick the name *Bob* for a Hurricane. Then they levied a sur-charge tax on all flashlights, batteries, and plastic tarps made in the United States because they reasoned that flashlights and batteries and even tarps creation and purpose was primarily due to the existence of tropical storms, even though most all of the flashlights and batteries and tarps sold in the United States are now made in China, Mexico, and other various non-democratic third world countries. The government also created a new bureaucracy called the *Department of Cultural Climatic Nomenclature (*the DCCN) consisting of 4,371 employees whose only accomplishments after its first full year of existence was the creation of the *Earth Science African-American Cultural Sensitivity Awareness Program,* (the ESAACSAP). The DCCN's ESAACSAP course is now required for all radio and television weather people, as well as all HAM radio operators, before they can be licensed and actually be permitted to say the names of tropical storms over the air waves. The DCCN's only other achievement was to produce 5,000,000 copies of a small five-page brochure printed on imported recycled paper, the production of which was contracted to a defense firm at $1,329 per dozen copies, plus shipping and handling. It was a very attractive colorful brochure with a satellite picture of a massive hurricane and five minority children dramatically superimposed in the eye of the storm, all looking like they just found out that Santa Clause wasn't real. The brochure listed in alphabetical order fifty-six African American names that could be used for naming tropical storms, none of which were pronounced the way they were spelled and none of which ever even existed in any language in either the United States of America, Africa, or anywhere else on the planet prior to their invention by illiterate single mothers in the 1980s. An additional 800,000 similar brochures were later produced in Spanish, Croatian, Vietnamese, Russian, Arabic, Portuguese, Farsi, Mandarin Chinese, and braille. Copies of the brochures are of course available free for the asking from the Federal Citizen Information Center in Pueblo, Colorado. The DCCN was also charged with the responsibility of monitoring and scientifically evaluating the rate of inception of illegitimate minority children during the hurricane season as opposed to national holidays and leap years, and teamed with NASA to research the possiblility of using other minority names for solar storms on the sun.

Regardless of Washington's stupidity the government appearantly had done everything right as far as the Dawn Patrol surf natives were concerned because hurricane Tyamekwa (pronounced *To-oa-mick-az*) was cranking bodacious waves at Sebastian Inlet, currently at six feet and rising fast.

As the members of the surfary cruised down the road counting how many bare asses were hung out the windows of passing vehicles, Dude Slicer, driving the VW buss, tuned in the surf report on AM radio station W-O-R-T. The surf report show was sponsored and produced by a local surf and dive shop in Melbourne Beach, and featured the talent of a high school drop out part time sales clerk full time beachnick named Skank Sitchian. Skank was updating everyone within radio range of the current surf conditions with reports that were sourced from information being called in by surfers up and down the coast. This wasn't an easy task because Skank always got a lot of crank calls from surfers who just wanted to bust his balls or see if they could get away with saying the word *fuck* on the air before Skank could cut them off. Just the same, Skank usually maintained an even strain and managed to get the surf info to the needy. (Usually)

> "*'Um... oooh... um 'kay, like, the waves are really bitchin' due to the climatic influences a hundred miles off the coast by Hurricane Tya... uh... Too... uh... Toochee...kwaz. Uh, yeah, like, improving up around the Space Coast at oooh bout three or four, but hey man, that's okay cause it ain't the usual beach break, know what I mean. And like gettin' real serious down Sebastian way,*

dudes. Goin off big time, like outside at five and six feet and growin' fast is the latest word. Gonna be a big one, dudes. So, like, let me know what's happnin down there dudes, "kay?. So, like give ol' Skank a call here at WORT, 'kay?"

In the background could be heard another voice, that of Skank's employer Ralph "Curley" Carney, who used to be a high school shop teacher until he cut off his left index and pinky finger on purpose so he could sue the school system and go on permanent disability. With his lawsuit winnings, his union and State benefits, and the security of his disability compensation check from the Federal government, which was more than enough to cover his alimony payments, he bought a 60 foot house boat and opened a surf and dive shop next to a Winn Dixie grocery store. It was located in a strip center in what used to be the location of the Home & Hearth Financial Services Office. The Home & Hearth Financial Services Office no longer exist because it was raided and closed down for giving sweetheart deals to government officials, bad mortgage deals backed by the government to unqualified home owners, and financing and distributing crack cocaine. So now Curley Carney has the keys to the place and goes to work in shorts, sandals, and cool looking surfer T-shirts, and is admired day after day by young surfers and little grommets who probe him for wave wisdom and credit of which he gives niether.

"Read the ad," Curley could be heard growling in the background to Skank. "Don't forget to read the damn ad."

"Oh yeah, right man like, read the… 'Kay all you dudes and dudets headin' for the waves don't want to forget to stop by Curley's Surf & Dive Shop in Melbourne Beach before you go, 'kay? 'Cause we got stuff for sale like two for one Sex

Wax, and... um, ten percent off all our Sea Slug custom boards, and... um, oh yeah, don't forget to stock up on Curley's own Goofy Foot brand coconut and banana scented sun tan lotion that's also good for rashes and stuff. And it really works, man, cause, like, I got this rash once from my board in this really inconvenient place and, like, my girl rubbed it on and it really worked dudes, so try it, 'kay? Oh, and like we got lots of free Sea Slug stickers left too, so, um, you know, like get 'em while they last, 'kay? 'Kay, man, like we got a phone report comin' in from some dude named Squeeze MacDougal down at Sebastian. 'Kay, you're on the air Squeeze dude so tell us what's happnin at the Inlet?"

"Waves, dude."

"Yeah, right, 'kay, so what's happnin?"

"Uhhh, like I'd saaaay... liiiike, maybe... umm... on a scale of one to ten... umm... really bitchin."

"Yeah, 'kay, good, so like, how high, dude?"

"Hey man, I ain't high. Don't be sayin' on the radio that I'm high and shit man cause I ain't high."

"No man, like I ain't sayin...

"I mean you can't be sayin' that shit, ya know? Cause I ain't really high. I mean I ain't had any weed since, um, well ya know. So don't be sayin' I'm high on the radio cause you ain't never sure if the feds or the Republicans are listenin', ya know? So don't be doin' that."

"Yeah, 'kay dude, so tell me about the surf conditions at the Inlet, 'kay dude? All the surfers are listenin' and wanna know what's happnin down there."

"What? Where?"

"Tell us what you're seein' at the Inlet, dude."

"The Inlet? Hell, I dunno. That's why I called you. Don't you know? We're sittin' at the Waffle House, dude."

Dude Slicer played with the radio knob searching for another surf report but it was the original 1964 radio that came with his 1964 VW Micro bus and it only picked up AM radio stations. He tuned in shows like the Temple of Solomon Hour with Rabbi Joseph Goldfarb, sponsored by the Center for Hebrew Awareness. It had people who called in and talked about how Muslims suck. And there was the Psychic Cooking Show starring that amazing blind chef Angelina Potter, sponsored by the Mid Coastal Burn Center. And then there were the myriad of foreign speaking stations playing foreign music. Some catered to illegal Mexicans but there were mostly Cuban stations with angry illegal alien Cuban refugees talking about how Fidel Castro sucks in between hot salsa songs that all sounded the same. There was also a Haitian station that advertised voodoo services, and an Arabic station that talked about how Jews and American infidels sucked and asked for donations to support nuclear research. Dude Slicer gave up searching and returned to the surf report on W-O-R-T.

"Dude there ain't no waves in the Waffle House. I mean, duh."

"Well yeah, dude. If there was waves breakin' in the Waffle House then like all the waffles would, like, get all gushy and shit."

"Hey, dude. Like, you can't say that on the radio."

"Say what?"

"You know. That."

"What?"

"Shit. You can't say shit on the radio."

"Can't say... Well hey, man, like you just said it."

"Dude, you just can't say that, 'kay?"

"What? Can't say what?"

"Shit, 'kay? So why'd you call if like, you don't know what's happnin at Sebastian?"

"Well, yeah, dude. You know, it's that hurricane Tyu... Tooa... my... ass... thing, out there... and stuff."

"But you don't know nothin', 'kay? So why'd you call in if you're sittin' in the Waffle House and you don't know nothin' bout the waves?"

"Because, dude..."

"Because what?"

"Well... cause, you know?"

"No I don't know. What?"

"Like to find out stuff and... uh, stuff."

"You know what I think. I think you're a dumbass idiot, that's what I think, 'kay? I think you're a dumbass stoner who's sittin' in the Waffle House on the I-95 right now and probably in possession of illegal drugs. That's what I think. I think you're a poser. I don't think you even know how to surf cause you're a dumbass stoner. That's what I think."

"Hey man, like you gotta be careful what you're sayin' on the radio cause you don't know who's listnin, ya know? Like maybe the DEA or the CIA or IRS or PTA or those other initials."

"What?"

"Or the Republicans or those Homeland people or somethin' might be listenin' and shit."

"Hey, I told you, you can't say that on the radio."

"Yeah I know, cause they might be listnin and shit."

"No, I mean don't say 'shit'."
"Yeah, I know, cause ya might get busted.

Dude Zeus, riding in the Celestial Rocket with Bean, reached over and turned on the radio.

"Dude?" he said to Bean, meaning, *do you mind if I turn on the radio?*

Somehow Bean understood. "Sure, go ahead," he told Dude Zeus.

On came W-O-R-T.

"I hope the CIA is listenin'. I hope the whole damn government is listenin' and they put you on the terrorist most wanted list and then bust your stoner ass and then send you to Gitmo where you can't call any more radio stations... ever, never again, 'kay? Cause it's surfers like you who give surfers like us a bad name cause you're just a dumbass stoner."

"Whoa, like, you should mellow out dude. You know, like chill. Like get you some weed or ludes or somethin' and just... you know, just... Oh, hey man, like my waffles are here so I gotta go cause I'm really hungry, ya know? Oh shit man, they burned the bacon."

"I hope you choke on your bacon. I hope you choke and... I hope..."

Dude Zeus changed the dial on the radio to a hot salsa number and started gyrating in his seat to the beat. A rusty old pickup truck with oversized tires and surfboards sticking out of the back passed them on the left. Just as it drew parallel to the Celestial Rocket three bare asses with faces drawn on them that looked a lot like Tammy Faye Baker, popped up over the side panel.

Ho chi mama, thought Fruitcake.

chapter 10
Big Thursday!

Upon their arrival they could see Sebastion Inlet State Park was already filling up fast with every manner of vehicle that could carry a surfboard and every kind of surfer that could ride one. From the parking lot they were all migrating to the sound of the breakers like so many newly hatched sea turtles emerging from the sand and desperately scooting to the sea. Beaner, Chi Chi, Fruitcake and the Dawn Patrol joined the migrating mass and went up and over the dunes feeling like the children of Moses rushing into the Promised Land. Over the crest of the dunes there appeared on the beach before them a colorful array of surfers with hundreds of boards planted and protruding out of the sand as though they somehow grew there from seed.

Bean had never seen so many people at one time on a beach before. In fact Bean had never seen so many people at one time anyplace before, nor had he ever seen so many surfboards in one place. There were little grommet surfers whose mothers probably didn't even know they were there. And there were liberated girl surfers who thought they had something to prove for the sake of socially enslaved women all over America, or because they had disappointed fathers who wanted a boy and didn't get one, or because they were gender confused and had something to prove because they were gender confused. There were also the sponsored competition surfers who collected oversize plastic trophies and got their pictures in the surfing magazines and got lots of free surfer stuff like surfer clothes, and free custom surfboards, and free rides to all the tournaments in new air conditioned custom painted RVs, and free motel rooms, and all the Whopper hamburgers and KFC chicken they could eat. In contrast there were also the soul surfers, the older independent guys who preferred to surf alone and looked down on the crowds and commercial competition side of surfing. They felt that surfing was a soulful event, a function of the inner being, a near religious experience, just man and wave, mono-e-mono, becoming one with the sea and the universe. They're also the ones who blew their chance to be sponsored commercial competiton surfers because they either weren't good enough or they were always stoned or serving time in juvie.

They were all there, every kind of surfer known to the Florida sands, all vying for the same big bitchin' waves sent to the Inlet by hurricane Tyamekwa (pronounced *To-oa-mick-az*), the biggest waves to hit Sebastian since, well… since hurricane Auntueweine (pronounced An-twan) that passed off shore the year before. And they were all ready to put their lives in danger, not from the waves but from the multitude of surfers who were all trying to catch the same wave.

Into the hopeful mass of wave riders on the beach there entered the Dawn Patrol surf natives and their newfound companions Bean, Chi Chi, and a paranoid Fruitcake, who was nervously looking for fat guys with guns.

Nearby, two young surfers stood with their boards tucked under their arms, their eyes firmly fixed on the incoming swells.

"Wow, man. It's awesome," observed the one young surfer with the bleached hair tips and single fake black pearl stud in the left side of his nose.

"Yeah, crankin' maybe eight feet now," said the other young surfer with the most zits and the buzz cut that he thought made him look just like Kelly Slater, famous Florida native and multiple world champion surfer.

"Nah, not even. More like ten if it's a foot."

"Whoa, it's *Big Wednesday*, dude," said the Kelly Slater wannabe with the zits, referring to the famous surf movie.

"No, dude, it's Thursday."

"*Wednesda*y, dude. You know, like, *Big Wednesday*."

"No dude. I told ya, it's *Thursday*."

"Yeah but no, I mean yeah Thursday, but you know, *Big Wednesday*, man."

"Man, like I just told you, it ain't *Wednesday* it's *Thursday*. I know cause Skank's workin' at Curley's and Skank only works at Curley's on Tuesdays, Thursdays, and Saturdays, dude, and Skank's doin' the surf report this morning so that means he's working and it's *Thursday* cause it ain't Tuesday or Saturday."

"No dude, I mean *Big Wednesday*. It's Big Wednesday with the giant waves and shit."

"Man, you don't know what the hell you're talkin' about. Who the hell cares what day it is anyway? Oh, hey man, you know what just hit me? This is all kind of like that movie with those three guys and those giant waves."

"Yeah dude, *Big Wednesday*."

"Oh man, will you quit with that damn Wednesday shit."

"Hey dude, look at those guys," said the Kelly Slater wannabe as he checked out Bean and his new friends. "Check it out, dude. That's some radical lookin' natives. Didn't have those in Big Wedenesday."

"Will you quit with that Wednesday shit."

The Dawn Patrol surf natives moved cautiously through the crowd looking out and checking the surf as they went.

"Whoa," said Dude Slicer, as he looked upon the impressive incoming swells, swells that were so inundated with surfers that they looked more like giant sausages being attacked by an army of ants. "Not cool, dudes," he said, referring to the crowded surf.

A depressed harmonious collective "Dude" of agreement and disappointment emanated from the other seven surf natives.

"Ho chi mama," said Chi Chi, who, in her biker leathers, looked as out of place on the beach as a street hooker in a monastery. "Ho chi mama. Dis worse'n Sunday on Me'ahmi Beash."

About that time she spotted an unattended beach bag with what looked like a bikini top hanging out of it. Both Chi Chi and the bag disappeared in the wink of an eye.

The surf natives finally found a clear spot in the crowd where they planted their long boards and their asses in the sand.

"Dudes," said Brah Buster, gesturing to the gridlock on the waves and meaning, *this sucks.*

"Dude," agreed, Dude Hammerhead, meaning, *you got that right.*

"Dudes," said Dude Kahuna Bob, meaning, *I told you guys this was a lame ass idea.*

Dudes, thought Fruitcake, meaning, *like, where's the food, brah.*

Just then there came the sound of a loud horn, one of those compressed air things that come in a can that people take to football games so they can destroy the eardrums of the people sitting near them in the stands, or are sometimes used to drive the visiting team insane when they're sitting down by the sideline. At the sound of the horn everyone on the beach paused, then all looked in the direction of the obnoxiously loud sound to discover… THEM!

It was… *THOSE GUYS!*

And *they* had arrived, as everybody feared they probably would but everybody hoped they wouldn't. And… *they* had just signaled with an irritating can of compressed noise that *they* were taking over the beach and claiming all the bodacious hurricane Tyamekwa (pronounced *To-oa-mick-az)* waves for themselves.

They were the infamous feared bad ass Surf Nazis! Known and seen on beaches all over Florida and occasionally all the way up as far as Cape Hatteras, North Carolina. They ruled the beaches by way of fear and intimidation, and disgusting appearance and bad hygiene.

All talk and movement on the beach came to a complete halt and all the surfers in the water quickly bellied down and paddled to shore, relinquishing their right to surf. The feared bad ass Surf Nazis had laid claim to the Big Wednesday (Thursday) moment and not even the Sebastian State Park rangers who were packing side arms would dare confront them simply because they didn't get paid enough and valued the tires and windows on their vehicles as well as the lives of their children more than their jobs.

There were six of them, fearsome, intimidating, all looking like they had been born in hell of Satan himself, or the product of bad over the top movie casting. Each of them was adorned from head to toe with tattoos that proclaimed some form of anarchist message, disproportionate nude women, meaningless but artistic spider webs and strands of barbed wire; tattoos showing a total disrespect for motherhood, and demonstrating a misspent youth that obviously didn't include watching Captain Kangaroo or reading Boys Life magazine. Three of them had shaved bald heads, and two of those heads were covered with spider web tattoos, one of which included a spider. One even had tattoos on his eyelids depicting his favorite four-letter word. Two of the Surf Nazis had multi-colored dreadlocks and one, though bald headed, sported a two and a half foot braided Chinese ponytail. They all had silver or gold rings through their lips, ears, navels, noses, and toes, as well as studs in places that even a doctor wouldn't examine. Just the sight of them caused most people to move aside, as much to avoid communicable diseases as from fear of conflict. The surfboards tucked under their arms were all custom-made east coast shredders with custom paint jobs depicting bloody violent acts of rape and fornication by Dark Age dungeonous creatures that made a day with Rambo seem like a church picnic. A small three-inch logo on the aft end of each board depicted some sort of cyber snail graphic with the logo words *SEA SLUG,* and underneath in smaller letters it said, *Curley's Surf & Dive Shop, Melbourne Beach, Florida.*

"What's going on?" asked Bean.

"Nazis," answered Dude Slicer.

"What's a Nazi?" asked Bean.

"Bad news," said Dude Hammerhead.

"Dudes," said the other Dawn Patrol surf natives, meaning a concerned, *dudes!*

Some people started to pack up and leave the beach. Mothers covered the eyes of their children. Others just moved aside, stood and watched with intense curiosity as the Surf Nazis paraded through and ignored everyone on the beach as though they didn't exist. That is until they came upon the members of the Dawn Patrol. For some reason, to the Surf Nazis, the Dawn Patrol represented dissent, contempt, or competition, and this caused them to pause. They stood and stared, the rings in their noses and eyebrows twitching with anxious anger, the sun beating down on their sweaty dark tanned unshaved faces, dripping perspiration from the mass quantities of beer and tequila consumed the night before. The Dawn Patrol rose and stared back. The more emotionally disturbed Nazi, the one with the tattooed eyelids seemed to be restraining some form of convulsive rage, causing the four-letter word on his left eye to flutter like a defective neon sign.

Everyone on the beach watched with apprehension, not knowing what to expect but expecting the worse. After an intense long silent moment during which the Surf Nazis sized up the Dawn Patrol, the emotionally disturbed one with the fluttering four-letter word on his eyelids finally spoke.

"Duuuude," he said with demonic intonation.

Soft whispers of *"Whoa, Uh Oh,* and *Oh shit,"* came from the crowd.

Following another long silent moment there finally came an impulsive reply from Dude Slicer of the Dawn Patrol. "Duuuude," he replied.

The crowd on the beach stirred with excitement and there came a loud quake of conversation as hundreds of onlookers began passing the word of a possible rumble on the waves. The Surf Nazis had thrown down the gauntlet and the Dawn Patrol had accepted.

Then the six Surf Nazis exploded into wild animalistic roars and screams of sadistic joy as they turned and sprinted for the water. The Dawn Patrol stood motionless, staring across the beach at the raging Surf Nazis screaming like banshees as they ran into the oncoming surf and paddled out to meet the ever-growing swells. The crowd turned and stared expectantly at the Dawn Patrol surf natives.

"Dude," said Dude Kahuna Bob to Dude Slicer, meaning, *what the hell did you just do?*

Dude Slicer stood silent, almost as though he were in shock. The other surf natives of the Dawn Patrol shuffled their feet uneasily as they looked to Dude Slicer for an answer.

"Dudes," said Dude Slicer, meaning, *sorry Dudes, it was a natural reflex and it just sort of flew out of my mouth when I wasn't thinking and...*

"I don't understand," said Bean. "What just happened?"

"We're going to get our asses kicked is what just happened," said Dude Kahuna Bob. Slicer just accepted a *surf-off* challenge by those socially abhorrent assholes."

Bean was surprised at the sudden change in demeanor and speech of Dude Kahuna Bob.

"But that's okay because you guys are better surfers aren't you? I mean, you're the Dawn Patrol, seekers of waves, harmony, and inner peace… and cool chicks," said Bean.

"Hey kid, I'm an orthodontist," said Dude Kahuna Bob. "I put cages on the crooked teeth of zit faced adolescents who think Pop Rocks are a food group. Dude Hammerhead there is a proctologist, Dude Zeus is a gynecologist, Dude Cuda is a pediatrician, Dude Banzai's a cardiac specialist, Dude Buster's an anesthesiologist, Dude Bird is an accountant, and our fearless leader Dude Slicer over there is a divorce lawyer. Get the picture?"

"Yeah kid," said Dude Hammerhead the proctologist. "Kind of hard to get a lot of surfing in when you're looking up people's asses all day."

Bean just stared, not knowing what to make of Dude Kahuna Bob's revelation.

"Kid, what I'm trying to say is we aren't really big time surfers. We're more like… late bloomers. We just… well… we kind of… we're actually kind of posers. It's a kind of alternative lifestyle we take on sometimes to shake off the drudgery of our dreary daily lives. I mean we can surf a little, respectable enough, but mostly we just work out at the club and cruise the beaches to pick up chicks and keep up our tan."

"Oh," said Bean, accepting but not really following Dude Slicer's explanation.

"So I guess what we do now is slink out of here before those Nazis come back and kick our asses," said Dude Cuda the pediatrician.

"Ho chi mama. Are chu kidden me. Chu guys are juss a bunch'a fakers?" said Chi Chi.

They all turned, shocked to discover Chi Chi standing there in an extremely hot sexy red bikini. Bean stared, his mouth falling open in disbelief. She had a perfect well-formed body that was only marginally noticeable before in her leather biker duds. She was even prettier than those girls he always saw on his beach at home, the ones that flew around in waterspouts or the ones in the surfer magazines at the Quickie Stop & Shop.

"Um… well, we can surf some but we can't come close to even thinking about competing with those guys," said Dude Zeus, the gynecologist.

"So whassa big deal? Wha dem Nazi guys gonna do?" asked Chi Chi.

"If you lose they take your boards and sell 'em for beer money," said the nearby young surfer with the bleach tipped hair and fake black pearl in his nose. "And sometimes they take your chick and you don't even wanna know what they'll do with her."

"Whoa, this is gettin' *better'n* Big Wednesday," said the zit faced Kelly Slater wannabe.

"Man, I told you, quit with the Wednesday shit. It's Thursday."

"Hokay," said Chi Chi. "So maybe *now es a big deal.* So wha chu gonna do bout it? If dis wass Kooba we juss choot 'em."

"Shoot 'em sounds good," said Brah Buster, the anesthesiologist.

Shoot 'em!, thought Fruitcake. *Did somebody say, SHOOT 'EM!*

"We can run away," suggested Dude Cuda, the pediatrician.

"No," said Dude Banzai, the cardiac specialist. "If we do that we'd never be able to show our faces on the beach again, and maybe even… oh lord, never get laid again."

All the Dawn Patrol surf natives let out a moan of dread at the very suggestion of a curtailed sex life.

"The odds don't look too good," said Brah Bird, the accountant.

They all looked to Dude Slicer, the divorce lawyer, for advice. Dude Slicer appeared to be in shock and offered no solution because he could think of no known precedents.

"Shoot 'em sounds good to me," repeated Brah Buster, the anesthesiologist.

"Hey, juss a minute," said Chi Chi. "My friend Bean can do it. My friend Bean sess to me lass night dat hees a surfer. Chu a real surfer ain't chu Bean?"

"Um, yeah, I can surf," said Bean.

"Dere, chu see wha I min?"

"Is that true kid?" asked Dude Kahuna Bob, the orthodontist. "Do you surf a lot?"

"Um... every day actually," answered Bean. "Since I was three years old."

Dude Slicer, the divorce lawyer, turned and looked at Bean. "You must save us," he said with all the fear he could muster. "Take my board. Save us Brah Bean. Save the girl."

"Yeah, man," said the zit faced Kelly Slater wannabe. "You gotta save the chick. It's your Big Wednesday moment, man."

"Listen dude, you don't quit with that Wednesday shit, you're gonna be walkin' home," said his bleach tipped friend.

The crowd joined in, first mumbling, then breaking into a growing chant, "Save the chick. Save the chick! BRAH BEAN SAVE THE CHICK! BRAH BEAN SAVE THE CHICK!"

"Yeah, SAVE DA CHICK," said Chi Chi. "Cause I'n da chick."

Bean was overwhelmed. Not only had he never seen so many people in one place before in his entire life but they were all chanting - for him.

Dude Slicer, the divorce lawyer, handed Bean his seldom used expensive custom longboard and a piece of board wax, and pointed to the sea. "You must stay on the board. If you eat pie, you know wipe out, then you're out of the surf-off and we lose and they take our boards... and the girl."

Bean took a big gulp of courage and looked to the breaking surf and the rising swells. Beyond them the Surf Nazis sat waiting on their boards. Hurricane Tyamekwa (pronounced *To-oa-mick-az)* was now pushing in waves at eight feet, bigger than any Bean had ever seen, but the chanting of the crowd filled him with courage and encouragement. He waxed the board, kicked off his Margaritaville flip flops he had gotten from Sister Moonbeam-Goom-jigi for his last birthday and had recovered from the ruins of his house, looked at Chi Chi in her newly acquired really hot and sexy red bikini, and trotted off toward the surf.

"SAVE THE CHICK! SAVE THE CHICK!" shouted the crowd.

"SAVE THE CHICK! Save our boards. Save our sex lives," said the Dawn Patrol surf natives.

Save my ass, thought Chi Chi.

Did somebody say SHOOT 'EM? thought a nervous Fruitcake.

"That guy is dead meat," said the zit faced Kelly Slater wannabe.

"So, es chu really a chynecolochist?" Chi Chi asked Dude Zeus, the gynecologist.

Dude Zeus, the gynecologist, smiled.

"So meng, dat min chu a Doctor Dude, huh?" said Chi Chi.

Dude Zeus, the gynecologist, smiled.

With Bean heading into the surf, Fruitcake was now left on the beach without his master for security. He nervously surveyed the crowd for fat guys with guns as he slinked in between the long boards belonging to the Dawn Patrol surf natives. *Did somebody say SHOOT 'EM?*

Bean reached the waters edge, attached the ankle cord of the longboard to his leg and jogged into the surf. He duck-dived under the breakers and then paddled until he reached the swells beyond. There on the high rolling swells sat the waiting Surf Nazis, staring at him, each intimidating enough to frighten and run off a four time incumbent Chicago gangster politician. But Bean, having never faced such adversity before, returned their fierce frowns with a naïve smile of such veracity that it launched them into a rage of determination.

"DUUUUUUDE!" growled the emotionally disturbed Surf Nazi with the four letter eyelids, meaning, *I'm going to kill you and your little dog too.*

"ARRRRG DUUUUDE!" echoed the other five Surf Nazis, meaning, *yeah, what he said,* as they all pointed menacingly at Bean.

"Hi," smiled Bean. "My name is Bean."

The Surf Nazi with the two and a half foot Chinese ponytail reached to his lower leg beneath the water and pulled out a shiny new dive knife that he'd stolen from Curley's Surf & Dive Shop two days before. Curley saw him steal it but didn't bother trying to stop him or to call the police because Curley knew the Surf Nazis would make trouble or possibly even burn down his store. He also knew that calling the police would bring scrutiny to the nearly entire stock of dive gear he suspected was stolen from somewhere near St. Petersburg that he bought from a shady Haitian from Miami. He bought the entire truckload because the Haitian told him to and he was afraid the Haitian would put some kind of voodoo curse on him if he didn't.

The Surf Nazi grew a devilish smile and pointed the knife at Bean. "Duuuude," he growled.

"DUDE!" called out one of the other Surf Nazis, meaning, WAVE COMING!

Bean looked back. The on-rushing swell was the biggest he had ever seen. His heart began pounding with excitement as he studied and judged the wave's potential. It rolled in and all the surfers bellied down and took off. All except Bean, that is, because Bean had also seen the swell behind that one and it was bigger and better.

While the Surf Nazis ripped and shredded their wave, Bean waited patiently for the big one and in it came. He bellied down and paddled, then popped up on his feet and felt the rush of free flight as he dropped in and angled the board along the full length of the wave. It was his first time on a classic longboard and he was amazed at the sensation, ease, power, and grace that the board gave him on the big wave. The ride seemed to shoot some form of energy through his body, heightening the experience and his ability to master the moment. The crowd on the beach roared with approval as Bean's ride took him over the surprised heads of the Surf Nazis bobbing in the water having had completed their ride. They cursed and threatened him with their fist as they ducked under to avoid him, then paddled back out and sat waiting for Bean to return. While they waited they formed their plan of action for the next wave. For the next round they would all wait until Bean launched, assuring them they would all be on the same wave. Then they would attack.

Meanwhile the waves were getting even bigger, now at ten feet. The biggest waves to hit Sebastian since hurricane Bob (pronounced *Bob*) in 1968, one of the first hurricanes named after a man because somebody in Washington, who didn't have anything else to do, held a press conference one day complaining about hurricanes always being named after women which would lead to the general populous assuming that all women, like all hurricanes, were real bitches.

Bean paddled back out after his first successful ride, waited and watched until another big swell rolled in and he paddled for the crest. The Surf Nazis followed suit and all caught the same wave simultaneously. Beans bigger board gave him an advantage, holding the wave as he angled down. At the same time two of the Nazis cut and pulled up in front of him. It was a suicide run intended to take out all three surfers but making the remaining Nazis the winners. Bean's eyes grew large as he faced the oncoming collision.

He squatted, shifted his weight and guided the board down just enough that he only bumped the noses of the boards of both of his attackers, sending them into the air in an unrecoverable spin in front of the wave. Their crash dive took them out of the competition and the crowd on the beach roared with approval for Bean who recovered and finished the wave.

"SAVE THE CHICK! SAVE THE CHICK!" they yelled with new enthusiasm.

Once again the surfers reset and once again the Surf Nazis formed a plan. This time they would pull out all the stops and force this punk kid onto the rocks, a long arching jetty wall constructed of large rocks and concrete that protected the inlet entrance, the existence of which was why the waves were usually exceptionally good at Sebastian. For surfers the wall was a blessing but also a curse, causing serious harm to wave riders who were untalented or unwary or just plain stupid.

In rolled another huge wave and off they went with the Nazis staying to Bean's right and dropping left, forcing him to avoid them by dropping in left as well. When he looked ahead he saw the peril of the fast approaching rocks.

"Told ya he was dead meat. Ain't savin' no chicks today, man," said the zit faced Kelly Slater wannabe watching from the beach.

"Hey man, what's the name of that movie? You know, the one with those three guys and the giant waves and stuff," asked bleach tips.

"Big Wednesday."

"Oh man, you're an idiot."

The rocks grew closer as did the pursuing shredding four remaining Nazis behind him who were crisscrossing all over the wave like a strand of DNA. Bean couldn't slide and cut right without running head-on into them so he applied his short board experience and cut the heavy board left, up, and over the crest of the wave in a 180 turn, crashing down through the four oncoming surfers, the front three of which froze at the sight of his dive bomber move and failed to see... *the rocks.*

While lifeguards and other onlookers reluctantly helped retrieve the three bloodied and broken Nazis and their broken grotesque custom Sea Slug boards, Bean and the only remaining Surf Nazi, the one with the two and a half foot Chinese ponytail, reset for another go. In an odd move, the Surf Nazi paddled away, putting more space between himself and his competition. Bean had no idea why.

"Uh oh," said Dude Slicer, the divorce lawyer.

"Oh shit," said Dude Zeus, the gynecologist.

"Ho chi mama. Why chu say oh chit?" asked Chi Chi, the not yet movie star trophy chick.

"A banzai," said Dude Banzai, the cardiac specialist.

"Hokay, so whassa banzai?" asked Chi Chi.

"He's gonna get rammed," said Dude Hammerhead, the proctologist.

"The Surf Nazi is gonna ram Bean," said Dude Banzai, the cardiac specialist. "A full speed head on collision that could kill him. Maybe send the pointy nose of the board right through him. "

"Ho chi mama. Good thing chu guys a buncha doctors, huh," said Chi Chi, crossing her heart.

HOLY CHIT! thought Fruitcake.

On it came, the biggest swell of the day, rolling into what would have to be a fifteen footer. Both Bean and the Nazi eyed the swell with intense caution. Closer and closer it rolled until it was on them and they both bellied down and dropped in, both catching it just right. Bean stood, slid down and cut right. The Nazi cutting left. The size and wall of the wave shot them both forward faster than either of them had ever gone on any wave before, Bean's long blonde hair flying back in the wind, the Nazi's long black braided Chinese ponytail flapping in the breeze. Faster, speeding ever closer and closer to impact as the wave began to break.

"Dead meat," repeated the zit faced Kelly Slater wannabe on the beach.

"Ho chi mama. I dun wanna see," said Chi Chi, covering her eyes but looking through her fingers.

"SAVE THE CHICK! SAVE THE CHICK!" yelled the crowd.

Twenty yards and approaching fast! Fifteen yards... ten!

The Nazi squatted, forcing his board on ever faster. When he did, he reached down and pulled out the dive knife that was attached to his leg that he stole from Curley's Surf & Dive Shop that was stolen from some place in St. Petersburg by a shady Miami Haitian who might or might not put voodoo curses on people.

"SAVE THE CHICK! SAVE THE…!"

The crowd on the beach gasps at the sight of the glistening blade. One girl actually fainted, not from the fear of witnessing a horrendous bloody lethal incident on the surf but because she just realized she had lost the beach bag with her mother's $689 red sexy Aldior Fuqua designer bikini recently purchased from the Che Poope Boutique on Worth Avenue in Palm Beach.

"SAVE THE CHICK! SAVE THE CHICK!"

"HO CHI MAMA! HO CHI MAMA!" said a concerned Chi Chi.

"Dead meat."

Bean spotted the knife just as the Nazi shot for the upper part of the wave. The outstretched blade was heading fast right for Bean's throat. Bean twisted and cut for the top of the wave. The Nazi did the same. The two surfers came together with a mighty CRACK that signaled to the crowd on the beach that the boards had collided. Both surfers caught air with the Nazi's Sea Slug board breaking in two and its rider twisting into a headlong spill behind the wave. Bean, squatting and holding onto the rails of the longboard, flew into the air a good six feet, then somehow managed to turn the board and land on the crest of the wave and continue his ride. In front of him rolled a perfect tube and in he shot, into a surreal moment of magic that closed him off from the rest of the world. He walked to the front of the board and exited the tube, standing tall and hanging ten on the nose just like he had seen in a magazine. And the crowd roared.

"HE SAVED THE CHICK! BRAH BEAN SAVED THE CHICK!"

When Bean reached the shore he was met by the surf natives of the Dawn Patrol, lifted on their shoulders and paraded through the jubilant crowd with everyone yelling, "BRAH BEAN! BRAH BEAN! BRAH BEAN SAVED THE CHICK!"

"Whoa sweeeet, man. Like that was way better than Big Wednesday, dude. Like outstandingly bodacious."

"No dammit, I told you it's *Thursday*, dude. *THURSDAY!*"

"HE SAVED THE CHICK! BRAH BEAN SAVED THE CHICK!"

"So, dude, es chu really a chynecolochist?" asked Chi Chi as she affectionately took the arm of Dude Zeus, the gynecologist.

Dude Zeus, the gynecologist, smiled.

News of Bean's defeat of the infamous hated Florida Surf Nazis spread like wildfire via Skank and the airwaves of W-O-R-T, and soon became the stuff of legend. A picture of his great victorious banzai collision depicting the Nazi taking a dive and Bean catching six feet of air over a hurricane Tyamekwa (pronounced *To-oa-mick-az)* record size Sebastian wave would soon be featured world wide on the cover of *Surfer Magazine*. Curley would order extra copies and frame and hang the famous magazine cover on the wall in his surf and dive shop in Melbourne Beach because it featured one of his custom Sea Slug boards. Not long after that however, the shop would burn down taking the Winn Dixie with it. Half a dozen more of the surf combat photos were scheduled for inside the magazine as well but three of them would be pulled and replaced with pictures of the really hot chick in the bodacious red bikini for which the now famous Bean Buffett had risked his life.

Told of what to expect by his admiring crowd of surfers, none of the immediate adulation or obvious future notoriety affected Bean's focus on his mission. He still had only one goal and that was to fulfill Sister Moonbeam-Goom-jigi's final wish and his own burning desire to find his father. So at the end of the day it was adios amigos. Bean sat behind the wheel of the Celestial Rocket saying his final farewells to his newfound Dawn Patrol friends and many other new friends at Sabastian Inlet, which included a goodby to Chi Chi who had become attached to Dude Zeus the gynecologist and decided to stay on. All of the Dawn Patrol had given him their business cards and offered their services and lifetime friendship, and especially their gratitude for saving their dignity and ability to continue picking up cool chicks on the beach. "Hereafter," they told him, "*Brah Bean* would always be a full fledged surf native and member of the Dawn Patrol with free dental and medical and divorce representation."

It was a joyful occasion as all waved good-bye to their hero. Fruitcake was happy as well. He had feasted on two ham sandwiches and Vienna sausages, was enjoying being associated with and a member of the now famous Bean Buffett entourage, and of course,was finally getting his seat back. But as Bean and Fruitcake pulled away in the Celestial Rocket, before they had gotten twenty feet they heard a cry from behind.

"WAIT!"

Bean hit the brakes and looked back to see Chi Chi running to catch up with him. Reaching the car, she tossed in her newly acquired beach bag and jumped in, again shoving Fruitcake aside.

"What about Dude Zeus?" asked Bean.

"Oh, hees hokay. Buh hees a chynecolochist an chu juss dun know where dose chynecolochist bin. Chu know wha I min?"

Bean shrugged, not really knowing what she meant. He was just happy she decided to join him.

"Bissides, I'n gonna be a moofy star and I can be no moofy star married to no chynecolochist."

"That's a nice outfit," observed Bean, approving of her designer shorts and high priced T-shirt that said *Royal Commodore Palms Beach Club,* embroidered in gold thread over the left tit.

"Oh, thanks. Es from da sane store es my bikini."

She ripped it off. I saw the whole thing, thought Fruitcake. *Just like she ripped off my seat. Go back to Kooba lady.*

🌴

Watching them wave good-bye and drive away, there sat on the far side of the parking lot in his red 1958 Caddy convertible with the plastic bobbing head figure of Jesus on the dashboard, one Guido Fulgenzi, alias Five Nose Freddy the mafia hit man, alias Father Alphonso Sabatino, talking on his cell phone.

"Yeah, Albert, it's me. I found the kid again down here at Sebastian Inlet. Heard somethin' about him on my car radio. Damn thing only picks up AM stations and they don't have shit for AM radio around here. All they got is…"

"I don't give a damn about your radio. So what's all this Sebastian stuff?" said Albert.

"Yeah, it's a beach freak show for surfers. You know, kind of like Woodstock with Coppertone. Your boy's some kind of local surf hero or something."

"What? A Hero? Okay, so what's happening with the kid now?"

"I almost had him up in Cocoa Beach. Wasn't for some Cuban bitch I woulda sliced his throat."

"WHAT?" said a surprised Albert on the other end of the line. "What the hell you mean *you woulda sliced his throat?!* Are you crazy? I ain't payin' you to slice his throat!"

"But you said to take care of the kid. How the hell can I take care of this punk if I don't *off* him?"

"No, stupid. I meant the regular *take care of him* kind of take care of him, not the *New Jersey kill him* kind of take care of him."

"That don't make no sense," said Father Sabatino.

"Yeah well, maybe it don't make sense to people who live in New York or New Jersey but it makes sense to everybody else who don't live in New York or New Jersey."

"But you said you wanted the kid out of the way."

"That's right. That's what I said. But I meant the *normal out of the way* kind of out of the way, not the *New Jersey* kind of out of the way out of the way."

"Hey, I ain't some kind of damn babysitter. What you think, I'm some kind of damn babysitter? I ain't some kind of damn babysitter."

"Hey, you're gettin paid ain't ya? You're gettin' a piece of the action ain't ya?"

"Damn right I am. Damn well better if I'm gonna be some kind of damn babysitter."

"So quit your bitchin' and just do what I say and take care of the kid. And I mean the *normal* kind of take care of the kid not the *New Jersey* kind of take care of the kid. Shadow him and buy us time and keep the kid outta the way so's I can take care of business. And make sure he doesn't come to no harm. We just might need him later."

"You know it's a good thing Gloria's my cousin or I'd be taking care of *your* ass... the *New Jersey way*," said Father Sabatino just before he flipped the cell phone off, discontinuing the call. He pulled a flask from his pocket and took a swig, cursing under his breath as he started up the Caddy. "Thinks I'm some kind of damn babysitter."

On came his classic radio. It was WORT.

"Hey man, like, so what's wrong with the Waffle House anyway? I mean, lots of surfer dudes go to the Waffle House man. I mean, so... that's a righteous thing, right dude? Right? Right?"

"But you can't surf in the Waffle House you dumbass, 'kay? So why do you keep callin' me from the Waffle House about the surf? There ain't no surf at the Waffle House, dude. There ain't never any surf at the Waffle House you stoner freak."

"Hey man you gotta be careful what you say... uh, cause... well you know. I mean, you don't know whats out there, ya know? I mean, they got surfer cops too, right?"

"Shut up. Just shut up and hang up the phone!"

"Cause... cause you know, the CIA or Obama or somebody might..."

"SHUT UP! JUST SHUT THE HELL UP! AND GET OFF MY PHONE. JUST GET THE HELL OFF MY PHONE!"

"Okay, so, I mean, sometimes they burn the bacon and shit and that's not cool, man, but, you know... hey, it's the Waffle House, dude. I mean... like, what the hell, right? Right?"

"I hope you choke on your burnt Waffle House bacon you stoner freak. I hope you overdose in the Waffle House and choke on your damn burnt bacon so you can't call me anymore. I hope you..."

chapter 11
Me'ahmi Beash

Somewhere down the coast around Fort Pierce, Bean
began thinking of how during his journey everything along
the road sort of looked the same, and it seemed the closer
they got to Miami the more of the same stuff there was to
see, even though some stuff was bigger and newer than
other stuff. At least that's how it seemed to Bean who had
never been anywhere but St. Augustine. He was
contemplating this while he was standing at a roadside
souvenir fruit stand with a bag of newly purchased Indian
River oranges, sipping on a Coke and listening to the Bob
Roberts Society Band play to tourists and a group of old
folks who just got off a blue bus that said Palmetto Palms
Senior Center on the side.

"Hey, is that an honest to God Nash Metropolitan?"
asked a very old man making his way towards them with a
walker.

"Yes sir it is," Bean responded politely.

The old man and his walker maneuvered to the side of
the Celestial Rocket. He shook his head, puzzled as he
checked out the exotic paint job then looked over the
interior with great affection, obviously remembering
another time and place.

"I had one of these once. Back in the fifties after the
war," he said, shaking his head. "Couldn't get a date for
shit. All the damn broads thought it was a joke. Had to get
me a big Plymouth so I could get a piece of ass. If I was you
kid I'd dump this thing. 'Specially with that faggy paint
job," said the old man. "Or you ain't never gonna get laid."

"Um… yes sir," said Bean.

"Ugly dog," mumbled the old man as he hobbled away to listen to the band and get some free orange juice.

"I thin' maybe dat old bird was no lucky wit da ladies causs he wass a asshole," said Chi Chi as she opened the car door and got in.

Bean just shrugged as he got into the car. He was meeting all kinds of new people, old and young, that he had never met or seen before and decided it best to reserve his opinions, at least for the present.

With the Florida build up over the years the coast road had been moved, merged, and diverted so many times that it could hardly even be considered a coast road anymore. To Bean sometimes old State Road A1A just seemed like one long shopping stripcenter. There were strip centers from the '50s running into strip centers from the '60s that ran into strip centers from the '70s, that ran into strip centers from the '80's, '90s and into the new millennium; interspersed, of course, with motels, restaurants, and various tourist traps. And it seemed as though Bean had seen nearly every evolutionary benchmark of architecture that ever existed in the history of Florida motels, not to mention the Publix Super Markets that sported designs spanning from those that appeared as though they came out of an old Buck Rogers flick to the Spanish and the understated town and country styles of the day. And then there were the thousand different convenience stores and used car lots, and used car lots that used to be convenience stores. There were stretches where old Florida had turned into run down low rent crap that butted right up against new Florida closed communities of high priced exclusive neighborhoods, condos, marinas, and private golf communities with immaculately manicured landscapes, fences, gates, and security. It was a land that seemed to never be finished or was unable to make up its mind, a place where its people seemed to just keep building stuff just so they could keep on building stuff. It was both new and exciting yet old and neglected, with both having a kind of desperate fraudulent temporary character that made Bean uncomfortable and begin to wonder if maybe he should never have left home.

Eventually Bean, Chi Chi, and Fruitcake found themselves right in the middle of Miami Beach where he nosed the Celestial Rocket over and parked in a slanted slot in front of an old but restored part of town where the stores were well dressed and painted in an assortment of tropical pastel pinks, blues, and greens. Across the street was a sizable popular waterfront establishment called *The Tropical Moon Restaurant & Lounge*. A triple-A restaurant and lounge that extended up and out for two floors with large decks that seated 200, and had live entertainment nightly on *Captain Svenson's Poop Deck*. The enormously successful establishment was owned and operated by a popular Miami entertainer and northern transplant from Oshkosh, Wisconsin.

"Well kid, dis es my stumpin' dirt," said Chi Chi.

"Your what?" said Bean.

"Chu know. My stumpin' dirt. Me'ahmi, where I liff."

"Oh," said Bean. "You mean you live here."

"Yeah, kina," she said with hesitance.

"Kina?" repeated Bean.

"Hey, es chu makin fun of my assent?"

"Oh no. Um, I wouldn't do that. Um, what accent?" said Bean in an effort to be polite. Bean, like everyone else, was often hard put to understand much of what Chi Chi was saying much of the time, but he understood enough to realize her limited mastering of the English language was exceptional being she learned it from scratch as a street urchin on her own in Miami.

"Hokay now, chu remember how I tolt chu. Chu take da cussway an den chu go leff on Biscayane causs das da road wass gonna took chu to chure papa in Key Wess."

She exited the car and closed the door. Fruitcake immediately jumped in the vacated seat.

"Hokay. I mean okay," said Bean.

"Hokay, so I gonna go now," said Chi Chi, backing away from the car.

Bean just smiled and shook his head.

Hokay, chu can go now, mango mama, thought Fruitcake, mocking her accent as he rolled over, balls to the sun. *Chu can go an I'n gonna take back my seat.*

Chi Chi paused, "So es chu chure chu gonna be hokay?" she asked.

Bean nodded an insecure yes as he nervously looked about.

"Oh, hokay. Well, so long den," said Chi Chi as she turned and walked away.

Bean started the car and was about to pull out when there came a quick short burst of a siren and the sudden appearance behind him of a Miami Beach Police patrol car blocking his way.

Chi Chi, who had walked only a short distance away, turned to see a large hulking police officer exiting the patrol car and heading for Bean. *Ho chi mama,* she thought, immediately realizing that Bean was going to get busted as an unlicensed under-aged driver.

Officer Leroy Fordhook was a six foot-five inch tall mass of a man who obviously spent a great deal of time in the gym, the result of which was an impressive display of muscles that fit into his uniform as though it were made of spandex. In fact it seemed Officer Fordhook even had muscles on his muscles that were often commented upon by the women to whom he was about to serve tickets for traffic violations. But quite often Officer Fordhook would forgo writing those tickets if the ladies in question would instead write for him their phone number. This was pretty much the essence of Officer Leroy Fordhook's life ever since he was cut from the Miami Dolphins' football team because he had difficulty remembering the playbook. Not the *plays* in the playbook but the playbook itself. In fact he held the record for the number of playbooks lost by any one player in the entire history of professional football, causing (though it was never proved) the worst losing season the Dolphins had ever experienced. It was suspected that thanks to Leroy Fordhook, every team in the NFL, as well as most college and high school teams now possessed a copy of the Miami Dolphins playbook. Copies were even going for $3.95 plus shipping on E-Bay.

So now Officer Fordhook, ex-Miami Dolphin wide receiver and sometimes tight end, rides around in his air-conditioned patrol car looking for lone blonde women in convertibles, of which there was no shortage in Miami Beach, to pull over and engage with a possible traffic violation. He always chooses blondes because he assumes blondes are too stupid or too timid to ever divulge any brief sexual encounters or relationships with police officers.

Officer Fordhook is blonde.

Having only seen the back of Bean's head and his long blonde hair, Officer Fordhook was about to encounter what he thought was another lone stupid blonde in a convertible – albeit a very strange convertible.

"Turn off the engine please, ma'am," said Officer Fordhook in his most impressive deep official law enforcement voice, the voice he always used when flexing those muscles on his muscles and approaching what he thought were lone stupid blonde chicks in convertibles. The rest of the time he spoke in his normal voice, which sounded like a poor facsimile of Clint Eastwood and sometimes resulted in normal drivers getting written up for extra traffic violations because they would laugh or chuckle, thinking he was putting them on.

Bean shut off the Celestial Rocket's motor and looked up. Seeing that Bean was actually a young blonde male and not a typical hot Miami Beach blonde woman or even a fake blonde woman with dark roots, Officer Fordhook deflexed all the impressive muscles on his muscles, leaving only his usually impressive muscles, which still fit into his uniform like it was made of spandex.

"Young man, you got a license to drive this clown car?" asked Officer Fordhook, now in his Clint Eastwood mode.

Oh, shit! We're busted! thought Fruitcake, wondering if there were any mean fat guys in the Miami jail.

Then, just as Bean was about to speak.

"Ho chi mama! Diddent I tell chu to no play wit da car when I wass in da store!" said Chi Chi as she came charging into the conversation. Ho chi mama. Dass where I leff da kees. Hoops, I goofs again."

Bean's eyes expanded in surprise at the appearance of Chi Chi but again began to answer Officer Fordhook's question. Chi Chi immediately cut him off because she knew that one of Bean's most prominent faults was that he always told the truth.

"Dun chu makes no scusses young meng. Chu knows chu no spose ta be messin' wit da car kees."

"Is this your car, ma'am?" asked Officer Fordhook.

"It's my…" Bean started to say, but again was cut off by Chi Chi.

"Now Bean, dun chu talk an get all flusterated," ordered Chi Chi. "Oh, I'n so sorry officer. Chu see hees my stepbrother and he dun know what hees doin' causs hees retarded."

"Oh," said Officer Fordhook.

Officer Fordhook knew that the issue of a mentally challenged individual created a whole new scenario of procedure as dictated by and involving the new official *Miami Beach Law Enforcement Officer's Politically Correct Handbook*, his copy of which Officer Fordhook failed to study closely because - he couldn't find it. And then there was Chi Chi's Palm Coast wardrobe that extolled the *Royal Commodore Palms Beach Club,* one of the most exclusive establishments in all of Florida, embroidered in gold thread over her left tit which might or might not mean she was a rich bitch with connections that could somehow backfire and cost Officer Fordhook his job. So now because of the strategic change in the situation due to Bean's handicap and Chi Chi's possible prestigious social status, he was not quite sure how to proceed or sure of what to say. Officer Fordhook's situation had become a whole new procedural ball game.

"Um… that your dog?" asked Officer Fordhook in an effort to make amends by making small talk.

Hey, who the hell you callin' a dog? thought Fruitcake.

"Ches. Hees nem es Fruitscakes," said Chi Chi. "Hees retarded too an heem belong to my retarded brother."

Hey, speak for yourself, lady, thought Fruitcake angrily. *First you take my seat then you take my dignity. And you can't even say my name right.*

"He's only got one ear," observed Officer Fordhook.

Oh, your so observant. Typical cop. Sheese, thought Fruitcake.

"Wow meng, chu really got sung big muscles," observed Chi Chi.

"Uh… yeah," said Officer Fordhook, reverting back to his deep official voice. "Use to play for the Dolphins. Wide receiver. Tight end."

"Ho chi mama! Are chu kiddin' me… Ho chi mama, da Me'ahmi Dolphins? Are chu serious?"

"Sure am."

"Oh, wait. Now I know who chu es."

Officer Fordhook puffed up, thinking he was about to be recognized for his former football glory days.

"Chu es dat guy! Chu dat guy use'a do da coochie coochie wit Maria," said Chi Chi. "Oh, dun chu worry," she smiled confidentially. "I chure no gonna tell nobody. I'n no efen gonna tell Maria's husband," she winked.

Officer Fordhook was taken aback and looked around nervously to see if anyone was near enough to overhear their conversation.

"Oh, uh… Okay. Appreciate that, ma'am," said Officer Fordhook.

"Now chu get back in dat seat where chu belungs," she ordered Bean.

Bean, totally confused, did as instructed and scooted to the other side of the car. Fruitcake was not happy to once again be relegated to his status between the seats. Chi Chi hopped in behind the wheel.

"Well, I'n gotta get my stepbrother to da retard doctor, hokay? It wass so nice meeten chu and I tell Maria chu say hola, hokay?"

"Oh, okay," said Officer Fordhook who retreated to his patrol car and backed it out of the way.

Chi Chi cranked up the Celestial Rocket and sped off in the direction of the MacArthur Causeway, leaving Officer Leroy Fordhook sitting in his air-conditioned patrol car trying to remember which Maria Chi Chi was referring to. In truth, Chi Chi had just taken a chance, knowing that just about every male cop from Fort Lauderdale to Homestead has had an affair with a Cuban girl named Maria.

"I'n thinkin' maybe I chould go wit chu to Key Wess," said Chi Chi. "Causs I dun thin chu gonna make it by chureselfs."

This made Bean very happy and also confirmed what he had suspected during their already brief time together; that Chi Chi had no place else to go.

"Oh, okay," agreed Bean with a smile. "By the way, what's *retarded* mean?"

"Oh, dun takes dat personal causs I wass juss layin' some bullchit on dat cop so I can gets chu outta troubles."

"I was in trouble?"

"Boy, sung tines I thin chu dun know how much troubles chu in," said Chi Chi. "Yep, I thin I better takes care of chu for a while."

"I'm hungry. Do they have cheeseburgers in Miami?" asked Bean.

"Ho chi mama. Sung tines I thin dis boy dun haff a clue," she said to herself.

Hey, I think that's a perfectly legit question, Mango Mama, thought Fruitcake, his tail and one ear popping up with excitement at the suggestion of food. *Where's the food! Where's the house! Where's the food!*

Ten minutes later the Celestial Rocket was sitting at a drive-up fast food joint on a corner near a busy intersection where its three occupants sat about to consume cheeseburgers and fries when suddenly Chi Chi perked up at the sound of *Cuban* music rolling down the street in their direction. She spied the source of the music emanating from a custom low rider 1953 blue chopped top Mercury. Seeing this she quickly slid down in her seat to avoid being seen. In doing so what she didn't see was the 1961 pimped out mystic green Buick coming from the other direction. When the two vehicles passed the occupants of both cars stared and glared at each other, as much to demonstrate their cruising cool as their shared animosity. That is all but one of the four occupants in the pimped out Buick who happened to catch a glimpse of and quickly recognize Chi Chi before she ducked down in her seat. He promptly pulled out his cell phone and hit his quick dial.

"What's wrong?" asked Bean.

"I thin dass sung bad guys," she said in a low whisper. "If dey see me I maybe gonna be in big troubles."

"How come?"

"Ess some old Kooba troubles. But dis ess America and I'n dun care a damn abou no old Kooba chit."

"Oh, okay," said Bean, having no idea what she was talking about. "That guy over there looks hungry," he said, pointing to a vagrant on a nearby corner of the intersection.

"Oh, dat guy. Hees crazy or sungthin," said Chi Chi as she looked around to make sure the chopped top Mercury was gone. "Hees alwaze hangin' out on da corners wit hiss sign and beggin' for moneys. Hees a bum. Hees fulla chit."

"But he looks hungry," said Bean.

"Dun chu worry abou dat guy. Hees a bum. He dun deserf nuttin from nobody."

"But... that's kind of mean. I think I'm going to get him some food," said Bean.

"Hokay. I know I'n a heartless bitch buh sungtines chu gotta be heartless to survife. Chu knows what I min?"

"No," said Bean as he got out of the car and walked over to the street-side beggar.

The vagrant was a black man of medium height and though he appeared older in his current grungy state, he was actually only twenty-seven. His clothes appeared as though they hadn't been off for a washing in months, stretched out of shape and coated with dirt to such an extent that it was even difficult to realize his knee-length Bermuda shorts were once a combination of bright red, blue, and yellow plaid. The original color of his T-shirt was a true mystery although parts of the words *Florida* and *Sunshine* as well as a faded palm tree could barely be made out on the front. On his feet was a pair of formerly red well-worn and shredded old faded high-top Converse All-Star sneakers, the left one of which had four toes exposed. The only other visible remaining item in his attire was a bandana covering his head that mocked the popular reality TV series by reading *Survivor Sea Circus Cruise,* an item someone most likely produced to capitalize on the Sea Circus Cruise incidents of mass passenger food poisoning and other mysterious illnesses. What appeared to be the rest of his worldly possessions were stuffed into a green plastic kitchen garbage bag that hung by his side from one hand. In the other hand he held a sign made from a torn piece of cardboard on which was scrawled WIL WERK 4 FUDE. On the reverse side of the cardboard was stamped in large black letters WAL-MART and MADE IN CHINA. This was the side he unknowingly and mistakenly was displaying to all the cars passing through the intersection, which most likely accounted for his lack of success of collecting job offers or sympathy funds, and his subsequent current state of depression and appearance of hunger. Seeing that side of the sign people just assumed he was a disgruntled protesting Wal-Mart door greeter or one of those millions of Americans who lost their jobs because Wal-Mart, the behemoth retail chain that said they would always buy American, now always buys Chinese. Though everyone who drove by felt sorry for the presumed victim of Wal-Mart corporate greed they really didn't give a shit because this was Miami where nobody really gives a shit.

"Um, excuse me," said Bean as he approached.

"Huh?" replied the beggar.

"I was wondering if maybe you were hungry?" said Bean.

"Huh?" said the begger, turning and gawking at Bean through languid eyes.

"We're having some cheeseburgers and fries and we were wondering if you would like some. Would you like a cheeseburger and fries?"

"Huh? What?"

"Ho chi mama. Now dat boy thin hees Sister Teresa or sungthin," said Chi Chi as she exited the car.

That's 'Mother' Teresa, Miss Chi Chi the I'n no famous yet moofy star, thought Fruitcake who suddenly found himself faced with a dilemma. On one seat sat two cheeseburgers and fries and the other seat, *his* seat, lay vacant and available for the taking. What should he do, chow down on the cheeseburgers on the driver's seat or reclaim his mobile throne? Could he do both successfully?

"I mean, are you hungry? If you're hungry you can… I mean I'll be glad to buy you something to eat," offered Bean.

"What?" said the beggar, still not sure if he could believe this offer of kindness.

"Hey chu stupid chit! The boy wanna feed chur sorry ass so dun just sten dere like a retard, say sungthin," demanded Chi Chi, crashing into the one-sided conversation.

"Oh, uh, okay," said the beggar.

"Hokay den, so get a moof on, meng."

The begger responded to Chi Chi because he was afraid not to. And the idea of food sounded pretty good.

"That seemed kind of mean. Is that what you meant by heartless?" Bean whispered to Chi Chi as the three of them walked to the car.

"If chu wanna survife in dis world den sungtines chu gotta be a asshole and sungtines chu gotta be a angel. But mosta tine chu gotta be a asshole."

"Oh," said Bean.

"Dun chu worry. Sung day chu gonna figure it out." Chi Chi scrunched her nose and moved away from the beggar. "Pew! Dis guy dun need no cheeseburger, he need a damn wash job."

Bean winced and nodded in agreement.

The beggar walked along, unaware of the odorous impression he was making on his new aquaintences. He seemed to be in some zone of depression or aloofness or emotional detatchment, a social zombie who wandered the streets alone.

The chopped top Mercury came cruising back up the street, this time without the booming Cuban music. Inside were three Cuban men who perceived themselves as bad ass gang-bangers but in truth they were just working stiffs who didn't want anyone to know they were just working stiffs because being a *Kooban* gang-banger carried much more prestige. Jorge, Juan, and Jesus were their names and they referred to themselves as the *3Js*.

Jorge worked at the Sun City Dry Cleaners that was owned and operated by a family of Muslim Palestinian refugees who were always talking mysteriously in their native tongue about what Jorge thought were plots to blow up Miami. The truth was they weren't plotting anything but were actually just bitching about having to deal with an over-population of Jews and complaining of Miami being just as bad as Palestine. This made Jorge a nervous wreck each day at work because there was nothing he could do to remedy his paranoia. He wanted to save Miami but he was sure he couldn't report the Muslim terrorists to Homeland Security because he was an illegal alien and might be deported. Then again if he did report them and it turned out they were actually terrorists he would save Miami and be a hero, but still lose his job when the Sun City Dry Cleaners got shut down by Homeland Security, and then maybe he'd still be deported. And of course, if he reported them and it turned out they weren't terrorists they would get seriously pissed off and fire him and then report him as an illegal alien and he would probably still be deported. All the options were negative which worried Jorge to no end, and to make it even worse he thought of what would happen if he reported them and it turned out that they actually were terrorists but Homeland Security, true to form, decided they weren't terrorists and let them go. Then they would come back to the Sun City Dry Cleaners and grab him and maybe kill him by cutting off his head live on the Internet and Al Jazeera TV because he knew they were really terrorists. So Jorge decided to keep his mouth shut and keep his job, all the while hoping he wouldn't get blown up or beheaded, or even worse - deported. And in Jorge's mind, somehow being a pretend gangbanger helped relieve the tension from not being able to save Miami.

Another member of the 3Js, Juan, worked part time at a Denny's Restaurant as a fast order breakfast cook and part time at an auto chop shop just north of town, which is where he came by the knowledge, tools, and materials to customize the 1953 Mercury that he bought hot for $300 from a Seminole Indian alligator wrestler named Chester who lived somewhere on the far side of Lake Okeechobee.

Jesus, the other member of the 3Js, worked as an orderly at an exclusively Jewish Retirement Home owned by the Temple of Solomon Corporation, where he sometimes had to break up arguments among the residents about whether or not Kosher food was necessary or just a rip off, and where he often had to listen to the old folks bitch about how the Muslims were taking over the dry cleaning business in Miami and how they weren't as good as the Croatians who where taking over the dry cleaning business in New York.

As the 3Js once again cruised around the corner, Juan glanced over at what appeared to be some kind of small clown car parked at the fast food drive in. It was then he caught sight of Chi Chi walking to the car with Bean and the beggar.

"Hey meng, ain't dat dat chic?" he asked of the other two Js.

"What chic, meng?" asked Jorge.

"Chu know. Dat chic, meng. Wit the reward."

"Oh chit! Dat Chic?"

"Yeah, meng. Dat Chic."

"Ooooh wow, meng. Wha da hell es chee doin' here, meng?" asked Jesus.

"I dun know. But chu know dass some serious coin out dere for dat chic."

"So wass she doin?" asked Juan as he slowed down the Mercury.

Just then a hairy head popped up behind the steering wheel of the Celestial Rocket.

"Hey meng, look at dat ugly dog drivin' dat clown car," said Jesus. "He no got no ear."

Jorge pulled out his cell phone and punched his quick dial. When someone answered on the other end he said with serious concern, "Hey meng, chu ain't gonna belief dis…"

🌴

When Bean, Chi Chi, and the smelly beggar reached the car they found Fruitcake belly up, balls to the sun. The cheeseburgers were gone and a few remaining French fries and wrappers were strewn all over the driver's seat and floorboard.

"I thin Fruitscakes eats our cheeseburgers," said Chi Chi. "Wrappers an all."

"That's okay," said Bean. "I'll go get some more."

"That your dog?" asked the vagabond.

"Yes," said Bean.

"He only has one ear."

"I know," said Bean, offering no explanation.

"He's funny looking," said the beggar.

Everybody's a damn critic, thought Fruitcake, just before he lct out a French fry fart.

They ordered more food and instead of eating in the car they sat the beggar in the open trunk and scooted down the street where they decided to get a room in a nearby motel called the Oceans Horizon Waterfront Resort Inn.

The Oceans Horizon Waterfront Resort Inn wasn't anywhere near the ocean and in fact was on the backside of the island. From the Oceans Horizon Waterfront Resort Inn you couldn't even see the ocean much less the horizon, but you could see Biscayne Bay if you were in one of only three second floor rooms with a view. All the other rooms faced the wall of a newer nicer taller hotel. Rooms with a view cost extra but Bean didn't have to pay extra for a room with a view because Chi Chi threatened to call the INS if the clerk charged extra. The clerk didn't even charge extra for the dog. Chi Chi could spot illegal aliens a mile away.

In the room with a view at the Oceans Horizon Waterfront Resort Inn (that didn't cost extra) they ate their cheeseburgers and fries, after which Bean and Chi Chi persuaded the beggar to take a shower. When he was finished they dressed him in Bean's extra set of clean clothes, including a brand new pair of Fruit of the Loom underwear from Uncle Albert's three-pack gift. Bean and even Chi Chi were surprised to discover there was actually a real person under all that dirt which led to a more cordial relationship.

"My name is Bean," said Bean, offering his hand now that the stranger's hand was clean. "And this is Chi Chi and this is Fruitcake."

"Huh, sounds like a vegetarian dinner," chuckled the stranger.

"Nice to meet you," said Bean.

"Um… nice to meet you too," said the beggar. "And um… thanks for… you know, the food and stuff."

"Chu gotta nem?" asked Chi Chi as she carefully collected the beggar's old clothes with only two fingers and dropped them into his plastic kitchen garbage bag. The bag was then shoved into the trashcan. Chi Chi had decided it held nothing of value, which was a torn rain poncho, a small inflatable pillow, a ragged copy of Soap Opera Digest, a half used roll of toilet paper, and a dog eared paperback novel titled *Monkey*.

"A name? Yes," said the beggar.

"Hokay, so wha da hell es it?"

"Oh, um, it's Rochier," said the beggar. "Name's Rochier."

"Roacher?" said Chi Chi. What chu min, like da creepy crawly bug?"

"No. Rochier. Like *Roshie-air*," said Rochier.

"Soun like Roacher to me. Chu gots any other nems?"

"Rogers," said Rochier.

"I thought you said Rochier," said Bean.

"I did," said Rochier.

"But chu juss sess Rochers," said Chi Chi.

"No, not Rochers. It's Rogers," said Rochier.

"But chu sess Roachie," said Chi Chi.

"No he said *Rogers*," said Bean.

"No, not Roachie. It's Roshier, *Roshie-air*," said Rochier to Chi Chi.

"Not Rogers?" asked Bean.

"Yes, Rogers," said Rochier.

Holy cow, thought Fruitcake as he lay on the bed listening and eyeballing the leftover French fries. *And I thought understanding Sister Moonbean-Goom-jigi was tough.*

"I thin dis guy es sung kina whack job," said Chi Chi. "He dun efen know hees own nem."

"Sure he does," said Bean. "His name is Roger."

"No," said Rochier. "It's Rochier."

"Then what about Roger?" asked Bean.

"Yeah, who da hell es Roacher?" asked Chi Chi.

"No, it's not Roger, it's *Rogers*," said Rochier. "My name is Rogers. *Rochier Rogers.*"

"I thin I'n juss gonna calls chu Roachie," said Chi Chi.

"Me to," agreed Bean.

"Um… Okay," said Rochier Rogers, now *Roachie,* who wasn't hard to get along with and willing to compromise, even if it meant a new name.

Rochier Rogers, now Roachie, was a regular fixture on the streets of Miami and Miami Beach with his plastic bag and cardboard sign that he found under a highway overpass. He found the sign nearly nine months ago and decided to try using it. On the first day he raked in $14 and pigged out at the Burger King on six one-dollar-special Jr. Whoppers, two orders of fries, and two chocolate shakes. The next day he made $17 and bought a clean set of clothes at a local Humane Society second hand store, then pigged out at the Burger King again on one-dollar special Jr. Whoppers, fries, and a chocolate shake. Roachie usually ate fairly well at the Burger King except when it rained. People didn't like to roll down their car windows and hand him money when it rained. Sometimes a cop would come along and chase him off, forcing him to find another corner in another part of town. It always surprised him that no one ever stopped to offer him work but just gave him money instead, except the one time an old woman with blue hair and a dog in a metallic silver Mercedes offered him a bath, a meal, and twenty dollars to have sex. Even though she was much older then him, he guessed in her mid to late 60s, he was desperate and about to say yes when she told him the sex would be a birthday present for her mother, then he kindly begged off. She got pissed and sped away, causing a chain reaction collision. All the drivers blamed Roachie, forcing him to find a new corner at a different intersection.

Roachie wasn't always a vagrant by trade. He was actually an MIT graduate with a Masters Degree in Computer Science and an additional Masters in Nano Technology from Stanford, not to mention the founder of the much lauded Rochier Roger's Research Corporation better known as *Triple R Corp* that was traded on the stock exchange as 3RC. It was a leader in nano science technology and research with numerous money making patents and an income potential of billions of dollars. The rumor around Wall Street was that Roachie had suffered a nervous breakdown and simply disappeared. Other rumors whispered of a takeover conspiracy that forced him into obscurity. Either way, Roachie went from millionair to homeless and found himself living under a highway overpass with his life in a plastic bag and depending on a poorly crafted cardboard sign that he sometimes unknowingly held backwards while standing in a hazy funk of depression at busy intersections. Every once in a while the old lady with blue hair would drive by in her metallic silver Mercedes and honk and shoot Roachie the bird.

Bean decided to adopt Roachie but Chi Chi was concerned about where they would put him, not sure if riding in the open trunk of the little clown car with the Kibbles & Bits, Sugar Pops, and Yoo-hoos was legal.

Just up the street from the Oceans Horizon Waterfront Resort Inn sat the four guys in the 1961 pimped out Buick, watching the second floor motel room with the little clown car parked in front while they casually conversed in their Haitian combo French-Spanish-African-Creole accent.

Just down the street, out of view sat Jorge, Juan, and Jesus, alias the 3Js, in their 1953 chopped top Mercury, casually conversing in *Kooban* Spanish while they too watched the motel room with the little clown car parked in front.

Covertly backed out of sight in an alley located midway between the Haitian's '61 pimped out Buick and the Cuban's '53 chopped top Mercury, and directly across the street from the motel, there sat in his red 1958 Caddy convertible with the plastic bobbing head figure of Jesus on the dashboard, one Father Alphonso Sabatino, AKA Guido Fulgenzi, AKA Five Nose Freddy the mafia hit man, also watching the motel room with the little clown car parked in front. He was talking on his cell phone.

"Well, how the hell should I know? Now there's three of 'em and that ugly frigin' little dog. And that ain't all. They got company following them around and they don't look too friendly."

"Whatcha mean, they got company that don't look too friendly?" said Albert on the other end of the call.

"Some kinda gangbangers takin' a serious interest in our boy is what I mean," said Father Sabatino. "Hey, did you know that dog's only got one ear? And that ugly hairy little shit tried to bite me when I snatched his cheeseburgers."

"You took the dogs cheeseburgers?"

"Hey, I was hungry. I was gonna eat at some damn Conch place that looked pretty good and had some guy croonin' Jimmy Buffett songs but the kid got into it with some damn giant cop and I had to hang lose and make sure he got out of it okay. You know, in case I had to take care of the cop or something. I mean, you know, the take care of him kind of take care of him, the *New Jersey way*. Anyways, I didn't get a chance to eat so's I snatched the dog's cheeseburgers and that ugly little mut tried to bite me."

"Who gives a shit about the dog? What about the cop?"

"No problem."

"Shit, you whacked a cop!"

"No."

"But you said…"

"No I didn't. I said in case…"

"Okay, so what about the gangbangers?"

"What about the gangbangers?"

"What the hell do they want?"

"Well how the hell should I know?"

"Well, maybe you should find out dammit… before something serious happens. You gotta take care of the kid, remember?"

"Maybe I should take care of the gangbangers," suggested Father Sabatino.

"Take care of the gang bangers? What are you crazy. You're supposed to take care of the kid."

"No, I mean take care of the gangbangers the *New Jersey way*, not the other way. So's they can't take care of the kid or nothing. You know, the *New Jersey way* I mean. So's I can take care of the kid, the other way. But I ain't no babysitter. What, you think I'm some kind of damn babysitter, like I'm gonna maybe baby-sit a bunch of damn gangbangers. Why the hell should I do that? I ain't gettin' paid to do that."

"That sounds kind of messy. The *New Jersey way*, I mean. On the gangbangers, I mean. In case... I mean. Not the kid. Cause the kid you gotta take care of the other way."

"Yeah, the kid. I got it. Like I'm a goddamn babysitter. I got it."

"So, you're gonna take care of it, right?"

"Take care of what? You want me to take care of the gangbangers or take care of the kid. I mean... you know, the *New Jersey way* and all that or what?"

"Just do what you gotta do to take care of the kid the regular way. Got it?"

"Yeah, I got it. But I ain't takin' care of that scraggly ass dog. That ugly little shitbird tried to bite me. Hey, you know that damn dog's only got one ear?"

chapter 12
Me'ahmi Mayhem!

While Bean and Roachie were getting acquainted by sharing the stories of their lives, both of which sounded safe and secure to Chi Chi, she strolled out onto the back balcony of their second floor room (with a view that didn't cost extra). The sun was setting behind Miami and Biscayne Bay and thousands of lights both bright and small began to flicker on through the twilight filling the skyline with a sense of magic. Just then a white seaplane with a large round logo on the tale rumbled across the surface of the bay and took flight.

Planes dat come down and take off on da water, thought Chi Chi. *Ho chi mama, anythin' can happen in Me'ahmi... and in America. Sung day I gonna haf me a plane when I'n a big moofy star.*

Chi Chi thought back to when she first arrived here six years ago, alone and frightened, not knowing any English (not that she's improved much), struggling on her own to survive and stay one step ahead of those who wanted to send her back to Cuba. The experience had made her cold and calculating, sometimes even heartless, but she was determined to stay free and live the American dream. She didn't really need Bean and she sure as hell didn't need the added responsibility of Roachie, but for some reason for the first time she felt someone needed her, that they both needed her, and feeling needed was an entirely new experience.

The only other time she came close to feeling needed was when she was taken in by an ex-Vietnamese prostitute named My Pi Lin whose English was worse than Chi Chi's, if that can be imagined. Because of her poor english My Pi Lin had a habit of getting into confusing arguments with almost everyone she met. My Pi Lin would most often resolve the arguments by throwing up her hands in frustration and saying "ho chi mama" and walk away. Sometimes Chi Chi would salvage the conversation as best she could, having more patience than My Pi Lin. But that all ended when My Pi Lin eventually moved to the west coast after marrying a famous over-the-hill one-hit-wonder movie director who hadn't made a full length movie since 1969. The movie was called *Cowboys and Indians* but had absolutely nothing to do with cowboys or Indians. It was actually a Vietnam War protest movie that was somehow centered on an Irish terrorist and a gay Polish communist, filmed on location in Greece. The film hit the big screen just before the young director fled to Canada to avoid the draft. It was a critical success in small circles and a box office disaster in large ones. Now he lives under a different name and survives by making short three-minute spoof flicks for viewing on You Tube on the internet and third world crisis documentaries that nobody ever sees but somehow always get financed rich left wing activists.

"Hey," Chi Chi called back into the room. "Chu gise wanna go walk onna beash. Es kina nice out en deres a place where chu can sit and see da stars and watch da wafes splashin' in and listen to some guy singin' Chimmy Buffett sungs up on a poop deck."

Bean jumped at the idea. He hadn't heard any Jimmy Buffett music since the day of the big waterspout and, except for the day at Sebastian Inlet, hadn't really spent much time on the beach, having lost his surfboard along with his home.

"Sure," said Bean. "Wanna go walk on the beach?" he asked Roachie.

"Uh… okay," said Roachie.

145

"And we'll stop off somewhere on the way and get you a new pair of sneakers," added Bean.

"Oh… okay," said Roachie, hardly believing his good fortune.

When they exited the motel room (the one with a view and no extra charge for the dog) they caught the attention of the occupants of all three of the cars staked out nearby.

"Hey meng, dere es da girl," said Jorge to the other two 3Js in the '53 chopped top Mercury.

"Hey mun, look it. It's da girl," said one of the Haitians in the '61 pimped out Buick.

"Shit," said Father Sabatino at being interrupted. He was kicked back, shoes off, feet on the dashboard, checking out the stars, sucking on a cigar, about to unscrew the top of his flask, and listening to Frank Sinatra on the AM radio croon a soft romantic song about a lost love. The song reminded Father Sabatino of the time he took care of Big Fats Berkowitz (the *New Jersey way*) and tossed him off the Brooklyn Bridge, then went and had a wonderful romantic evening with Sybil Francetti at Mama Rosa's Little Nopoli Café. He and Sybil had a great relationship until Sybil refused to date him anymore after she discovered he was the one who took care of her Uncle Ralphie Scanzaroli (the *New* Jersey way). He was never very successful when it came to relationships, especially when the women found out what he did for a living. Never the less Father Sabatino really liked Frank Sinatra. It was kind of a rule that he learned somewhere back in the day when he was in mafia hitman school, that all mafia hitmen (and women) are supposed to like Frank Sinatra, especially Italian hitmen. So Father Sabatino liked Frank Sinatra and especially liked Frank Sinatra's song *September of My Years* which, according to the DJ on the radio, was the song coming up next.

Father Sabatino was also beginning to like Miami. It was as though someone took New York City and its jammed up freeways and big boxy buildings and even its miserable people and ran it all through a wash cycle and a fluff dry cycle in one of Fast Eddy's laundry mats, then just set it all down on the coast in the south Florida swamp and sunshine, then threw in a bunch of palm trees and beautiful girls in bikinis. And the water, unlike the Hudson River, was so clear that he would have to think twice about polluting it with something as atrocious as the bodies of a Big Fats Berkowitz or Ralphie Scanzaroli. As Father Sabatino grudgingly slipped his imported Italian loafers back on his feet and sat up, he contemplated the possibility of retiring in Miami where, he thought with a smile, they even have Frank Sinatra singing on the AM radio.

One day you turn around and it's Summer,
Next day you turn around and it's Fall...

Arriving at the car, Bean, having raised the top and buttoned the Celestial Rocket up for the night, put the top back down and opened the trunk for Roachie.

"Maybe Roachie he chould sit in da front," suggested Chi Chi.

"But where are you going to sit?' asked Bean.

"I can sit on hees lap. Es hokay now. Hees all clean now and he dun smell so bad and we dun needa go too far to da beash."

Great, thought Fruitcake, *now they're gonna shove my ass in the trunk.* He was wrong. They shoved him back between the seats again as usual.

Just then they heard tires screech and looked to the street. Approaching fast was the Haitians' '61 pimped out Buick. It sped down the street then took a violent turn into the parking lot of the Oceans Horizon Waterfront Resort Inn. Three of the four Haitians intended to jump out and grab Chi Chi.

"OH CHIT!" said Chi Chi, jumping into the passenger seat. "Get in da car quick!"

"What?" said Bean.

"What?" said Roachie.

Now what? thought Fruitcake, popping his scraggly one-eared head up between the seats.

"GET IN'N DRIFE! DRIFE! HURRY!" yelled Chi Chi.

Bean jumped in behind the wheel, injected the key, and cranked up the engine.

"Uh… What…" said Roachie.

"GET IN! GET IN!" repeated Chi Chi to Roachie.

"But… where…" said Bean.

"JUSS DRIFE, DRIFE DA CAR! DRIFE, HURRY!" she said, bouncing up and down in her seat, looking back at the approaching pimped out Buick.

Roachie, not sure what to do, hopped into the trunk as before just as the Celestial Rocket blasted off. Not wearing any shoes and not wanting his feet to drag on the ground the way they did on the way to the motel, he lifted his feet up, turned sideways and brought his knees to his chest in order to fit into the small space. Then he noticed something was poking him in his ass, which reminded him of when he had his colon checked three years ago. He twisted and contorted himself until he could get his hand behind his butt where he discovered the discomfort was caused by a bottle of chocolate Yoo-hoo. He pulled it out and was about to screw the top off when Bean sped out of the motel parking lot and onto the street. When he did, the curb bump jerked the hood of the trunk down on Roachie's head.

"OW!" yelled Roachie.

"ES CHU HOKAY, ROACHIE?" asked Chi Chi.

"WHAT?"

"Oh, hees hokay," said Chi Chi. "Drife! Hurry! Drife!"

The '61 pimped out Buick was quick to follow, sparks flying from its chrome duel tailpipes when they scraped the curb at the parking lot exit. Another set of screeching wheels revealed the 3Js '53 chopped top Mercury as it shot from its discrete stake out spot and into the street to join the chase. Immediately behind came the subtle but powerful rumble of the red '58 Caddy convertible's 8 cylinder flathead engine as it emerged from the alley in pursuit of the pursuers.

With Sinatra crooning and not missing a beat.

And the Springs and the Winters of a lifetime,
Whatever happened to them all?

Off they all went into the Miami Beach night, three classic automobiles all occupied by characters of questionable character, in pursuit of yet another classic, Sister Moonbeam-Goom-jigi's 1955 Nash Metropolitan convertible, the Celestial Rocket.

"Shit," grumbled Father Sabatino. "Like I'm some kind of damn babysitter."

🌴

Officer Fordhook was at the corner of 15th and Lenox Avenue near Flamingo Park and looking forward to getting off duty in about 20 minutes, especially after just getting a fresh phone number from a blonde named Sissy in a mauve colored BMW convertible whose windshield frame he was now leaning on while flexing the muscles on top of his muscles.

"...of course I won't write you up," he said in his impressive deep official catch a blonde voice. "I wouldn't do that to a pretty thing like you."

"Wow, are those real muscles?" said the blonde, thinking, *this guy I just gave that fake phone number to is a friggin' idiot and I'll say anything to keep from getting another damn ticket.*

"Uh, yeah. As a matter of fact I used to play for the Dolphins. Wide receiver. Tight end."

"Still looks pretty tight to me," said the blonde with a sly smile, thinking, *okay, lets get this shit over with you ignorant disgusting prehistoric man-beast, because I got a hot date with my sexy new girlfriend.*

While Officer Fordhook flexed his muscles and his tight end, he glanced up to see the lights of four vehicles approaching fast from the west end of 15th. At first glance he thought it was one of those classic car club caravans until he realized they were driving way too fast. Then he recognized the little car in the front of the pack with the weird paint job and the half-ass manatee on the hood as that little clown car with the Cuban girl and the retarded kid with the retarded one eared dog. The four speeding vehicles slowed just a bit when they saw the flashing lights of Officer Fordhook's patrol car, but seeing he wasn't actually in the car, all four punched it and sped on.

"What the fu… Oh, sorry ma'am. Duty calls," said Officer Fordhook as he studied the passing speeding cars and their occupants. Then looking back to the blonde, "But I'll be in touch… real soon," he said with a wink.

She winked back, thinking, *don't count on it dickhead.*

Officer Fordhook quickly mounted his vehicle, flipped on the siren and spun out in pursuit of the speeding classic car caravan, thinking, *I bet that blonde chick thought that was pretty damn cool.*

The blonde in the BMW slowly pulled out and headed in the opposite direction, thinking, *Jesus, what a tool. Yuk.* She immediately pulled out her cell phone and dialed her lawyer. Her next call would be to the Miami Beach City Hall.

Bean had never driven so fast in his entire short life and was gripping the steering wheel as though it were likely to fly out of the car. Chi Chi was bouncing up and down in a panic, encouraging Bean to go faster. Fruitcake was frozen with fear, his head extended up from between the seats, his one ear flapping in the breeze. Roachie was still bouncing around in the trunk holding on for dear life with one hand while trying to get the Yoo-hoo to his lips without breaking his teeth on the bottle with the other. On the street behind them they left a wake of derailed cars that ran amok trying to get out of their way.

The trunk hood popped down.

"OW!"

"ROACHIE, ES CHU HOKAY?"

"WHAT?"

"Hees hokey."

The Haitian's '61 pimped out Buick was only two car lengths behind the Celestial Rocket. Its driver, a dark-haired, dark-skinned, dark-eyed, dark-spirited, determined man was intently focused, looking for any opportunity to waylay the little car and the girl. Behind the Buick trailing by only a car length raced the '53 chopped top Mercury carrying the 3Js, all of which were pointing and talking excitedly at the same time (in Kooban). Bringing up the rear, nearly running up the tailpipe of the Mercury was the red '58 Caddy convertible driven by the cool, calm, and confident Father Sabatino who was humming along with Frank Sinatra except when he mumbled, "Shit. Like I'm some kind of damn babysitter."

And Frank Sinatra not missing a beat.

As a man who has always had the wandering ways,
Now I'm reaching back for yesterdays...

"Unit one-niner to Central. Over," said Officer Fordhook into the radio mike in his normal but excited Clint Eastwood voice.

"Come in one-niner. Over," came a calm clear woman's voice in reply.

"Central, I am in high speed pursuit of four vehicles going west, I mean east on 15th... No, check that..."

At Chi Chi's insistence Bean had just made a drastic right turn onto Pennsylvania Avenue that nearly flipped Fruitcake over and didn't go too well with Roachie in the trunk who was just about to get the Yoo-hoo to his lips. The force of the turn shot some of the delicious chocolaty drink right up his nose and again brought the hood of the trunk down on his head.

"OW!"

"ROACHIE, ES CHU HOKAY?"

"WHAT?"

"Hees hokay."

"Speeding vehicles now proceeding south on Pennsylvania. Over," Officer Fordhook informed Central Dispatch.

"Central to one-niner. We copy. Other cars dispatched. Please identify subject vehicles. Over." answered the woman from Central Dispatch.

"I got four vehicles in what looks to be a chase of some kind. Leading vehicle is a... uh... little... uh... convertible clown car of some kind with a manatee on the hood being driven by a... uh..."

Just then Officer Fordhook realized that the driver of the little clown car was the retarded kid he had come across earlier that day. He also realized that he had yet to read the new official *Miami Beach Law Enforcement Officer's Politically Correct Handbook* that informed him of the proper language and procedures to use in situations involving minorities and people of special circumstances such as being mentally challenged, because - he had lost it - and was therefore not quite sure how to proceed verbally with his high speed situation report.

"Say again one-niner. You're transmission apparently broke up. Over" said the Central Dispatch woman.

152

"I said, the lead vehicle is a multicolored little clown car with a manatee on the hood being driven by an under aged young male *retard* with a *Spic chongo* female, a one-eared *retarded* dog and a... uh... what appears to be a drunken *Negro* in the trunk. Over."

"One-niner, did you just say..."

"They are being pursued by four foreign looking *negros* in a light colored early 60's pimped out Buick that is being pursued by three *Spic cholo* gangbangers in a purple chopped top early 50's Mercury which is being pursued by a... uh... I'll be damned... a *Catholic priest* in a red Cadillac convertable. Um... Central are they shooting any movies or TV shows out here tonight? Over," said Officer Fordhook; assuring himself he had used all the proper politically correct references he had learned over the years in all the locker rooms where he had spent most of his social life and gained most all of his cultural reference.

"One-niner, did you say a *Catholic priest*? Over."

"That's affirmative. Over."

"One-niner, did you say a *retard?* Over."

"That's affirmative, Central. Over"

"And did you say *Spic*? Over."

"That's affirmative. Over."

"And did you actually say, *NEGRO?*" said the Central Dispatch lady who happened to be a racially sensitive black woman with an excessive weight problem and bi-polar disorder by the name of Shanakitra Jackson, and who after hearing all of Officer Fordhook's ethnic slurs and the word *Negro,* just snapped and was now so royally pissed off at Officer Fordhook that she forgot to shut off her microphone.

With her microphone on, Officer Fordhook could hear everything said in the Central Dispatch center.

"Did that stupid asshole actually say *NEGRO?*" asked the angry black Central Dispatch woman of no one in particular.

"I heard something about a retarded manatee and a one eared dog. Or was that a retarded one eared Negro with a retarded dog?" said someone.

"No, it was a retarded Negro and a one eared Spic, wasn't it?" said another.

"Was it east or west on Pennsylvania, or..." said someone else in Central Dispatch.

"Isn't that that dumb shit that lost all those Dolphin playbooks that cost us the whole damn season? I lost a lotta money that season cause of that dumb son of a bitch."

"Yeah, me too."

"Oh yeah. The blonde guy with all the muscles, thinks he's Clint Eastwood," chuckled Officer Charley Harley as he popped a palm full of M&M peanuts in his mouth and followed them with a swig of Mountain Dew soda. Officer Charley Harley was temporarily desk bound because he had been bitten three days earlier on the inner thigh by a bad tempered pitbull that belonged to an old woman with blue hair. At least that's how he reported it. He claimed the pitbull got away. Rumor was he was actually bitten by the bad tempered old lady with the blue hair. The various speculations regarding what she was doing down there in the first place were many.

"Uh... Central. One-niner here. I could use a little help here," said Officer Fordhook over the sound of his siren and while expertly weaving through the chaotic traffic mess caused by the speeding cars of the classic caravan as though he were running a pass pattern for the Dolphins. "Suspect vehicles have just merged onto Washington, southbound. Over."

"One-niner, did I hear you right? Did you actually say drunken *NEGRO?*"

"Um... that's affirmative Central. A drunken Negro in the trunk of a little clown car with a chongo chick, a retarded kid and a one-eared retarded dog... in a clown car… being pursued by Negro pimps, Spic cholo gang bangers, and a priest. Over."

The dispatch woman was getting angrier by the second and could no longer contain herself and launched into an animated tirade.

"I gonna kick yo ass, one-niner!" said the Central Dispatch woman, now standing at her station, again failing to turn off the mike. "I gonna kick that white mo'fucka's ass. You just wait 'til that mo'fucka git back to dis station. I gonna kick that muscle bound redneck insensitive racist mo'fucka's ass… and then I gonna kill 'em."

"Uh oh. Shanakitra's goin' on another tirade," said Officer Charley Harley as he popped in some more M&M peanuts and took another swig of Mountain Dew. "Hey, did somebody say that retarded dog was driving?" he mumbled through the stuff in his mouth.

Officer Fordhook looked at the speaker of his patrol car radio in disbelief. He tapped the radio a few times with his knuckles, thinking it might be malfunctioning and picking up some foreign transmission. "Uh, Central, you wanna run that by me again?"

"I said I gonna kick your mo'fu…"

"Officer Fordhook. This is Sergeant Fernandez," said Sergeant Fernandez, formerly of the San Francisco Police Department, taking over Shanakitra's mike. "Now I'm going to ask you a question and I want an honest answer. Son, have you… I mean, are you possibly… under the influence? Over."

"What? Under the what?" replied Officer Fordhook.

"Oh, nothing in particular. Maybe some sort of drugs or alcohol or possibly some prescribed mood manipulator," said Sergeant Fernandez. "It's okay to admit it, son. We have programs to help, you know. Everyone needs a little help once in awhile. Nothing to be ashamed of."

"Uh, negative, Central. I am in high-speed pursuit. Vehicles in question have just turned right and are now proceeding on 5ᵗʰ and heading for the MacArthur Causeway. Can you set up an intercept? Over."

"I'll intercept yo white ass you redneck racist mo'fu…"

"Now Shanakitra, you just calm down," said Sergeant Fernandez, the same Sergeant Fernandez that helped create and write the new official *Miami Beach Law Enforcement Officer's Politically Correct Handbook* soon after he transferred to Miami Beach from California. "I'm sure Officer Fordhook didn't mean to be offensive. He's in a stress situation and we need to keep our heads, be professional, and assist him in any way we can. Don't forget Shanakitra, the guidelines and principals of the new *Miami Beach Law Enforcement Officer's Politically Correct Handbook* apply to all of us."

"Handbook? Calm down? Calm down my ass. I gonna call the NAACP! I gonna call the Urban League! I gonna call the Civil Liberties Union! I gonna call ACORN! Hell, I might even call the Reverends."

"The Reverends? What Reverends?" asked Sergeant Fernandez.

"Al Jackson and Jesse Sharpton," said Shanakitra.

Without her medications Shanakitra sometimes got confused and turned things around, like the first names of the Reverends and like the time she dispatched cars on an officer needs assistance call, informing them that an old lady with blue hair had attacked an officer and bit him in the thigh.

"That's right, you heard me. You got that right. The reverends will fo sho stir up some shit. Fo sho they will. You'll see. And then I gonna sue. I gonna sue ever'body. I gonna sue the police department. I gonna sue Miami Beach. I even gonna sue yo ass, you west coast pussy. No sir, I ain't gonna put up wit dis Jim Crow bullshit, usin' a word like *Negro*. A white boy cop usin' a word like *Negro*. Why, dat dumbass sum'bitch white boy just insulted and demeanered every black person in Miami. Every black person in allllll Florida."

"Don't you mean *Jesse* Jackson and *Al* Sharpton," corrected Sergeant Fernandez.

"Oh, the Reverends. Yeah, those guys," said Officer Charley Harley. "Hey those guys ever have a real job?" asked Officer Harley as he searched through the bag and picked out only blue M&M peanuts and tossed them in his mouth. "I mean, like, I wanna know how'd they get so rich if they never had a real job?"

"Don't you be tellin' me what the hell I mean," said Shanakitra to Sergeant Fernandez. "I know what the hell I mean. I gonna call the reverends and they gonna git down here and demonstrate and maybe start a movement and git all da black folks to boycott and stuff. Maybe boycott the whole damn Miami Beach Police department. Maybe even the whole country's police departments."

Sergeant Fernandez was about to object until the thought crossed his mind that a black boycott of police departments might not be a bad thing, depending on your point of view.

"Now Shanakitra," said Sergeant Fernandez, "you just need to calm down. Have you taken your medicine today?"

Shanakitra hadn't taken her medications. Shanakitra didn't calm down.

"And if dat don't work then I'll call... THE MAN HIS'SELF. Dats what I gonna do."

"What man? You mean the Mayor?" said Sergeant Fernandez.

"Oh hell no. Dat fool ain't good fo nothin'. I mean the man his'self. My man BARACK HUSSEIN OBAMA! And maybe even his woman, Michelle. Now there's a bitch don't take no shit."

Now Shanakitra, I'm sure it was just an unintentional mental error on the part of Officer Fordhook, made in the heat and haste of the moment. Nothing to get excited about."

"Excuse me, Sergeant Fernandez," interrupted one of the 911 operators. "We just got a call from a woman named Sissy Rominski, you know that woman who's always on TV talking about gay rights. She says Officer Fordhook pulled her over near Flamingo Park and tried to solicit sex."

"What? Sex? Solicit sex? From a gay woman? WHAT? ARE YOU SHITTIN' ME?" exploded Sergeant Fernandez. "God dammit! I'm gonna tear that brainless idiot a whole new asshole when he gets in here. High speed pursuit my butt. Call all those cars back. You just wait 'til that spaced out redneck moron gets back in here, I'm gonna kick that big oaf's friggin' ass. And did I hear him say *spic chonga?* Did I hear him say *spic cholo?* I'll be damned. And harassing a gay woman. I'll be damned."

"Something about a retarded dog…" said Officer Charley Harley, "…driving a manatee. He took a sip of his Mountain Dew. 'So much for that handbook I guess."

"No neck, redneck, sexist, male chauvinist, racist, honky asshole pig mo'fucka!" chimed in a ranting Shanakitra whose head was sliding from side to side with each word as though it were going to launch right off her shoulders, and who by now, like Sergeant Fernandez, was definitely not adhering to the new *Miami Beach Law Enforcement Officer's Politically Correct Handbook.*

"Oh Shanakitra, shut the hell up and sit your fat ass down," demanded an angry Sergeant Fernandez.

"What! You can't talk to me like dat you Spic bastard! I'm gonna call…"

"Shanakitra, I have a gun. Shut the hell up. Sit down."

"Oh, okay," said Shanakitra, sitting down.

"OW!"
"HEY ROACHIE, ES CHU HOKAY?"

"WHAT?"

"Hees hokay."

In the pimped out Haitian's Buick the driver hit the speed dial of his cell phone. "Dey headin' for da MacArthur. Cut 'em off."

"OW!"

"HEY ROACHIE, ES CHU HOKAY?"

"WHAT?"

"Hees hokay."

In the chopped top Mercury, Jorge pulled out his cell phone and hit the speed dial. "Hey meng. Chee es goin' for da MacArthur cussway. Chu gotta heads er off, meng."

"OW!"

"HEY ROACHIE, ES CHU HOKAY?"

"WHAT?"

"Hees hokay."

In the red Caddy convertible Father Sabatino turned up the radio to compensate for the noise of other cars, the wind from the increased speed of the chase, and Officer Fordhook's irritating siren. "Shit. Like I'm some kind of damn babysitter."

And Sinatra not missing a beat.

And I find that I'm sighing softly as I near... September,
The warm September of my years.

"OW!"

"HEY ROACHIE, ES CHU HOKAY?"

"WHAT?"

"Hees hokay."

"Was that a one-eared retarded dog driving a clown car with a manatee in the trunk or...? Oh, hey, there aren't any more blue ones. Hey, who the hell ate all the blue M&M peanuts?" asked Officer Harley through a mouth full of blue M&M peanuts.

chapter 13

Party Crashers!

Due to his lost credibility Officer Fordhook was now the only patrol car in pursuit of the three vehicles that were in pursuit of the Celestial Rocket. Sergeant Fernandez, now convinced that Officer Foordhook was under the influence, recalled all of the other patrol cars that were sent to assist in his *alleged* high-speed pursuit. The Miami City police on the mainland, however, had been monitoring the radio, and being familiar with the Haitian's 1961 pimped out Buick and knowing they were bad guys, decided Officer Fordhook was on the up and up and so decided they would intercept the high speed caravan when it reached their turf at Watson Island on the west end of the MacArthur Causeway.

"OW!"

"HEY ROCAHIE, ES CHU HOKAY?"

"WHAT?"

"Hees hokay," said Chi Chi to Bean as they sped onto the MacArthur Causeway. "We gotta loos dees guys. We gotta get across da cussway and den we gonna loos 'em in Me'ahmi for chure. Hey, dun dis little clown car go no faster?"

"I don't know," said Bean. "I never had to…"

Chi Chi slammed her foot on top of Bean's foot that was on top of the accelerator pedal and the Celestial Rocket gained another ten miles per hour which wasn't much compared to the power of the cars pursuing them. It came at an opportune moment however, just as the Haitians had gained a chance to pass and cut them off near the causeway's turn off to Star Island. When Bean looked to his left the Haitian's '61 pimped out Buick had pulled up beside them and was about to force them off the road. Chi Chi mashed both their feet all the way to the floor, increasing their speed again to a Celestial Rocket personal best of nearly 75 miles per hour. This caught Bean by surprise and caused him to swerve left, forcing the Haitians to do the same and nearly fly into the median. When that happened, the 3Js in their chopped top Mercury moved up on the Celestial Rocket's tail. The Cubans squeezed their heads and arms out of the low narrow chopped top windows and began desperately waving and yelling in *Kooban* Spanish, which of course no one could hear because of Officer Fordhook's siren and the noise from the wind and other cars on the MacArthur, so of course Roachie had no idea what they were saying.

"WHAT?" said Roachie, who finally managed to get the Yoo-hoo to his lips for a taste and hopefully was about to do it again to finish off the bottle.

The Haitians recovered control of their pimped out Buick and, eager to get back in the chase, tried to force their way in between the Cuban's chopped top Mercury and Father Sabatino's '58 Caddy.

"Hey you old bastard, get da hell outta de way, mon!" one of the Haitians yelled at Father Sabatino.

Father Sabatino looked at them, smiled, reached into his jacket and pulled out a Coonan 357 Magnum Automatic, "Have a nice evening gentleman," he said just before he expertly shot out their rear tire.

The Haitians swerved, fell behind and ran off the shoulder of the road, nearly taking Officer Fordhook's patrol car with them, then swerved again and ran back on the road sliding sideways where they were hit by an oncoming white Cadillac Escalade driven by a prominent Miami plastic surgeon by the name of Dr. Norman Bloomenstein. The Escalade was then struck by a mauve

BMW occupied by two blondes, and the BMW was then almost hit and crushed by a Cosco eighteen-wheeler that nearly jackknifed before it slid to a halt, blocking all traffic in the westbound lanes of the MacArthur Causeway. Dr Bloomenstein the plastic surgeon cursed the Haitians. Sissy Rominski, the gay rights activist and driver of the BMW along with her hot new girlfriend date cursed Dr. Bloomenstein. The good ol' boy bubba Cosco truck driver who was from out of town cursed all of Miami, swearing he was never going to drive the Miami route again.

"Like I'm some kind of damn babysitter," mumbled Father Sabatino as he replaced his Coonan 357.

And Sinatra not missing a beat.

And I find that I'm sighing softly as I near... September.
The warm September of my years.

The 3Js continued to yell and waive at Chi Chi and Bean, only to get a minimal response from Roachie in the trunk between his attempted gulps of Yoo-hoo.

"WHAT?" Roachie asked the Cubans.

"HEY ROACHIE, ES CHU HOKAY," asked Chi Chi.

"WHAT?" Roachie asked Chi Chi.

"Hees hokay," Chi Chi said to Bean.

"OW! I think I chipped my tooth," said Roachie to nobody in particular.

"WHAT?" asked Chi Chi.

"WHAT?" asked Roachie.

What. Whatta ya mean what? What's all this what crap? What my ass. Get me off this thing," thought Fruitcake as loud as he could think it, hoping like hell somebody was paying attention. *Okay, you can have the front seat; just give me back my papa-san chair. Where's the house? Where's the house?* Fruitcake was not exactly the high-speed type and preferred to just hear about anxious moments in paperback novels like Sam Slade Ace Detective.

On the west end of the MacArthur Causeway four Miami Police cars with lights flashing and sirens screaming were just approaching the bridge to Watson Island. Arriving ahead of the police and also heading for the island were two other vehicles. In one were Cubans, seven of them, all jammed into a yellow Taxi Cab, all talking excitedly and looking ahead intensely for a little clown car being chased by Haitians and cops. The other vehicle carried five Haitians riding in a used chocolate brown UPS delivery truck. The truck had been restored and looked exactly like a chocolate brown UPS delivery truck because it actually had been a chocolate brown UPS delivery truck (duh). This brown UPS delivery truck however sported an altered logo on each side that said "ubs" which nobody ever seemed to notice (the Haitians weren't great spellers either). The Haitians liked that nobody noticed because a "ups", or in their case a "ubs" truck could go anywhere without question or suspicion, which was helpful when stealing things or transporting things that were already stolen or that were otherwise illegal. The Haitians' chocolate brown "ubs" delivery truck that usually served as a roving illegal operations center also included a tricked out engine under the hood for extra speed, a bodacious sound system with a collection of all the latest violent gangsta rap music, a large flat screen TV, and a DVD player that only played the movie *Scarface*. It was also fitted out with a myriad of high tech communications gear that allowed them to monitor most every manner of law enforcement and military communication frequencies in the state of Florida.

As the Celestial Rocket, the Cuban's chopped top '53 Mercury, the '58 Caddy, and officer Fordhook's patrol car reached the east end of Watson Island - and the Cubans

Yellow Cab, the Haitians "ubs" truck, and the four Miami police cars reached the west end of the island, four large brilliant civil defense spotlights came on suddenly from the island's south side and shot skyward. Out of the dark night sky and into the broad beams of bright light there slowly appeared the huge bulbous figure of none other than the famous Goodyear Blimp. Everyone within miles of the majestic sight, including Bean and Chi Chi, immediately fixed their attention on the huge dirigible above the small island, which gave Chi Chi the idea to grab the wheel and aim the little car to the off ramp, taking them to the island's north side.

"What are you doing?" asked a surprised Bean.

"Get off here. Onto the island," said Chi Chi, looking back to see if their pursuers were still distracted by the blimp. And distracted they were, all of them, and when they finally looked back to the road there was no little clown car with a weird black guy curled up in the trunk.

"Hey meng, where da hell es dat leetle car?" said Jesus.

"I dunno," answered Juan. "We was right behind dem and now dey ain't dere. Maybe dey wass obduckeded by dat big thing. Chu know, ly on dat X-File cho wit dat leetle chort lady. Maybe dat ain't no blimp. Maybe dass a big Chu-F-O."

"Oh yeah," said Jorge. "Chu mean dat TV cho wit da lady dass always wearin' a trench coat. How come chee always wearin' a trench coat anyways when it ain't rainin' an how come dey never turn on da lights on dat TV cho? Dey always usin' them leetle flashlights when all dey gotta do es turn on da light switch."

"Yeah meng, dass kinna stupid," agreed Jesus. "I'n thinkin' I be turnin' on some lights if some big alien blood suckin' worm wass gonna' get me, meng."

"Aliens?" said Juan. "What da hell es chu talkin' about, meng? Where's da girl! Where's da leetle clown car?"

Jorge looked back off the main road just in time to catch a glimps of the Celestial Rocket at the end of the off ramp near the Ichimura Miami Japan Garden.

"I see 'em! I see 'em!" shouted Jorge. "Turn around!"

Juan hit the brakes and slid into a 180-degree turn, then smoked the tires as he shot back toward the exit. Father Sabatino did the same followed by Officer Fordhook.

"Like I'm some kind of damn babysitter," mumbled Father Sabitino.

"Hey meng, who es dat priest guy?" said Jorge.

"I dunno," said Juan. "But hees a priest so what chu worried about?"

"Hees a priest with a pretty cool car," said Jorge. "Like maybe dat priest business ain so bad. And look at dat Pope guy. He gots all kina blingy gold and chit and chu know wha, he dun even pay no taxes."

"Yeah, meng. Dass a pretty cool car," agreed Jesus.

"Chu mean da Pope dun pay no taxes? Hey meng, dat ain fair."

"Hey, meng. Ain none of does preacher dudes payin' no taxes."

"Wha, you min all dem fathers no pay no taxes?"

"Wha chu care, meng. Chu dun pay no taxes neither."

"A babysitter. Like I'm some kind of damn babysitter," mumbled Father Sabatino in the car behind them.

And Sinatra not missing a beat.

As a man who has never paused at wishing wells,
Now I'm watching children's carousels,

"Central, Fordhook here. The clown car has exited onto Watson Island," reported Officer Fordhook as he spun his vehicle around and headed for the off ramp. "And I think I heard shots fired."

"I don't give a shit what your imaginary retarded manatee and one eyed dog are doing with their little clown car, son. I don't give a shit if they got a cannon. I don't give a shit if they launched to the moon. I told you to get your ass back here. And that's an order," shouted Sergeant Fernandez.

"Um… that's a one *eared* dog, sir," corrected Officer Fordhook. "And the manatee isn't real. I mean it's really there but it's on the hood but not… shit," said a frustrated Officer Fordhook.

"Dats right, dammit!" injected Shanakitra the irate dispatch woman. "You get yo lily-white honky self back here so's I can kick yo…"

"Shanakitra! Gun! Shut the hell up!"

"Yes sir."

"OW!"

"ROACHIE, ES CHU HOKEY?"

"WHAT?"

"Hees hokay. Uh oh. Here dey comin' again. Quick, turn arounds and go back on da big road."

Bean began to turn the Celestial Rocket around and drive back onto the off ramp.

"No no!" said Chi Chi, quickly changing her mind when she saw how fast the Cubans were approaching. "Dun go on da big road. Go dat way."

"But you said…"

"GO DAT WAY! GO DAT WAY!"

Bean, confused, turned a half circle and headed in the direction of Chi Chi's finger that was bouncing up and down and sideways just like Chi Chi was bouncing with excitement. The bouncing finger led him around a corner and into a parking lot then out of the parking lot and straight into the approaching Cubans again who were followed closely by Father Sabatino. Bean, Chi Chi, and Fruitcake closed their eyes and braced for a head on collision but Juan yanked the wheel of the chopped top '57 Mercury, swerving right just in time to avoid the crash. Father Sabatino swerved left to do the same. When Bean opened his eyes there was a near miss flash of a police car passing then there were no cars and only clear road ahead. They were away.

Following turn after turn on the service roads of the Parrot Jungle, not knowing where they were heading, they eventually found themselves on the west end of the island driving under the east end of the bridge, the part of the causeway that connected the island to the mainland. They entered the south side of the island where there suddenly appeared before them a large open-air tent surrounded by lights and people in formal evening attire, and a live band singing, *"Up up and away in my beautiful, my beautiful balloon."* The huge spotlights in the sky highlighted and swept across the mammoth Goodyear blimp while it slowly descended overhead.

Inside the cockpit of the blimp the pilot was bitching to the co-pilot because earlier that day they had to take a number of VIPs for short rides over Miami. On the very last excursion that included the Mayor and his wife, the Mayor's wife who is prone to fits of intestinal panic got air sick and barfed. The co-pilot wasn't really listening because he was too worried about being blinded by the great big Hollywood premier lights and crashing into the nearby Children's Museum building.

Bean slammed on the brakes, cut the engine and headlights, and stared at the scene in total amazement. Until that moment the biggest thing he had ever seen floating in the air that close was a pelican and two teenage girls in a waterspout.

"Ho chi mama," said Chi Chi. "Es juss like dat Close Encounter moofy."

"Moofy?" replied Bean.

"Chu never seen da alien Close Encounter moofy on TV? Chu know. Da one wit dat stupid guy what makes mountains and stuff with mashed potatoes an den at da en chu wanna cry. Oh no, wait, dats da ET moofy dat wanna makes chu cry."

"I've never seen TV," said Bean.

"Ho chi mama. Chu es one depraved young meng."

The word is "deprived," mango mama, thought Fruitcake. *Now how bout gettin' us outta this place before the bad guys show up.*

Back in the day Watson Island was once the home base of the famous Goodyear Blimp. As Goodyear increased their fleet they moved on to bigger digs up the coast. The island has since been developed into a cultural center, or in layman's terms, a tourist trap, consisting of a children's museum, Island Gardens, Parrot Jungle Island, Japanese Garden, the old established Miami Outboard Club, the Miami Yacht Club, and the Visitor's and Aviation Center, all of which is split down the middle by the MacArthur Causeway freeway and most all of which is pretty much hated by most Miami locals who wanted to keep the island natural, that is if a man made island can be considered natural. On this particular night the Miami community fathers were having some kind of a goodwill dog and pony show hootenanny to promote their proposal to turn most of the island into an exotic exclusive high-priced high-rise hotel complex, something equivalent to the oil money developments in Dubai, or in the opinion of some folks, a vision out of a sci-fi movie. Not to mention the enhanced development of their personal financial portfolios. For this very special occasion they brought back the Goodyear Blimp to show their respect and appreciation for the historic value of their treasured man made island.

The Haitians in their "ubs" truck were just crossing the west end of the island where naturally there attention was drawn to the events involving the blimp when they spotted the little clown car and headed for the exit. The Cubans in the Yellow Cab had gotten the word from the Cubans in the chopped top Mercury and did the same. Monitoring Officer

Fordhook's radio, the four Miami police cars all followed suit and exited onto the island as well.

🌴

Back at the east end of the MacAuthur Causeway the traffic was still at a standstill due to the wreck caused by the Haitians in the pimped out '61 Buick with the bullet damaged back tire. The exchange between those involved in the pile up was becoming heated. The Cosco truck driver, a very large man from south Georgia, now had one of the Haitians pinned up against the big grill of his big truck and was raining down on him all kinds physical intimidation and horrific good ol' boy threats, while Sissy Rominski, who owned the now heavily damaged BMW and was a fourth degree black belt, was beating the shit out of the Haitian driver. The two remaining Haitians were held spread eagle and face to the ground by Sissy's new hot girl friend who backed up her demands with the threat of a special edition Glock 27 automatic pistol known as the *Sarah Palin Moose Minder*, the latest accessory craze of women all over Miami. Dr. Norman Bloomenstein, the high priced plastic surgeon with the white Escalade, was content to just stand back and let everyone else fight it out while he decided which ones he would sue and which ones to suggest his services to after the bloody conflict. Either way he anticipated financial gain with minimal risk.

🌴

The Haitian's in the "ubs" truck caught sight of the four police cars and slowly glided in behind the Children's Museum, parked and killed the engine. Meanwhile the chopped top Buick Cubans and Officer Fordhook found their way under the bridge and were converging on the Celestial Rocket at the same time as the Yellow Cab Cubans. The four Miami police cars aprocahed from the other direction. With lights flashing, sirens blaring, the Miami cops slid to a halt and exited their vehicles with weapons drawn (which was nothing new in Miami). At the same time the Cubans slid to a halt, babbling excitedly in Spanish as they exited their vehicle (which was nothing new in Miami). All the action was centered on the little clown car with a one eared dog and a guy in the trunk sucking on a Yoo-hoo, (which *was* something new for Miami), and it brought the crowd of nearly three hundred people to silently freeze in their tracks. That is all except the Mayor's high strung wife who panicked and immediately barfed her exotic seafood dinner, three martinis, and a Fuzzy Navel, all over the flowing white silk robe of the Saudi Arabian Prince who happened to be the principal investor in the proposed unwanted hotel/condo resort destination development.

When the sirens ceased, the Miami cops, not finding any bad guy Haitians quickly decided the next best thing to point their weapons at were the occupants of the little clown car because that's what cops do, especially in Miami, and especially when the Mayor was watching. That is until his wife re-regurgitated on the Mayor's new custom tailored tuxedo. Chi Chi quickly threw up her hands in surrender. Bean, seeing this, did the same. Fruitcake hid between the seats, and Roachie, happy because he finally was able to finish the Yoo-hoo, just smiled and said, "What?"

Everyone stared in silence at the little clown car expecting it to soon become a little bullet magnet not unlike the end time of the infamous Bonnie and Clyde, when from somewhere through the quiet anxiety and the drone of the Goodyear blimp engines there came the voice of old blue eyes.

And I find that I'm smiling as I near… September.
The warm September of my years.

"Like I'm some kind of damn babysitter," mumbled Father Sabatino as he slowly approached the scene in his red Caddy. He quickly assessed the situation, drew his magnum automatic and shot three times in the air.

The people screamed and scattered for cover in all directions, most of which couldn't find any and so took cover behind the flashing cop cars where the cops were also taking refuge because they were unsure of the origin of the shots.

Father Sabatino then shot out one of the nearby Hollywood searchlights, feeding the people's panic even further and inspiring them to huddle behind the police officers. Father Sabatino then followed up by expertly shooting out one of the engines of the Goodyear Blimp.

The blimp shuttered and turned drastically in the direction of the big white party tent as it began to descend. Before the pilot could regain control Father Sabatino shot out the other engine.

"OH SHIT!" said the pilot as he struggled with the controls.

"OH SHIT!" echoed the co-pilot.

"I knew I should have signed on with those Jap Fuji people," said the pilot.

The massive blimp came in low; its gondola dragging across the tops of the police cars, ripping off the flashing lights then crashing into and dragging the large tent. It then severed the cables that fed power to the entire gala affair. Women screamed. Men screamed. Cops screamed. All scattered in all directions as everything went suddenly dark. The huge blimp careened into a nearby light pole that ripped it open along its side, letting lose countless thousands of pounds of pressurized helium that spewed out in a sightless cloud engulfing everyone at the scene. (Oh, the humanity!)

As Bean tried to adjust his eyes to the sudden darkness and focus on the incredible sight of the crashing blimp, he felt the passenger door open and heard Chi Chi scream. When he turned she was gone.

"Chi Chi?" yelled Bean.

"What?" said Roachie.

Then suddenly he heard voices in the dark speaking a foreign language. The little car bounced as someone plopped down in the seat beside him and slammed the door shut.

"Dey took her, meng!" yelled Jorge to Bean over the constant noise of desperate panicking screaming people.

"What?' said Bean.

"What?" said Roachie as he tossed away the empty Yoo-hoo bottle.

"Dem damn Haitian dudes, meng. Dey took her. We wass tryin' to warn chu guys but chu wouldent stop." Jorge looked around nervously and spied an approaching cop. It was Officer Fordhook coming on fast and about to draw his weapon. "Quick. Chu gotta drife. Go, hurry, before da cops get chu."

Bean stared at Jorge, not knowing what to make of him. Not only did he talk with an accent like Chi Chi's, but in mid sentence he began to sound like a tiny little munchkin or one of those little chipmunks he heard on the radio one Christmas at the Beachcomber.

"But what about Chi Chi?" questioned Bean, surprised that he too suddenly sounded like a chipmunk, not knowing it was the result of being engulfed by the mass of helium spewing out of the huge blimp.

"Chu can no help Chi Chi if chu in jail, meng. GO! GO!" said Jorge, wondering what the hell was happening to their voices. He looked back just in time to see Officer Fordhook slip on the Yoo-hoo bottle and fly head over heals, his gun discharging into the sky. The Miami cops immediately responded with a barrage of fire in all directions.

"Shit!" said Officer Foordhook, covering his head as he crawled back toward his vehicle.

"Oh, sorry," said Roachie to Officer Fordhook. "Oh sorry," said Roachie again because he wasn't sure it was his own voice that sounded a lot like a Chipmunk. "Oh sorry. Oh sorry," he repeated, now laughing at the silly sound of his own voice. "Now is the time for all good men to come to the aid of their country," quoted Roachie while laughing in the tiny munchkin voice. "Oh sorry. Oh sorry... She sells sea shells down by the sea shore. Oh sorry."

Bean cranked up the Celestial Rocket and sped off, carefully dodging whatever wreckage popped up in front of his headlights as well as a mass of panicked people in formal evening attire who were running in all directions, all babbling and screaming with little munchkin voices.

"Hey! Hey, stop that car!" yelled Officer Fordhook in a Clint Eastwood munchkin chipmunk voice.

Behind the Children's Museum the back door of the "ubs" truck flew open and in was dragged a kicking, biting, cursing (like a munchkin chipmunk) Chi Chi. The Haitians quickly gagged and tied her. The "ubs" truck pulled away slowly so as not to draw attention and slid away from the chaos and confusion surrounding the crashed blimp. Bean, with Fruitcake still hiding behind the seat, his new mysterious passenger Jorge, and Roachie still in the trunk feeling around for another Yoo-hoo, pulled away safely as well, but getting a little frustrated because he was stuck behind a slow cumbersome "ubs" truck.

"Oh sorry. Oh sorry. Now is the time for all good men... Ask not what your country can do for you... I have been to the mountain top... Oh sorry," laughed Roachie. "Oh sorry..."

Father Sabatino saw Bean make his escape then saw the Cuban chopped top Mercury slink away into the darkness back around under the bridge the same way he and they had arrived. He was quick to follow, leaving the cops and confusion behind. "Take care of the kid he says. Sure, take care of the kid. I'll take care of the kid. Take care of the kid my way, the New Jersey way. Like I'm some kind of damn babysitter," he mumbled in a bad-ass chipmunk munchkin voice as he angrily shoved his magnum automatic back in its holster. "Like I'm some kind of damn babysitter. Take care of the kid my ass."

A medical rescue truck had finally made its way to the scene of the accident on the east end of the MacAuthur Causeway. Upon arrival the paramedics discovered a very large truck-driving Georgia boy sitting on top of three Haitians while examining and admiring the Sarah Palin Special Edition Glock 27 Moose Minder automatic pistol, and trying his best to impress and make time with the two hot blondes. (He didn't have a clue) The Haitian driver lay in a bloody broken heap next to his '61 pimped out Buick.

"What happened to him?" asked a paramedic.

"He made the mistake of calling the lady a bitch," said Dr. Norman Bloomenstein.

The paramedic seemed puzzled so Dr. Bloomenstein decided to change his story.

"Oh, um… thrown from his car I think," said the good doctor. "Looks as though he might need some reconstructive surgery," he added, remembering he had stuck a business card in the damaged Haitian's shirt pocket.

After the Miami Police ceased shooting and he rose and walked toward his patrol car, Officer Fordhook rubbed and favored his sore back where he had slipped and landed on Roachie's discarded Yoo-hoo bottle. Through the invasive sound of more than 300 panicked little chipmunk voices there came the sound of the dispatch room from his vehicle's radio.

"You can't talk to me like dat! I'll kick yo Chicano beaner butt and then I'll sue yo ass! I'll sue ever'bodies ass! I'm callin' Jessy! I'm callin' Barack! I'm callin'…"

"God dammit Shanakitra, I told you to sit down and shut the hell up!"

BANG! came the sudden crack of a gunshot over the radio.

"Oh well, there's always the Canadian League," said a frustrated Officer Fordhook to himself in his little munchkin chipmunk Clint Eastwood voice as he turned to see the huge Goodyear blimp roll over on its side.

"Oh shit," said the pilot.

chapter 14

The Voodoo King

"So youuuu beeeee da one dat *himself* be wantin' soooo bad?" came the deep slow voice.

"What?" answered Chi Chi.

"Yes, youuuu beeeee da *one*. Da one dat Fidel soooo desire," said the strange intimidating man seated on a large throne of a chair in a dark corner of the dimly lit room. Small candles surrounded him above and to each side, interspersed with an assortment of voodoo symbols and paraphernalia, yet his face remained shadowed and mysterious. All but his eyes that is; penetrating, searching, threatening eyes. He spoke slowly, drawing out occasional vowels of occasional words as though he suffered from some odd speech impediment. Each drawn out vowel was emphasized with a widening of his eyes that would capture and hold the attention of his audience. If he was stressed or simply impressed with his own diatribe his elongated words would sometimes be repeated back to back. "Fidel he want youuuu, youuuu missy. Him want his *Corena Maria Castro* back in da fold."

"Fidel es a dick," said Chi Chi heatedly, as she strained to free her hands and feet. It was hopeless. They were bound tightly to an exquisite elaborately hand carved rosewood chair situated in the center of a large room with a high ceiling. The room was filled with many other expensive furnishings as well as mysterious items from Haiti that could just as easily be displays in a Ripley's Believe It or Not Museum. "Me yamma es no Castro," she continued. "An chu es a dick too, chu voodoo freak."

"Do you know whoooo I am?" he asked as he slowly rose and crossed the room and stood towering over her, looking down.

"Everybodies know who chu es," answered Chi Chi. "Chu es da Haitian. Da Voodoo King. But chu ain no king, chu es juss a dick. And I'n no afraid of chu."

"Afraid?" laughed the Voodoo King. "Oh please missy, beeeee not afraaaaaid, not afraaaaaid at all. You have nothing to fear. Quite the contrary, you be da jewel. Youuuuu little missy be Fidel's million dollar baaaaby."

"What?" said Chi Chi.

"A cooooool one million dollar, missy. Dat be da price Fidel put on you," he continued as he slowly paced around to the back of the chair and began stroking her hair. "A cooool, cooool one million, and da Voodoo King is goin' to collect dat one million."

"A million," said Chi Chi. "Da price es go up."

"Fidel, he look for you tooooo many year. He is an old man and heeee's not long for dis world. Soooon to pass over to da udder siiiiide." The Voodoo King leaned down close to her ear, "Many people say dat be a gooood ting but now daddy want his baby come home to Havana soon and heeeee be willin' to pay big time."

"He es no my papa. He es a pig… juss like chu," said a defiant Chi Chi. *"Y usted puede besar mi asno,"* she said, spitting on the Voodoo King's very expensive Persian carpet.

The Voodoo King threw up his hands and roared with laughter. "Youuuu, youuuu beeeee a wild one," he said. "You most certain be Fidel's seed my million dollar child. Moooost certain."

Chi Chi had to flee Cuba because Fidel Castro, the cruel revolutionary and long time communist dictator thought she was his daughter. Her mother, who was forced to work as domestic staff in the dictator's home because she was exceptionally beautiful, became pregnant with Chi Chi by her husband to whom she was secretly married. Often Castro, while sampling too much fine Cuban rum, took sexual advantage of his young staff of supposedly all single selective lovelies, but after those drunken episodes he often didn't remember who he had forced into his bed. And so he was delighted at the news of the pregnancy, thinking the child was his. An unlikely event since most often the girls who weren't wrongfully ambitious either ran away, aborted, or committed suicide if they thought they had been impregnated by their bearded fearless leader.

Fidel's assumption was wrongheaded because Chi Chi's mother kept a very low profile and had always managed to avoid him. He had in fact never touched her. Just the same, to show his gratitude for her bearing him a beautiful child, he granted Chi Chi's mother free reign of the house without any threat of future sexual advances. Her only responsibility was to care for Chi Chi. So while growing up Chi Chi had to endure years of personal visits and doting by the man she despised and always considered to be... *a dick*, all the while being forced to conceal the truth and hide her love for her true family and biological father. When they could no longer endure the situation Chi Chi's parents shipped her off on the first available raft to America and then went into hiding, hoping to join their daughter later, but they never arrived, leaving Chi Chi to fend for herself.

Rumor brought over by newly arrived refugees was that Fidel's brother, Raul, knew of her parents' deception, searched them out and executed them to preserve the secret and spare his aging brother's emotions. Now the old ailing soon to be late Fidel Castro was offering a cool million dollars for the return of his precious favorite little girl Corena Maria, which certainly appealed to more than a few unscrupulous would-be bounty hunters. Money hungry unprincipled people like the Voodoo King and even some Cubans.

Somewhere in a chop shop in North Miami the 3Js and the Yellow cab Cubans stood gathered around the Celestial Rocket explaining all this to Bean and Roachie. Fruitcake took it all in as well and though it sparked some honest concern for the girl who confiscated his bucket seat, it didn't take priority over his thoughts of a serious desire for some belly filling Creola. That, plus his wondering how the hell all these people managed to understand each other when speaking in that fast foreign language, especially when they all sounded like little munchkins as they had back on Watson Island.

The 3Js also explained they were all part of an organization of young Cubans who planned to overthrow the communist government as soon as that old cigar sucking bastard Castro croaked. *Los Hermanos Cubanos Para La Libertad* (The Cuban Brothers for Liberty) is what they called themselves and they were ready to rumble at the drop of a hat. So they thought. The *Los Hermanos Cubanos Para La Libertad* had arranged for and/or accumulated a cache of weapons and ammunition, an armada of three old working Desco Marine shrimp boats, a collection of Radio Shack walkie-talkies, and a 1940 Stearman bi-plane usually used to fly beach banners but which they intended to use to drop bombs on Fidel's head. And of course they were all graduated conditional black belts from the YMCA's six week Tae Kwon Do crash course. All of which led them to believe themselves Rambo-ready for just about anything. Not to mention they had a softball team that played in the city league on Thursday nights. It was all gibberish to Bean but he was certainly impressed with their enthusiasm and willingness to help rescue his friend Chi Chi.

"Guns and boats and planes. Wow. How did you do all that?" asked Bean.

"Connections," said Jorge. "Cussins mostly. Everybody got a cussin in Me'ahmi. Most of dees guys right here are my cussins."

"Why we no juss go in and get her?" suggested one cousin.

"Are chu kiddin', meng? Dat place es like a castillo an hees gots guards with guns," said another. "I know causs I know da guy who sold 'em. Hees my cussin."

"We gots guns," said Juan.

"Das right, meng. But dat Voodoo King, he es one bad dude. He catch chu and den he mess chu up wit all dat voodoo chit," said another cousin.

"But we es *Los Hermanos Cubanos Para La Libertad,*" argued Jesus.

"Yeah, but dass in Kooba. Dis ess Me'ahmi, meng. Me'ahmi es serious chit. Dun chu read da peppers and watch da TV newses?"

"Hey meng. All heem wan es da monies so why we no juss gives heem da monies?" suggested Jorge.

"Oh, hokay. Das a good idea. Here I gots a million bucks right here in my pockets causs I juss got paid," came a satirical response from Juan.

"No, I min at da table," clarified Jorge. "Everybody know da Voodoo King he ly to gamble and he go to da islands all da time to gamble. So maybe we get Chi Chi dat way. We do him a stinger. Chu know, a con job."

"Yeah, but everybody know he dun ly to lose to nobody. If chu beats da Voodoo King den chu gonna be a big loser anyways."

"Dass right. I hear dis one dude he beats da Voodoo King and da Voodoo King pay heem his monies hokay but den da next day dis guy, day fines heem wit no eyeballs an a dead voodoo chicken up hees ass. I dun know bow chu meng, but I no wan no dead chickens up my ass, specially if dat chicken no wass dead before it wass put dere."

"Ain nobodys can beat dat guy anyways, meng," said Juan. "He es a big time gambler an like chu say, everybodys lose to heem causs dey dun wan no chickens up no asses."

"I can beat him," came a voice from inside the trunk of the Celestial Rocket where a bent over Roachie emerged with a smile and Bean's last Yoo-hoo. "Piece of cake, actually."

They all knew who Roachie was because they had all seen him standing on the street corners with his bum bag and little cardboard sign, so of course none of them were prepared to take him seriously. They stared a brief moment then turned away.

"It's just simple math," continued Roachie as he shook the Yoo-hoo then screwed the top off and took a swig.

"Wha chu min, meng?" asked Jorge.

"Winning at cards. It's just simple math," said Roachie. "Paid my way through college and started my business that way. Playing cards I mean. In Las Vegas. Then I quit cause I only needed two and a half million dollars."

"Este tipo está loco," said one of the Cuban liberators.

The rest shook their heads in agreement.

He's a friggin' genius you morons, thought Fruitcake. *You should see what I hear inside his head. Hey, any of you underground heroes got any Creola?*

"I don't understand," said Bean.

"Me neither," said Jorge.

"Counting cards. Works in most any card game," said Roachie. "The casinos don't like that very much but actually it's not illegal. So the trick is to not get caught."

"So wha chu sayin', meng, dat chu kina ly dat leetle chort guy in da moofy dat talk funny an wass counten toothpicks an bangin' on hees head? Dat leetle guy he es retarded and no hokay in da brain, meng," said Jesus.

"Hey, meng, es chu tellin' da truth?" asked Jorge. "Did chu really win two millions?"

"Yes he is. He went to MIT and Stanford and used to own a big high tech Wall Street research corporation," said Bean. "Whatever that is."

"No I no thin so. He es juss a bum wit a cardboard sign," said Juan.

"His wife and her boyfriend, a Harvard lawyer, stole his billion dollar corportion," said Bean.

"Ahhh," said the entire group in unison, all being former victims of one degree or another of female deception and expressing their sympathetic acceptance of Bean's explanation.

"So, wha chu got in mine, meng?" asked Jesus.

"Um… a game," said Roachie.

"Ahhh, a game," said Jesus. "I thin maybe he gots sungthin dere."

Jorge, who worked at the Sun City Dry Cleaners, smiled as he formulated a plan, looked to Roachie and asked, "Hey meng, what size suit do chu wear?"

Roachie shrugged then smiled in return after finishing off his newly discovered favorite drink. "Hey, you guys got any Yoo-hoos?"

The Voodoo King, whose real name was Jean-Francios Laguerre, was a master of intrigue. He began his lucrative career by stealing a 16 foot outboard boat that he used to hijack and steal a 90 foot luxury yacht just off the coast of Porte Prince. Disposing of its crew and owners, he then traded it to a Frenchman for $20,000 and a very fast 48 foot charter fisher that the Frenchman had stolen somewhere off the coast of Aruba. The money financed his first load of drugs smuggled into the States on the fisher and from there he expanded his enterprise into a small empire of crime. He was known to smuggle any and everything that would bring a profit, from drugs into the U.S. and guns out, to people both in and out and all about the Caribbean and South

America, the latter proving to be exceptionally lucrative and ingenious. He would sometimes sell his services as an intelligence and security enforcer to various wannabe power mongers throughout the islands, then invent or create some form of imaginary threatening opposition, and then get paid large sums of money to eliminate that same imaginary threat or to smuggle his client to exiled safety, usually somewhere in Miami or Venezuela. It was on such operations that the Voodoo King moniker came to be known when he would spread the rumors that he eliminated all enemies with black magic. Those occasional examples of his ruthlessness might include a snake, dead chicken, or feline placed in various orafaces of his victims. It was more than enough to maintain the legend. When business was such that he had to keep a low profile he would then put his boys to work at more simple criminal endeavors such as highjacking trucks or breaking into wholesale warehouses full of imported Florida souvenirs or car tires or diving gear such as that sold to Curley Carney in Melbourne.

The Voodoo King's latest commodity of trade would be Chi Chi who was to be handed over to Fidel Castro in Havana for a million bucks and a boat load of Cuban cigars that were priceless on the black market.

"Jean-Francios," said one of his henchmen softly as he quietly opened the door to the Voodoo King's media room.

The Voodoo King sat sprawled comfortably in a large leather reclining chair, sipping a drink and watching the news about a Miami Beach police officer who was suspected of going crazy and shooting down the Goodyear Blimp. He waved his man into the room and nodded approval for him to speak.

"A message from the Arranger. He say a man come to town. Dis man he asking about you. He say he a big time gambler. He say he can... um."

"What?" demanded the Voodoo King.

"Arranger say dis man say he can kick your ass. Say nobody can beat him at cards. Not even da famous Voodoo King. And he say… um…"

"What?" demanded the Voodoo King.

"He say you just some kind small time wimp if you no come to da table wit him."

"When?" demanded the Voodoo King.

"He say tonight."

"Call the Arranger. Tell him the Voodoo King… is nooooo afraid of noooo bullshit high roller. Tell him I meeeeeet him tonight."

"But…"

"What?" demanded the Voodoo King.

"But… Jean-Francios. He say he only play a millions dollar table wit no limit. We no gots dat kind cash right now. We just make a big buy in Columbia. We no got dat kind cash for five or six days. Maybe then we got fifteen or twenty millions cash for da tables."

"Not to worry. The Voodoo King noooo lose no millions to noooooobody, noooobody. Make da call," demanded the Voodoo King. "Make da damn call."

chapter 15

Roachie's Royal Flush

Who do Voodoo was the name splashed in gold across the transom of the glistening 59ft, 15 passenger high speed monohull yacht. It was a made in China Feng Huang custom special, not the largest of his fleet but the pride of Voodoo King's collection and probably one of the few possessions he ever actually paid for. He had first tried to win the boat in a poker game from a Chinese diplomat but was foiled when the little guy came up with cash to cover his losses. He then tried to trade for the boat with government military secrets which he had manufactured from the assembly plans for Star Wars toys, but the little Chinese guy didn't go for it because he had already bought the same plans from a former 1960's radical anti-war revolutionary appointed as a Deputy Secretary of Defense at the Pentagon by President Obama. The Deputy Secretary purchased them three months previous from a Miami arms dealer who had purchased them earlier from the Voodoo King. So finally the Voodoo King gave up and purchased the yacht outright with $550,000 cash, a priceless Stetson hat that he swore had belonged to John Wayne but was actually bought at a local feed store near Ocala for $17.95, a stuffed ten foot albino alligator that he found in an orange stand souvenir shop gas station on I-95 just north of Jacksonville, and the feast de résistance, an all-nighter with actress Halle Berry who was actually a Halle Berry look-a-like named Margie Cornwell. The Chinese diplomat never knew the difference and left the country happy as a pig in squalor.

Who do Voodoo glided to the side of the dock of the small private island and the location of the South Island Club. The Voodoo King, Jean-Francios, disembarked after his men secured the area, took a long deep breath as he looked around and smiled with the confidence he was about to have a challenging and profitable night at the table.

As per the two parties' agreement, the game was to take place on neutral ground, in this case a small private gaming club located on a small private island in the Bahamas. That is small in terms of frequency of use and function but large in terms of accommodations as it spread over the center of the island like a grand hotel. A multi-level structure built in classic island fashion, a mix of stone and meticulously crafted wood surrounded by beautiful tropical gardens. It was owned by a British Lord who worked in the Secret Service Special Branch of British Intelligence, but for legal and traceable record purposes it was listed as an establishment owned and operated by an Italian closed corporation known as the South Island Company, which of course was hidden behind a number of holding companies. Its primary purpose for existence was to lure in high-rolling enemies of the state who had a proclivity for gambling. The place was rarely used for anything else except as an occasional vacation spot for select Brits and friends. The main event at the club was the annual invitational gaming extravaganza each April that lasted five days. Games of all sorts took place, everything from backgammon, chess, craps, a variety of card games such as poker and bridge, and all with stakes so high and a potential for enormous winnings so tempting that only the confirmed wealthiest of gamblers were invited – along with the Secret Service's targets of interest at the time. It was known that entire fortunes were made and lost in a single night at the club therefore few underworld enemies or wannabe power mongers could say no to such an invitation. And those same few hadn't a clue they were having their brain picked for intelligence by participating government ringers while they were gaming and by well trained ladies of the evening when they were not. Not to mention a few who disappeared altogether after all the fun and games were over.

A known high stakes gaming arranger had been contacted about the challenge to the Voodoo King and for his usual fee of 5% of the pot had arranged for the game to take place at the South Island Club. His name was Steven Hicks but he was known in the trade simply as the Arranger. He came by his career as a gaming arranger fraudulently when he first provided the service as an undercover CIA agent working on a joint venture with the Brits. He was so good at it that word got out among certain circles creating a demand for more of his services. Hicks still works for the CIA but unknown to the CIA he now moonlights with the lucrative sideline of arranging illegal high stakes gambling gatherings at various covert locations. The sideline enterprise also affords him the opportunity to occasionally gather juicy intelligence, which keeps the CIA happy, not to mention padding his retirement fund.

Another reason Arranger Hicks is in such demand is the fact that he personally guarantees and stands for anyone he brings into the games and is responsible for their losses if they fail to come through and pay up. He's only had to deliver on that guarantee one time when a really talented phony from Brazil weaseled his way into a game and lost over $1,500,000. Of course Hicks had no intention of coughing up the money so he took care of the problem quickly and efficiently by assassinating both the phony looser and the winner, claiming they were working together to fleece the other players. Everyone accepted this explanation and his credibility rocketed to new heights, increasing business considerably.

The Arranger's only flaw is that he has a weakness for Cuban girls named Maria but the Arranger, Steven Hicks, is a married man who has to keep his wife happy in order to keep the CIA happy. One particular Maria happens to be another one of Jorge of the 3Js cousin. Hence, Jorge arranged for the Arranger to put forth the challenge and arrange on the QT the high stakes game with the Voodoo King on behalf of the *Los Hermanos Cubanos Para La Libertad.* The Arranger gave it his best shot and set them up with all the fixings at the exclusive South Island Club. As far as the Voodoo King was concerned, who had heard rumors of the club, the arrangement was proof of the resources, credibility, and influence of his opponent and the importance of the game. The bigger they are the harder they fall thought the Voodoo King confidently. As far as Roachie was concerned, well… it was all fun and games and a hell of a lot better than standing on the corner with a cardboard sign that said WIL WERK 4 FUDE with the hopes of maybe getting a Whopper Jr. and a chocolate shake at the end of the day.

When the Voodoo King and his squad of four bodyguards strolled into the club's lobby they were met by the Arranger who introduced himself and informed them that only players and club staff were permitted to enter further, and that his men, just like Mr. LaBongo's security men, would have to remain there in the lobby. The Voodoo King turned to find four of the Cubans, all dressed in suits pretending to be his opponent's security detail, sitting silently against the wall across the lobby. He nodded agreement and motioned for his men to remain.

"Please make yourselves comfortable gentlemen," said the Arranger while casually noticing the bulges from the weapons holstered under their jackets. "A member of the staff will bring you refreshments directly."

"Tell meeeee of this LaBongo, this arrogant player whooooo would challenge the Voodoo King," insisted the Voodoo King.

"He's from South Africa," said the Arranger. "He owns diamond mines and trades in rare metals and minerals. He is here in Miami on a working vacation. I hear he has purchased the Royal Commodore Palms Beach Club and is currently attempting to buy the Miami Dolphin's and their Land Shark Stadium."

"Hmmm," said the Voodoo King. "And he bets high?"

"Of course. Very," said the Arranger. "Known to go a million or more a hand."

The Voodoo King nodded approval.

"As agreed by both parties, the game of choice will be Texas Hold'em," continued the Arranger. "You understand of course, as you have both also agreed to unlimited stakes that my usual guarantee will not apply here."

"Not to worry, mun," said the Voodoo King. "Youuuu just begin counten your five per cent of my winnin's, which I believe will be quite substantial. Now take me to this foooool who tinks he can come here and defeat the great Jean-Francios."

"Of course," replied Hicks the Arranger. He turned and opened two large doors that revealed a large extravagantly decorated room with a high dome ceiling, sky lights, tall windows, large tropical plants, and a mix of plush sofas and tropical wicker and rattan furnishings. There were stairs on each side that wound to the upper level residences and three sets of double doors that led to a dining room, a smoking room, and gaming rooms. The two men continued to and through the doors that led to the gaming rooms. Upon entering, the Voodoo King found himself in the main game room, the hub, with three other smaller gaming rooms going off in separate directions. All the furnishings had been set aside with a single table and three comfortable velvet clad chairs set in the center, one for each player and one for the dealer. Next to each player's chair was a small table with water, napkins, and ashtray. Exactly three feet behind each small table a personal lovely young waitress for each of the players stood poised to accommodate any request.

The Voodoo King was impressed. Even at the very best casinos in the islands he had not seen such opulence geared only to the pursuit of gambling. His blood began to sear quickly through his veins in anticipation of the upcoming contest.

"Jean-Francios Laguerre of Miami, may I introduce Mr. Pogo LaBongo of Johannesburg, South Africa," said the Arranger, sincerely hoping that from this point forward all would go as planned, and wondering what the hell they would do if it came apart.

Roachie, introduced as the now alias Pogo LaBongo of South Africa, turned from where he stood peering through one of the large tall windows to face his opponent. He was impeccably dressed in an expensive custom tailored tuxedo that Jorge had *borrowed* from the Sun City Dry Cleaners. A tuxedo that had been dropped off by someone from the Mayor's office claiming the Mayor's wife had barfed on it the night before when she witnessed all the mayhem that took place at that gala affair where the Goodyear blimp crashed. The owners of the Sun City Dry Cleaners expressed their sympathy and blamed it on the Jews. Jorge also managed to help himself to the full wardrobe of an upcoming wedding so that the Cuban members of the *Los Hermanos Cubanos Para La Libertad* posing as male staff at the South Island Club strutted around convincingly in formal tales. Their girlfriends posing as waitresses and staff were outfitted in costumes that were in for dry cleaning from a local theater production of *The Dancing Harlots of Rangoon*. *The Dancing Harlots of Rangoon* was an all male gay production but Jorge didn't know that. Just the same the costumes seemed to fit just fine even though they appeared overly seductive and a little tacky. The Voodoo King barely noticed however, having not an ounce of genuine class from which to pass judgment.

Pogo LaBongo turned to discover the Voodoo King. He looked him up and down, raised an eyebrow and offered a cursory smile, then silently walked across the room and took his seat. Everything seemed to be going well except for one unsure element being that Roachie could not pull off a foreign South African accent to save his mother's life even though he had been coached all day, so Jesus managed to come up with a solution.

"I have been asked to inform you that Mr. LaBongo does not speak any language other than his own tribal native tongue and that it will be necessary for him to occasionally utilize an interpreter," said the Arranger to the Voodoo King. "However, he will indicate the amount of his wagers with his fingers. With his left hand he will indicate amounts of one-hundred thousand dollars each finger, therefore no wagers of his will be less than one-hundred thousand dollars. With his right hand he will indicate one million dollars each finger. If that is acceptable you may begin play."

The Voodoo King afforded an impatient nod of agreement, at the same time taking notice of his opponent's lack of maturity. He called the Arranger to his side and whispered, "This mun seeeeem awfully young to be sooooo rich and successful."

"He is the nephew of Nelson Mandela," the Arranger replied softly.

"Ah," said the Voodoo King. "That explains a great deal."

Jesus, dressed in a finely tailored business suit (also courtesy of the Sun City Dry Cleaners) stepped to LaBongo's side, "Good evening sir. My name is Reginald, Mr. LaBongo's interpreter," he said to the Voodoo King with a more than adequate South African accent he had learned from repeated viewings of the movie Lethal Weapon II.

LaBongo made a hand motion similar to that of a royal greeting that brought Reginald (Jesus) to bend and listen to his whisper that was inaudible to the Voodoo King.

"Mr. LaBongo wants to know if you would like to bet on the cutting of the cards?" said Reginald to the Voodoo King.

"Why not," replied the Haitian. "What does he propose to bet?"

Reginald whispered in LaBongo's ear and LaBongo held up all five digits of his left hand then placed $500,000 in chips in the center of the table.

"Five hundred thousand," said the Voodoo King, surprised but smiling. "Sure, why not," he added as he slid his chips to the center.

The dealer, the only member of the entire farce who was actually an agent of the club and the charter fishing partner of Hicks the Arranger, opened a new pack of cards, shuffled and placed them in the center of the table, saying only, "Gentlemen."

LaBongo raised his hand to reach for and make the first cut thinking it was his honor as he was the visitor, but an eager and tactless Voodoo King superseded his effort, reached out and made his cut producing the Queen of spades.

LaBongo at first seemed just a bit surprised by the Voodoo King's lack of protocol but then collected himself and made his cut, producing a disappointing eight of hearts. Seeming indifferent about his low draw and the loss of half a million dollars, he gently dropped the cards back on the pile.

The Voodoo King smiled as he pulled away the chips, thinking this to be a good omen of things to come.

Bean, Juan, and the remaining members of the *Los Hermanos Cubanos Para La Libertad* had recently arrived and were waiting aboard an old shrimp trawler moored on the opposite side of the island. They were receiving a message over the radio from one of their cohorts on the mainland assigned to watch the Voodoo King's fortress mansion in case the Haitians decided to move Chi Chi while everyone was occupied at the gaming club. The Cuban spy had some hot news but was at first unable to relay the message because he couldn't get his Radio Shack radio to work. When he finally figured out it had no batteries and ran to the nearest convenience store to get some, the Haitians had already arrived at the island and the game had begun.

"Kooba red one to Kooba blue six!" came the excited voice over the boat's radio. "Kooba red one to Kooba blue six! Juan. Hey meng. Anybody!"

"Kooba red wha to wha?" was Juan's answer from the trawler.

"Dis es Kooba red one to Kooba blue six!" came the excited voice once again.

"Yoyo, es dat chu meng?" asked Juan.

Yoyo was pretty much the dumbest of all the *Los Hermanos Cubanos Para La Libertad,* which is why he was the one left behind to hide in the bushes and watch the Voodoo King's place, and why he always played right field when he wasn't on the bench keeping the beer cold at the Cuban's softball games.

"Ches es me," answered Yoyo, standing at the water's edge looking east as though it would somehow help his voice travel better. "Who da hell chu thin it es, meng?"

"Yoyo, wha da hell es chu doin' wit all dat Kooba red Kooba blue chit, meng?"

"Es da code callin', meng. Wha da hell chu thin it es? Dun chu watch no moofies, meng?" said Yoyo.

"Chu dumb chit. We ain't got no codes," said Juan. "But if we has sung codes it would be red one and *red* six not red one and *blue* six, dummy. Now wha da hell chu callin' abou?"

"So, why dey say dem colors in da moofies anyway?" asked Yoyo.

"Wha moofies?" asked Juan.

"Chu know, dem moofies wit da codes," said Yoyo.

"Forget da damn moofies, Yoyo. Wha chu want call for?"

"Hey meng, chu guys gave me a radio wha diddent gots no batteries," said Yoyo.

"So how chu callin' me on da radio wit no batteries?"

"I went an got sung batteries at the Quicky Stop."

"So how come chu didn't use your cell phone, dummy?" said Juan.

"Oh,"

"Hokay, so why chu wan make da call about on da radio anyway?" said Juan.

"Es da girl, meng."

"Yeah, hokay. So wha abou da girl, meng?"

"She ain here, meng."

"Wha chu min she ain dere, meng?" asked Juan.

"She es gone, meng," said Yoyo.

"Wha chu min shee es gone, meng?"

"Dey took her, meng."

"Wha chu min dey took her, meng?"

"Da Voodoo King, he took her, meng."

"I know da Voodoo King took her. Das why we es here, dummy."

"No, I min da Voodoo King he takes her again, meng."

"Wha chu min da Voodoo King takes her again? Da Voodoo King ain took her again. Da Voodoo King he es here."

"Das wha I min, meng. Da Voodoo King, he put da girl on da boat, *Who do Voodoo*."

"Who do Voodoo? Wha da hell dat min *Who do Voodoo?*"

"Da boat, meng."

"Wha boat, meng?"

"*Who do Voodoo*, meng. Das da Voodoo King's boat, meng," said Yoyo.

"So who care wha da boat's nem es?" said Juan.

"Chu gotta care, meng," said Yoyo.

"How come?"

"Causs da Voodoo King put da girl on da *Who do Voodoo* and I hear dem talkin' and say he gonna takes her to Kooba on dat *Who do Voodoo* boat to give her to Castro after he get done wit da gambling with the Africa guy. Das wha I min, meng. Causs I see him load her on da *Who do Voodoo* boat and I hear 'em talkin, is wha I min."

"Wha, chu min Chi Chi she es here, meng?"

"You mean she's here?" echoed Bean who was standing by and listening with the others.

"I'n gonna tell da guys at da club," said Juan as he jumped into the dingy and rowed away before anyone else could join him.

"I'm going to Voodoo's boat. Maybe we can save her," said Bean as he hopped over the side of the trawler and swam for shore, quickly followed by two of the Cubans.

I'm stayin' here, thought Fruitcake. *This island might have fat guys with guns.*

"Kooba blue six, es chu dere, meng? Hola? Juan? Anybody? Holaaaaa! Hey, hokay. Chu guys can be red code and I be blue code, hokay? Hey chu guys… Chu know chu guys got to pay me for dem batteries, meng. Hey, Juan, duss chu wan me to stay here now or wha, meng. Causs I thinnin maybe since da girl es gone… Hola? Juan? Hey mcng, I gettin' kina hungry now. Hola…"

From the radio Yoyo heard what he thought sounded kind of like a bicycle horn. Actually it was only Fruitcake who just realized everyone had jumped ship and headed for the island. He was left all alone and had visions of being stranded again like after the waterspout had destroyed the beach house.

"Hey Juan, meng. Chu no soun so good," said Yoyo. "I thin maybes chu chould see a doctor, meng. Hola? Blue six? Anybodys?" Yoyo gave up trying to get an answer and plopped down on his ass in frustration. "I dun thin dis thing es workin' to good. Maybes I chould take back dem batteries," he mumbled.

Juan went into the back entrance of the club and informed Jorge of the situation with Chi Chi. They quickly began thinking of ways to alter the plan but were hard pressed to come up with anything other than pulling the fire alarm. Then they decided that wouldn't work simply because there wasn't any fire alarm. There wasn't any fire alarm because there weren't any building safety codes on the small private island and because the small island didn't have a fire department anyway.

Meanwhile Bean and the two Cubans had scurried across the island and were now huddled in the nearby shadows observing the Voodoo King's boat. As best they could see there was only one guard who paced impatiently up and down the dock, checking only occasionally in the boat's cabin below where the Haitains must have stowed Chi Chi.

Bean quickly formed a plan of action and whispered it to the others, then quietly sped off and slid into the water without making a sound. He stealthily swam to the rear of the boat, out of sight of the guard. Then the Cubans stood and casually strolled out of the darkness toward the dock, conversing in Spanish and pointing to the boat as if admiring it. When they reached the dock the Haitian guard perked up and moved to intercept them.

"Hey mun, you can't come here. Stay away," said the Haitian, his hand slipping under his jacket in case he needed to quickly withdraw his weapon.

The distraction gave Bean the opportunity to quietly slip up over the transom and onto the boat. Worried there may be other Haitians aboard, he paused, crouched low, and moved slowly to below deck where he found only Chi Chi laid out on a bunk, bound and gagged. He motioned for her to be silent as he freed her with a knife he found in the yacht's galley.

In the gaming room things were getting intense as the betting that had been favoring the Voodoo King to the tune of nearly $4,000,000 was now beginning to go the way of the South African diamond baron. All going as Roachie, alias LaBongo, had planned. LaBongo didn't have to be dealt good hands; he only had to know what the other guy had in his hand in order to bet favorably. The cards ran through his mind like rain drops in a storm and his brain counted and sorted them as efficiently as a National Security Agency super computer. Roachie was having fun, realizing that it had been a long time since he embraced any form of satisfying challenge requiring his natural intellect and mathematical skills, a satisfaction rarely achieved during lonely evenings under the highway overpass reading his outdated Soap Opera Digest and discarded old cheesy novels.

The Voodoo King was an intense, aggressive, and impatient player, and obviously a bad looser, be it the loss of a single hand or an entire game. Roachie knew this and teased him along, betting to give him a win here and there, then a big loss on subsequent hands. The object of course being to keep him hungry and hopeful but eventually drain him of all his funds until his only betting chip left would be Fidel Castro's million dollar baby.

The time had come and LaBongo went for the jugular with the largest bet of the evening. He held up five and then five more digits of his right hand and shoved ten million dollars in chips to the center of the table where nearly twenty million had already been wagered. He could see the Haitian had only about eight million of his own chips left. If the bet was to be matched he would have to come up with something else of value. As he placed the bet LoBongo's confident deadpan face took the Voodoo King by surprise, causing him to hesitate before making the decision to call or fold in defeat.

While the Voodoo King hesitated, LaBongo whispered to Reginald his interpreter who in turn whispered to LaBongo's personal waitress. She quickly exited the room and returned a minute later to fill LaBongo's request in the form of a perfectly chilled Yoo-hoo - shaken not stirred. The drink was poured expertly into a crystal goblet and received by LaBongo who took a long satisfying drink, then casually tapped away the chocolate residue from his upper lip with a silk napkin from the small table.

The Voodoo King stared in astonishment at this obviously super rich man indulging himself, not with the finest and most expensive of spirits but with a child's chocolate drink. This and the ten million bet had set the Haitian Jean-Francios Laguerre's game askew and for the first time ever infused self doubt as to his gambling skills. To level the field, the Voodoo King requested a bottle of champagne and waited patiently for its arrival before he would respond to LaBongo's bet. The waitress returned, treading gracefully across the soft carpet of the gaming room, carrying the container of the Voodoo King's ice chilled champagne and dutifully set it on the small table next to him. All the while the Voodoo King's eyes stayed locked on LaBongo's, searching for any indication that the bet could be a bluff.

LaBongo took another leisurely sip of his Yoo-hoo and again padded the chocolate residue from his upper lip with the silk napkin as though nothing short of a volcanic eruption could distract him.

This mun be one cool African, thought the Voodoo King, *I'll be damned if Jean-Francios gonna lose to him.* His hands reached slowly for his pile of chips and was about to shove them across the table when suddenly the

Voodoo King's concentration was abruptly broken when he heard a voice say the fateful words...

"Chu es still a dick, chu Haitian asshole."

He looked up just in time to unexpectedly discover that his personal waitress was now Chi Chi his million dollar baby, who came down on his head with the full bottle of champaign. The Voodoo King fell forward, unconscious, symbolically matching Roachie's large bet with his own head as it crashed atop the multimillion dollar pile of chips. The sudden action of the bottle popped the cork and the high priced bubbly sprayed the room.

"Hey, I was about to beat him," complained Roachie. "I had a royal flush."

"Oh, I so sorry Roachie. I juss could no resiss causs he es such a asshole an I wanna teaches him a lesson. Chu know wha I min?" said a smiling Chi Chi while she wrestled with the spraying bottle as though it were an out of control fire hose.

"Holy cow," said Roachie. "Is that bottle what I think it is?"

"Yes," said their lamenting Arranger and host. "It's a bottle of Dom Pérignon Oenothèque. About fifteen hundred dollars worth."

"Oh," said Chi Chi, handing the bottle to the Arranger. "Sorry. I dident know it wass the good stuff."

Into the room came Bean and the others sporting smiles of victory. "We rescued Chi Chi from the Voodoo King's boat. There was only one guard and the guys knocked him out and tied him up."

"Good," said the Arranger, "Now we have to switch to plan B, which by the way is already in motion."

"Plan B? Wha es a plan B?" questioned Jesus.

"Plan B is we get off this island pretty damn quick because it's about to be invaded by the British."

"What? The British are coming?" asked Bean.

"Well you see, I figured that no matter what the outcome of tonight's game that this Haitian here was still going to be pretty pissed off and start sticking dead chickens up everybody's ass because if he won there was no money to pay him off and if he lost, well... So I decided he would somehow have to be neutralized or maybe even eliminated. We drugged his bodyguards who are passed out on the floor in the lobby. I calculated the time it would take to play the game based on Roachie's near perfect estimate then made arrangements for a communiqué to be sent to the Brits telling them the island was being overrun and occupied by Haitian drug smugglers. And I was going to sabotage the Voodoo King's boat so he couldn't follow us and he'd be stuck here to deal with the Brits. But now we can use it and the other boat to get the hell out of here before this guy wakes up and the Brits arrive. You see, I originally figured that with this Haitian and his men stuck on the island that we could storm his mansion in Miami and rescue the girl."

"Are chu kiddin', meng," said Juan. "We es pretty good softball players but I no thin we really ain no commandos."

"Sure you are," smiled the Arranger. "I've been watching you guys for years. You got heart and desire. All you need is a little guidance which I think I might persuade the CIA to provide."

"Oh, I dun know, meng," said Jorge. "Dat didn't work so hot las tine at the Bay of Pigs."

"Oh yeah, well. Sorry about that," said Hicks.

"Ho chi mama. Why we doin' all dis talkin'," said Chi Chi. "Less get da hell outta here before dem Brits come and thin we es da bad guys too."

The trawler and the *Who do Voodoo* sped swiftly away from the island. On the Voodoo King's sleek yacht were Bean, Chi Chi, Roachie, the Arranger, the dealer, and the 3J's and their girlfriends. The trawler carried the rest of the *Los Hermanos Cubanos Para La Libertad* and their girls, as well as Fruitcake who sat frustrated because he couldn't understand a damn word any of them were saying or thinking as they laughed and popped the corks off a number of bottles of Dom Pérignon Oenothèque. Cruising for the coast and safety of Miami they could see miles behind them in the distance to the east, the lights of a formation of British helicopters loaded with SAS assault teams soaring in to retake the South Island Club.

On board one of the choppers an assault team member communications expert fiddled with his radio to bring up a broken signal that he thought might be the Haitian drug runners.

"Kooba red one to Kooba blue six, I min red six. I min... hokay, I'n no gonna do da codes no more. Hey, come on chu guys. Dis es Yoyo. Talks to me. How comes chu guys dun wan talks to me?"

The Celestial Rocket had taken a few licks during the traumatic events of recent days, resulting in a loose exhaust system, a sputtering engine, a slightly dented quarter panel, a couple bullet holes, and a now malfunctioning convertible top, all of which the 3Js volunteered to fix for free, estimating it would take at least three days. Meanwhile Bean, Chi Chi, Roachie, and Fruitcake stayed in the Oceans Horizon Waterfront Resort Inn (for which they didn't pay extra) where they treated themselves to a much needed rest, new clothes, and a gracious dinner at the The Miami Moon Restaurant & Lounge, topping things off with an evening of listening to Jimmy Buffett songs by Captain Svenson on the Poop Deck.

The next day as they sat on the balcony of their room with a view, watching the boats come and go along Biscayne Bay, there suddenly came the sound of a musical car horn playing the notes of Jimmy Buffett's *Cheeseburger in Paradise*. It repeated twice more until out of curiosity they went and looked out to discover sitting in the parking lot was Bean's once runty little weirdly painted clown car, the Celestial Rocket, that had been magically transformed and stretched to an imported leather upholstered four-seater convertible with a custom five stage two tone pearl white and candy apple red paint job, classic fifties style wire spoke wheels, a top of the line Bose CD/radio surround sound system – and, of course, a pair of fuzzy dice on the mirror. Behind the newly pimped out Nash Metropolitan stood the entire compliment of the *Los Hermanos Cubanos Para La Libertad,* all sporting broad smiles of achievement.

Bean and company were speechless as they walked around and toured the born again vehicle. Bean paused, especially taken when he reached the spare tire continental kit on the trunk where there was neatly scribed in real 14k gold lettering the name…

Celestial Rockit

(With an 'i' because The Cubans couldn't spell too well either)

"Wow!" said Bean.

"Wow!" said Roachie.

"Ho chi mama!" said Chi Chi. "Dey sung kina pimped out chur ride, meng."

Holy crap. Look at all those seats, thought Fruitcake. *Finally, the respect I deserve.*

"We hope chu like it, meng," said Jorge. "I min sungtines chu white boys dun always like…"

"I love it," interrupted Bean. The others nodded in agreement. Fruitcake's tail was flipping around at high speed as Bean lifted him into the car. He scooted around, sniffing the fresh soft leather on all the seats.

"Yeah, we figured maybe chu guys needed some more room wha wit Roachie jammed in da trunk all da tine," added Jesus.

Juan lifted the hood to proudly reveal a spotless rebuilt engine with enough chrome and technical upgrades to impress a team of NASA engineers.

"I'n really proud of dis leetle baby, meng," he said. "Now chu can really leaf dem bad guys behine, chu know wha I min? Dis es no leetle clown car no more, Bean meng. She go maybe one-twenty or thirty wit'out a hiccup and maybe sung more if chu need it. An da suspension to match too, meng."

"Look in da trunk," said an excited Yoyo.

"But... um... This looks awfully expensive," questioned Bean.

"Look in da trunk," repeated Yoyo.

"No problem, meng," said Jorge. "We got lots of money now. Some from when we sell dat *Who do Voodoo* boat an lots more moneys comin' from da CIA after dey look at us take over the Voodoo King's compound. An all we gotta do for it es go down to Kooba once in a while and blow chit up and blame it on Fidel."

"Look in da trunk," said Yoyo again.

"Oh, okay, Yoyo," said Bean as he popped open the trunk.

"It wass my idea," said Yoyo. "An I do it myself."

Built into the trunk was a refrigerated cooler that ran off the power of the engine.

"Hey, that's nice," said Bean.

"Yeah, that's nice," said Roachie as he peered into the trunk.

"Open it," said Yoyo.

Bean opened the cooler to find it stuffed with chilled chocolaty delicious Yoo-hoos.

"Oh, that's extremely nice!" said Roachie who had acquired quite a taste for the drink.

"Dere wass some junk in chur trunk so I stuff it behine da cooler, hokay?" said Yoyo.

"Oh sure," said Bean. "Thank you very much, Yoyo. The cooler is a great idea." He looked to all the *Los Hermanos Cubanos Para La Libertad*. "I don't know what to say, guys."

"Chu no gotta say nothin'," smiled Jorge. "Chu es one of us now."

"Yeah, dass right, meng. Now all chu gotta do es go fine chur papa," said Juan.

"Dass right" said Chi Chi, taking Bean and Roachie by the arm. "We gonna go fine Bean's papa an we ain gonna quit no way until we do."

Roachie and Bean smiled and shook their heads in agreement as Yoyo drew out Yoo-hoos from the cooler and passed them around. Roachie's smile widened.

Across the street, backed into the ally, Father Sabatino sat in his '58 Red Caddy convertable, his arm resting on the sill of the door. He leaned his head heavily into his hand as he watched Bean and his friends hop into the newly pimped out stretched out Celestial Rocket for a test run.

"Like I'm some kind of damn babysitter," he mumbled to himself. He then grew a slight smile and snickered as he remembered how he had left the Voodoo King for the British commandos at the South Island Club - naked, bound, and very angry - with a chicken up his ass. Father Sabatino always did his research and was not one to ignore local culture, customs, and the traditions of his friends - and enemies. He was beginning to like Miami more and more each day.

chapter 16
Down Island Dead End

Chi Chi rose in her seat and stretched up above the windshield of the Celestial Rocket, spreading her arms as though she were going to lift off and fly away, her face aglow, her long dark hair whipping freely in the warm gulf wind.

"Míreme. Estoy libre y puedo volar como un pájaro!" she shouted to the sky.

"What?" said Bean.

"She said, Look at me. I am free and I can fly like a bird!" Roachie interpreted from the back seat as he nursed a Yoo-hoo through a straw and read his old dirty dog-eared copy of *Monkey* that he had salvaged from the trashcan in the motel room. He especially liked the part where the giant gorilla saved the hero from the cannibals.

"Oh, you can speak Kooban? I mean Cuban?" said Bean.

"Spanish? Sure," said Roachie. "And German and Italian. Not that difficult actually. Learning a language is kinda like learning math."

"Estoy libre! Puedo volar! Estoy libre! Puedo volar!" Chi Chi yelled with sincere passion.

"What's she saying now?" asked Bean.

"She's still free and she's still flying," Roachie loosely translated.

And she still has my seat, thought Fruitcake from the other back seat next to Roachie where he lay bottom side up, balls to the sun. *But okay this is cool. I can live with this.*

They were all feeling exceptionally happy, Chi Chi having found a new family in her new friends, Roachie, having moved out from under the overpass to rediscovering his brain and soap and water, and newly discovering chocolate Yoo-hoo, and Fruitcake finally getting his own seat in the new custom Celestial Rocket. While Chi Chi flapped in the breeze, Roachie began to sing one of his favorite songs between slurps of his Yoo-hoo.

"But he's got... hi-igh hopes. He's got... hi-igh hopes. He's got... high apple pie in the... skyyyy hopes."

"Hey Roachie, es chu hokay?" asked Chi Chi.

"What."

"He soun hokay to me," laughed Chi Chi.

"Oops there goes another rubber tree plant," Roachie continued singing.

Ahead of them stretched five more miles of the famed Seven Mile Bridge, the longest of the many bridges connecting the Florida Keys. Beyond the bridge as they continued their way south, the mid day sun and spaciousness of the sea combined with hot salsa music on the radio seemed to feed their high spirits.

Bean began to wonder for the first time since he departed St. Augustine what he was going to do or say when he found his father. He was getting anxious and his anxiety turned to near fright as they finally drove slowly along Duval Street in Key West to discover a spot and park directly across from Jimmy Buffett's Margaritaville Cafe. Following a long five minutes of Bean's motionless silence while sitting behind the wheel of the Celestial Rocket, Chi Chi finally spoke up.

"Well, wha chu gonna do now? Es chu gonna juss sit dere or chu gonna go finds chur papa?"

Chi Chi, Roachie, and Fruitcake all stared at Bean, waiting for a response but he continued to just sit there, silent.

"Hokay," said Chi Chi. "I get it. Chu es spookied causs chu dun know heem. So chu juss wait here. I'n gonno go get chur papa first and let heem know dat he es gotta kid an dat kid es chu."

Chi Chi exited the car, strutted across the street and into Margaritaville where she discovered a crowd of diners and drinkers, none of whom were the famous Jimmy Buffett. Making her way to the long crowded bar, she asked of the bartender, "I'n lookin for Chimmy Buffett. Es he here?"

"Yeah, sure kid. You and everybody else in Key West," said the bartender. "Sorry but you just missed him. Actually he doesn't spend much time here."

"So maybe chu juss tell me where he lif causs I gotta tell him hees…"

"Oh, he doesn't live here any more."

"He dunt? But es very impordant. Es about hees boy."

"Don't know what to tell ya, kid. He's on the road all the time. Busy man, ya know?"

Chi Chi accepted the bad news and turned slowly to unexpectedly discover Bean, Roachie, and Fruitcake standing behind her. They overheard the bartrender and their faces showed the same disappointment she was feeling. Even Fruitcake's one ear drooped in dismay.

"Wow, that sucks," said Roachie, placing his hand on Bean's shoulder for comfort.

Yeah, that really sucks, thought Fruitcake as he surveyed the entire establishment for fat men with guns. *Can we go home now?*

Bean slowly looked up and around Margaritaville. He was finally here. After a lifetime of living with the world of Jimmy Buffett through the appreciative but forgetful mind of Sister Moonbeam Goom-jigi, he had finally arrived here at the mecca of the man, the man who had filled her life and in turn his life with joy and contentment. At every glance there were reminders of him and his music in the form of photos, album covers, and memorabilia depicting his songs and philosophy. It was on the walls, behind the bar, hanging from the ceiling, even the music that filled the air and mixed with the laughter of the cheerful patrons. Bean had finally arrived and should have been awed by the experience yet he was far from it. He instead found himself wishing that Sister Moonbeam-Goom-jigi could be here as well. Arriving at the one and only original Margaritaville didn't mean he had succeded in his quest to fulfill his mother's dying wish. *Where,* he thought, *where is my father? And where do I go from here?* He turned sadly and walked out the door.

Roachie and Chi Chi followed Bean as he wandered slowly up one side of Duval Street and down the other with Fruitcake at his side. He seemed oblivious to everything around him which included a growing parade of tourists, bikes, motor scooters, and even a pickup truck full of gay men in the back who offered up a concert of cat calls and invitations to the long-haired young Bean. It was that time of evening and Duval Street was rolling out its nightly freak parade.

"I think you have some admirers," Roachie said to Chi Chi.

"I dun thin so," said Chi Chi. "I dun thin dose guys in dat truck wan nothing to do wit any girls ly me. I thin maybe dey whistlin' to Bean or chu or maybe even Fruitscakes."

Oh lady. You got one serious imagination, thought Fruitcake moving closer to Bean's side, scanning the street for fat men with guns. *So, when are we leaving this burg anyway? Can we go home now?*

"What, you mean they're…" came Roachie.

"Yep," replied Chi Chi. "Dis town es wackier den a Dole fruitcup. And day alls come out at night."

"Oh," said Roachie.

Bean continued, unaware of the sound of people's laughter and music drifting from places like the The Hog's

Breath Saloon and Sloppy Joe's. He paid no attention to the strange long haired man sitting on the sidewalk playing the violin. The man's dog, wearing a straw hat with protruding dreadlocks, a Hawaiian shirt, and sun glasses, sat dutifully next to him holding a donation basket in its mouth. Nor did he notice the group of transvestites dressed for exhibition, assembling in front of the old theater who smiled invitingly while keenly giving him the once over. He simply ignored everything and wandered along to eventually be caught up in the migration of people making their way to Mallory Square.

Mallory Square was a large open area on the west side of the island where the cruise ships dock and where people gather each night to take in the carnival ritual centered around watching the sunset. A traditional gathering that seemed to feed on itself as it drew both the curious and the certifiable.

As they approached the crowd near Mallory Square's bulkhead, there appreared in the distance over the water a white sea plane that lifted off the surface, gained a little altitude and turned northwest over the gulf as it chased the setting sun into an incredible golden sky. Balancing the perfect picture was a three masted barcentine in full sail on the horizon. It was a quintessential tropical scene of the melding of man and mother earth at their finest, but it was all wasted on a disheartened Bean Buffett who could only think of his failure to find his father.

"It's not real," said a secretive voice near Bean's ear.

Bean came about to find himself face to face with a stranger who was shaking his head vertically to emphasise the honesty of his words.

"Not real. None of it," said the wide eyed young man, now shaking his head horizontaly to emphasise the negative.

Chi Chi was busy splitting her attention between a magician with a monkey on his head and a juggler who was entertaining a circle of people with his talent for tossing a mix of sharp kitchen utensils and fake body parts in the air. The magician was very good at making things disappear, especially people's money. Roachie's attention was set on a man with a long white beard and matching hair, dark glasses, and a broad straw hat decorated with assorted fake fruit and flowers. He was playing a guitar, harmonica, symbols, drum, flute, and an assortment of bells and whistles, all of which were somehow attached to his body. When Chi Chi and Roachie heard what was said to Bean they turned to discover a strange barefoot man in a shabby pair of cut-off faded jeans and a raggedy old sweat shirt with cut-off sleeves. The sweat shirt had been decorated with an orange indelible Sharpy and read *Maynard G. Krebs Lives!* across the front. On the back was the face of a space alien and it read *The Truth Is Out There*.

"It's not real," repeated the desperate strange looking man, his eyes darting around like a paranoid lizard. "You see... you see all this. It's not real. That boat out there, it's not real. That monkey on that man's head, it's not real. That's what they want you to think. That's what they want you to think and then they gotcha. And then, and then when they getcha they really gotcha. Ya know?"

Bean, confused, shook his head yes then no.

The more the strange man talked the more excited he became and the more excited he became the more his many homemade bracelets and necklaces full of little tin trinkets and bells and sea shells would jump and jingle and make noise, and the more his many bracelets and necklaces would make noise the more excited he seemed to become. He was like a perpetual emotion machine with a million things to say and no one to listen, so when he did finally find someone to listen he would automatically go into overdrive.

"But *I know. I know.* They don't know that I know but I know. And I know that they don't know that I know or they would... or... I mean, so that's why I'm telling you so you'll know too. But don't let them know that you know too or else... um... or else... um, you know?"

"Huh?" said Bean.

Whoa, thought Fruitcake. *And I thought the guy with the fruit on his head was weird.*

The strange man seemed to get a grip and slow down. "Oh um, yeah," he seemed to say to himself as he reached down and grabbed a small school bell that hung with a shoestring from a loop on his cut off jeans. He rang the bell except it made no sound because it didn't have a clapper but apparently *he* could hear it and it reminded him of something.

"Oh, um, yeah. I forgot. Um... could you spare a dollar for a disabled Vietnam veteran? Abused and um... abused and neglected by an ungrateful nation and tossed on the streets to... um. A dollar. Just a dollar."

"Hey meng, chu ain old enough to be no Vietnam veteran," observed Chi Chi.

"Oh... um... did I say Vietnam. I meant Korea. No, I mean... um, I mean the war in the desert."

"I thin chu es full of chit," said Chi Chi.

"Chit? What's chit?" said the nervous little man.

"You need a cardboard sign," said Roachie.

"Who are you?" asked Bean.

"I'm... Oh no. I can't tell you because then you'll know and then they'll know you know and then they'll know. You know?"

"HEY!" threatened Chi Chi loudly.

"BONER!" replied the strange nervous man, jumping and jingling in fear of Chi Chi's threatening tone. "BONER!"

Some people nearby gathered up their children and quickly moved away.

"What," said Bean.

"JONES!" jingled the excited strange man.

"I thin dis guy hees sung kina pervert," said Chi Chi. "An he chure ain no veteran. He dun even know hees own nem. He juss say pervert stuff."

"Boner," repeated the little man.

"See. I telt chu he es a pervert," said Chi Chi, waiving him off and turning to watch the sunset.

"Boner Jones," said the strange man. "Um… you, you can call me Boner. Boner Jones."

"Boner? What kind of name is Boner?" asked Roachie.

"Oh, um… nickname. From junior high school. It just kind of stuck. Um… I really don't like to talk about it," said the strange man, embarrassed.

He again rang his bell that didn't have a clapper but the action seemed to ring a bell in his head and help when he was confused or forgetful. The therapeutic soundless ringing of his bell also reminded him of his principal purpose for mingling with the sunset crowd.

"Um… a dollar… please?" he said.

"Are you hungry?" asked Bean.

"Oh no. Here we goes again," said Chi Chi.

The man shook his head and jingled a yes.

"Come on," said Bean. "I'll buy you a cheeseburger."

"He's very strange," Roachie whispered to Chi Chi as they all headed back to Duval Street.

"Yeah, but he dun smell as bad as chu did back in Me'ahmi Beash," she replied.

"Oh," said Roachie. "Sorry."

"That your dog?" asked Boner Jones.

"Yes," answered Bean.

"He's only got one ear," said Boner Jones.

"Yes, I know," said Bean.

"Very strange," repeated Roachie.

chapter 17

Cayo Hueso Joe

They made their way back up Duval Street to finally turn into the Hog's Breath Saloon for a bite to eat. Chi Chi suggested they eat at Margaritaville but Bean's heart just wasn't in it. Making their way past the bar to a table they were held up by the Hog's Breath manager.

"Listen here Boner, I thought I told you to stay outta here and quit bothering my customers," said the manager as he extended his arm to block Boner's passage. "Is this guy bothering you folks?" he asked.

Boner began to look a little confused and his necklace and bracelets began to jingle a bit as he looked to his newfound friends for assistance. Chi Chi was quick to accomadate him.

"Hey chu," she said to the manager. "Wha chu thin chu es doin'? Dis Boner guy he es with us and we gonna eats here. Dun chu know who we es? Dis es Chimmy Buffett Jr., and dis es Meester Rochers. Hees a rich hightech genius."

"You sure he's not bothering you folks?" asked the manager, looking at the one eared dog and doubting what Chi Chi just told him. *Jimmy Buffett and Mister Rogers my ass,* he thought. *And I'm the Cookie Monster.*

"No sir, he's not bothering anyone," said Bean.

"Because he's always coming in here pan handling and bothering people with his conspiracy theories and end of the world alien crap."

Boner began to jingle a little louder as he nervously anticipated being tossed from the Hog's Breath Saloon... again.

"No. He es hokay and he es wit us and if chu dun wan heem here den we gonno go spend our moneys sungplace else, hokay," said Chi Chi.

"Well, as long as he stays with you and doesn't start bothering people," replied the manager.

They turned and took a table in a corner of the dining room, ordered cheeseburgers, fries, and Cokes all around and sat quietly staring at Boner which made him a bit nervous.

Fruitcake sat next to Bean's chair waiting for some fries to rain down from the table when he spotted a cat wander in from the bar. It was one of the many polydactyl cats unique to Key West. He was considering following a mysterious primordial inner psychological drive to attack the cat until he noticed the fairly large feline had seven toes on each foot instead of the usual five, and he deduced that seven toes meant twenty-eight very sharp claws capable of doing some serious damage to an undersized one-eared dog. Leaving the polydactyl cat alone, reasoned Fruitcake, was the prudent thing to do. He also decided not to lose face over his decision, concluding that it was equal to Sam Slade Ace Detective deciding not to go up against a Tommy gun with a pee shooter. Instead he directed his focus on looking around the Hog's Breath Saloon for fat guys.

Boner was becoming even more nervous and decided to break the uncomfortable silence with some conversation. "I'm a Conch," he declared with an odd sense of pride and a nervous smile.

"Yeah, right, chu es a conch," said Chi Chi. "An I'n a mermaid."

"No," replied Boner. "It means I was born here in Key West. If you were born here, a decendant of Bahamian immigrants, you're a Conch. So I'm a Conch. A regular Bahamian bohemian."

Bean, Roachie, and Chi Chi simply nodded their heads politely.

"Um… if you weren't born here then you're not a Conch," continued Boner.

"That stands to reason," said Roachie.

"Um… right. So… um, you're a Freshwater Conch."

"What?" said Bean.

"If you come down-island to live but you weren't born here then you're a Freshwater Conch," explained Boner. "Did you come down here to live?"

All three shook their heads no.

"My folks go way back to when the island was called Cayo Hueso. My great-great-great-grandfather Flevis was a pirate and my great-great-grandfather Fareley was a pirate and a ship wrecker. Used to put fake lights out in the straights to misguide ships so they'd wreck on a reef and then go out and salvage their cargo. My great-grandfather Otis was a wrecker too and a sponge diver and then a cigar maker. So ya see I'm a Cayo Hueso Conch."

"What about your grandfather?" asked Roachie.

"Oh… um, he got into politics. We don't like to talk about him."

About that time the food arrived, making Chi Chi happy that she could now eat and not have to converse with this odd man. It also made Fruitcake happy because Bean wasted no time tossing him a french fry. They were all hungry and dug into their burgers immediately. That is except for Boner who first dissected and inspected all of his meal's components. Once satisfied that it was safe he reconstructed the burger and began to eat.

"Why did you do that?" asked Bean. "Is there something wrong with the food here?"

"Microphones," said Boner. "You can never be too careful, ya know. And transmitters. They're tiny little dudes and you swallow them and they travel through your blood and go in your brain and then they know everything because they can hear everything. It's that nano science stuff, um… nanobots. They're using them to take over the world. Can read your mind. Even control what you say and do. That's why I wear these bracelets and necklace… interferes with the reception and transmissions so they won't know. Ya know? But they don't know that I know. Gotta be careful. Specially in places like McDonalds and Burger King."

"Ho chi mama," said Chi Chi as she was about to toss a French fry into her mouth but then paused and inspected it for nanobots.

"Well, actually," entered Roachie, "I know quite a lot about that sort of thing and that's not so far fetched because…"

"Buffett?" said Boner, interrupting Roachie. "You're lookin' for Jimmy Buffett?"

"Yes," said Bean. "How did you know that?"

"I heard," said Boner. "When she got outta the car and went into Margaritaville. I heard. I can help. Um… that's why I followed you to the Square. I wasn't sure but now I'm sure. Because you're nice. Not like lots of folks who come here. They all think I'm crazy."

"Hmm, wha a surprise," mumbled Chi Chi.

"How can you help?" asked Bean.

"There's an island. A secret island. And I know a man, an old Cayo Hueso Conch who can tell you how to get there. That's how I can help."

"What's an island got to do with Bean's dad?" asked Roachie.

"It's a special island," whispered Boner. "It's only for special people. People who know. Like you people. Jimmy Buffett's people."

"Will you take us to this old man," asked Bean, perking up now at the prospect of again finding his father.

"Sure," smiled Boner. "No problem. Soon as we eat. Remember the Maine?" he said without skipping a beat as though it were all a single thought dealing with the same subject. The others stared, confused, as they often were when Boner was talking. He took a big bite of his burger and followed it with a fry after a quick inspection for micro cameras. He pointed to the cheeseburger and as he chewed looked side to side to be sure no one was listening when he whispered, "McDonalds, Burger King, don't never… cause it's them and the stuff is loaded with nanobots." He shook his head to give emphasis to his warning then continued, "Hey, did you know that the USS Maine conspiracy was hatched right here in Key West," he said as he chewed his food. "It was really Cayo Hueso Conchs that sank her down there in Cuba and started the Spanish American War. Yep, it's true," he continued through another bite of burger. "It was all about sugar and rum. And Cuba has lots of sugar and rum. You see, Teddy Roosevelt made a deal with the space aliens who needed sugar for food and rum for fuel for their flying saucers and in return they promised to make him President. Space aliens are the secret fourth branch of the government ya know, always have been, very powerful, usually mascarade as Democrats and Progressives. But don't let them know that I told ya, okay? Cause they don't know that I know. Ya know?"

"Ho chi mama," said Chi Chi.

Space alien? What's a space alien? thought Fruitcake.

After that brief revelation Boner fell silent while he inspected one particular French fry more closely then the others. He then wrapped it in a napkin, placed it on the floor and stomped on it, then looked to the others, put his finger to his lips and whispered, "Shish. They're listenin'."

They all finished their meal in silence except Fruitcake. *What a terrible waste of a perfectly good French fry*, he thought just as one of Bean's fries dropped on his head. *Ah, that's better.*

An hour later the group was walking along the docks of the marina at Key West Harbor. It was dark and quiet except for the muffled noises filtering from nearby clubs and restaurants. Along in the more secluded part of the marina there was only the sound of water lapping against the boat hulls and nylon lines tapping the tall aluminum masts of the sailing yachts as the gentle waves rocked them back and forth.

"He comes here and sits on the same bench every night," said Boner. "Looks out to sea remembering the old days before all this rich tourist stuff and strange people got here. He's an old merchant sailor. He tells me about when Key West used to be a workin' man's island. You know, back in the day. Ever since I was just a little shitter I'd come over every once in a while and talk with him. He's the only one round here don't think I'm crazy. Him and old Sally Jewel. But old Sally Jewel's crazy so she wouldn't really know anything anyway. Sally Jewel went crazy when she was dumped by that movie star Rock Hudson back in 1964 when he ran off with some guy. Couldn't take the rejection. Claims they were married but never could prove it."

"I don't think you're crazy," said Bean.

"Well, that makes two," replied Boner, "or maybe three if you count Sally Jewel." He paused and looked to a dark area between two buildings where stood a few benches and a trash can under a dim lamp post. Sitting on one of the benches staring out to sea was an old black man wearing baggy gray shorts, sandals, and a flowery faded pink souvenier T-shirt with the words *It's Better in the Keys*. Tipped back on his head he sported a crumpled old blue baseball cap that said *USS Indiannapolis* on the front. An unlit corncob pipe hung from his mouth. He looked dead.

"Is that him?" asked Bean, pausing to keep a polite distance.

"Yeah," answered Boner.

"He looks dead," said Roachie.

"Yeah, he looks dead," said Bean.

"Ho chi mama," said Chi Chi as she made the sign of the cross.

"No, he's just kind of zoned out," said Boner.

Boner approached quietly and sat next to the old man. The others followed and stood nearby. "Hello Joe Papa. How are you tonight?" asked Boner.

The old man blinked, his glazed stare beyond the horizon dissolved and his eyes drew in to settle on Fruitcake who was sitting at his feet looking up to see if he was really dead.

"That ugly ass dog's only got one ear," said old Joe Papa who stared at Fruitcake for a long silent moment before he continued speaking. "Had a dog once. Name was Shitstick. Got run over by a drunk lady from Boston who was fightin' with her husband at the time cause she caught the ol' man porkin' a Conch. Said she was sorry and paid me fifty bucks. Most money I ever seen back then. I took the money and bought me a boat and buried Shitstick at sea. When the Conch lady's ol' man come back to port and found out what happened he killed that Boston fella. Then he run off with the Boston lady who run over Shitstick. Now ain't that a damn hoot. Like a Greek tragedy or somethin'."

Fruitcake decided the old man wasn't dead, walked away and pissed on the trash can, then parked his ass next to Bean. Old Joe Papa watched with interest.

"Joe Papa, these are friends of mine. They need to get to the island," said Boner who then leaned over and whispered confidentially in Joe Papa's ear. When he was finished Joe Papa looked at Bean, inspected him more closely for a long moment, then shook his head in agreement.

"Weren't always like this round here ya know," said the old man to everyone and no one in particular. "Used to be a workin' man's dock back in the day. Joined the Navy. Went off to the Pacific to kill Japs when I was a kid, then worked the merchant ships. Came back home to retire and found all these questionable folks come here with their big money and strange ways. Turned our ol' Bone Key into a damn circus is what they done. Oh hell, ain't been right anyways since Henry run that Goddamn railroad is what my daddy always said. Is what I think too. Is what God almighty thought too. Took a storm and washed that damn train right off the tracks is what the almighty did. Old Bone Key's had its moments I s'pose. But ain't the same, that's for sure. Damn freak circus now. And ain't nobody can complain neither cause they's all gotta be socially correct while they is busy being social deviates. Ain't that some bullshit?"

The old man pulled the corncob pipe from his mouth and looked up at Bean, then briefly inspected the others and shook his head with approval. After a long silent moment he blasted out an elongated fart and acted as though the exceptional flatulence never took place. He followed it up with a healthy belch then replaced the pipe.

"Ho chi mama," said Chi Chi, shocked at the old man's impertinence.

Whoa, thought Fruitcake. *Could shoot down a Pan Am heavy with that ass cannon.*

"Can you help us?" asked Bean.

"Spose so," said Joe Papa. He then sat silent, waiting.

Boner got up and went to Bean and whispered, "Um… I think maybe you should offer him something. Maybe a few bucks, ya know."

"I thin dis es a hustle. I thin he es pullin' chur chain," said Chi Chi. "An dat leetle crazy pervert, he es helpin' too."

"Ah, Cuban. We got us a Cuban girl here, eh?" said Joe Papa. "Been to Cuba I have. Used to run guns to Castro when he was hidin' up in the hills, him and his blood thirsty gang of killers. Can't say I liked him much. Always thought he was full of shit myself. And that Argentine commie butcher Che Guevara comrade of his. Now there was a half rigged vessel if ever I seen one. Beat him at poker once and ol' El Che got so damn pissed he stomped off and shot three of his own revolutionary compatriots and a mule right there on the spot. Nope, can't say I liked those boys much. Money was good though."

"I thin maybe chu choulda run one of dem guns right up Castro's hairy ass," suggested Chi Chi.

Joe Papa chuckled, "I think I like this girl."

Bean pulled a twenty from his pocket, sat down next to the old man and offered it to him.

"Don't want your money kid. I got plenty."

"So, you'll help us then?" asked Bean.

"Only one man can get you there, kid. That be Purdey Boon."

"Purdey Boon? Who's Purdey Boon?" asked Bean.

"Got a boat. Only boat that goes there. Only one they let in. He'll run ya in. Just tell'm Joe Papa sent ya. Tell'm ya gotta get to the island. He'll know."

"I know Purdey Boon," said Boner. "I can take you to him. His boat's just down the marina a ways."

"You go see Purdey in the mornin'. He'll get ya there. But don't be tellin' nobody else," instructed old Joe Papa. "Don't be sayin' nothin' to nobody bout that island, ya hear?"

"No sir, we won't," said Bean. "And thank you very much."

They left old Joe Papa alone on his bench, sitting and reminiscing and passing gas, and they headed back to town.

From a concealed location in the darkness nearby where he had listened to the entire conversation Father Sabatino strolled over and sat on the bench next to old Joe Papa.

"Nice night tonight isn't it old man?" he said.

"Yep," replied old Joe Papa as he adjusted his pipe. "Be even nicer if you'd get lost. Ain't no need for any religion round here tonight," he said just before he let a loud, menacing fart. "I been to hell and back more'n once. Ain't nothin' you can do for me now preacher man."

Father Sabatino rose quickly to avoid the gasseous comment, then walked away. "Crusty old bastard," he mumbled.

They were approaching the Celestial Rocket when Roachie brought up the subject of what they were going to do regarding overnight accommodations.

"I guess we're going to sleep in the car, huh?" said Roachie. "Or maybe on the beach."

"No," said Bean. "We'll find a motel."

"Um… how bout you stay with me?" offered Boner. "I got plenty of room. I don't mind."

Bean agreed and they all piled into the car. Boner being an extra body meant Fruitcake was forced to sacrifice and was once again relegated to an uncomfortable spot between the seats.

Okay, this sucks, thought Fruitcake. *What do we have to do, get a damn school bus?*

Boner directed them around and through a number of narrow streets in the older part of town until they arrived at a large neglected two story grand Victorian house with chipping white paint and sagging shutters, surrounded by an elaborate rusty wrought iron fence.

"Well, um… this is it," said Boner with pride.

Bean managed to fit the stretched Celestial Rocket in a space at the curb in front of the house, secured the top and windows closed for the night and entered the house with the others. When they entered the grand foyer they faced a grand winding staircase that rose to the upper level. The detail and old world craftsmanship was exceptional all about the house and the architectural opulence easily impressed the few people who were ever fortunate enough to see it. Another prominent feature was the furnishings, or lack of. The large house was pretty much empty except for a series of portraits of long dead family members including great-great-grandfather Farely Elsworth Jones, the wrecker turned sponge diver, legitimate Sea Captain, importer and exporter, and cigar manufacturer. And they all showed an uncanny likeness or extreme family resemblance to Boner himself. Along the wall was a series of wooden crates on which sat a small 12 inch TV and five or six polydactyl cats all named after characters from Hemingway books, except for one named Mister Spock. Faded stenciling on the crates read *F.E.JONES & CO. FINE CIGARS.* There was also Boner's rusty bicycle with baskets mounted on the front and back that he often used to take his cats for a ride.

The site of the cats moved Fruitcake to take refuge behind Bean, even though the cats completely ignored him and the others.

"See, I told you I have lots of room," smiled Boner. "Pick any room you want. Plenty of bedrooms upstairs too."

"Chu lif here all by churself?" asked Chi Chi.

"Sure," he replied. "Boner Jones was born here. Upstairs, first room on the right. Great-great-grandfather Farley built the place. Just me and the cats now. Oh, and the chickens in the back yard. My mother and father got divorced when my dad caught mom in bed with a Brazilian woman. I was just a kid. She left the country, went to Brazil with her lover. A few years later my dad got caught in a hurricane when he was out in his boat. He was a shrimper and a diver. Nobody's heard from him since. Somebody told me once they thought they saw him on some small island near the Caymans living with a Jamacan lady from Kingston. Said he had a shack that sold jerk chicken, rum smoothies, and ganja. But I don't know."

"Beds upstairs?" asked Roachie.

"Um... no. Just bedrooms. Sorry. Most of the furniture has been sold off. To pay the taxes. Sorry. The city says this place is worth twelve million bucks so I got some pretty big tax bills. I got a lawyer who's sueing the city to stop the big taxes. He says when this house was built the whole damn island wasn't worth twelve million bucks and that us Conchs gotta stick together and defend our rights before all the Freshwaters take over and own everything including our souls. But I think it's them, you know, the government. They want to sieze this place cause they think old Farley Jones' fortune and the family treasure is buried here along with some important documents that prove who really owns the island. That's how the local legend goes anyway, and the family stories too, that old Bone Key as it was called was bought by my great-great-great-grandfather Flevis. Ya see, it belonged to the Indians first, then the Spanish, then the British, then the Spanish again, and then the Governor of Cuba gave it to some Spanish army dude who was some kind of con man and sold it three times over back in the early 1800's. Allegedly one of the buyers, the first one, was my old great-great-great-grandaddy, the pirate. So who really owns the island has always been in question. It gets complicated, you know, politics and money and all that crap. But I know their secrets and I think they know I know their secrets so I think they're keeping their distance for now. Afraid I might squeal."

"Squeal about what?" asked Roachie.

"About what they think I know," answered Boner.

"What's that?"

"Don't know for sure. But I got an idea they want to turn this whole island into a space port so they can land their intergalactic fleet when they take over the world."

"So what your saying is that all of Key West might belong to you?" asked Roachie.

"Guess so," said Boner with a shrug as he picked up a cat and stroked its soft fur.

"But chu can sell diss place and be a rich man," said Chi Chi.

"Already rich. Got everything I need right here. Born here. Stayin' here. Me and Mister Spock here."

His reason for living in apparent poverty and obscurity was beyond Chi Chi's comprehension who had survived on very little for a very long time. It pretty much confirmed to her that he was indeed a few garbanzo beans short of a salad. "Ho chi mama," she mumbled.

🌴

When they awoke the next morning Boner was no place to be found. What they did find was a note directing them to the slip at the marina where they could find Purdey Boon and his boat. So without concerning themselves further about the whereabouts of their odd new friend and host Boner Jones, they walked to the marina stopping only at a convenience store for a quick bite of breakfeast in the form of Yoo-hoos, honey buns, potato chips, Twizzlers, and Snickers.

At the marina there were only two boats moored at that particular dock, one being an old beat up wooden hulled cabin cruiser charter fisher named *Lost & Found*, and the other a pristine fully restored and fully functional WWII era PT boat.

They stood on the dock looking around, finding no one until the cabin door opened on the cabin cruiser and out popped a bearded man sporting dark sunglasses and an old boonie hat. He wore an open dirty paisley shirt, wrinkled fish stained baggy khaki pants, and faded blue canvas deck shoes of which each had holes worn at the big and little toes.

"You the folks Boner said was comin'?" asked the man in a raspy voice.

"Boner told you we were coming?" asked Bean. "Are you Mr. Purdey Boon?"

"Nope. Ain't him. Name's Nemo. Cap'n Nemo. This here's my charter fisher," said the man, turning away and opening the hatch to the engine below the deck. He grabbed a wrench, gave Fruitcake a quick glance, then plopped down on his knees and began to fiddle with the engine. He reached down leaving his back and the crack of his ass to the group on the dock as he continued speaking, "Cap'n Boon says for you folks to meet him a half hour after sunset. Says to meet him at the Schooner Wharf Bar exactly one half hour after sunset, and if you ain't there then he's leavin' without ya."

"Uh... okay," said Bean. "The Schooner Wharf Bar a half hour after sunset. Yes sir. Thank you."

The man on the boat didn't look back but simply grumbled acknowledgement by waving the wrench above his head.

Bean and company turned and walked away, admiring the PT boat. Fruitcake paused and looked back. The man rose, lowered his sun glasses a bit, looked at Fruitcake and winked, then returned to his task.

"Sungthin' funny bou dat guy," said Chi Chi. "Dun chu guys thin deres sungthin' funny bou dat guy?"

Bean answered with a negative nod.

"Cap'n Nemo?" chuckled Roachie. "I'd say there's something funny."

If you guys are that dumb then you're not getting any hints from me, thought Fruitcake. Then the entire conversation shot straight from his mind when he suddenly spied a fat man sprawled over a lounge chair on a nearby yacht. The fat man looked straight at Fruitcake then reached for something.

Oh shit! He's got a gun! Fruitcake thought as he moved quickly to put his three companions between him and the weapon. Nervously looking back he saw the man was only reaching for a bottle of suntan lotion. *Whoa, that was a close one.*

"So, wha we gonna do all day 'til we meet dis Boon guy?" asked Chi Chi.

"Well, guess we can just walk around and see what's to see," suggested Bean.

"Lot's to see," added Roachie.

But what if there are fat guys with guns? thought Fruitcake. *Hey Bean, I'm hungry! Where's the house? Where's the food? Creooooolaaaaa!*

Bean paused and pulled a can of Vienna sausages from his pocket. "Oh, here Fruitcake. I got these for ya at the store when we got breakfast. Sorry, I forgot about 'em."

Bean opened the can and dumped the little sausages on the walk where they were eagerly gobbled up by Fruitcake. In mid gulp Fruitcake paused and looked up to Bean because he suddenly realized this was the first time Bean had actually responded to his comments. Prior to that moment he had only had discussions with Sister Moonbeam-Goomj-jigi and those rare occasions were dependent on what sort of brain expanders she had consumed on that particular day or night. Connecting with Bean, however, was an all time first, a defining moment in Fruitcake's life. Elated, Fruitcake wolfed down the sausages then gleefully trotted along with the band of friends, enjoying his new status as they ventured on to explore the town.

Thanks, thought Fruitcake.

"You're welcome," said Bean.

Those were really great little sausages, thought Fruitcake.

"I thought you'd like 'em," said Bean. "Want a Twizzler?"

Sure, thought Fruitcake. *I'll try anything once.*

Standing not far off in the marina where he was unlikely to be seen was Father Alphonso Sabatino. Apparently he too had made a stop at a store for it appeared he had gone native. He was now wearing leather sandals, cargo pant shorts, a straw hat, and an open Hawaiian shirt over his still existing clerical pull-over with clergy collar. He looked somewhat like a Pacific island missionary run amock as he stood there smoking a thin Cheroot cigar spaghetti western style. He studied the bearded man on the charter fishing boat with extreme interest until the man retreated into the cabin. Father Sabatino then meandered away to follow Bean and his friends.

chapter 18

Parrothead Nation

A half hour past sundown, before they had even reached the entrance of the Schooner Wharf Bar, a man stepped out of the shadows and intercepted them. He was dressed in 1940's period Navy issue bell bottomed denim jeans and shirt with a signature white Navy seaman's cap. "You there," he said in a secretive whisper. "You the people spose to meet Capt'n Boon?"

"Yes," answered Bean. "Joe Papa sent us."

"Follow me," the man said as he turned and walked away.

He led them to the end of a dock where sat the restored World War II PT boat they had seen earlier that day, its engines idling in anticipation of their arrival. Another similarly dressed crewman busied himself on board preparing for their departure.

"Is this the boat that'll take us to the island?" asked Bean.

"No questions," said the throwback sailor as he led them up the ganglank and handed them all life jackets. "Put these on and have a seat there next to the torpedo tubes until we're under way, then you can stay there or go below. But don't wander. Can't have anybody going over the side. That your dog?"

"Yes," answered Bean.

"Looks like it's only got one ear. Can it swim with only one ear cause we don't have a life jacket to fit a dog."

"Yes," said Bean. "It can swim and it can surf, too."

"Ya don't say."

With that said and the passengers settled, the two sailors cast off as another man, Captain Purdey Boon, dressed in period Navy officer's tropical khakis, emerged from below deck and took his place at the helm on the bridge. Bean couldn't quite see the man's face in the shadows but for some odd reason he thought there was something familiar about him. The Captain reversed the boat away from the dock then guided it slowly forward until it rumbled clear of the marina and into the darkness away from the island.

Fruitcake made his way from Bean's side to the bridge where he sniffed the leg of the man at the helm. *Hey, remember me?* thought Fruitcake.

The Captain glanced down briefly then returned to his task.

Fruitcake plopped his butt next to him and repeated his thought. *Hello there. This is Fruitcake speaking. Remember me?* After his major breakthrough with Bean earlier in the day, Fruitcake felt empowered and was determined to get a rise from this guy as well, even if it didn't involve any Vienna sausages.

The man just stared ahead into the darkness, ignoring Fruitcake altogether.

Hello. Hello. Hello. Anybody home up there?

"I thin dis es a leetle spooky. Dun chu guys thin dis es leetle spooky?" whispered Chi Chi.

"Maybe this is for security. You know like for the President," said Roachie. "Bean said his dad was a famous person and President of Key West. Maybe this is the Key West Navy."

"Hey Bean," said Chi Chi. "I dun wanna rain on chur parades but Key Wess ain got no presidents. Es part of the U.S.A. and belonks to the President of Florida."

"Florida has a president?" asked Roachie. "When did that happen?"

"Well, chu know wha I mins. Key Wess es da sem es all dose other states like um… Atlanta," clarified Chi Chi.

The man at the helm motioned to one of the crewman who quickly joined him on the bridge. They exchanged a few words then the crewman came off the bridge and spoke to their passengers.

"That's Cap'n Boon at the helm. Says for you folks to sit tight but be ready for action. We'll be cruising through the Straights, runnin' dark cause there's a report that the Japs are patrolling heavy tonight. We're also short handed so we might need your help on the guns if we run into trouble."

Bean, Chi Chi, and Roachie stared at the crewman without comment, waiting for a punchline to what they thought was surely some kind of joke, but none came and they realized that he was serious.

Guns! thought Fruitcake as he quickly jumped off the bridge and took refuge next to Bean. *Did somebody say guns?* After assuring himself there were no fat guys around he returned to the bridge.

"Japs?" said Roachie, looking up at the big intimidating 40mm gun mounted aft. Roachie's only experience with a weapon was when he was six years old and his sister's home-made rubber band gun nearly took out his left eye. He decided then that all weapons were things to avoid, especially if they were pointed at him.

"Yes sir, Japs," answered the crewman, staying in his 1940s character. "But don't worry. We'll get you to your destination even if we gotta sink a few Jap cruisers to do it."

"Ho chi mama," said Chi Chi. "How come I'n always gettin' da whack jobs?"

Bean looked up at the bridge to the Captain at the helm. Only his back was visible as the man reached over and cut off all the running lights except for a dim light in front of the wheel that made the boat's instruments visible. He reached over and shoved the throttle forward and the PT boat revealed its impressive power as its bow rose and shot forward. Captain Boon snugged his hat down against the wind to keep it from flying off. He partially turned his head, first glancing down at Fruitcake then briefly at his passengers. When he did the dim light created a strange facial silhouette that exposed a heavy mustache and gotee, and an unlit cigar under a drooping well seasoned khaki Navy saucer cap. It was a classic recruiting poster of a WWII attack boat hero. Bean thought he caught a glimpse of a half grin but it was too dark to be sure.

Everyone in Key West knew about Captain Purdey Boon but nobody except his crew actually knew Captain Purdey Boon. For the most part Captain Purdey Boon was a complete enigma. The only time anybody ever saw the Captain was when he was on his boat. During the day the PT boat took tourists for joy rides, giving them a small taste of the excitement that was the war in the Pacific in the 1940's, but Captain Boon rarely went along, leaving the pastel sunburnt tourists to his capable crew. Only on occasion would he command the boat during a day's tourists run, such as when it was chartered by a group of sorority girls from some university looking for cheap thrills. What the hell, he was only human. As for where he spent the rest of his time was a complete mystery.

It was at night that Captain Boon really came alive. At night when he went on his mysterious cruises to who the hell knows where, and at night when he went out searching for Japs. Rumors around town likened him to some sort of seafaring immortal that was a little left of keel, an ocean vampire or ancient mariner, reliving his WWII glory days back in the Soloman Islands. Rumors also somehow linked him to every colorful waterborne legend in the Caribbean, from the original explorers, to pirates, to being the spinner of the tales that inspired some of the writings and characters of local favorite son and author Ernest Hemingway. Stories gathered by Hemingway while the two men of adventure spent days and nights together consuming cheap Teacher's scotch at old Sloppy Joe's on Green Street. Others whispered that he was a drug runner but the Coast Guard had long ago proved that rumor false after secretly planting satellite tracking devices on his vessel. All the rumors aside, like everthing and most everyone else in Key West, Captain Purdey Boon was basically just another weird egg.

It was an exceptionally dark night with the moon only a slither hovering above in a starry sky. The only sound was the repetitious deep rumble of the boat's powerful engines as it glided over a relatively calm sea for more than an hour. Finally it slowed and there came a distant sound, slight but audible. It sounded somewhat like music. Bean looked about as best he could from his seated position next to a torpedo tube but saw nothing. The sound came again and he stood and looked out forward past the bow to discover in the distance ahead of them pulsating or flashing lights that would periodically reveal what looked like part of an island.

"Look," said Bean, "there's something out there."

Chi Chi and Roachie rose to view the mysterious vision. A strange carnival of lights shot up through the scrub brush and palm trees into the night sky as though it were some imaginative dramatic Hollywood production of visitors from space in a pulsating UFO. The sound included the beat of drums and people crying into the night air, sometimes in unison, sometimes just screaming.

"Sounds like the natives are restless," said Roachie.

Eventually the vision clearly defined itself as an island with light eminating from its center. As they drew nearer the sound defined itself as music, familiar music. Bean recognized the song as Jimmy Buffett's *The Pascagoula Run*, and his heartbeat increased with anticipation. They approached a small lagoon just large enough for the boat to enter. Captain Boon reversed then cut the engines and they glided in, coming to rest beside a narrow dock that led into the darkness of the treeline. Just then the music stopped.

"This is it folks," said one of the crewman. "Capt'n says you're on your own from here. Says we'll be back to pick you up in two days."

Bean started to approach Captain Boon to thank him but saw he had already vanished below deck.

"Where's Captain Boon?" asked Bean.

"Two days," repeated the crewman. "Be ready to leave in two days or else you'll be stranded here for… well, just be ready to go. Midnight, two days hence. Understand?"

"Yes sir," acknowledged Bean.

"Good. Now go ashore quickly. There's Japs out there and we have to patrol the area."

"Ho chi mama," said Chi Chi.

You got that right, thought Fruitcake as he lept to the dock followed by Bean and company.

At the end of the dock a path led them through dense broad-leafed vegetation and tangled twisted overhanging branches of low growth scrub trees interspersed with palms. Flickering tiki torches lit the path ahead as it widened, leading them ever closer to the source of additional music. When the music ceased they could hear voices and laughter. Through the trees they could now see bright lights that nearly turned the night into day, then came the clanking of a cow bell that was joined by drums, then other instruments. Bean recognized it right away. The instrumental intro sounded bigger than life, resonating throughout the island into the night sky and out across the gulf waters.

"Listen! Do you hear?" said Bean as he hastened his way along the path. The others increased their pace to keep up.

"What?" said Roachie.

"The music," said Bean as the all too familiar singer jumped in on the song and the voices of an obviously large group of people started whooping and cheering. "It's him!" exclaimed Bean.

"It chure does soun ly heem," agreed Chi Chi.

They moved along even quicker now until finally they burst into a clearing full of lights and people, lot's of people. Some were dancing, others gyrating in time with the music, and most were singing word for word along with the song. Bean and company froze at the sight. These were perhaps the strangest people he had ever seen in his entire life. They were not only acting strange but were dressed strange as well. Many of the men wore grass skirts and half coconuts shells over their breast as did many of the women. Many others just wore shorts and Hawaiian shirts. Some of the women in grass skirts went without the coconuts or anything else over their breast. Some were bizarrely painted from head to toe. A few men wore Halloween type shark suits and were accompanied by women in bikinis and foam hats in the form of a parrot or a shark fin. One man had a large blow up Corona beer seaplane on his head and was making the sound of engines as he rode on the shoulders of another man in a Hawaiian shirt and black speedo. At every glance there was another surprise, another freak, all seemingly having the time of their lives and all not even noticing the new arrivals. It could just as well have been a regular wild New Orleans Mardi Gras or Bahamian Junkanoo. It was the most extraordinary thing Bean had ever seen.

As the song reached its famous chorus the entire crowd of what appreared to be nearly a thousand people or more turned toward the source of the music, clasping their hands above their heads forming a pseudo shark fin and began swaying to the left then the right as they sang along with Jimmy.

Can't you feel 'em closing in, honey?
Can't you feel 'em schooling around?
You got fins to the left, fins to the right,
And you're the only bait in town.

Bean couldn't see to find the source of the music so he wandered into the swaying crowd, quickly swallowed up by the mass of crazies as he was drawn toward the lights, to the man singing that famous familiar song, to the object of his mother's life's passion and the objective of his quest, to find... his father. The mass of people continued to sing and sway as he snaked his way through to finally break free of them and discover... an empty stage. There were no musicians, no back up singers, no steel drums, no... Jimmy Buffett anywhere. It held only four very large speakers, a table of sound equipment, and a half naked Korean DJ named Mooch Daddy wearing an assortment of Hawaiian leis and a baseball cap with a palm tree growing out of the top. On each side of the hat was mounted a can of beer with straws that curved to his mouth. Above him over the stage was stretched a large banner that read PARROTHEAD NATION FESTIVAL. At each side of the stage was a large flag on which there was a parrot holding a Land Shark beer circled by the words *Parrothead Nation – Give Us Paradise or Give Us Death.*

Bean's heart sank.

When Chi Chi, Roachie, and Fruitcake finally managed to make their way through the crowd they found Bean just staring at the empty space where he thought he had finally found his father.

"Ho chi mama. Dis dun look so good. Wha da hell we gonna do now?" said Chi Chi as she looked about to discover on one side of the area a large concession stand. The sign above the stand read BEER & MARGARITAS. On the other side was another concession, its sign read simply CHEESEBURGERS, OYSTERS & BOILED SHRIMP.

The Fin song ended and Mooch Daddy the DJ changed the mood as he put on the slower paced Buffett classic, *Tin Cup Chalice.* The wild crowd of Parrotheads morphed into couples and danced slowly as they hummed or sang along, some kissing, some just leaning or holding each other upright, some nearly falling over in a drunken stuper. All were attuned to the music while Jimmy sang,

I want to go back to the island,
Where the shrimp boats tie up to the pilin'.
Give me oysters and beer for dinner every day of the year,
And I'll feel fine, I'll feel fine.

A man in a shark suit stumbled on his own tail, falling to the ground with his dance partner, colliding and taking two other couples with him. The crowd laughed and doused them with beer.

"I think I have an idea. Be right back," said Roachie as he split from the group, hopped up on the stage and approached the DJ.

"I thin maybe es tine for chu to go home," Chi Chi said to Bean who could hardly hear her due to the impact of the very large speakers just a few feet away. She was trying her best to be sympathetic but prudence wasn't exactly her forte. "I min, I dun thin chu es ever gonna fine chur papa now. An I thin maybe dat ain so bad. Maybe he es juss a asshole anyway like dat English guy on dat American Idol cho. I min chu know how dem famous peoples get. Maybe he dun even wanna know abou chu anyhow. Like I tells chu before, sungtines chu gotta be a angel and sungtines chu gotta be a asshole. Maybes chu gotta be ly me and mostly be a asshole causs chu ain't got nobody, juss like me. An den maybes chu forget all abou chur asshole papa."

"What?" said Bean.

"Ho chi mama," said Chi Chi, realizing her entire heatfelt offering had gone unheard.

Then suddenly the music stopped and DJ Mooch Daddy flipped on his microphone. "Helro out there. Risten up all roo Parrotheads. I have important announcement."

DJ Mooch Daddy was only a few years removed from Korea and was still mastering the English language, especially having a great deal of trouble with his Ls and Rs as well as a good bit of the rest of the alphabet. Most of the time he sounded more like Scooby Doo than a DJ but usually nobody cared because usually they were too drunk to notice.

All the parrotheads paused and the island grew silent except for the drunken shark on the ground who was still mumbling, "Fins to the left. Fins to the right and... fins... and... fin stuff..."

"Re have wery special guest," continued Mooch Daddy. "Light here in fwont of stage is Jimmy Buffett Jr. That light people that rhat I say. Jimmy Buffett Jr. come join us at our fessibal. Ret's all give big relcome to Jimmy Bean Buffett who come all the ray flom St. Augustine."

"What did he say?" Bean asked Chi Chi.

"Es chu askin' me? Huh, I dun know. Es sound li sung kina foreign chit to me."

Even though nearly every parrothead in the crowd knew just about everything there was to know about the famous singer, none of them were in a state of mind to remember that there was no known record of a James William Buffett Jr., alias Bean Buffett. However, in their current state of revelry just about any Buffett would do, and so they erupted into cheers and applause, pushing forward just to touch and be closer to any perceived amount of actual DNA derived from their idol and object of worship. After all, they were perhaps the most intensely dedicated parrotheads on the entire planet and Bean had just landed dead center into their private island roost. They formed around him, taking his hands, touching his hair, patting him on his back, and even hugging him. Bean's eyes widened with a combination of surprise and fear. One woman even offered him her body and in his most inexperienced way he determined it was a pretty nice body at that.

Not only had Bean never been in a crowd of so many people before, he had never known so much affection or admiration, especially all at once. And all he had done was show up. He kept backing away until his back bumped into the stage where he turned and climbed up to avoid and stand above the crowd. Seeing this, the crowd settled down and grew silent, waiting reverently as though they were at the Vatican waiting for the Pope to say something relevant that would make their day. A thousand people waiting for Bean Buffett to do or say… what? It was an eerie uncomfortable moment until from somewhere back within the mass of people came a distant voice that yelled, "Give us a song!"

The crowd nodded and mumbled in agreement, all of them assuming that if this was truly Jimmy's son then he would have no problem singing Jimmy's songs.

Standing next to DJ Mooch Daddy, Roachie assumed the same thing and leaned to inquire, "You got any Buffett karaoke?"

"Sure," answered Mooch Daddy. "Re alrays have a big karaoke contest on day two. Big part of fessibal."

"Day two?" asked Roachie.

"Day two," repeated Mooch Daddy the DJ. "It tree day fessibal remember? Then evlybody go home. You no know that?"

"Um, oh sure," said Roachie. "Um well, just throw something on cause Bean knows 'em all." Roachie was assuming a great deal. He actually didn't even know if Bean could sing. All he wanted to do was cheer him up and show him how lucky he was just to be alive and have friends.

"Yeah, give us a song," came another voice from the crowd.

Bean, obviously nervous as hell facing the biggest crowd of his life, looked down to Chi Chi for support. She offered an encouraging smile and nod of confidence in return which Bean wasn't sure was very encouraging. DJ Mooch Daddy placed a microphone on a stand in front of him who then turned and looked to Roachie who offered a thumb up and a sheepish smile. Then out of nowhere Fruitcake appeared at his feet. *Come on, you can do it big guy. I know you can*, thought Fruitcake.

"You really think so?" Bean asked, looking down at Fruitcake, his heart thumping wildly.

Fruitcake jumped for joy, elated that this time there was no question he and Bean were connected just as he and Sister Moonbeam-Goom-jigi had been. He started sounding off with his little bicycle horn bark so that the entire crowd could hear. His actions filled Bean with the confidence to give it a whirl. The crowd of parrotheads broke into applause.

Suddenly the music rose, the parrotheads grew silent, and the strum of a six-string was joined by a Hawaiian guitar. Bean immediately recognized the song and smiled. It was one of the songs Sister Moonbeam-Goom-jigi used to sing to him long ago when she put him to bed at night. Or at least she would sing part of it until she realized she couldn't remember the rest of it and would then put on the recording. Bean closed his eyes, remembering those tender moments and began to sing.

I really do appreciate the fact your sittin' here.
Your voice sounds so wonderful but your face don't
look so clear.

The crowd of parrotheads roared with approval and joined in as he sang the chorus.

So bar maid bring a pitcher, another round of brew,
Honey, why don't we get drunk and screw?

A broad smile spread over Bean's face and their overwhelming acceptance quickly wiped away, at least temporaily, the realization that he had once again failed to find his father. Roachie, relieved that his plan had worked, joined in, as did Fruitcake and even Chi Chi.

"Why dun we gets drunk and screws," sang Chi Chi as she watched but paid little attention to DJ Mooch Daddy behind his layout of technical gear. Mooch Daddy's face had grown serious as he eyed Bean and dialed his satellite phone.

Bean had won them over with a single song, each and every one of them, but it didn't stop there. His confidence now restored, he was quick to jump in on the next song that popped up, *Pencil Thin Mustache*, and again the crowd cheered and partied. As the night went on Bean realized there wasn't a single recorded song by Jimmy Buffett that he didn't have committed to memory thanks to Sister Moonbeam-Goom-jigi's dedication, and being he had never in his entire life actually listened to any other music or singer except for his very brief exposure to the Bob Robert's Society Band at the fruit stand and some Latin Salsa while in Miami and on the car radio, he had no trouble at all duplicating his famous estranged father to the most minute note and syllible. He even admired himself for doing so. Bean was fast succombing to that strange emotional high and deceptive feeling of entertainer Godliness that encompasses sports idols, rock stars, and presidents like Obama. He suddenly had dreams of filling stadiums around the world with adoring crazed fans. Were it not for the coming of dawn the next day he may have been lost to that drug-like fantasy altogether. This, he concluded, was even better than the adulation he received after defeating the surf Nazis during hurricane Tyamekwa (pronounced *To-oa-mick-az*). Could anything this wonderful actually be this easy, he wondered.

chapter 19

Pirates in the Caribbean?

The warm Caribbean sun rose to find them everywhere, spread haphazardly around the island like a carpet of bodies mysteriously dropped from the sky, unconscious in a pooped out post party state of near comatose due to too much revelry, too much beer, too many margaritas, and too little night time to continue having more. It had been a very special first night at this particular Parrothead Festival because this time they actually had a Jimmy Buffett clone live on stage to enhance the celebration. On this morning, the beginning of day two, the nearly one-thousand parrotheads rested in an undignified stooper and dreamed of more fun to come.

Among the many exoticly dressed and undressed bodies there lay our intrepid searchers as deeply passed out as the rest of the tribe. Roachie, asleep and hugging a palm tree, had somehow managed to come by a grass skirt, Hawaiian shirt, and a foam parrothead head-dress. In his lap was an unconcious strange woman with a head full of feathers and a permanently fixed smile. Chi Chi lay unconscious as well. She had managed to get her face painted in an assortment of tropical colors along with the rest of her body that was left exposed by her shorts and the coconut shells on her chest. Somehow she had managed to confiscate the plastic blow-up Corona beer sea plane which now rested on her head, deflated. Fruitcake had discovered the free hamburger booth and managed to use the influence of his increasingly powerful mental telepathy to subliminally convince the chef to continuously drop burger patties on the ground throughout the night. Or so he thought. Truth was the chef was drunk as a skunk and as a result had become spatula challenged. Fruitcake was now passed out on his back, balls to the morning sun, with a satisfied bloated gut full of burgers and wearing a doggy shirt that sported a picture of Kermit the frog and the words *Caribbean Amphibian,* which meant that somewhere in the festival crowd was another four legged creature passed out shirtless. Apparently it was a milestone night for all of our wayward travelers.

Among the singing tropical birds, the soft rustle of the ocean breeze flowing through the tall palms, and the repetitive crashing of the nearby surf, there came the sound of whispers and soft footsteps moving cautiously among the living dead parrotheads. Suddenly the serene tropical morning symphony was shattered by the earsplitting violent repeat of shots fired from a Russian AK47 assault rifle. A thousand severely hungover parrotheads groaned in unison.

Then someone yelled in Spanish, "Nadie se mueve o le tiraremos!" Meaning, "Nobody move or we will shoot you."

Everybody moved... and groaned... and moaned... and held their heads in pain. Someone crawled behind a bush and barfed. Those near him moaned in sympathy.

"DIJE, NADIE MOVIMIENTO O LE TIRAREMOS!" repeated the man who had fired the assault rifle into the air. This time he meant business and emphasized his repeated demand with another burst of gun fire over the heads of the physically pathetic all-night parrothead partiers, but the result was the same, more moans and groans and throbbing heads as well as another dry heave from behind the bushes.

"El don't le entiende estúpido. Son todos los Americanos," scolded a woman standing next to the man who fired the weapon. Meaning, "They don't understand you stupid. They are all Americans."

"Oh," said the bad-ass guy. "Dunt nobody moof or I gonna choots chu," he yelled in his best English. He then pulled the trigger to fire off another round of shots but the result was just a subtle click because the clip of the weapon was empty. Embarrassed, he quickly ejected it and reloaded with a full one.

The single click roused Bean from a deep sleep, where he was lying, his body covered with lipstick and phone numbers, dreaming of rock star fame and glory. He smiled, stretched and opened his eyes to find the business end of no less than four AK47s pointing directly at his head. Each time he moved they came closer.

The men holding the weapons were all serious, rugged, mean looking dudes, dark tanned and sweaty with a three or four day dark stubble, dirty long black hair, and obvious dark intentions. They even smelled bad, like a combination of sardines, garlic, and cheap whiskey. Machetes hung at their sides like simatars, and knives and pistols hung from their broad leather belts or shoulder holsters or both.

One particular dark mean looking man had a brown leather patch over his left eye with a nasty two inch scar just below in the shape of an upside down Nike symbol. A large tattoo of Donald Duck also wearing a patch over one eye and with a cutlass in each hand could be seen on the man's bare chest behind his bandoleer of ammo clips. On his right arm was a tattoo proclaiming *Rambo Rules,* bordered in blood and underlined with a facsimile of Rambo's famous all purpose survival knife, an exact copy of which hung from his belt. On his left arm were tattoos of Donald Duck's nephews, Huey, Dewey, and Louie, each making an obscene jesture with their middle finger. On his head he sported a well worn dirty old ball cap that said *Planet Hollywood* on the front. His name was Oswaldo but his fellow pirates referred to him as *El Carnicero Feliz* (the happy butcher) because he always laughed when he killed his victims.

"Morning, gringo," Oswaldo said to Bean through a fiendish smile that revealed two gold teeth next to a space where there were two teeth missing.

"Oh chit," Chi Chi said to Roachie. "Pirates."

"Pirates. Are you serious?" replied Roachie as he quickly sat up, dropping the strange feather-headed woman to the ground.

Pirates, thought Fruitcake. *Oh no! Are you serious? What's a pirate?*

Bean smiled nervously, "Oh, um… Good morning."

Are those guns? Do they have guns? Do pirates come in fat size? Can we go home now? thought a very nervous Fruitcake.

Back in Key West Father Sabatino had poked around the marina and inquired around what seemed like half the town of Key West before he finally found one of Captain Boon's other PT boat crewmen and persuaded him (the *New Jersey* way) to spill the beans. What he got was a strange story about some mysterious island where diehard Jimmy Buffett fans known as Parrotheads gather once a year for an extreme three day festival. For the most part they were wealthy or otherwise important people, who couldn't be known or seen as whacked out crazed fans of a rock star without endangering their highbrow social, corporate, or governmental status which would in turn affect their livelihoods. In their everyday social circles they had to tow the line of responsibility, respectability, and dignity, and couldn't afford being labeled eccentric or extremists who might be too blissfully mired or vulnerable to, or influenced by, pop culture. But for three days each year on *Parrothead Island* at their private pagan festival they could let it all hang out and live all the carefree Buffett experience they could possibly imagine or could endure. They arrived by boat, float plane, and helicopter; swarming over the four square mile island like flies to road kill, all voluntarily overdosing on three days of unparalleled, unabridged, unscrutinized fun and festivities. It was their own exclusive regular annual Woodstock, Caribbean style, which included everything they could imagine or associate with their musical object of worship and affection except for the man himself who, oddly enough, was never invited for the simple reason he would draw too much attention and compromise both the secret island and their annual festival.

This all sounded kind of ridiculous to Father Sabatino who never really concerned himself with what other people thought of him. If for example, he said he liked Frank Sinatra and anyone expessed their displeasure with his opinion, he would simply deal with them right there on the spot, the *New Jersey* way. And as for the reason all those society types gathered incognito on their little island each year, Father Sabatino thought that was a little ridiculous as well. After all, he thought, who were they all trying to hide their secret parrothead activities from if not from each other? Father Sabatino simply never could make sense of what he referred to as that Whitebread Crowd.

Father Sabatino was doing his best to hold down his breakfast as his shanghaied crewman steered the confiscated small cabin cruiser, Captain Nemo's *Lost & Found*, toward the island. As boating goes it was pretty much smooth running, just a normal cruise on a normal sea, but Father Sabatino, being a lifelong city dweller that spent his entire existence on asphalt and concrete that never moved, didn't quite see or feel it that way. He was sea sick and at first blamed it on the crewman piloting the boat. He seriously considered putting a bullet in the boat pilot's head until he realized that wasn't a wise thing to do because he had no idea where the hell he was or what to do with a boat on the ocean. Oceans, thought Father Sabatino, were for dumping New Yorks garbage by the barge full and bodies without noses and making cool WWII movies with big Navy ships and submarines, not for 32 foot cabin cruisers that bobbed around making life difficult for city boys who had trouble keeping down their cookies. He even thought about turning around and heading back to Key West, but knowing they were half way to their destination he decided that wouldn't improve his situation or achieve his mission. He was stuck there, sea sick and out of control and about to hurl and there wasn't a damn thing he could do about it. It was the worst he had ever felt in his entire life. Even worse, he thought, than when he was 12 years old and stole a quart bottle of Seagrams whiskey from MacFinny's liquor store and drank the whole damn thing after eating a half pound of his grandmother's gnocchi. In fact he felt so bad now that for a brief moment he even considered putting a bullet through his own head just to end the misery.

"Like I'm some kind of..." he tried to say as the boat rocked and rose with a wave and his breakfast dropped and swirled in his stomach. He was fast growing pale, clammy, and getting weaker.

"Like I'm some kind of damn babysi..." he tried to say again as the boat rocked and dropped down over the wave and his breakfast rose and swirled in his stomach. He was quickly going from warm and clammy to breaking into a full cold sweat.He was determined not to be a victim of the sea, to not let a simple thing like a ride in a little boat get the best of him and turn him into a sniveling barfing fool. But it was a losing endeavor.

"Like I'm... Like... I'm... Oh... Oh shit," he said, just before he leaned over the side and hurled. It was one of those disgusting, foul tasting, continuous, uncontrollable, wretched, rank, regurgitations that included everything within the human body that wasn't attached to something, and maybe some things that were. The kind of hurl that impels a man to realize he is the most inconsequential organism in the entire universe and inspires him to yearn for death, yet leaving him too helpless to make it happen or even request it from another.

On Parrothead Island all the parrotheads had been rounded up by the pirates and herded to the clearing in front of the stage where Mooch Daddy the DJ directed them to surrender all their booty. It wasn't a difficult process since most all of them were in a state where they probably would have surrendered their entire fortunes just for a glass of water and two Alka-Seltzers. Into an empty Land Shark beer box went all their valuables as it was carried around to each of them by the smiling one-eyed Donald Duck henchman with the gold teeth. Watches, wallets, money, jewels, and everything of value went into the box, including the last of Bean's cash and the pre-paid credit card he was given by Uncle Albert.

After the booty was collected Bean was separated from the others and tied to a tree while Mooch Daddy and the leader of the pirates along with the boss pirate's girlfriend were in conference. The subject of their discussion was James William "Bean" Buffett Jr. and the ransom they could get for him from James William Buffett Sr., the rich and famous singer.

Mooch Daddy the private party DJ for hire was formerly a Private by the name of Kwang Ho in the North Korean Army until he deserted and escaped from North Korea three years ago. The three main reasons he deserted were, 1; he had taken a real liking to the American rock & roll he used to hear coming from the GI barracks across the minefield on the DMZ where he always pulled guard duty, 2; he never really quite got the hang of that goose-stepping marching thing because he thought it looked silly and felt abnormal, and 3; he had let slip that he thought the "Dear Leader" North Korean communist dictator Kim Jong-il was an effeminate transvestite midget who should be skewered and used for squid bait. Kwang Ho had been casually digging an escape tunnel to South Korea for seven months and had only 49 feet left to go when he heard that he had been put on Kim Jong-il's shit list and was destined for a life of torture, starvation, hard labor… or death. Knowing he wouldn't have time to complete his escape tunnel and knowing that Kim Jong-il's secret police were only 10 minutes away from arresting him, he quickly developed a plan B for his escape.

It was once said (probably somewhere in Asia) that there is wisdom in simplicity. Obviously not a philosophy applied in most Asian alphabets but certainly applied by Kwang Ho with the plan he quickly devised that night; a plan that was certainly simple and wise, if not genius. In desperation, Kwang Ho meandered up to the North Korean main guard hut near the bridge that led across the DMZ to South Korea. There he darted into the restroom, stripped completely naked, burst out and ran past the North Korean communist guards and across the bridge like a crazed orangatang with rabies waiving his arms wildly in all directions, all the while screaming the only English phrases he knew, phrases he had learned from a song he heard drift across the DMZ mine field almost every night.

Hey Mamma, look at me!
I'm on my way to the promised land!
I'm on the highway to hell,
And I'm going down,
All the way down.
I'm on the highway to hell!

Those were the song lyrics he screamd as he ran toward the American and South Korean guards, except when Kwang Ho yelled the words from the heavy metal AC/DC song it sounded a little more like,

*"HEY MOMMA, ROOKAT ME! I ON MY RAY TO
PLOMISED RAND! I ON HIGHRAY TO HELL. AND I
GONNA DOWN, ALL RAY DOWN. I ONNA HIGHRAY
TO HELL! AHHHHHHHHHHHHHHHHHHHHHHH!"
PLEA NO SHOOT! PLEA NO SHOOT! PLEA NO
SHOOT! PLEA NO SHOOT! PLEA NO SHOOT!"*

The sight of a wild naked man sprinting across the
bridge screaming lyrics to *Highway to Hell* was just too
much for the guards from both countries on both sides of
the DMZ to mentally process in time to properly react.
Protocal required them to shoot the naked idiot dead. By the
time they recovered from the shock of the sight of him and
decided to take action, Kwang Ho had long disappeared into
the night and was halfway to Seoul, South Korea where he
made arrangements to be shipped out of the country in a
container full of digital cameras and blu-ray DVD players
destined for a Wal-Mart central distribution center in the
U.S.A.

Kwang Ho, alias Mooch Daddy, now passes as a part
time DJ for hire from Miami. The rest of the time he is a
marginally successful half-ass hustler and slimeball with
connections to lots of other slimeballs around the islands.
On this particular occasion he had jumped at the
opportunity to pull off the ultimate slimeball crime with the
help of a band of pirates he met in Belize when he was
tryng to marry a 78 year old rich widow who died at the
alter before she could say *I do*. The pirates he was now in
cahoots with were led by a man who went by the handle of
Capitan Errol but whose real name was Alajo Alajo Alajo.
Their original plan was just to rob the parrotheads but that
changed when a jewel of an opportunity in the form of Bean
Buffett fell into their laps.

Alajo Alajo Alajo was a Mexican revolutionary turned
pirate because he sucked as a revolutionary. His girlfriend,
Bertha, had convinced Alajo Alajo Alajo there was no

future in the revolutionary business because the Mexican drug cartels were too much competition, and she was right. She was also smart enough to know that even when you are victorious in a Mexican revolution it always results in your getting assassinated in somebody else's revolution or by your most trusted friend, or by one of the drug cartels.

Alajo Alajo Alajo was the illegitimate son of a hotel maid in Cartagena, Colombia named Lucinda who fell in love with a traveling salesman named Alajo. Alajo the traveling salesman did what traveling salemen always do when he lied, romanced, and impregnated the lovely but naïve young hotel maid and then left town. Lucinda was so incensed with Alajo's desertion of her that when their baby boy was born she named him Alajo Alajo Alajo so that everywhere her son would go in Columbia everyone would know that Alajo was Alajo Alajo Alajo's father. To Lucinda this made complete sense but for her boy it was a curse because no one would ever take him seriously, always accusing him of having three of the same names because he was too stupid to remember just one. And of course, everyone had no problem at all remembering the *bastard* kid, eventually the man, with the same three names. They would always say, "There goes Alajo Alajo Alajo, the dumb bastard with three same names." Actually the three names were all a wasted effort anyway because little did Lucinda the hotel maid know that Alajo Alajo Alajo's father's real name was not Alajo at all. It was Ralph.

All this made Alajo Alajo Alajo a bitter and vengeful person which was not good because Alajo Alajo Alajo wasn't really smart enough to back up his rage and was almost always getting in trouble with the powers that be, whether they be legitimate or criminal or, as is often the case in Colombia, legitimately criminal. This brought Alajo Alajo Alajo to the attention of Hugo Chavez in neighboring Venezuela who considered Alajo Alajo Alajo to have the perfect personality profile, motivation, and individual drive to start a revolution in Mexico. It seems Chavez, the self consumed dictator of Venezuela, is fast outgrowing his little oil blessed domain and has designs on most all of Latin America, not to mention Las Angeles, Pheonix, Albuquerque, and Dallas. So Hugo Chavez recruited Alajo Alajo Alajo, gave him a hundred-thousand U.S. dollars, 500 Russian AK47 assault rifles freshly minted in his new arms factory built for him by the Russians, and promised him 72 Muslim virgins and a General's commission when the job was finished. It was a lucrative deal, one that even the marginally intelligent Alajo Alajo Alajo couldn't turn down.

Three months later Alajo Alajo Alajo found himself sitting in an open-air adobe bar at an obscure dusty crossroads in the Mexican desert with no money and no revolution and no revolutionary army. Most of his mercenary army deserted as soon as they got their first paycheck because they had no faith in their leader or his undefined cause, and because they wanted to get home in time to watch the World Cup of Soccer. Then Alajo Alajo Alajo lost the rest of the revolutionary funds in a poker game to some traveling salesman named Ralph. It didn't actually matter however, because it was apparent that the people of Mexico had already been through so many revolutions that they didn't really care for another, preferring the more subtle tasteful graft and political coups of modern times which didn't interrupt their siestas. So after raiding a goat farm, seizing a town of only 11 people, and capturing a single over-the-hill semi-retired alcoholic overweight Mexican Federale named Paco who had no intention of resisting in the first place, Alajo Alajo Alajo's revolution was a total flop. Not to mention the fact that the revolutionary mantra of *Viva Le Alajo Alajo Alajo!* didn't exactly roll off the tongue with ease or lend itself conveniently to spray paint graffiti, and was not likely to catch on any time soon.

So there he sat discouraged, crying in his cerveza, and trying to decide his future while his girlfriend Bertha, who he had kidnapped from the goat farm, hounded him into changing professions. Bertha was no fool. She read People Magazine and TV Guide and had seen old Errol Flynn movies when she visited her grandmother in Bacanora. So Bertha had all the answers. Bertha decided they would sell off most of the guns to the drug lords and use the money as a start-up investment to get into the pirate business. She was convinced that pirating was the quickest way to get a lot of money and Alajo Alajo Alajo was definitely going to need a lot of money because Bertha was high maintenance and had big dreams. Bertha wanted a canary yellow 1960 Chevy convertible with wire wheels and a Bose sound system for her Ricky Martin CD collection, and Bertha wanted to possess no less than three Wal-Mart credit cards, and as if all that wasn't enough, Bertha wanted to live in Beverly Hills. Alajo Alajo Alajo took Bertha's demands quite seriously because Bertha was without a doubt the most luscious, most voluptuous, most beautiful, most sensuous, and most passionate Latina woman he had ever bedded, therefore all things considered there was no alternative to Bertha's desires and demands. And so Alajo Alajo Alajo and his remaining revolutionary army of eight men turned to piracy. To seal the deal Alajo Alajo Alajo, the Venezuelan backed Colombian failed Mexican revolutionary, changed his title to - *Capitan Errol, Pirate and Terror of the Seven Seas,* which in reality consisted of only the Caribbean.

On Parrothead Island Capitan Errol and Bertha and Mooch Daddy were in a heated discussion over just how much money they were going to demand from Jimmy Buffett in exchange for their captive Bean Buffet. Bertha wanted money, millions, and wasn't particular as to an exact figure as long as the word million remained plural. Capitan Errol wanted to ask for a big new boat and an unlimited Capital One credit card. It seems Capitan Errol always had a bit of a problem grasping the concept of consumerism, especially unlawful consumerism. Mooch Daddy thought $10,000 and a full collection of autographed Jimmy Buffett CDs was a reasonable demand but then Mooch Daddy was still thinking in North Korean economic terms where the local currency is totally worthless and the U.S. dollar goes a long, long way. As far as the other eight revolutionaries-turned-pirates were concerned, they really didn't give a damn because they didn't like soccer and had no lofty ambitions about riches and creature comforts. They were too busy fantasizing about what they were going to do with all those hot half-naked parrothead chicks. Ravaging the women was what they always considered the best part of being a pirate. These were practical bird in hand kind of guys who realized that what they had, such as a Land Shark beer box full of booty and a bunch of hot parrothead women, was far better than what they usually get from most of Errol and Bertha's diabolical screw ups, so they decided to just cling to their guns and crotches until the big three brains finished arguing.

"Hokay Mucho Doggy, now chu makes da call sose we can get some millions of moneys," demanded Bertha.

"Mooch Daddy," corrected Mooch Daddy.

"No estúpido. Chu no gonna call churself, chu gonna calls the Chimmy Buffett rich gringo," said Bertha.

"I mean, it's *Mooch Daddy* not Mucho Doggy," said Mooch Daddy. "When you say Mucho Doggy you got it long."

"*Long*? Wha da hell chu talkin' abou? I said *Chimmy Buffett*. Es chu gonna calls dat Chimmy Buffet dude or wha?"

"How chu gonna calls heem?" asked Capitan Errol.

"On phone," said Mooch Daddy as he pulled the satellite phone from his belt.

"Es chu got hees phone numbers?"

"No."

"So how es chu gonna calls heem?" asked Capitan Errol.

Capitan Errol wasn't very sharp when it came to today's technology. Even though he had a GPS system on his big beautiful stolen boat the pirates spent a great deal of time lost at sea but they were often fortunate enough to bump into islands or other boats which presented the opportunity to do what pirates do.

"Yeah Mucho, chu dun gots hees phone numbers," said Bertha. "How es chu gonna calls heem?"

"*Mooch* dammit," corrected Mooch Daddy. "Not Mucho. I call information and I show you. You know, information, huh? Helro."

"Wha for chu gonna calls information? Dun chu know chour own nem?" said Bertha.

"Sure I know my name," answered Mooch Daddy. "It Kwang Ho."

"Kwang Ho. Who da hell es Kwang Ho?" said Capitan Errol.

"Me," said Mooch Daddy.

"But chu sase chu was Mucho Doggy," said Bertha. "If chu ain Mucho Doggy and chu sung kina Kwang Ho den maybe chu ain who chu sase chu es an we no can trust chu."

Bertha pulled a U.S. Army surplus .45 automatic from her belt and, BANG, shot Mooch Daddy dead in the heart.

"Icarumba! Look at dat. Chu chooted heem," said Capitan Errol. "Now wha we gonna do?"

Nearby one of the pirates pulled some cash out of his pocket, separated a twenty and reluctantly surrendered it to the pirate standing next to him who accepted it with a knowing smile.

"See," he said as he took the money. "I toll chu she would choot dat leetle chink guy. She dunt like no complications."

"So I thin maybe we better no make no complications, huh," replied the pirate who lost the bet.

They both laughed and returned their attention to evaluating the breasts of various parrotheads.

Bertha bent down and relieved Mooch Daddy of his satellite phone and handed it to Capitan Errol.

"Wha chu whan me to do weeth dis?"

"Make da calls," said Bertha.

"I dunt know hees numbers," said Capitan Errol.

"Call information," said a voice from the group of captives.

They turned to find Roachie sitting nearby with the group of parrotheads.

"Call information like that Kwang guy said. You can get someone's phone number from the information service."

"Chu know how to calls this information thing?" asked Capitan Errol.

"Sure. You just dial 411 and ask for the number of the person you want to call," said Roachie.

"Chu wan me to choots heem?" asked Bertha, raising the .45 and pointing it at Roachie whose eyes nearly doubled in size. "Maybe I juss choots heem causs hees a smart ass gringo."

"Hees no a gringo. Hees a black guy," said Capitan Errol.

"Well, hees talks ly a gringo. I gonna choots heem."

"He can no help it. Das how dey makes the black guys talk in da U.S. Dey no let dem talk no African no more. Diddent chu see dat Roots moofy?"

"Honest," said a very nervous and desperate Roachie. "411. Just try it."

Capitan Errol stared at Roachie suspiciously for a long moment, thinking this could be some sort of trick, then decided to give it a try. He dialed 411 and waited.

"Information," said the voice of a woman on the other end of the line. "Your call may be recorded so that we may monitor and insure quality service to all our most gracious customers. How may I help you today please?"

She was speaking English but the voice sounded odd, even to Capitan Errol. That was because the lady on the other end was a Rajasthani Indian speaking from somewhere in Calcutta… India.

"Information?" asked Capitan Errol.

"Yes please, this is information. How may I help you?"

"Um… I need a phone numbers. Can chu gets me a phone numbers?"

"What number would you like, please sir?"

"Chimmy Buffett," said Errol.

"*Jimmy. Jimmy* Buffett," corrected Roachie loud enough for the information operator on the phone to hear.

Bertha quickly threatened him with her .45, "Hey chu. Chu chut up."

"Jimmy Buffett, sir?" asked the woman. "Please, what city is Jimmy Buffett sir?"

"What?"

"I say, what city does Jimmy Buffett live in, please thank you sir?"

"U.S.A.," said Capitan Errol.

"Yes please. That is not a city, kind sir. That is a country of the United States of America."

"I know es a country. I need da numbers in da country."

"There may be more than one Jimmy Buffett in the United States of America, sir. Where does your Jimmy Buffett live please sir thank you?"

"More den one. I know es more den one. I know dat causs I gots one wi'me righ now."

"Oh, he is with you right now, sir?"

"Ches, he es right here. I lookin' at heem."

"Does not he know his phone number, please thank you sir?" asked the Rajasthani information lady.

"I dunt know. Wait a minutes," said Capitan Errol as he turned to Bean. "Hey kid, doos chu know chur papa's phone numbers?"

Bean shrugged his shoulders, "No sir."

"No, he dunt know," said Capitan Errol into the phone.

"Oh, I understand sadly, sir. Please does he know what city, please sir thank you sir?"

"Hey kid, doos chou know where's chour papa lif?"

Bean shook his head no.

"What? How comes chu dunt know chur own papa's phone numbers an wheres he lif?" asked Capitan Errol.

"I never met him," answered Bean.

"Oh. Das too bad. Hey, chu know wha. I ain never met my papa too. My papa he run away efen before I wass a leetle nino. Some day I gonna finds heem and I thin maybe I gonna choots heem. Are chu gonna choots your papa if chu finds heem? If chu gonna choots heem chu make chure chu choots heem real good juss in case he..."

"Do you know the city, please sir?" interrupted the information lady.

"Wha... oh um... hell no I'n not knowin' da city and I dunt know da numbers. Das why I calls chu, lady. I need hees numbers causs I dunt know hees numbers. Chu know wha I min?"

"I am showing many Jimmy Buffett phone listings in the United States of America, sir. Which number would you like, please thank you."

"Um... juss gimmi da one on top," said Capitan Errol, assuming that the richest and most important Jimmy Buffett would be listed first.

"Would you like me to connect you, please sir?"

"Chure hokay, chu can connects me," said Capitan Errol.

"One moment sir while I connect you to the party to which you are choosing to speak. It is always a pleasure to be of service kind sir please thank you. Please thank you for your patience and most gracious consideration. Your connection is a success. You are now connected. You may continue to your desired communication now please sir thank you good day."

Capitan Errol smiled triumphantly, having just conquered this great technical hurdle and anticipating a rich comfortable life in Beverly Hills with Bertha and her yellow 1960 Chevy Impalla with wire wheels.

The connection was made and a phone on the other end rang.

"J. J. Buffett's Plumbing and Mechanical," answered a deep voice.

"Es dis Chimmy Buffett?"

"That's right. J. J. Buffett here. What can I do for ya?"

"I gots chur kid," said Capitan Errol.

"What? You got what?"

"I sase I gots chur kid, gringo."

"What kid?" asked J.J. Buffett.

"Chure kid. I gots chur kid. Hees a preesoner and I gots heem and if chu wants heem back den chu gotta half to pay me two millions of dollars. If chu dunt pay den Bertha she gonna choots heem."

"What's this some kind of damn joke. I ain't got no kids. Hey Larry is that you? Are you messin' with me again. What I tell ya about messin' around when you're on the clock? Listen man, just because I creamed your ass bowling last Tuesday night… Well, hey man, tell ya what. I'll give ya a chance for some pay-back, okay? We'll go again Friday night and I'll give ya a second chance, okay? Loser buys the beer, okay? Now quit messin' around with that phony Chicano accent and get that old lady's toilet fixed so we can pay some bills around here."

The phone went dead with a click and buzz followed by silence.

"Wha heem sase," asked Bertha.

"Heem sase he es busy workin' but he wanna go bowlin' on Friday," answered Capitan Errol.

"Wha?" said Bertha.

About that same time Father Sabatino arrived at the island on Captain Nemo's cabin cruiser the *Lost & Found.* He was still in a cold sweat and weakened and his mood was less than cheerful. He decided someone was going to pay for his less than comfortable voyage, but just who and how he wasn't quite sure. In his current state of mind he wasn't particular and he was even considering reinstating his trademark habit of collecting noses as he angrily made his way through the tropical underbrush to where he expected to find only a bunch of screwed up overpaid fun loving whitebread parrotheads.

"Like I'm some kind of damn babysitter," he mumbled under his breath. "First I gotta get sick and retch on a boat and now I gotta sneak around in a damn jungle like Tarzan, like some damn monkey man. It better be worth it. It better damn well be worth it. Ya hear me Albert? It damn well better be worth it."

What Father Sabatino discovered as he sneaked about and peered through the dense growth were a thousand very strange looking hung-over people with their hands above ther heads sitting in a cluster on the ground like a heard of sick cattle. On occasion one of them would just pass out and fall to the ground; others simply leaned against each other because it was all they could do to just sit up. At first he thought they were in some sort of trance or involved in some kind of religious cult ritual. Following closer scrutiny and after seeing a man in a shark suit turn away from the rest and barf on another man dressed as a parrot, he realized that the entire bunch were actually in a post stoned stupor. Either that or they had all eaten three-day-old sushi. He also noticed roving among them was a hand full of threatening degenerates with assault weapons and machetes that seemed to be very interested in some of the lesser dressed parrothead women. Father Sabatino who has a natural nose for danger, wasted no time determining there was something wrong with this picture. Then he spyed Bean sitting near the stage tied to a palm tree and the obvious object of an intense heated discussion between an armed man and woman who seemed to be running the show. At Bean's feet he could see the body of a little oriental guy with beer cans growing out of his hat and a bloody hole in his chest which prompted Father Sabatino to pull out his Coonan 357 Magnum Automatic. "Well, well, what the hell do we have here?" he mumbled to himself.

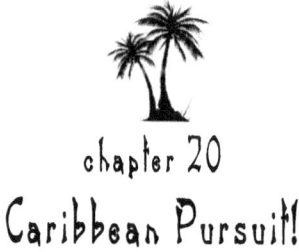

chapter 20
Caribbean Pursuit!

"Wha da hell chu min dat gringo wanna go bowlin' on Friday?" asked an angry Bertha.

"I dunt know. Das juss wha heem sase. Heem sase dat heem ain got no kid an heem wanna go bowlin'... on Friday," replied Capitan Errol. "I thin maybe hees no tellin' da truth. I thin maybe hees a cheep gringo who dunt wanna pay no monies for hees kid and maybe das why heem leff da kid when da kid wass juss a niño."

"I thin dat gringo need a bullet in hees head es wha I thin buh first I whan hees monies," said an angry Bertha. "I thin chu better calls heem back some more."

"But heem dun wanna talk. Heem juss wanna go bowlin'," argued Capitan Errol. "An I dunt know nothing bout no bowlin'."

Since their rude awakening by the pirates, Fruitcake had been nervously pacing back and forth, in and out from under the protection of the stage, partially hidden while wracking his brain in an effort to decide whether to run and hide or stand by his friends and probably die. Though he saw no fat men with guns he did hear the shots, saw the pirates with guns, and unfortunately witnessed the demise of Mooch Daddy. It was then and there Fruitcake decided that being Sam Slade Ace Detective, cunning man of action and courage, was actually a fictitous crock of shit.

Run or die? Run or die? Run or die, thought a desperate Fruitcake. *Where's the house? Where's the house? Where's my damn papa-san chair?*

Just as Fruitcake was about to take refuge under the stage again and possibly out the other side of the stage and into and through the bush to the beach to make a swim for the nearest continent, he saw a man dash out from behind a tree, club a pirate on the head with a big gun and drag him back into the bushes. All of it done so quickly that it wasn't even noticed by any of the other pirates, and the parrotheads who witnessed it were too far hungover to care. On the edge of the clearing where the *Happy Butcher* Oswaldo was about to fondle a terrified female parrothead, the mysterious man popped out again, cracked Oswaldo on the head and dragged him away. Fruitcake immediately recognized the man as the cheeseburger thief he had bitten in Miami and quickly decided everthing was getting a little too serious, mysterious, and complicated for him to deal with so he ran for safety. He ran until he reached the dock at the cove where Captain Purdy Boon had dropped them off. There he saw Captain Nemo's cabin cruiser and seeing the boat he put a few facts together, helping him to realize the cheeseburgler must be an ally of some kind and that the cheeseburgler's bonking bad guys on the head was a good thing. The enemy of my enemy is my friend deduced Fruitcake, even if this enemy of my enemy was a cheeseburgler.

Fruitcake became inspired. Regaining his faith in the Sam Slade philoshophy of heroism, he began to formulate a plan and returned to the scene of the crime in progress. His plan was to try his best to pretend he was just a dog, though he was not fully confident he could pull it off. After all, he thought, if most people were going to treat him like a dog just because he was short, hairy, and had a couple extra legs, and for some reason they sometimes actually thought he was a dog then why not pretend to be one. But Fruitcake had never really spent a lot of time with dogs other than the ones he saw in the waiting room once a year at the doctor's office where they would stick that cold thing up his ass.

And those dogs at the doctor's office, he recalled, just sat there and scratched, none of them ever striking up a conversation allowing him to judge their intellect or character or if they liked pickles the same as he did. Therefore not quite sure how dogs behaved he simply assumed that, compared to himself, most dogs were just stupid animals.

Returning to his friends, Fruitcake wandered around stupidly, sniffing, pausing and pissing, and hoping his newly acquired Kermit the Frog Caribbean Amphibian shirt wouldn't give him away. Once he worked his way behind the tree to which Bean was tied, and he was out of the sight of Capitan Errol and Bertha, he began chewing on the rope tied around Bean's wrist, all the while letting him know his plan.

We're going to make a run for it, thought Fruitcake to Bean. *Wait until I make my move and then grab the guys and run for the dock. There's a boat there.*

"A boat?" said Bean.

Well sure, you don't think we can swim for it do ya, thought Fruitcake, forgetting that he was going to try and do that very thing only minutes before.

"But what about all these people?" asked Bean.

Don't worry. There's somebody here to help them, thought Fruitcake.

"Oh, okay," said Bean.

"Hey chu. Who da hell es chu talkin' to?" demanded Bertha, as she pointed her gun at Bean.

"Um… just… um… just my dog," said Bean, who in all of his 14 years had never learned how to lie. Not even to deadly pirates who were threatening to kill him.

"Wha dog es chu talking to?" asked Errol.

"Honk," came the sound of Fruitcakes pathetic bark from behind the tree. Quickly finishing off the knot on the rope, he again tried to portray a stupid dog as he wandered out to be seen by Errol and Bertha.

"Oh chit. Das a ugly perro," said Bertha.

"Es only gots one ear," observed Errol. "Why es only gots one ear?"

"I don't know," answered Bean as he felt the rope begin to give way. "He's just always been that way."

Fruitcake let out a few more cute little honks and pranced about trying to be as cute and stupid as he could to draw Capitan Errol and Bertha's attention away from Bean. He at first approached Bertha who immediately pointed her gun at him, warning him away. He freaked and involuntarily raised his leg and pissed. Fruitcake then tried to appeal to Errol both mentally and theatrically.

Look at me moron. I'm just a cute little stupid dog. Don't you think I'm just a cute little stupid dog? I'm going to jump up now, thought Fruitcake as he jumped knee high in front of Errol.

"Icarumba, I thin maybe dat cute leetle thin es just a stupid dog. Look hees gonna jump up. I thin maybe hees ly me," said Errol.

"I gonna choot it," said Bertha.

"Why chu wanna choot it?" asked Errol.

"Cause es a stupido perro an es only gots one ear," reasoned Bertha. "I gonna put it outta hees misery."

Fruitcake's heart leapt into his throat. He thought only fat guys shot dogs. Now he has to worry about beautiful Mexican women pirates too and this one's already got a gun. His increased heartbeat threw his brain into high gear. *No no,* thought Fruitcake as hard as he could think. *Chu no gonna choot dis cute leetle stupid dog!*

"I thin hees tryin to jump in my arms," observed Errol as he slung his weapon over his shoulder. "Dunt chu thin he es a cute leetle dog?"

Das right. Es juss a cutes leetle dog, thought Fruitcake in as much Spanish as he could conjure.

"I gonna choot it," replied Bertha.

Fruitcake repeated his thought with even more intensity like he was pulling off some kind of Jedi mind trick, something he recalled from the only movie he had ever seen. The movie his first master, a very old man, was watching in the nursing home where he lived. The old man died just before a big gross thing called Jabba the Hut appeared on the screen and scared the shit out of the very young Fruitcake. After Jabba the Hut and the old man's death Fruitcake decided to beat feet and hit the road, later to be found by Sister Moonbeam-Goom-jigi where he was bumming French fries and licking up dropped ice cream in the parking lot at the Dairy Queen.

Chu no gonna choot dis cute leetle stupid dog! thought Jedi Fruitcake.

"No no, I no gonna choot dis leetle guy," said Bertha, who was immediately confused by her quick reversal of intent.

Fruitcake was immediately relieved and growing more confident in his new ability to communicate with strangers, especially the stupid ones. Having dealt with the woman, he focused on the man and jumped again to be sure he could make the right height. With Capitan Errol stretching out his arms and smiling with delight at the little dog's antics, Fruitcake made his final leap straight into the pirate's crotch… teeth first! He clamped his jaws shut tighter than a hungry crocodile on a dinner mission, catching Errol's cahonies in as painful a circumstance as any man could possible imagine. So painful in fact that Capitan Errol could not even manage to scream and instead only managed to let loose with a pathetic helpless noise that sounded a great deal like squealing tires on asphalt.

"Ho chi mama!" exclaimed Chi Chi.

"Oh wow! Right in the gónadas!" said Roachie.

The other pirates along with most of the men in the group of hostage parrotheads groaned in painful empathy, including Father Sabatino who had just conked another of the roving pirates over the head.

Bertha's immediate response was to aim her gun at Fruitcake which wasn't a response that Errol, even with his limited intellect, thought was very wise, because Errol, even in his current state of severe pain was lucid enough to know what critical body parts might be in jeopardy if she actually pulled the trigger.

"¡NINGUÌN NO. DE NO! DON' ¡LANZAMIENTO DE T! DON' ¡LANZAMIENTO DE T! DON' LANZAMIENTO DE T!" squealed Captitan Errol. Meaning, NO NO NO! DUNT CHOOT! DUNT CHOOT! DUNT CHOOT!

At first Bean was taken aback by Fruitcake's surprising act of courage as well as imagining the pain it must have caused, then he snapped to and took advantage of the moment of confusion to yank his bindings loose, jump to his feet and throw a body block into Bertha that sent her crashing into Errol and sent the .45 pistol flying through the air.

"Come on!" Bean yelled to Roachie as he grabbed Chi Chi's hand, yanked her to her feet, and sprinted for the boat.

Bertha quickly recovered, snatched the AK-47 from Errol's shoulder and expertly aimed it at the escapees. She was determined to shoot Fruitcake first who with his pathetic little horn honk of a bark was fast catching up with the group. Just as she was about to pull the trigger a shot rang out, a bullet struck the weapon and careened it out of her hands. Surprised, she turned to discover she had just been shot at by... a parrothead priest? Before she could regain her senses the parrotheads screamed and rose to become a frightened and panic stricken mob running in all directions, trampling their pirate captors and even their would-be rescuer Father Sabatino.

"Shit," said Father Sabatino as he dodged the mass panic of the thousand oddly dressed parrotheads. "Like I'm... ouch! Shit! Hey, watch out! Shit!"

When Bean and company reached the boat they found its unwilling pilot tied and gagged.

"Who es chu?" asked Chi Chi as she untied him and removed the gag.

"Some guy made me…"

"Never dun chu mind," interrupted Chi Chi. "Chu juss get us outta here or we all gonna be dead!"

The man was quick to react and the confiscated cabin cruiser was soon cruising at full speed out of the cove and away from the island.

As they sped away Bertha arrived at the dock followed by a waddling Capitan Errol, both hands tenderly massaging his gónadas. Bertha managed to get off a single shot but the boat was now out of range.

"We no gonna let dose Gringos get away!" yelled an angry Bertha. "Get to da boat!"

It wasn't long after the cabin cruiser was in open water that they saw the pirate's high speed intercepter in pursuit.

"Who's that?" asked their pilot.

"Pirates," answered Roachie. "And they're not very nice."

"No kidding," said the pilot as he jammed the throttle forward. "There's no way we can out run them in this boat. They'll be on us in five minutes."

Roachie studied the pirate's boat closely. "There are only two of them. The woman and the dumb guy," he said.

"Maybe it juss be two of dem but dey gots guns," added Chi Chi. "Ho chi mama!"

The boat driver reached for the ship to shore radio to call for help.

They watched in despair as Errol and Bertha closed the distance between them, Bertha raising the assault weapon. She fired, the bullet tearing into the stern and killing their engine. She fired twice again with the same results. Then again, this time hitting the radio.

"Oh chit!" said Chi Chi.

Oh chit!, thought Fruitcake.

"Me too," said Bean as they all hit the deck.

Roachie suddenly found himself desiring a Yoo-hoo. For some reason he had become conditioned to want to drink Yoo-hoo during times of high anxiety like during high speed chases.

Just then a rapidly fired stream of bullets tore across the forward section of the pirate's boat sending Bertha back onto the deck, her weapon discharging wildly, just missing Errol standing at the helm. Another burst of automatic fire followed and ripped across their bow, and yet another killing the engine that began to smoke and sputter. Errol dove to the deck next to Bertha as their boat slowed then floundered.

"Wha wass dat comes from?" said Errol.

"I dunt know," said Bertha. "Get the gun and choots 'em!"

Errol grabbed the AK-47, popped his head up to find the source of the incoming rounds and then stood to take a shot, but another round of heavy fire ripped across their boat and he quickly dove back to the deck.

"I dunt thin so," he said as he handed the weapon to Bertha.

Bean and his companions aboard the *Lost & Found* looked to discover Captain Purdey Boon standing at the big fore-gun of his PT boat as it rumbled toward them. The cabin cruiser slowed and Captain Boon's PT pulled alongside. A crewman tossed them a rope, instructed them to rig for towing then helped them aboard. With the big duel guns of Purdy's boat trained on Errol and Bertha, the PT idled up and pulled away for Key West without further incident.

When Capitan Errol and Bertha peered out to sea, frustrated that their prize bounty had escaped, they suddenly realized their boat was sinking.

"Oh chits," said Capitan Errol.

"I toll chu I chouda choots dat ugly dog," said Bertha, just before she slapped him.

🌴

Okay, the jig is up, thought Fruitcake as he joined Captain Purdey Boon at the helm of his PT boat. *Time to come clean.*

They were nearing the marina at Key West and the crewman on board the *Lost & Found* had just detached from the PT boat when Captain Boon agreed with Fruitcake.

"Yeah, I guess you're right," replied Captain Boon, not realizing he was talking and listeneing to a dog. He took one hand from the wheel, pulled off his sunglasses, stripped away his mustache and goatee, turned to his passengers as he removed his hat and wig and said, "Looks like you folks had a pretty good time on that island."

They all stared in disbelief. The man at the helm and the man who had rescued them from a terible fate at the hands of deadly pirates, the man they all thought was Captain Purdey Boon was none other than their strange paranoid conspiracy freak, Boner Jones.

chapter 21
Gulf Coast Bound

"So, the son of a son of a son of a pirate saved us from pirates. That seems kind of incongruous doesn't it?" observed Roachie as a waitress placed their food on the table.

Boner nodded his head in agreement. "Never thought of it that way but I guess you're right," he replied as he dissected and inspected an onion ring. He popped it in his mouth and while chewing he added, "I been after those pirates for a long time. They were a disgrace to the profession."

"You left them stranded to maybe die out there. That wasn't very nice," said Bean who was busy looking at all the memorabilia that contributed to the ambiance of the Margaritaville Cafe. He was particularly taken by the record album covers on the wall next to their table that featured Jimmy Buffett's picture. They represented various stages in his career and somehow seemed to fill in missing years worth of memories Bean had missed out on. That is until a girl with red, green, and blue striped hair and so many tattoos that they blended with her camouflage print sleeveless tank top walked by. She took a seat at the bar, distracting Bean from both the walls and the conversation at the table.

"Yeah, buh hey Bean, dose dudes was bad peoples and dat Bertha bitch chee choots dat leetle Chinese Moocho guy," said Chi Chi. "An chee choots him dead an chee try to choots us too, even Fruitscakes."

Bean was still observing the girl with the striped hair as though she were some strange exotic animal in a zoo and barely heard Chi Chi's words.

"Oh, I didn't leave them to die. I called the Coast Guard. So all they had to do was avoid the sharks until they were picked up," assured Boner. "And the parrotheads too, the Coast Guard will find 'em… I guess."

Chi Chi looked to Boner suspiciously, "So Boner, do chu gots any other peoples inside chu dat we dun know abou?" asked Chi Chi. "Ly maybes chu es a guy wha wears a tight suit and can fly? An wha nem we gonna calls chu anyhow? Es chu Boner or Purdey or Nemo or wha?"

"You mean he was Captain Nemo too?" said a surprised Bean tuning back into the conversation after finally accepting the girl with the striped hair as an earthling.

You just now figuring that out? thought Fruitcake. *Man are you guys slow. I mean it's not like you guys don't have noses. Maybe you all should work on improving that whole olfactory thing.*

"I wass thinin heem wass a leetle whacky the first tine. Now he es pretendin' to be a fish and a Navy dude and stuff," said Chi Chi.

"A fish?" said Bean.

"Yeah, chu know, *Nemo,* ly in da moofy."

"You mean the sea captain," corrected Roachie. "Nemo was a sea captain. You know, like in the book."

"No, ly da fish in da moofy. Chu know, dat poor tiny loss Nemo clown fish… in dat moofy."

"No, it's *Nemo, Captain Nemo* in the book with the submarine," said Roachie.

"Actually, when I bought the boat, the old guy who lived on it called himself Captain Nemo so I thought it was a good idea to just keep things the way they were. Most I could do since the nice old guy died on the boat," said Boner, who by now had changed back into his about-town

Boner the pan handler attire, complete with all his jingling necklaces and bracelets and paranoia. "That old man's brain was a little sun seared. Every other Wednesday he used to get naked and cruise once around the island singin' old-time sea chants. The tourist loved it."

"Sounds about right for this place," said Roachie.

"How chu buy his fish boat and dat big Navy boat if chu no can efen buy chu sung French fries and furniture?" asked Chi Chi.

Boner's bracelets jingled as he shook the onion ring over an open palm and looked closely to see if any nanobots fell out. "Like I told you before, I have everything I need," he smiled.

"I guess that old Jo Papa was wrong," said Bean who also dissected and searched his food for nanobots.

Chi Chi, observing the two of them scrutinize their food, looked down at her's, lifted the top of the cheeseburger bun, then refusing to give in to their paranoia quickly replaced it. "Dis hole thin smell kina fishy to me," she said.

"Is there something wrong with the food?" asked the waitress as she passed by their table.

"No," answered Chi Chi. "But I thin dere es sungthin' wrong wit dem people whas eatin' it."

"Oh… um, okay," said the waitress, who walked away confused.

"What?" said Bean, his attention again focusing on the tattooed girl with the striped hair who had just been joined by an equally tatooed tall skinny man with rings in his nose, ears, lips, and eyebrows, and who was shaved bald except for a two inch thick three foot long clump of blonde hair coming from the left side of his head. It was braided with beads and every time the man turned his head it would fly about like a horse's tail. To Bean it seemed to make the man's entire body extremely lacking in symmetry.

"Nope, nothin' fishy here," continued Boner. "Rumor was that Jimmy Buffett was going to be on Parrothead Island this year for sure. Maybe that's why those pirates showed up. Then again maybe Jimmy heard that pirates would be around and didn't show up because of it. Maybe that's why he headed for Alabama. Or was that Mississippi?"

"Alabama?" said Bean, turning back to the discussion at the table. "My father's in Alabama?"

"That's what I think," said Boner as he scowled at a small piece of onion ring, dropped it on the floor and stomped on it to destroy the nanobots.

"What makes you think that?" asked Roachie.

"Cause that's what Girdy said."

"Who's Girdy?" asked Bean as he handed Fruitcake a pickle.

Fruitcake's one ear perked up with delight because Fruitcake is possibly the only dog on earth that likes pickles. Probably because Sister Moonbeam-Goom-jigi sometimes included pickles in her Creola, and Fruitcake dearly loves and misses Sister Moonbeam-Goom-jigi's Creola.

Where's the house? Where's the food? Where's the house? thought Fruitcake as he devoured the pickle. *I miss my chair. Where's my papa-san chair? Creeeooooolaaa.*

"Girdy's the bartender over there," answered Boner.

They all looked to the bar. The bartender in question was talking to the couple with the strange heads and tattoos.

"Das a man bartender," observed Chi Chi. "I no see no Girdy."

"Yeah, that's Girdy," said Boner.

"A guy named Girdy?" questioned Roachie. "I had an aunt named Girdy… but she wasn't a guy."

"Hey, this is Key West," shrugged Boner. "Whatcha expect?"

"Uh, okay," accepted Roachie.

"So what did Girdy say?" asked Bean.

"Girdy said Jimmy went home and if anybody knows where Jimmy went it would be Girdy and I trust him cause he's one of the very few folks on this island that doesn't work for the Fourth Branch. You know, those aliens that put the nanobots in everything. They don't like guy-girls much but they pretend to."

"Chu see wha I min? Dat Boner, he es a whack job. He es no efen know'n' who da hell he es and hees dun know if he es comin' or goin' and he es talkin' to boy-girls and he es thinin we gots aliens. He es a whack job," declared a frustrated Chi Chi. "I hates to tell chu Bean buh I thin maybes chu chould go home. I thin chu ain gonna fine chur papa. Chu juss gonna fine a buncha whack jobs ly dis guy and get disappointed an depressed."

"But in Miami you said…"

"I know wha I sase. But now I'n know we never gonna fines chur papa no matters how much we look."

"Yeah, maybe you're right," agreed Bean. "Maybe I'll never find him. Maybe I should go home. I'm out of money anyway. The pirates took it all. I don't even know how I'm going to get home."

"No no," said Boner. "You have to trust me. I wouldn't steer you wrong."

"Whack job," said Chi Chi.

Can I have another pickle? thought Fruitcake.

Bean dropped him another slice of pickle. It was devowered in less than a second.

"I'll prove it to you," said Boner.

"How can you do that?" asked Roachie.

"Well, um… well, I'll go with you."

"What?" said Bean.

"I said I'll go with you. And I'll even pay for the trip."

"How es chu gonna pay?" asked Chi Chi. "When we meets chu, chu wass pretendin' to be a veteran from three different wars and askin' for some monies. How es chu gonna pays?"

"He's paying for our burgers," said Bean.

A wide smile crawled over Boner's face, "Like I said, I got everything I need... and maybe a little more."

"Okay," said Bean. "But where are we going?"

"That way," said Boner, throwing a thumb over his shoulder. "I heard he lives in St. Barts. But then Jimmy was born in Pascagoula, Mississippi. So we gotta go to Alabama."

"But you said St. Barts?" questioned Roachie.

"An chu sase Mississippi," said Chi Chi.

"He was but then he's from Mobile, Alabama. So we should go to Alabama. I'm pretty sure or is it the other way around. Well, what the hell, I'm pretty sure it's over up there on the gulf coast."

"I heard he lives in Palm Beach or was it Hawaii?" said Roachie.

"Ho chi mama," said Chi Chi. "Dun chu guys know we only can goes in one direction at a tines?"

Is that all the pickles? thought Fruitcake. *Anybody got another pickle?*

Without even thinking about it all four of them tossed a pickle slice to Fruitcake who not only enjoyed eating them but enjoyed the knowledge that they all now accepted and included him in their conversations.

"Yep. Pretty sure it's up there south," said Boner as he picked off a piece of his burger, dropped it on the floor then crushed and twisted it with the ball of his well worn flip flop.

Wow, what a waste, thought Fruitcake after viewing the demise of a perfectly good piece of burger.

"You mean north. You mean up there is north," corrected Roachie, while observing Boner's curious interest in his food. Seeing Boner's curiosity led Roachie to examining his own food in a like manner.

"Nope, nope," disagreed Boner. "This here is down island all by itself. Up there is the south of north."

"Sose chu es sayin' we gotta go north to get south?" said Chi Chi.

"Yeah… something like that."

"Ho chi mama."

"Well, that's what I said isn't it?"

"Ho chi mama."

"South of north… up there. What I said isn't it?"

"Ho chi mama. He es no efen not knows hees own nem but he es no efen knows where he es."

Any more pickles? Fries? Some cheese would be nice.

A handful of fries and another pickle rained down on Fruitcake's head. He was in heaven.

Oh wow, thought Fruitcake. *This is real heaven. It's raining food. I could stay here forever. Just stay here chowin' down and waistin' away in Margaritaville.*

After a full day's driving from the Keys to Alligator Alley through the Everglades and up along the west coast of Florida, they stopped and checked in at an old '50s era place named the Dixie Palm Motel. It sat alone on the side of the road nestled among tall pines and palmettos. The nearest alternative lodging was 38 miles away. As for the name, the nearest palm tree was a quarter mile down the road but as are many things in Florida; it's all in the name even though it's all the same... or not. For Bean's part the stop-over was just a polite way of putting an end to the last 200 miles of audible torture created by Roachie and Boner in the back of the car singing *99 Bottles of Beer on the Wall*. Bean had joined in as well and it was actually fun in the beginning and even for most of the first 50 miles, but when Fruitcake joined in and tried to howl in harmony it became more than Bean could endure. Roachie pretty much carried the melodic load because Boner couldn't sing a note to save his life and tried to make up for it in volume. Somehow Chi Chi managed to sleep through the entire 1200-plus bottles of beer and when they pulled into the motel she awoke refreshed and smiling.

The Dixie Palm Motel had over a half century of varied pastel colored flaking paint layered over cement blocks and sun-cracked wood surrounding crank-out jealousy windows that no longer cranked out because the crank handles had long since been broken off back in the '60s. Their room had walls of old pine paneling that had deepened over the years to a dark red and smelled of a half century of cleaning with

Pine-sol. There were two beds with lumpy mattresses, a constantly dripping shower that smelled of sulfur water, well used unmatched furniture, and an overall décor that fell somewhere between French modern cubism and something resembling the old sixties cartoon *The Jetsons*. On the wall over a bed hung a picture of a Greek fishing boat rotting away on a beach. Over the other bed was the same picture of a Greek fishing boat rotting away on a beach. The air conditioner barely blew cold, smelled musty, and sounded as though somewhere inside its rusted metal housing was a hamster running around in a wheel full of marbles.

For entertainment there was a television set that looked as though it had been around so long it may have once played the original broadcast of Crusader Rabbit on Captain Kangaroo. When Roachie turned it on it somehow still functioned but managed to only receive one station that consisted of only one show. It was the Reverend Bucephelus T. Fassbender's Hour of Christ that broadcast repeatedly all day long on the public access channel because there weren't any other programs to show except a brief production made by the 6th grade students of the local county middle school about the metaphorphosis of a caterpillar. Few people actually watched the Reverend's Hour of Christ but lots of people watched the 6th grader's show because their teachers exposed cleavage was in the background of all the close up shots. And there were lots of close up shots.

On the air now the good reverend was busy talking enthusiasticaly about the end of the world, a horribly frightening revelation that affected him so intensely that he would often close his eyes and segue into a desperate emotional prayer that ultimately and inevitably morphed into a desperate tearful plea for money. The only entertainment alternative to listening to Reverend Bucephelus T. Fassbender or watching the 6th grade teacher's cleavage at the Dixie Palm Motel was to go swimming in the small kidney shaped pool that sat in the middle of the parking lot, a pool none of the few guests ever used because of the motel owner. The owner was a Pakistani named Abdul-hafeez, a name that means *to serve the master*. Abdul-hafeez was always lying around the pool in nothing but his dirty yellow BVDs, intimidator sunglasses, a three-dollar Wal-Mart straw cowboy hat, and listening to ear-piercing Pakistani music from his portable cassett player. Though the condition of the motel along with a Pakistani in his underwear by the pool often turned away travelers, none of these shortcomings seemed to bother local patrons who referred to the establishment as the *Motel No-tell,* the place where they could rondesvue with their other significant others or get a one hour special with no questions asked if they payed the guy in his grundies at the pool twice the going room rate, which already exceeded what the dump was actually worth.

Abdul-hafeez came to America in search of his dream and his dream was to no longer have to serve the master. Once having arrived in the U.S. he wasted no time at all assimilating to his southern American environment. He now called himself *Bodean* and drove a faded orange rusty twenty year old Ford F-150 pickup truck with no tailgate that was once the property of a South Georgia utility company. When Abdul-hafeez wasn't lying by the pool in his underwear he was playing grab ass with the half-dozen Pakistani maids he had imported to service his ten room luxury resort motel. But because Abdul-hafeez was so touchy-feely friendly most of the Pakistani maids wouldn't stay with him for very long, which probably explained why there was never enough toilet paper or enough of those cheap scratchy rough worn thin towels with faded red letters that said Howard Johnsons or Property of Saint Julius Mental Hospital, and why the bedding was rarely changed. Even the phone books were six years old which actually wasn't of any consequence because Bodean Abdul-hafeez had long since removed all the telephones from the rooms to save money, and so he could charge a buck a call for the use of the only remaining telephone on the premises located in his registration office. It was a lucrative deal until cell phones saturated the entire population.

Bodean Abdul-hafeez, who was too damn cheap to buy a bathing suit, never really cared if his lying around in his underwear scared away potential customers because he didn't really need the business in the first place. The Dixie Palm Motel was actually just a means to an end because he received regular shipments of money and fresh motel maids from a group of cousins in Pakistan. Having a sponsor like Bodean Abdul-hafeez in the United States who was in good standing with a thriving business concern offering gainful employment put the Pakistani women ahead of the immigration line; that plus the State Department's eager willingness to keep the Pakastanis happy in order to propagate the war in Afghanistan. Of course once they arrived and gained citizenship they would buy their own motel or gas station or convenience store with guaranteed government minority business loans, then bring over the rest of their clan who would repeat the process and who would then bring in even more Pakistani relatives. In this manner Bodean figured half of the population of Pakistan would eventually be in the motel or gas station or convenience store business in America in one short decade. But not before he got his. For now, being paid $30,000 per maid with an average three new maids per month, Bodean lived comfortably in his underwear by the pool where he bided his time between pilgrimages to Las Vegas each spring and fall. Even though he lost most of his money there he liked Las Vegas because there he discovered that whatever he decided to do in Las Vegas stayed in Las Vegas and he didn't have to take any shit from unwilling Pakistani motel maids.

Surprisingly there was little guilt on Bodean's part while he enjoyed his luxurious American lifestyle because he was well aware that the money he received put no strain at all on his extended family's resources in the old country. Bodean Abdul-hafeez just continued to enjoy playing grab-ass with the virgin motel maids at each opportunity in the comfort of knowing that all of the money he received from Pakistan was actually courtesy of the good old U.S. Government. It was money that had been sent to Pakistan to help fight terrorism. In fact, Abdul-hafeez, AKA Bodean, a Muslim, was proof that the U.S./Pakistan Joint Terrorist program was working because Abdul-hafeez, AKA Bodean, a Muslim, was once a terrorist himself who specialized in blowing shit up. He learned to blow shit up from his cousin who was now high in the Pakistani Defense Ministry, the same cousin who sends him virgin maids and money. The money sent to Bodean is intended to train more terrorists and turn them loose on America, which is what he did at first only to find himself tracking them down in Las Vegas where they learned no matter what the great Mohamad says, it was better to party than to terrorize. This, concluded his students as well as Abdul-hafeez, AKA Bodean, was far better than being a part of the *serving the master in the once in a lifetime suicidal blowing shit up club.* So who the hell needs 72 virgins in the hereafter when you can have a full buffet of experienced female company in Las Vegas and get paid for sunning in your grundies by the pool at home, reasoned Bodean.

"How come dat preacher man es always askin' for monies?" said Chi Chi. "Where da hell es he gonna spend it if es gonna be da end of da world?"

"Maybe he's going to have to buy his way into heaven," said Boner. "You know, to compensate for all that bullshit he's shoveling on the tube there."

Religion's in the hands of some crazy ass people, thought Fruitcake.

"Yep, you sure got that right, Fruitcake" agreed Roachie.

"I'n hungry. I'n gonna go ask dat guy in hees underwear where es a good place to eat cause I'n no see no place around here when we come here," said Chi Chi.

"Good idea," said Boner. "Make sure they have cheeseburgers. Bean's gotta have his cheeseburger."

With French fries, added Fruitcake. *And pickles.*

When Chi Chi returned to their room ten minutes later Fruitcake was spread out on one of the beds, balls up and snoring. Bean and Roachie were sitting at the foot of the bed fixed intently on Reverand Bucephelus T. Fassbender who was near tears and an emotional breakdown while explaining why everyone should send him money even if it was their very last dollar because their reward in heaven would be worth more than all the gold on earth. Boner was wandering the room searching under, around, and inside everything he could put his hands on.

"Wha chu doin'?" Chi Chi asked Boner.

"Microphones and cameras," replied Boner. "Ya never know. Ya know?"

"Ho chi mama."

"Did you find us a place to eat?" asked Boner, his butt up in the air while looking under the bed. "Oh wow. You guys don't want to know what's under this bed."

"Up da road. Three miles den to da leff on da water. Da guy in hees underwear, he sase… Oh, I gotta tell chu guys, dat guy he smell funny too and heem try to grab my ass… anyways, he sase es called the Paradise Restaurant an it gots good food."

"He tried to grab your ass?" asked Roachie.

"Chess, an hees smell bad to. Like garlic and sour milk."

"What did you do?" asked Roachie, still fixed on Reverend Bucephelus T. Fassbender who was now talking to God about money.

"I tolt heem if he efer touches my ass again I wass gonna break his smelly arm."

"Oh," replied Roachie, making a mental note never to touch Chi Chi's ass.

"I could never lay around a pool in my underwear," said Bean, who sat fascinated with the TV and still fixed on Reverend Bucephelus T. Fassbender who was now saying that God said you can send him money on the internet with a credit card through PayPal.

"Why not? Why couldn't you lay around a pool in your underwear? Actually I don't think it would be that hard," asked Roachie as he stared intently at Reverend Bucephelus T. Fassbender.

"Because I don't wear any," replied Bean.

"Oh. Guess that makes sense."

Neather do I, thought Fruitcake who had come awake at the sound of the mention of food.

"Hey, didn't that preacher guy just say that God invented the Internet so everybody could send him money?" asked Roachie.

"Buh I thought dat Al Gore sase he invented da internets." said Chi Chi.

"The aliens invented the internet," said Boner as he sat next to them on the foot of the bed and joined in their fascination with the Reverend Bucephelus T. Fassbender's Hour of Christ. "So they can know what everybody is doing and talking about. I betcha he's one of them."

"Who, Al Gore," asked Roachie.

"No, that preacher on TV," replied Boner. "And probably Al Gore, too."

"Lets go eat," said Chi Chi.

"Okay," the three guys said in unison.

Now you're talkin', thought Fruitcake as he hopped from the bed and parked his ass next to the door, tail wagging in anticipation. *Where's the food? Where's the house? Where's the food? Creeeeooooolaaaa.*

chapter 23
Cheeseburgers in Paradise

The place had evolved over the years from an old fish and sponge camp sitting at the water's edge in a sheltered cove on the Gulf to the now popular open-air Paradise Restaurant that included a small marina, a boat ramp, and a temporary docking area. Boaters and fishermen regularly pulled in for gas, fish bait, food, and refreshments. The Paradise, as it was known locally, was a typical tin roofed and unpainted faded wood structure decorated with beach junk, maritime paraphernalia and those little white twinkling Christmas lights made popular by yuppie bistros. A twenty-four foot combination bar and bait shop faced the large deck and cove where a half dozen homemade wood plank tables sat outside under large unbrellas surrounded by palms. Near the water a pelican and a few seagulls sat on nearby pilings waiting for patrons to toss food, preferably steamed shrimp, or leftover fish bait.

A large hand painted sign hung over the bar that read "Live Bait & Dead Steak" next to another that said "Free Beer Tomorrow!" Behind the bar hung all the usual bar accouterments including a ten foot section with a small sign that read "Paradise Wall of Fame." It included a montage of a great many photos of famous people, most of which Bean and the others didn't recognize but a few they did, such as Sylvester Stallone and Angelina Jolie. Among the many other pictures of celebrities and famous folks were Walter Cronkite, Clark Gable, Johnny Weissmuller, Yule Brenner, John Wayne, Betty Davis, and Richard Nixon. In the center of the wall of fame hung an 8x10 framed dated photo draped in Hawaiian leis of the man himself, one James William Buffett.

"Look," said Bean pointing to the wall as the four of them took seats at the bar.

They all looked at the wall in front of them.

"Hey Bean, ain dat chur papa?" asked Chi Chi.

"You talkin' about the dude in the middle there," said a pot bellied jollie man in a Panama Jack hat. He appeared to be in his late sixties with a full belly, well tanned, balding with grey hair, and a full gray beard.

"Yes sir," answered Bean.

"Isn't that Jimmy Buffett?" asked Roachie.

"Sho 'nuff is," said the old man through an inviting southern accent and friendly smile. "Now what'll you folks be havin' today?"

"I'll have a cheeseburger," answered Bean.

"Me too," said Roachie.

"Cheeseburgers all around I guess," added Boner.

"Not for me. I wanna shrimps," said Chi Chi.

"Okay. Three cheeseburgers and a shrimp basket comin' up. You catch that order back there Rosco!" yelled the old man through a small pass-through window to his cook in the kitchen behind the bar.

Rosco the cook and general kitchen man was busy dancing to his own interpretation of a favorite old song by James Brown but paused long enough to confirm the order. "I got it boss. Three cheese and some steamed peelers."

"I like mine with lettuce and tomato," said Bean.

"And Heinze-57 and French fried potatoes," added Roachie.

"With a big kosher pickle and a cold draft beer, too," added Boner.

"So how come chu gots so many pictures up dere?" asked Chi Chi.

"My friends," said the old man. "Famous friends who been comin' here for years."

"Dose es all chur friends? All dose famous peoples? Efen da moofy stars?"

"You got it missy," said the old guy with a wink.

"I think some of those folks been dead a long time," observed Boner.

"How come Jimmy Buffett's picture is the biggest and in the middle?" asked Roachie.

"That's cause Jimmy's special. Made my place here famous. Stops here all the time for cheeseburgers, just like you youngins is doin' right now. Wrote him a song about it and made my place famous."

"You mean this is the Cheeseburger in Paradise place?" asked an excited Bean.

"You got it youngin. This here's the place."

"The one in the song? For real?"

"Sure 'nuff," said the old man.

Boner observed Bean's peaked interest but had reservations about the old man's integrity. After all, Boner was from Key West where tall tails and bullshit are a way of life and he didn't want to see his new found friend disappointed yet again.

"You mean he comes here for cheeseburgers?" asked Bean.

"You bet. Flies and lands that float plane right in the cove here he does, just like he did that very first day back in... in... ah... back that first day. Emergency landing it was. Out of gas is what he said. Him and his friends walked right up and sat right here at this very bar just like you folks. Said they were on there way back from Jamaica. Said them crazy Jamaicans shot at his plane cause they thought they were drug smugglers with a load of ganja. Said they didn't realize that those crazy Jamaicans had hit the gas tank until they were almost empty. That's when they saw the Paradise from the air and put her down. So I patched the hole, filled up the tank and fed em all cheeseburgers. 'Best cheeseburger he ever had,' is what ol' JB told me. And he's been flyin' in here for burgers ever since. Made my place famous is what he did."

"Not many people here for such a famous place," observed Boner.

"Uh, nights and weekends," said the old man. "You gotta come on the weekends. Can't hardly walk through the place. Nothin' but assess and elbows all day long and all night."

"Up'n smokin' Boss," yelled Rosco as he slid the food through the kitchen window to the bar.

"Name's Stanley. Stanley Smith," said the old man as he slid their food onto the bar. "But everybody just calls me Scratch."

"My name is Bean, James Bean Bu…"

"We're on vacation," interrupted Boner, preventing Bean from finishing his name and revealing himself as the son of the man in the featured photo. "This is Bean, famous surfer, and this is Roachie, he's a high tech entrepeneur. And this is Chi Chi, up and coming movie star. You've probably seen her on TV."

Chi Chi's TV fame came when she did a commercial once where she walked across the screen in the background pushing a shopping cart while some guy stood in front of the camera and announced the grand opening of a new Wal-Mart. She was paid twelve bucks and got free hot dogs and cokes. The commercial ran half a dozen times on local TV in Miami.

"Oh sure," said Scratch. "I should have recognized you. Have to put your picture on the wall here won't we."

"My name is Efrem Zimbalist Jr., Special Agent Efrem Zimbalist Jr., and I work for the FBI but like I said, we're all on vacation. They call me Boner."

The old man squirmed a bit at the mention of the FBI, which led Boner to believe his suspicions were correct; that Scratch Smith was full of shit and as phony as his southern accent.

Scratch Smith, whose real name was Theophilus Burklander, was proud that the Paradise was famous even though the fame was completely contrived. Scratch had spent eight years in a Federal penitentury as a cook because he was a con man who got caught in an FBI sting while he was conducting what he thought was a con intended to rip off a U.S. Senator who had ripped off a powerful lobbyest representing a major government contractor who was backed by the mafia. After his release from prison he gathered what funds he had stashed away, fled to the deep south and bought this failing fish camp; a safe and obscure place he was sure, to hide away from the Mafia and a vengeful Senator who was also soon to be released from prison. Unfortunately his newly purchased failing fish camp continued to fail and was about to go under completely when Jimmy Buffett released the Cheeseburger in Paradise song, giving Scratch the inspiration to make his place famous. With nothing more than a new name on a hand painted sign, a small ad in the yellow pages that actually didn't bring in any business at all, and a weekly half-hour broadcast on the public access channel that was put together by a local middle school video class and aired between Reverend Bucephelus T. Fassbender's Hour of Christ show, the *Paradise Restaurant* started to turn around and become profitable. In view of his masterful marketing efforts Scratch then considered himself a business genius. Efforts that also included a phony wall of fame, years of Scratch's bullshit stories, and a little help from a writer from Southern Living Magazine who happened to stay at the Dixie Palm Motel with a woman who wasn't his wife. When the writer let it slip about his little affair it gave Scratch the idea to blackmail him into doing a great travel piece about the Paradise, complete with complimenting photos and a raving review of the menu. The article was seen and read all around the country, inspiring people to cruise in from all over the gulf just so they could say they had an original cheeseburger at the one and only genuine famous original Paradise Restaurant of Jimmy Buffett song fame. That, and to listen to Scratch's bogus story of the wounded seaplane and its famous pilot. They showed up from everywhere, all with hopes of catching a glimpse of the singer himself while consuming cheeseburgers. Cheeseburgers, by the way, that *are* pretty damn good in spite of their fraudulent inception.

I'm with you, thought Fruitcake. *This guy's a phony. But his fries are pretty good. How bout a pickle?*

Here ya go, thought Boner to Fruitcake as he tossed him a pickle then began to inspect his food for nanobots.

Thanks. Ya think he's one of them? An alien? thought Fruitcake.

Nope, not a chance, thought Boner. *Not a good nuff liar.*

Boner wasn't aware he and Fruitcake had just made another breakthrough by communicating completely by thought alone. And to think, Boner had never even consumed Sister Moonbeam-Goom-jigi's Creola or any of her mind expanders. Boner let the old man and his lies slide, not wanting to rain on Bean's newfound joy at stumbling across the so-called original *Cheeseburger in Paradise* eatery, and touching what he thought was a piece of his father's life. They took their time, chowed down as they listened to a few of Scratch Smith's other tall tales then returned to the No Tell Motel where they all crashed while watching the Reverend Bucephelus T. Fassbender Hour of Christ and trying to figure out why he needed all that money. The good Reverend was relentless and neverending. Odd, they all thought, for a man who would soon come to face the end of the world.

The next day, long after the Celestial Rocket and its passengers had departed the Dixie Palm Motel and headed further along on their trip to Boner's south of north; old

Scratch's Paradise was over-run by law enforcement officers and emergency vehicles of all sorts. There were town cops, county cops, State Police, a couple of Forest Rangers, a rescue vehicle, a volunteer fire truck, the county coroner, the FBI, and even Reverend Bucephelus T. Fassbender in his yellow Hour of Christ Ford Pinto with a radio that monitored the emergency services band. He was there as a reporter because he also owned and edited the local weekly newspaper and the free monthly publication, the *Pennypincher Classifieds*. Most were there to witness the result of the most heinous crime to take place in that area since way back during the prohibition days when a moonshiner named Leroy Copperdome chopped up a dog that belonged to a Greek sponge diver who in turn chopped up old Leroy Copperdome. It seemed the dog took a liking to Copperdome's product and its repeated visits for samplings eventually led the Federal revenuers right to the old man's moonshine still that he had stashed way back in the woods near his turpentine works. The crime resulted in a hung jury on two occasions because the jurors who valued highly a well bred coon dog couldn't decide which was the worse crime; chopping up the dog or chopping up Leroy Copperdome, and also because the Greek sponge diver, Kyriaki Gianopoulos, was a woman.

The current crime at the Paradise wasn't quite as messy and gruesome as the historic chop-fest but none the less it was just as appalling. When the report of the crime spread over the radio waves they all rushed to the Paradise that morning with flashing lights and sirens, overwhelming poor old Rosco the cook with all their official questions and desire to get their picture in Reverend Bucephelus T. Fassbender's weekly newspaper. Rosco had made the emergency 911 call to report that he had discovered old Scratch Smith dead on the kitchen floor with a cracked skull and missing his nose. The only thing Rosco could tell the police was that just before he closed up and headed home the previous night an old friend of Scratch's had arrived at the Paradise. He wasn't quite sure but he thought the man looked kind of like a priest who kept calling Scratch *Theo,* and that the stranger said he was staying at the Dixie Palm Motel. Also something about old unfinished business for somebody named *Fast Eddy.*

chapter 24

No Deal in Mobile

"Hokay, I'n thinin dat maybe pretty soons I gonna go crazy," said an aggravated Chi Chi just before she took a sip of her Yoo-hoo. "Hey, chu know dis Choo Choo stuff es pretty good."

"Yoo-hoo," corrected Roachie.

"Das wha I sase, Choo-yoos, an dat es pretty good stuff."

The four of them were sitting on a large stone bulkhead chowing down again on cheeseburgers and fries, sipping Yoo-hoos, and looking out over the Gulf waters at a couple of passing shrimp boats escorted by a frantic flock of hungry seagulls. Chi Chi raised her sunglasses to better observe the boats then turned to observe her three companions who were disecting and inspecting their food for nanobots.

"Ho chi mama."

"Gonna go crazy? How come?" asked Boner.

"Are chu kidden me?" exclaimed Chi Chi. "We comes all da way to Mobile in Alabamas and we no finds Bean's papa and den we goes to a leetle plaze called Creola and ain nobody know where es hees papa dere too but dere es a policeman who sase dat Bean's papa es maybe back at dat big Margarita Hotel in Pensacola Beash in Florida an sose den we go all da ways back dere and day sase Chimmy Buffett hees done fly home again an den we drifes all da ways to here in Pascagaula in Mississippis where hees born from and day sase hees no liffs here no more for a long tine but sung tine hees here and sung tine hees no here. Ho chi mama, Bean, es no wonders we no can't fine chur papa causs dat man hees no can never make up hees mine where hees gonna be."

Yeah, I'm with her, thought Fruitcake. *And who names a town after food anyway?*

"Are you saying that we should give up?" asked Boner as he handed a french fry to Fruitcake who was mooching off each of them while he bounced from rock to rock.

Pickle please, begged Fruitcake after gulping down a fry.

"I thin maybes. Causs what else es we gonna do if we dun know wha ways we gunna go. Das pretty bad, right?" said Chi Chi as she tossed a slice of pickle to Fruitcake.

"It could be worse," Boner said to Chi Chi.

"Are chu kidden me. How can it be worser den goin' nowheres when chu es goin' everywheres? Das a lotta beers on da wall singin' chu know," declared Chi Chi.

"At least you're not being rectally probed by aliens," laughed Boner as he tossed a piece of cheese slice to Fruitcake.

"Whack job. I thin chu es a whack job. Das wha I thin. Causs chu no always makin' sense ly one of dose peoples who gots more peoples inside dem."

"You mean schizophrenic," said Roachie.

"Well, I may be schizophrenic but at least I have each other… um, most of the time," laughed Boner.

"Hah, that's funny," said Roachie.

"I don't think we should give up but I don't think going around in circles is going to get us anywhere," agreed Bean. He tossed Fruitcake a fry then picked a small round thing from his burger and extended it to Boner for inspection. "Is that one?"

"No," said Boner after close examination. "They're smaller than that with little tiny antennae. That's a sesame seed I think. Some of them have itty bitty little flashing lights too but they're really hard to see. But then they could be disguised as a sesame seed I guess. They're pretty sneaky, that fourth branch. Just like regular politicians."

"Oh," said Bean.

"Ho chi mama," sighed Chi Chi.

Nearby sat a very old woman with a long fishing rod in one hand and a longneck beer in the other. Everything she wore was covered with flowers or in flower print including her sneakers, a wide brimmed hat, and oversized sunglasses that partially hid a rinkled leathery face with a well seasoned tan that was decades old. When she laughed out loud at their conversation they all turned and looked at her. After a silent moment she laughed again then said, "That boy follows the stars. Always has, always will."

"What?" said Bean.

"Ya'll talkin' bout that Buffett boy, Jimmy, aren't cha?"

"Yes ma'am," answered Bean.

"Oh yeah, I member him. Had him in my class when I was teachin' school way back when." She smiled then sipped her beer.

"You know him?" asked an excited Bean.

She smiled again as she recalled the memories. "Might say that." She adjusted her hat against a sudden breeze and continued. "Daydreamer. Class clown. Pretty much a pain in the ass, I'd say. Yep, I member. Had to ship him off to the Catholic school to keep him out of trouble. Wasn't all bad though. Just distracted a lot. Girls mostly."

"What do you mean he follows the stars?" asked Boner.

"Head in the clouds. Follows the stars. Never would listen to nobody except his granpa and that crazy cajun lady over Bayou way."

"Cajun lady?" said Roachie.

"Bayou?" said Chi Chi.

"The boys in town use to slip over that way on the weekends to do what they couldn't get away with around here. A few would go see that witchie woman. Deep in the swamp there. Some say she was a lady of the evening. Others say she was a witchy gypsy woman who sold potions; if you know what I mean. The boys liked that back then. Now too I spose. That's an odd dog you got there. One ear. Odd. But kind'a cute. Wanna sell it? I could use some company."

Hell no! thought Fruitcake immediately before he caught himself and wondered if maybe the old lady knew how to make Creola like Sister Moonbeam-Goom-jigi, and if by chance she had a papa-san chair. *On the other hand, maybe...*

"Oh no ma'am," said Bean. "Fruitcake's not for sale."

"Who said anything about a fruitcake? I mean the dog. Do you want to sell the dog not a fruitcake."

"That's his name," clarified Bean. "His name is Fruitcake, but I could never sell him."

"Oh, well okay, if you say so. Cute though. In an odd ugly sort of way."

Probably just as well, thought Fruitcake. *Bean wouldn't know what to do without me.*

"So chu sase dis lady es a witch?" asked Chi Chi.

"They say she can read a man's soul and once she does... well, there's nothin' a man can do for the rest of his life that she doesn't know about or maybe even got something to do with," said the old woman. "Most likely then she'd know the whereabouts of that Buffett boy." The old woman propped the longneck beer between her legs and adjusted the fishing pole then retrieved the beer, took a swig and continued, "They say she's still around. Rumor has it she was the one concocted the potion that made young Jimmy what he is today."

"A *make chu famous* potion. Wow. Den dat witch maybes know hows to fine Chimmy?" asked Chi Chi.

"Chimmy? What's a chimmy?" asked the old woman.

"*Jimmy,*" claearified Boner. "*Jimmy Buffett.*"

"Find him? Oh, a reasonable assumption I guess. If you believe the rumors that is," replied the old woman.

Just then the line jerked on her fishing rod. She set the beer down, calmly adusted her hat for action, stood up and started to reel in her catch.

"Where can we find that gypsy lady?" asked Bean.

"In the Bayou. Name's Odalia. Some call her the Dark Queen, some the Swamp Queen, others call her Mother Odalia or the Gypsy Queen. Lives deep in the swamp out Bayou La Batre way is what they say." The old woman wrestled with the rod and reel to bring in her fish. "Ah hah, gotcha you whily bastard," she said to the fish as it flopped near the surface of the water then was reeled in to where she could grab it. "Rumor is you go to an old fish camp owned by a man called Bear Boudreaux. He's the only one knows that swamp and the only one that can take you back in there to where that witchy woman lives. Else you'd get lost in that place for sure. So they say. They say... well, even the gator hunters don't go in there where the witchy woman lives."

Chi Chi looked at Boner suspiciously.

"What?" said Boner.

"Chu es not dat Bear Boudreaux guy too, es chu?" Chi Chi asked, accentuating her suspicions with a strong glare.

"Uh, I don't think so," answered Boner.

"Are chu chour?" Chi Chi glared.

"Course. Don't be ridiculous," laughed Boner.

"Juss checkin'," said Chi Chi. "Cause chu already been four peoples since we meets chu."

The old woman reeled in what looked to be about a two pound fish of some kind. She expertly restled it off the hook and tossed it into her cooler with the beer. Then in triumph up-ended and finished off her opened bottle of beer, tossed the empty in the cooler, slammed the lid shut and gathered up her things. The cooler was rigged with wheels and a handle so she could roll it along like airline carry-on luggage.

"Are you sure that Bayou lady is still around?" asked Roachie.

"So I hear. Witchy woman been there forever is what they say. Probably be there forevermore," she said as she carefully managed her load over the large rocks of the bulkhead and then started for the road. She paused and turned with a quick bit of advice, "If you're gonna look for that Queen Odalia then you go over to Bayou La Batre and best find Bear Boudreaux first. But ya'll be careful over there in that Bayou. It's a dark and mysterious place. Some of our St. Ignatius boys went in there lookin' for fun and adventure once and didn't come back out for ten days. When they finally did they didn't remember a thing, not a damn thing, like they lost their minds and all sense of time. I'm thinking maybe they even lost their soul to that crazy witch. There's even old tales of a few folks went in there and never came out at all. Never. Yep, ya'll think twice before you go in that swamp. It's not a welcoming place for outsiders, and no matter what ya'll do be sure and never…" Her voice trailed off, her words of warning lost in the sound of a sudden gust of wind off the gulf, a passing truck, and the ear splitting screeches of a frenzied group of seagulls. She turned and waddled slowly away down the road, a walking floral arangement with her fishing gear over her shoulder, dragging her rattling cooler behind her.

"What did she say?" asked Boner.

"I'n no chure. I thin chee sase sungthin bou dun never eat nothin wit a spoon," answered Chi Chi.

"What," said Bean.

"No," corrected Roachie. "I think she said something about the moon, something about a full moon."

"So I guess we're off to the Bayou, huh gang?" said Boner.

"I guess so," agreed Bean.

"Hokay," said Chi Chi. "Buh chu guys better no be singin' dat bottles of beer song no more causs I thin I gonna go crazy if I hear dat ninty-nine bottles song again."

"We could do Yoo-hoo," Roachie suggested to Boner. "We could do ninety-nine bottles of Yoo-hoo on the wall."

"That would work," agreed Boner.

"How chi mama."

chapter 25
Jimbob and Jimbob?

"Are you sure this is the right road?" asked Roachie.

"That's what the man said isn't it," replied Boner sitting confidently behind the wheel of the Celestial Rocket. "Fifteen miles out of town then left at the old store with no roof and no windows and a rusty Texaco sign, then another six miles 'til the road ends then right and go 'til we come to Bear Boudreaux's fish camp on the left."

"Is that what he said?" asked Roachie.

"Yep," answered Boner.

"Is that what we did?" asked Roachie.

"Sure," answered Boner.

"Are you sure?"

"Sure I'm sure."

"How sure?"

"Pretty sure."

"I thought we went right at the old Texaco sign."

"Well, that depends on your point of view."

"Point of view?" said Roachie.

"Sure," said Boner. "On your point of view depending on which old Texaco sign you were looking at in the first place. I saw two Texaco signs."

"But the man said to go left at the old Texaco sign," said Roachie.

"No. He said go left at the store with the old Texaco sign."

"So we went left?" asked Roachie.

"Right," agreed Boner.

"But he said go left."

"That's what we did."

"But you said right."

"No, left."

"But I thought we went right."

"Sure, depending on you point of view."

"Then we did go right?"

"Why would we go right?" asked Boner.

"We went left then?" asked Roachie.

"Right."

"We went right?"

"No."

"I think we're lost," said Roachie.

"Euphemistically speaking, we are all lost," said Boner. "Or else we would all be somewhere else. Right?"

Roachie looked to Chi Chi sitting next to him in the back of the car, "Chi Chi, don't you think we're lost?"

"I'n no chure. I thin it all depends on who chu talkin' to. Ly maybes chu es talkin' to Boner Jones or maybes chu es talkin' to Captain Nemo, or maybes chu es talkin' to Purdy Boon, or maybes chu es talkin' to da FBI guy, or maybes chu es talkin' to da Easter Bunny. An I dun no nuttin abou no *eunomistic* stuff."

They all agreed that Boner should drive because a policeman in Bayou La Batre was giving them the hairy eyeball when they were going around town asking directions to Bear Boudreaux's fish camp. Also because they felt that Boner was better qualified to lie his way out of any official inquiries put forth by any law enforcement officers, although they weren't sure who Boner would be if such an occasion should present itself. And also because Boner was the only one who had a driver's license. Or so he claimed.

The road out of Bayou La Batre was lined with a few old majestic oaks and graceful fields, but the first turn put them onto a sandy washboard of a lane that meandered through a pine forest ending in a grassy wetland. From that road the directions they followed led to a rutted raised way that became progessively narrow. It was close in and bordered by dark water and a tall canopy of cypress trees draped with long haunting strands of grey Spanish moss. The swamp seemed to threaten the dark skinny road forcing them to instinctively slow down and progress more cautiously, feeling as though they had just become a form of prey wandering deep into some dangerous foreign jungle.

"What if we get lost? Because I think we're lost," Roachie said with concern as he looked all about the dim swamp. "And it's getting late in the day… I think."

"You must be a city boy," laughed Boner.

"Well okay, so what? I mean you're not exactly Grissly Adams or Davy Crocket, ya know."

"Are chu chure?" said Chi Chi. "He maybes es one of dose guys."

"Yeah, you're right there. Spent most of my time on the water. Same thing ain't it though? I mean you can get lost on the ocean just as easy as in a swamp. Maybe even easier."

"That doesn't make any sense," said Roachie.

"It does if you're lost."

"What? You mean we're lost?"

"Nope."

"How do you know we're not lost?"

"Because we're there, I mean, we're here," said Boner as he turned the Celestial Rocket into what appeared to be a junkyard time capsule of swampland survival and evolution of technology.

An assortment of rotting old wooden flat bottom boats, rusted old cars dating back to the '30s, and a stripped down old truck sat near a work shed by the water's edge. An old gas powered generator sat next to an even older steam engine. Tied to a shaky wooden dock was a 16 foot aluminum flat bottom with a small outboard motor and a cover rigged for duck hunting. It was draped with camouflage and sported a less than artistic camo paint job. On the side scrawed in red paint was the name *Swamp Thang*. Near the dock a rusty tin roof covered a multi-generational assortment of connected wooden and tin shacks with rusty screens and protruding stove pipes, the largest with a second floor extending over the water on stilts. Fuel cans, old tires, an old hand crank gas pump, a claw foot bath tub, assorted trash, and a long outside wooden table covered with dried blood sat near a fifty-gallon drum mounted over a butane fire. A steamy vapor rose from something boiling under the lid of the drum and expelled an unrecognizable stench. At one end of the table, mounted on old concrete blocks was a large wood burning grill converted from the hood of a 1938 dodge pick-up truck. Behind the table on the wall of the shack were mounted a few dozen alligator heads, assorted snake skins and the skins of a few unrecognizable furry creatures.

They exited the car cautiously and stood in silence while they surveyed their surroundings and the nearby swamp.

"Ho chi mama. I thinin maybes dey chould be callin' dis guy Mr. Gator stead of Mr. Bear," said Chi Chi as she moved closer to inspect the many alligator heads.

"I wonder where Mr. Boudreaux is?" said Bean.

"Maybe something ate him," said Roachie.

"Hokay, well, hees no here so I thin we chould go now," said a nervous Chi Chi as she started for the car. "Dis place given me da heebee geebees."

"He be in da swamp," a strange voice echoed through the fish camp. It seemed to originate from over near the dock.

"In da swamp," said another voice that seemed to come from behind one of the shacks.

"Bag dare in da swamp," came the first voice again, though now it seemed to be moving.

"Ho chi mama," said a nervous Chi Chi. "I thin dose spooky trees es talkin' to us."

"What, there's people in the trees?" said an anxious Roachie looking to the top of the tall moss covered cypress trees.

"Hello," said Bean. "Is anybody there?"

"Duz shew be a gang warden?" asked one of the voices.

"A what? A gang what," said Bean.

"No," said Boner. "We're not game wardens."

"Den wha shew be?" asked the other voice. "Shew talks like da gang wardens."

"We're looking for Mr. Bear Boudreaux. Are you Mr. Boudreaux?" asked Bean.

Both of the hidden voices began to laugh and move about. The sound of their laughter echoed off the trees and off the surface of the water throughout the swamp, disorienting our bewildered foursome. Bean wondered what was so humorous. He went to what he thought might be the door to the main shack and knocked. "Hello. Mr. Boudreaux! Are you in there?" When no answer came he began to enter.

"Dare be big crazy coon in dare! Mebbe bite at shew!"

"What?" said Bean, pausing at the door.

"Shew be a gaga mebbe he eat shew whole gone," laughed the voice from behind the shed. "Bite atcha! Bite atcha! Bite atcha! Ha ha ha."

"Maybe I better do the talking," said Boner. "This sounds Cajun just like the lady who lives next door to me down Island. The one used to wash dishes at the The Blue Heaven. She's Cajun from Louisiana."

"Chu mins chu can understand wha dey sase?" asked Chi Chi.

"Kinda," answered Boner. "Can't be any harder than understanding what you say."

"Hey, es chu makin' fun of my assent?"

"Of course not. I wouldn't do that," replied Boner.

"Kina? Den wha chu min, *kina?*" ask Chi Chi. "Wha happen if chu no get it right?" she said, looking at the many gator heads on the wall and thinking the worst.

Boner stepped forward and raised his voice, "Anh shaw, come outta hine dat shad so ah can talk atcha."

After a long silent moment a tall shirtless young man appearing to be nearly twenty years of age poked his head around the corner of a shed then quickly pulled it back again and said, "We funnin wit da coon bite shew fo sho not," he said from behind the shed. "Ain no coon in dere in dat shad. Ain no Dada Bear Boudreaux needa."

Another tall young man did the same, poking his head from behind the old rusty junk truck after working his way unseen from the dock. Then he slowly walked out and around the Celestial Rocket inspecting it closely until he let out a long whistle of approval, wiped his hands on his shirt and adjusted his dirty jeans and grimy worn and faded red ball cap that said Crawdaddy's Bar & Grill on the front. "Hooooo shaw, dat a sweet ting," he said of Bean's car. "Hoooo dat sweeta den jugar keen, dat iz. Dat some pretty like a crane bird dat iz."

The other young man had popped into the back door of one of the sheds then finally slinked timidly out the front, leaving the door open and exposing an old prohibition era moonshine still draped with assorted junk and a few gator hides. It was obvious it hadn't been used for many years. He stopped and stood silent with his hands in the pockets of his overalls and producing a broad smile as he stared wide-eyed at Chi Chi.

"Shew be da Bear Boudreaux?" asked Boner in his limited but passable Cajun. Boner wasn't sure but there was something odd about the two of them that he just couldn't wrap his mind around. Though they were tall and appeared to be of a certain age with all their faculties they seemed to be almost childlike.

"Ah be da Boudreaux sho nuf bu ah nah da Bear Boudreaux. Da mah dada. Dada Bear he out on da lake fo some shoepicks fo suppa. Crawfish is da bez bait fo catchin' da shoepicks. He go fo da crawfish an den he go fo da shoepick is how he do it."

Boner extended his hand, "I be Boner Jones."

"Anh, shew be da Bona! Gah dat me too most like shew also!" laughed the young man, grabbing his hat as though he expected it to pop off with excitement. "Oh me oh my, I be da *Bona* also an we bote be da Bona now ain dat sumpin? I be da *Bone*fish Boudreaux shew zee. Dat dere be Hambone me brudda alzo. Actual he be Jimbob Boudreaux an I be da Jimbob Boudreaux alzo. Dat be how come we be Bonefish an Hambone fo nah be nah mo confusin shew zee. Da Dada Bear he go make two dem Duperoult sistaz wit de babiez back den an den dem Duperoult mamaz done do uz bote wit da same name when we juz tee tee. Den da mamaz fight bout who git ta keep da name Jimbob zo Bear he say he fix it wit da Bonefish an Hambone wha see? Da way we da same buh difernt. An den da mama'z dada zay to Dada Bear, he zay, 'Fine dandy den you juz take dem two bone heads from mah girls an keep 'em.' An dat wha Dada Bear done."

"Dat be da trute of it alrighty," laughed Hambone.

"Ho chi mama," said Chi Chi, cautiously eyeing Hambone who seemed to be undressing her with his mind.

"We be lookin' fo de Bear," said Boner. "Da Bear Boudreaux."

"He still out gittin' shoepicks like I zay," said Fishbone.

"We waz gonna made some dat gumbo wit turtle ags but dere ain no more turtle cause dem alma dillins dig up al da ags," said Hambone, his eyes still fixed on Chi Chi. "Turtle ag gumbo good eatin' ya know."

"Dada Bear he comin' from bag dere wit da shoepicks den shew be talk at im soon nuf," added Bonefish.

Hambone's focus went from Chi Chi's breast to Fruitcake. Fruitcake had parked himself next to her where he sat staring at the many alligator heads mounted on the wall. He was wondering why the gator heads were there and was trying to imagine what the rest of the creature must have looked like before it lost its head. Since they're arrival at the fish camp, between the scent of death attacking his sensitive nose and the sight of the many dead things on the wall, Fruitcake was pretty much thoughtless except for his struggling imagination that was beginning to run wild.

"Dat dawg gat juz one eah," said Hambone. "Wha fo dawg like dat? Ain no coon dog. Dog can no do da coon runnin' ain for nuttin much but cookin'. Dat kine dog meat taze good in da gumbo."

Oh shit! They're cannibals! Thought Fruitcake.

"Dun chu worries Fruitscakes. I gots chur back ends covered. Nobody es gonna eats chu in no gumbo stuff," said Chi Chi.

"We're looking for Odalia," said Bean.

"Gah, dem folks wan fine de Queeny," said a surprised Bonefish to Hambone.

Hambone's eyes widened. He looked to the ground and shuffled his feet, demonstrating a reluctance to deal with the subject and expressing a desire to appear completely ignorant or at least silent regarding the swamp queen.

"Shew be lookin' fo dat swamp Queen woman?" said Bonefish. "Ah tinks mebbe shew nah like what shew goin' fine wit dat moodee witch. An if she nah take shew much den mebe she do da gree gree."

Oh, that sounds gross, thought Fruitcake.

"Dat da trute! She do da gree gree alrighty!" echoed Hambone as he shook his head in the negative, avoiding eye contact. "Gah, shew no wan no gree gree from dat woman, nah nah nah, ah garooontee."

"Gree gree?" Roachie asked Boner. "What's gree gree?"

"Oh nothing serious," said Boner. "Some old superstitious kind of mumbo jumbo stuff. You know, like a curse or something. Like when that Cajun lady next door back home said she put the gree gree on one of my cats because it came through her kitchen window and pissed on her toaster oven."

"Oh okay. Good. Nothing serious then," said Roachie with a breath of relief.

"Guess not. The cat's still around. But..."

"But? But what?"

"He's just a little weird is all."

"Weird? The cat's weird?" asked Roachie.

"I think it thinks it's a chicken. At least it acts like it thinks it's a chicken, or a rooster maybe. But like I said, nothing serious. I mean it's not like an alien abduction or anything."

"Can you take us to Queen Odalia?" asked Bean.

"Nah nah, we nah go dere. Dada Bear he beat us witta ugly stick we go dere. Dada Bear he be da ony one go dat plaze," said Bonefish. "Dat Queen lady she been roun long time, mebe two hunnard yeah. Dada Bear he take care on her juzz like hiz dada an granddada. Nahbody see dat lady sep but dey do wit da Dada Bear Boudreaux." Bonefish abruptly ended the conversation and went to the boiling steamy barrel where he used a hooked iron rod to flip up the lid, dipped it down in and pulled out an exceptionally large flesh bare alligator head that was nearly boiled clean to the bone. He dropped it back in after deciding it wasn't quite ready.

Cannibals! Oh shit! Cannibals! I knew it, thought Fruitcake after seeing the skull. *They're gonna eat us. Why can't they just be vegitarians like everybody else and eat Creola and cheeseburgers. Oh the humanity! Can we go home now? Where's the house!*

Suddenly the screeching and desperate flapping of birds launching and taking flight in the surrounding swamp echoed through the Boudreaux compound. When the birds cleared away everything fell mysteriously quiet. The Boudreaux brothers knew what that meant and exchanged a quick glance and a nod of confirmation. Then a quick splash in the water a few yards away next to the dock drew everyone's attention and they all turned to see a fourteen foot alligator disappear beneath the surface.

"Ho chi mama!" said Chi Chi.

"Gata know. He know," said Hambone with a giggle.

"The gator? Knows what?" said Bean.

"Know dada Bear comin'."

"Don shew worry nun. Dat gata be da General," said Bonefish after noticing Chi Chi's expressed concern. "He nah problem lez shew be a gubment man."

"Shew mean dat gata dere be name da General? Why dat?" asked Boner. "Why he no got hiz head on da wall?"

"Dat gata be call General Jackson. Dada Bear keepin' im roun all time fo some timez da swamp be chock a block wit da gang wardens an such. Dat git dada Bear da chew rouge. General Jackson chaze dem gubment folk away dey come here roun too much cloze. Mebbe some time dey git too damn cloze roun too much an mebbe dey no git away alwayz. General Jackson ony one knowz an he ain sayin lemme tell ya."

"What does that mean?" Bean asked Boner.

"You don't want to know," answered Boner.

It means they probably ate 'em! thought Fruitcake. *Like they're going to eat us! They're cannibals! Can we go home now?*

Everyone fell silent. That is everyone except Fruitcake who continued to nervously wag his tail and mentally mumble his concerns about cannibals. They turned their attention to an unseen interruption from beyond their view in the dense swamp. From over the water and through the tall cypress came a distant continuous mechanical purring that eventually came near enough that it could be recognized as the steady putter of an outboard motor.

"He comin'," whispered Hambone, seeming to express both warning and welcome anticipation.

In the distance the aluminum flat bottom boat cruised slowly into sight as it rounded an island of high weeds and swamp growth. It rode low in the water creating a gentle wake that rolled through and against the swamp grass and smooth bloated trunks of the cypress trees. The boat seemed to know where it was going with little assistance from the big man sitting with his arm resting on the control handle of the motor. He sat slouched near the stern, appearing almost bored to the point of falling asleep, the result of a lifetime of comings and goings in these very familiar surroundings. A beat up old broad-brimmed straw hat hung down over his dark tanned weathered face that sported a salt and pepper week-old beard. A very hairy shirtless torso could be seen behind the straps of faded overalls. Serious downturned lips shuffled a half burnt cigar. In appearance, first impression made Bear Boudreaux out to be a century old Bayou throwback, as unchanged as the creatures mounted on his wall.

Thirty feet from the dock, General Jackson surfaced near the path of the boat and waited. Bear reached down, picked up a large fish and tossed it in the water where the big gator attacked and consumed it with frightening enthusiasm. The man gave out a single deep chuckle at the sight then looked up to discover the four strangers and his two sons staring back at him. His transparent deep blue-grey eyes quickly changed to dark cautious slits as he slowed then cut the engine and glided the bow of the boat onto the bank at the side of the dock. Oddly, he just sat there staring at the strange visitors who stood looking back at him. Without taking his eyes away he reached down, grabbed a string of four twenty-nine inch shoepicks and tossed the large fish onto the dock. He reached down again with both hands and up came a dead five foot gator that was tossed with little effort next to the day's catch of shoepicks. Those items were followed by a bucket of crawfish. He then reached down and came up with an old Army surplus 1903 Springfield bolt action rifle, chambered a round then rose and stepped out of the boat.

"Hooooo shaw looky dat! We done got da gata tail fo eatin' night!" danced Hambone as he skipped off to the dock to retrieve Bear's catch of the day.

Bear stepped from the boat and started toward the visitors, his strides were long, cautious and slow, characteristic of his size and build. His bare feet extending from the bottom of his worn and shredded overalls landed heavily on the ground. He cradled the Springfield rifle in his arms with confidence, careful to keep his hand close to the trigger.

"Hooo chi mama," mumbled Chi Chi.

"Yeah," agreed Roachie while eying the pistol protruding out of Bear's pocket.

"Wow," said Bean. "That's the biggest man I've ever seen in my entire life."

"Now we know why they call him Bear," said Boner.

"Dada Bear be more den seven foot hagh," said Bonefish. "Juz like his dada and his dada'z dada fo im. Ain nahbody roun Bama bigga den Dada Bear. Mebe uz too be dat some day."

Bear walked toward them slowly, then for some reason stopped a careful distance away and glared, inspecting each of them fully from top to bottom with a second glance at Boner and his home made anti-alien jewelry. He then looked to Bonefish and cocked his head as if to ask a question. Bonefish was quick to answer.

"Nah Dada, dey ain nah gubment folk," said Bonefish.

Bear nodded then continued forward until he paused directly in front of Bean. Bean looked up and up again as though he was seeing a giant California redwood tree for the first time and until he finally found the huge man's eyes.

"Hello sir. My name is Bean Buffett. I'm trying to find Queen Odalia and I'm told that you are the only one who knows how to get me there."

The huge man stared down intensely into Beans eyes, saying nothing.

"I'm told she can tell me where to find my father and I would very much appreciate your help."

After a very long time the giant man finally looked to Bonefish, gave a slight tilt of his head and a shake of his hand, then turned away and entered the main shack.

"Sorry Bean. Looks like he's not going to help," said Roachie.

They hung their heads in disappointment and began to turn away.

"It be okay so so," perked up Bonefish. "Dada Bear say he take shew dere. He say shew seein' da swamp Queen on da sun up next day. He goin' take shew."

"He say dat?" asked Boner.

"Sure do."

"Buh he no say nuttin. He juz do da lookin'," said Boner.

"Dada Bear neva say nuttin. Dada Bear neva talk cause he nah like da talkin', buh dat okay cause we know," said Bonefish.

Well I heard him plain as day, thought Fruitcake. *But I didn't understand a word. Maybe that's because I don't speak cannibal! I said CANNIBAL! Can we go home now?*

"Gah oh boy da mean shew stayin' fo da night. Dat be a goo ting alzo cause we goin' got da shoepick gumbo a cookin' an da craw fishes and da gata tale. Shew goin' like dat eatin' lemme say. Ah garoooontee shew goin' like dat," said an excited Bonefish as he snatched up a large chopping knife and started for the fish and the gator that was dragged and placed on the long wooden table by Hambone.

Hambone smiled at Chi Chi as he flipped the dead gator over on its back to begin skinning it with a long slice down the middle. He pointed the knife at Fruitcake, "Shew keep a look on dat tee dawg, ma'am cause General Jackson he likin' da dawg meat."

OH SHIT! Thought Fruitcake as he jumped up in Chi Chi's arms.

chapter 26
Elvis and the Gypsy

Her ass swayed back and forth to the rhythm of the music as her bare feet slid lightly without effort from one side of the room to the other, throwing her yellow silk skirt around with abandon, the fringes at the hem tossing about wildly. Her long white and silver hair protruding from under a colorful bandana that covered the crown of her head hung down and floated alongside an orange and green floral print shawl worn over a purple paisley blouse. Her wardrobe presented a kaleidoscope of colors and patterns as she danced and twirled; her earrings, bracelets, and beads bouncing and jingling, the bold jewelry being tossed about as freely as her eyes that darted from place to place with the beat of the music. Eyes that missed nothing and could see beyond what could be seen by normal people, even when they were closed. She was a great deal older than she appeared but in body and spirit she had boundless energy, a testimony to the effectiveness of her potions, lifestyle, and comfort with who she was. And as any gypsy queen, her insight to the human element made her wise beyond her years.

The jive music filled the room and she drew it in with ease and relish like a creature of nature would absorb the warm sunshine.

Boo bop boo bop,
Boo bop boo bop,
Way down soooouth... in Bermingham,
I mean soooouth... in Alabam,

An old plaaaace... where people go,
To dance the niiiiight away.

The music of choice was the group Manhattan Transfer singing the subtle jazzy song *Tuxedo Junction*, one of her favorites from an extensive collection of jazz, jive, and big band records that she had collected during what she often referred to as her free years. The music was one of the ways the mysterious swamp queen looked back to a time before she perminently inherited her responsibilities as the resident witch of the bayou.

The song was easy and soulful and eminated from an old record player sitting on a shelf among hundreds of small bottles filled with potions and lotions and tins filled with a myriad of exotic powders, all with faded labels hand written in a strange ancient language that only she knew. Another shelf held canning jars filled with things like frogs, snakes, and varied parts of varied other small specimens from nature's kitchen. There were larger bottles full of odd colored liquids and a collection of wild herbs hung drying from the ceiling. The music filled the room; indeed it filled the entire swamp for nearly a quarter mile around as it drifted out the open windows and through the screen door. It was the way that life within her realm of the bayou woke nearly each day. The creatures of the swamp would rise and move to the rhythm while an easy morning breeze would toss the Spanish moss so that it too seemed to sway with the beat. With the music everything in her world came alive, even the sun as it often did and has for many years, preparing to stream down through the trees to set its warm glistening reflection on the surface of the still water. It was that magic time of new hope between the darkest part of the night and the full sunrise where things still lingered under the struggling heavy orange/red horizon, and when creatures came to rest after surviving a night of pursuit by nocturnal predators. Others would rise in anticipation, yet to begin their own cruel survival rituals in the daylight. The gypsy queen's bayou was a microcosm of the rest of the world but it was *her* small part of the world into which folks from the outside rarely ventured.

A tea pot whistled and she danced across the room, snatched it up and poured the hot liquid into a cup, mixed in her special morning ingredients, smiled as she took in and accepted its pleasant aroma, paused briefly, then rolled her eyes as she sensed something in the air. "Hmm, me ting we goin' have compny," she said softly to herself.

A half snore half growl came from across the room.

"Shew hear dat I say Elvis? I say me ting we goin' have compny."

Elvis, an exceptionally large dark shit-brown hound dog with a few extra, if not too many, rolls of body fat replied by opening one eye then closing it, showing little or no interest. In fact Elvis was probably the only creature in the bayou that didn't flinch during the gypsy queen's morning music ritual. The bayou witch Odalia had come by Elvis as payment for providing a remedy to a woman who couldn't have children. With the aid of one of Odalia's potions the woman gave birth nine months later, the gift of a beautiful baby child, and for her assistance Odalia received from the grateful woman a gift of a baby hound dog that she named Elvis in tribute to one of her past successes. Now, as a full grown hound when Elvis laid flat on his gut as he often did, he looked a lot like an overstuffed pig. That didn't bother Elvis however, simply because no one had ever bothered to mention it. But even if they had it wouldn't make any difference because Elvis didn't know what the hell a pig was anyway. Elvis was content with his limited knowledge of the world because he had a simple life that included mostly eating, sleeping, occasionally chasing down coons, and keeping the gators at a safe distance from Odalia's abode. The gators were only an infrequent nuisance so he focused mostly on eating and sleeping except when the moon was full. That was when Elvis spent part of the night howling, and Elvis could really howl at the moon. Elvis had a set of lungs like nobody's business, greater than an eighteen wheeler's air-horn, and his howling at the moon that echoed through the bayou at night was so impressive and chilling that it generated all sorts of myths, stories, and rumors among the locals. It created legends regarding ungodly beasts and creatures from hell that were more unpleasant than anything they could dream up in Hollywood. The gypsy queen thought all of that was quite humorous, especially the rumors that she and the frightening beast could possibly be one in the same. Of course the mythic beast was in fact only good old fat Elvis who mostly laid around looking like an overstuffed pig that occasionally enjoyed howling at the moon.

Odalia cradled her cup of tea with both hands, danced to the screen door, bumped it open with her butt and danced out onto the porch of her stilted home that overlooked the swamp. In the water below only a few yards away a pair of gators cruised slowly by as they made their way along the narrow channel, a fish jumped out of their path, then a crane landed on one of the pilings of her dock. The beautiful white bird sat facing the rising sun and tilted its head to the light. The gypsy queen took it all in, sipping her tea, turning her face to the morning sun as well, and swaying about as she sang along with the music. "It's a junction, where the town folk meet. At each function, and the bands will greet you."

Gypsy queen Odalia was the sixth generation of her kind to dwell in and practice their profession in the bayou, which accounted for all the stories that the same witchy woman has perpetually ruled there for over two hundred years. Very few people actually ventured into the swamp to seek her out unless it was absolutely necessary. Fear kept the others at bay, fear of the legends and fear of her son Bear Boudreaux. Most of those that came were the needy, of which she gladly gave aid and comfort, and the selfish who wanted shortcuts to fame, forturne, or love. The latter, unless pure of heart, most often would find there was always a price to pay – sooner or later. The rumors and mystery surrounding the existence of the gypsy swamp witch was more than supported by what these occasional visitors saw and later reported to their friends. It was her appearance caused by a family genetic or DNA *intentional* quirk of fate. It resulted in each new generation of her family having the same characteristics as those previous, be it male or female. That one consistency was what proved the two-hundred year theory to the outsiders. But their theory of a two-hundred year old witch was all wrong.

The true story passed down from Odalia's clan was that a member of her family had once been cursed after stealing the lover of another. The curse imposed by a powerful jilted gypsy woman on the two lovers that violated her trust was that their children and their children's children forevermore would suffer the *big* and *small* of their dirty deed in such a way that it would adversely affect their lives. And so the curse accomplished its goal, forcing the lover's offspring and that of subsequent generations to give up their nomadic lifestyle and settle in the bayou simply because their physical appearance was too exceptional to live, much less ply their trade, amoung normal folks.

In the case of Odalia, she just happened to be a twin which gave her and her sister the opportunity to alternate their time in the real world outside of the bayou without interrupting the family tradition as the reining swamp witch. It was during those occasional outside junkets that Odalia developed her fondness for music, especially jazz, jive, and big band. The occasional sorties continued until her sister died a few years back. But Odalia has long since relinquished her desires to occasionally visit the outside world and has settled down to accept her role in life in the bayou, all the while hoping that some day her only daughter, who was currently traveling somewhere in eastern Europe, would be ready to willingly replace her when the time comes to do so. Odalia had full confidence she would because she knew by experience that there would come a time in her daughter's life when it would become more preferable to be a swamp witch who sells potions, tells fortunes, creates fortunes, and dispenses the occasional gree gree, than to deal with the cruel consequences of the family curse while living in the so-called civilized world.

🌴

They were clumsily herded into the boat in the predawn darkness after being rudely awakened with a loud bang on the hood of the Celestial Rocket caused by Bear Boudreaux's large hand. As jarring as it was, the wake up demand was almost welcomed after a miserable uncomfortable night curled up and tangled together in bucket seats where when they weren't fighting mosquitos they were shoeing away curious racoons, or trying to psychologically deal with the many strange and frightening night sounds of the swamp. And then there was having to deal with the internal discomforts of eating the Boudreaux Bone brothers deep fried gator tail and shoepick gumbo. According to Roachie, it wasn't the gumbo and gator tail that created the intestinal demon but rather the apparently unwashed dirty old cast iron pots and the often re-used well seasoned grease the Cajun delights were cooked in that did the deed. The Bone brothers, concluded Roachie, must have intestines of stainless steel. The only sleep they managed to enjoy came after applying some smelly home brewed lotion concocted by Hambone that he said consisted of the essence of select local plants mixed with the organs of various swamp creatures, and was *garoooonteed* to keep away anything and everything, including leaches. Chi Chi insisted it smelled like a combination of road kill and goat turds, which was probably why it worked so well at keeping the coons and bugs away. Whatever the essence of its fumatory esthetics, it certainly wasn't conducive to sweet dreams.

Fruitcake was the only one who enjoyed being exempt from its use since he was small enough to benefit from its perimeter of effectiveness. The smell of Hambone's swamp stuff repellant reminded Fruitcake of a large decaying chunk of meat and bone with what appreared to be a single protruding fin wrapped in seaweed that had the occasion to wash up on the beach one day back home. It sat stinking in the hot sun all day while being picked and pecked at by sea birds and poked at by small children and curious tourists. He called it the great funky meatball and made a point not to be down wind of it. It was finally removed by a group of Florida State Parks Wildlife Conservation scientist who came all the way from Tallahassee in a big white truck. Fruitcake thought they looked more like astronauts from Cape Kennedy. They were dressed in biological hazard suits as though the big funky meatball had fallen from outer space and might be radioactive. After a great deal of careful study and scrutinization the scientists declared the pile of mystery meat was an unknown prehistoric species of sea creature that had somehow managed to survive for a million years only to succumb to ocean predators, the ravages of modern man, and global warming. Actually the mysterious stinky clump of creature was nothing more than the front quarter of a two-thousand pound Angus beef cow that had gone bad after one of the freezers failed on a Sea Circus Cruise Line ship and was tossed overboard in the middle of the night. Fruitcake had figured this out right off the bat due to his gifted sense of smell and his experience of once being forced to survive at the mercy of dumpster spills and parking lot cast me downs from fast food burger joints. The team of state scientists vacuum packed the big funky meatball and put it on ice to be shipped to some far away place where other scientists could take DNA samples and do experiments to determine how the prehistoric Angus beef-cow-fish managed to circumvent all the accepted theories of evolution.

As miserable an experience as it was spending the night in the car, they had unanimously decided it was preferable to accepting Bonefish's invitation to sleep in the Boudreaux house where, Roachie having been influenced by Fruitcake's unfounded paranoia ardently argued that if they bunked with the Boudreaux boys they might possibly wake up in a giant coldren of boiling gumbo with their heads mounted on the wall next to the heads of the many dead gators, or possibly even be served up as a midnight snack for General Jackson. The Celestial Rocket, he argued, would at least provide some protection and a quick get-away if necessary. Roachie said he knew all about cannibals and such because he read about them in his favorite dog-eared paperback novel *Monkey*. Deep down, Roachie was pretty much a coward, not liking and usually avoiding any degree of confrontation, which is why he lost his multi-billion dollar research enterprise to his unfaithful wife and her conniving sneaky-ass Harvard lawyer boyfriend. He was also uncomfortable when he discovered that Bonefish and Hambone, who were nearly six feet tall, were actually only twelve years old, and speculated that this might have something to do with their diet.

They departed the Boudreaux fish camp in the pitch black darkness of the pre-dawn with nothing more than a small lamp mounted on the bow of the slightly larger *Swamp Thang* duck blind boat. It was being guided by their giant host, Bear Boudreaux, standing at the stern, one hand resting on the long handle of the outboard engine and the other clasped for stability to the high bar of the canopy frame. At times he looked much like the George Washington figure crossing the Delaware in the famous painting, but most of the time he looked like he was asleep. They sat about the boat quietly listening to the puttering motor as the swamp swallowed them up, venturing ever further into the Bayou, uncomfortable and anxious by all they saw or couldn't see until the sun finally crawled above the horizon and added light and definition to the dark shadows and shapes around them. Nearly a half hour later, along with the sun came the far off indistinct sound of music and people singing. Eventually the big man turned the boat up a narrow canal where in the distance through the dimly lit morning mist they could make out the stilted dwelling of the swamp witch. Drawing nearer they saw the colorful woman on her porch sipping her morning tea and swaying to the music. Odalia paused and looked at them as they approached, then turned away into the house. Soon after the music ceased.

"Did you see that?" Roachie said softly so as not to be heard by Bear Boudreaux.

"Ho chi mama," whispered Chi Chi.

"Wow, that's the shortest woman I've ever seen," said Bean. "I didn't know big people came that small."

"I wonder…" said Boner.

"Wonder what?" asked Roachie.

"I wonder if maybe she's one of… them. You know… an alien," replied a nervous Boner as he played with his numerous jingling necklaces.

The boat came to rest at the side of the dock and Bear tied it off. Boner tied off the bow then Bear took up his rifle, got out and walked off into the swamp. A moment later Bear, now unseen somewhere in the swamp, let out a loud whistle and out through the door charged Elvis who jumped from the high porch and headed in his direction.

"Wha da hell wass dat thin?" said Chi Chi.

"I think it was a dog," said Bean.

"Looked like a big chocolate pig to me," said Roachie.

"Come on," said Boner as he exited the boat and started up the steps to the porch.

After they arrived at the door Bean stepped forward, peered through into the darkness then knocked.

Odalia had closed all the drapes and lit a number of candles about the sitting room, creating an atmosphere that made most people behave as though they had entered a chapel or even a mortuary. Odalia was always amazed at how such theatrics played with the minds of her guests and catered to their ignorant expectations.

"Enter," she said.

Bean opened the screen door and entered. The others hesitated then followed timidly as did Fruitcake, but only after he surveyed the area and was assured there were no mean fat men or pirates with guns, or famously named gators with a gastronomic preference for small useless four legged creatures.

"Sit," said Odalia as they entered the room.

There was an assortment of chairs about the room, none of which were there to be used by Odalia for obvious reasons, because Odalia was a dwarf of only two-feet-five and three-quarter inches tall and would have needed a stool to mount them. The chairs were there for her visitors as was the entire room with its lit candles, brightly patterned tapestries, exotic carpet, and a strange kind of incense burning in a small brass cup on a shelf above them. It sent a small stream of smoke just over their heads and was already beginning to affect them. Though this was the room where Odalia met her guests, her favorite room in the place was the back parlor that no one ever saw. It was there she had a scaled down recliner and a large flat screen TV hooked up to a satelite dish mounted high in a tree behind the house. And it was there she enjoyed her Frosty root beer and Keebler's wedding cookies, and reruns of Gilligan's Island, not to mention her black cherry tobacco in a corn cob pipe. Now, however, she had visitors and that meant it was time to ply her trade - and she was damn good at it too.

Bean and company politely sat as instructed, looking about the room if for no other reason than to avoid staring at the very small woman. Except of course for Fruitcake, who followed her every move and thought the entire situation was somehow familiar, flashing him back to the time he lived with the old man in the senior citizens home. For some reason he kept remembering the old man watching the movie Star Wars all the time. He remembered but couldn't quite make the connection. Then he remembered the old man died watching Star Wars and Fruitcake started to get very nervous.

Odalia moved slowly about the room, studying each of them carefully. She even scrutinized Fruitcake who was about to jump up in Bean's lap when she simply pointed at him and then pointed to the corner of the room. Fruitcake obeyed immediately and went to the corner where he quietly parked his ass for the duration.

Whoa, this little chick means business, thought Fruitcake.

Damn right I do, thought Odalia in response. *Now shew juz sit an wasch da show, tee dog.*

Yes ma'am, thought Fruitcake, amazed that a first time aquaintance, even a swamp witch, could tune in to his brain.

Odalia had parked Fruitcake in the corner because she was concerned with the possibility he might dispel her visitors thoughts and interrupt the affects of the incense which was now placing them into a trance. The pleasant smelling incense was more a subtle drug than a form of magic. It relaxed them and cleared the clutter from their minds, affording Odalia an easier task of looking into their thoughts and souls. Just then a rifle shot echoed through the swamp and the sound barely affected her guests telling her they were now ripe for the picking. She finally spoke.

"Shew come seekin'," she said as she slowly strolled up and down in front of her guests, the varied candlelight within the room filling her small stature with a sense of power and mystery. "Shew all be seekin what shew ting can't be found. A quest, all differnt buh each da same altogetta."

Their eyes widened a bit in surprise with each revelation that poured from the small woman's hypnotic voice. Strangely, no doubt as a result of the drug, they all had no problem understanding her Cajun dialect but in doing so found themselves having to deal with the woman's riddles. How does she know they wondered? They saw the gypsy's eyes were firm yet kind; eyes that seemed to penetrate their own to discover the truth of their hearts and souls. She paused in front of Roachie, reached up and placed two fingers under his chin, turning his head to peer into his eyes.

"You be wantin' go back. Full of da regret fo what shew never do and wha shew lost," she said to Roachie.

"Huh?" said Roachie.

"Done shew despair. Dis journey make shew clear in da heart and da head and dere be friendship give shew da courage shew be needin'. All will be again. Courage good man. All will be again."

She then turned to Chi Chi. She looked deep into her eyes, reached up and softly stroked her cheek and said, "Shew got da deep pain and anger in shew fo so long ma baby girl, buh shew so strong and shew goin' fine peace. Shew goin' fine da love again and be free from dat bad feelins an shew goin' shine in da night like da great nort star an ain nobody goin' not know dat bright star dat shew goin' be."

She softly caressed Chi Chi's face in both hands then slid away. Odalia's touch somehow sent a warm rush of security and reassurance through Chi Chi's body that she couldn't quite identify but embraced just the same.

Odalia turned to Boner and stared for the longest time then turned and walked away, strolling about the room puzzled, occasionally looking back at him until she seemed to come to a surprising conclusion. She came back across the room and leaned towards him with a knowing victorious smile.

"Yesssss," she said, moving ever closer to his face so she could peer into his eyes. "Yes, I see long long ago. Yes, I know. I know who shew be. Shew be da one who is many but only got one soul. A lost soul. I know. I know wha shew be. Shew be da old one. Shew be... da mariner... is who shew be. Fo so long, so very long. Da old Mariner of da far off sea who never come ta rest an can never go home cause home so long go. Dat what shew be. What fo why shew come wit deze chillen, mariner? What shew be doin' here? Dat I don't know but I see. I see time make shew be a good man so I ting I no goin' bodder cause I ting mebbe shew already conquer dat demon. Yesssss, I know who shew be. It be a good ting shew do mariner. A good ting. Mebbe shew long journey come to da end soon and shew no have be sailin' so many seas of time no mo. I ting love gone bring shew full circle soon, ... ancient mariner."

Boner looked back into the eyes of the small Gypsy and offered a slight upturn of a sly smile from the corner of his mouth along with a quick wink. She smiled in return, acknowledging their shared secret, then moved on where she finally came to Bean.

"Ahhhh, shew be dat baby what is an what ain't. Baby who searchin' buh hopin' mebbe shew no goin' fine fo what shew searchin'. Mebbe followin' a dream what no be your own is wha shew be tinkin. Shew taken a great journey. Dat great jouney make shew soon get lookin' wit new eyes and den shew know what fo shew lookin'. Remember, it nah da *who* dat shew search, buh da *why* shew be searchin, young buy. I tinkin mebbe what shew searchin'' already in shew and shew juz need look wit da differnt eyes. Yes, young boy, shew be oky doky come roun right time. Buh shew beware cause dere be evil come taken wha shours. Shew beware, baby boy."

Her words confused Bean completely so in his usual innocence he posed the question. "Did you know my father?

I'm trying to find my father and I was told that you… um, that you might know… where he is."

She thought a moment, weighing the consequences of her answer, then said carefully, "I know da one shew speak bout. He come to me way bag den. He wan big tings bag den dat one. When I search his soul I zee good stuff zo I help a little. Juz a little."

"Do you know where he is?" asked Bean. "Where I can find him?"

The tiny woman thought carefully then reached out and placed her hand on Bean's chest. "I search da zoul diz boy I zee heah," she said, her other hand touching Bean's hand. "I zee he got im a pure heart," she said to herself as much as to anyone else. She again moved about the room in deep thought, reluctant to send Bean on another long journey until she came upon Fruitcake parked in the corner looking up to her.

Give the kid a break, thought Fruitcake, pleading Bean's case.

She looked to Fruitcake and smiled agreement, then turned to Bean. "Da one you seek dis tahm now he be in da west, in dat plaze called Hollywood. Buh he ain goin' be dere long." She rested her hands together in front of her, "You go now ma baby boy. Da Bear be ready an waitin' at da boat."

Bean smiled, expressed his thanks and headed for the door. The others filed out behind him. Chi Chi, who was last, turned back to the small gypsy queen.

"Was it a potion dat chu gives to him an makes him famous?" she said, thinking she might score some of the same stuff that Jimmy Buffett got years ago that magically propelled him to world fame and fortune.

Queen Odalia smiled knowingly and answered, "No, baby girl. Dat boy don't need no pozons. He juz need a doze a da trute dat waz already in him… juz like shew, baby girl. Only da trute."

"Truth?" said Chi Chi.

"It already inside shew baby girl. An shew goin' find it soon."

Chi Chi smiled, turned away and followed the others.

Odalia sighed, her work was done, but when she turned around she discovered Fruitcake still obediently frozen in the corner of the room. Fruitcake had been ordered to the corner and there was no way in hell he was going to disobey a swamp witch who could put the gree gree on him and make him think he's a chicken or worse, turn him into one of those big things like the one that came out the door when they arrived. He looked to her with pleading eyes, his tail tucked and his single ear drooping, fearing his friends were going to leave without him. Odalia pointed at him then threw a thumb over her shoulder toward the door. Without hesitation Fruitcake took off to join the others, just making it out the door before it closed, grateful he was still just himself.

They sat about the boat, staring at a very large dead gator that Bear Boudreaux had shot and killed while they were in session with the giant man's mother. The Boat puttered away along the canal while each of them contemplated what the little gypsy queen had told them, each in their own way trying to interpret her strange words. And each wondering how such a very small woman could have such a very large son. Bear never said a word which of course offered no answers.

"She said he went to Hollywood," said Bean. "What's Hollywood?"

"Oh, that's a place where short wimpy affeminate guys go to make faces on camera and pretend they're tall macho heros," said Boner.

"Why would they do that?" asked Bean.

"Fame and fortune," answered Boner.

"I don't understand," said Bean.

"So they can get famous and everybody in the world knows who they are and so they can make lots and lots of money until they start to think their IQ is equal to their bank balance," answered Boner. "Big mistake."

"Why?" asked Bean.

"Dunno. Maybe because they were always the last kid to get chosen for the kickball game or because they used to play with dolls or their mother had a mustache. Who the hell knows."

"Hey, I dun thin day es all chort and wimpy. Sung day I gonna be a big moofy star out dere in Hollywood. Efen dat leetle witch lady sase so... I thin... an I es no chort and wimpy. Well, I no too chort anyhow," said Chi Chi.

"But you're a girl," said Boner.

"Oh, so chu figure dat out all by churself did chu?"

"Kind of obvious isn't it. And um... kind of nice, actually," said Boner with a smile.

Chi Chi smiled and started to accept the remark as a compliment but then her street conditioning survival instincts kicked in, "So how come chu knows so much abou Hollywood anyways?"

"Was there... for a while," said Boner. He then turned away to avoid the conversation.

She didn't tell me anything, thought Fruitcake while keeping a very cautious eye on the dead gator, amazed at its hairless lumpy body, short legs and fat tale. *Why didn't that little gypsy lady tell my fortune? What's wrong with me?*

There's nothing wrong with you, Fruitcake, thought Roachie as he lifted the ugly little dog up in his lap. *You're just... different that's all.*

Oh sure. Like I didn't know that already, thought Fruitcake. *Just don't tell me I'm retarded.*

The distant sound of music drifted once again through the bayou. Roachie perked up and listened intently until he thought he finally recognized it, "Hey," he said to the others. "Isn't that the theme from Gilligan's Island?"

The red '58 Caddy convertible sat baking in the sun next to Doodle Dan's Quicky Stop in Bayou la Batre while its owner, Father Sabatino, sat perched atop a picnic table in the shade of a couple of palm trees, crunching on a Nutty Buddy ice cream cone and talking on his cell phone.

"I'm tellin' ya I lost the little bastard. I had a kind of thing back down the coast, then caught up with them in Mobile, then lost them again when they started squiggling all around the Gulf coast," said Father Sabatino while quickly trying to consume the chocolate and nuts and cold ice cream before it melted in the high noon heat of the small fishing town. A piece of chocolate popped off the ball of ice cream and stuck to his chin. Having one hand occupied with the cone and the other with the phone he tried to reach it and lap it up with his tounge but only managed to knock it off. It landed on his cell phone and quickly melted. "Shit," he said, then licked it off.

"What? What did you say? A thing?" said Albert on the other end of the line.

"No. Shit. I said shit."

"No, not that. The thing. You said you had a thing. Whatcha mean a thing? Whatcha doing stopping off for a thing? You're supposed to be on the job taking care of the kid. You ain't supposed to be messing around with women."

"Not that kind of thing. A *New Jersey* kind of thing. I bumped into Theo Burklander."

"Oh that old hustler. I thought the mafia got him a long time ago. I thought he was dead."

"He is now."

"Oh."

"The ice cream started dripping down over Father Sabatino's hand and forearm. When he tried to wipe it off it again landing on the cell phone. "Shit."

"So what ya mean you lost 'em? You can't lose 'em. Hasn't anybody seen 'em?"

"Well sure people seen 'em but that just tells me where they been not where they're goin'. I mean it's hard not to see four idiots and a one-eared dog in a stretched out convertible clown car," said Father Sabatino while wiping a drool of ice cream from his chin. Another glob fell on his leg. "Shit."

"What do you keep shittin' about? And what the hell you mean *four* idiots?"

"That's right, four. They picked up some other guy down in Key West, some crazy guy who's always pretending to be some other crazy guy or... the other guy being him or pretending to be some other guy or some damn thing. Back when those pirates tried to kill 'em and all those parrotheads on that island. I caught up with 'em after I finally got away from the Coast Guard."

"What? What the hell are you talking about? Are you back on the sauce? You ain't no good to me if you're back on the sauce."

Father Sabatino looked at the phone then looked at the melting Nutty Buddy. More melted ice cream leaked out of the bottom of the softening waffle cone and ran down his arm. Then more ran all over his hand. "Shit." He was just about to tell Albert that he was giving up and coming home but in a split second the situation changed as he glanced up just in time to catch a glimpse of the Celestial Rocket and its five occupants flash by on their way out of town. "Oh shit!"

"Shit again? What the hell..."

"I got 'em. They're back. Gotta go," said Father Sabatino as he slid the cell phone in his pocket and tossed the Nutty Buddy over his shoulder. A splat of runny ice cream landed on his ear. "Shit." He jumped in and cranked up the Caddy only to realize he had just smeared melted ice cream all over the stearing wheel. "Shit." He quickly licked his fingers clean then started licking the steering wheel. When he looked up he discovered a woman and a small girl in the car parked next to him. They were both staring in amazement.

"Mommy, that man's eating his car," said the little girl.

"Shit," said Father sabatino.

chapter 27

The Hollywood Hooters

The I-10 seemed to roll on forever, meandering through Louisiana, across Texas, New Mexico, Arizona, and finally into southern California. It was just past midnight when Boner guided the Celestial Rocket to a stop on the Griffith Park Overlook atop Mount Hollywood. Everyone else in the car was asleep and for those few moments during the silence after the engine was turned off Boner sat and looked out over the lights that are Los Angeles, remembering another time, the time he spent as one of the elite in the world of cinema, another one of his many, many secrets.

The sudden lack of motion and road noise caused the others to wake, stretch, and sit up.

"Why are we stopping?" asked Bean.

"We're here," answered Boner.

"We are?" Bean said, sitting up, then getting out of the car.

The others joined him.

"I thought you'd like to see this before we went into town. That's LA and over there is Hollywood. Over there is the ocean," Boner told them as he pointed from one to the other.

"All that," said an astonished Bean.

"All that and more," said Boner.

From where they stood, nearly 1200 feet above sea level, the Los Angeles basin was a massive broad carpet of millions of lights, some towering into the night sky, all interlaced with streets and boulevards on which even more lights snaked along like streams of electricity through a circuit board.

"Ho chi mama," said Chi Chi. "Das efen bigger den Me'ahmi."

"That's a lot of lights," observed Bean.

"Guess they don't call it Tinsel Town for nothin'," said Roachie.

"Wow. How am I going to find my father in a city that big?" said Bean.

"Won't be easy," Roachie said as he twisted the top off a bottle of Yoo-hoo.

"Don't worry, Bean," said Boner. "Your old man is famous. If he's here we'll find him. Besides, I know a guy who knows everything about everything that goes on in this town. He'll steer us straight. And we can trust him because I know he's not one of them."

"One of who?" asked Bean.

"You know. One of them… one of those aliens from the Fourth Branch."

"Ho chi mama. Here we goes again."

"Hey, I think he might have something there," said Roachie. "I'm pretty sure I found a nanobot in my cheeseburger back there in El Paso. Can't imagine what they put in the Yoo-hoos though. I mean, how ya gonna check for nanobots in a Yoo-hoo anyhow?"

"No problem," said Boner. "Nanobots can't function in milk. They're lactose intolerant. You know, intolerant of that commercial kind of chemical lactose they put in the food after they take out the normal kind of lactose."

"Why do they do that?" asked Roachie.

"Who knows," answered Boner. "For that matter, who the hell knows who *they* are in the first place?"

"But Yoo-hoo isn't real milk," said Roachie. "It's mystery stuff."

"Oh. Well in that case you're screwed."

Roachie looked at his Yoo-hoo, thought of pouring it out and then decided; what the hell, there are some things in life that are just too damn good to give up no matter what the reason.

Holy crap, that's a lot of lights, thought Fruitcake as he jumped from the car and joined them.

"Yep, a lot of lights," agreed Bean.

"Sure is,"said Boner.

"Es mucho lights, hokay, Fruitscakes" agreed Chi Chi.

Roachie downed the remaining half of his Yoo-hoo, nodded agreement and belched, "Ahhh, take that you nasty nanobots."

The next day they were driving through San Ysidro Canyon of Beverly Hills, each of them rubbernecking as they passed one opulent mansion after another, one ornate estate security gate after another. San Ysidro was where it all began in Beverly Hills back in the 1920s with film stars like Mary Pickford and Douglas Fairbanks entertaining all of their famous friends in their mansion known as Pickfair. It was the golden years of Hollywood after the talkies came in that was on Boner's mind however, as he looked about making note of all the changes that had taken place since he was last here. Along with some of those memories came an occasional sly subtle smile. But now he hardly recognized much of anything.

"Ho chi mama, I diddent thin moofy stars lif ly dis. I min I thin it buh I no belief it," said Chi Chi.

"Believe it," said Boner.

"Sung day I gonna be a big moofy star an lif in a house ly dis."

"I'm looking forward to it," said Boner.

"So chu sase chu bin here before?" asked Chi Chi.

"Long time ago," said Boner.

"But chu sase chu es a down island Conch. Wha chu doin' in Hollywood?"

"There it is," said Boner, avoiding her question. He slowed and pulled to the side of the road where he sat and looked at a large elaborate iron gate with a film reel on each side and the letter K in the center. The columns on each side were topped with bronze statues of the Greek gods Poseidon and Athena. "At least I think this is it. It looks much bigger now but I know it's the right spot. Things have changed a lot around here."

"Whoooa, that's a serious house," said Roachie.

"You mean that's somebody's house?" asked Bean. "It looks more like a grand hotel."

"Yep, it's a house. Well, more a mansion actually," said Boner. "The kind of house that very rich folks live in."

The grand white three story art deco mansion that would have been considered modern in its day of origin, sprawled out from the top of a gentle hill and sat amidst ten acres of well planned well manicured majestic garden and landscaping reminiscent of the classic castles of Europe.

I bet a waterspout couldn't carry that place off, thought Fruitcake. *Where's the house? Where's the food? Where's my chair? Creeeooolaaa.*

"I bet you're right, Fruitcake," said Roachie.

"An chu sase chu know who lifs in dat house?" said Chi Chi. "How come a down island son of a son of a son of a pirate know somebody wit a house ly dat?"

"Long story," answered Boner as he pressed the gas and pulled up to the gate. The heavy iron gates were closed but a voice came from a small box extending from the side of the drive.

"May I help you?" came the voice of a woman.

"Arlen Pearl and company to see Mr. Kuester," said Boner.

"One moment please," said the nameless voice.

"I knew it. I knew dere wass more peoples inside chu," Chi Chi said to Boner. "I bet chu efen gonna be Donald Duck pretty soon," she declared.

"Did you say Arlen Pearl?" came the voice in the box a minute later.

"That's right," answered Boner.

Somewhere someone pushed a button, the big gate rolled opened and Boner guided the Celestial Rocket through and along the palm tree lined long curved drive that took them to the front of the huge mansion. There they were met by a tall elderly butler who opened the car doors and showed them in. The servant seemed to be well trained as he ignored their appearance and the odd little car. But then this was Hollywood, home of many great oddities so it was likely there wasn't much that would throw him off. The butler led them on an extensive walk that took them through the great house to finally exit in the rear where they came to face a very large rectangular pool surrounded by Royal palms, exotic plants and flowers, and twelve eight-foot marble fountains in the form of Hollywood's famous gold Oscar award. It was the same number of Oscars that were sitting on a mantle inside the mansion except the Oscars at pool side were noticeably placed there by someone with a great sense of humor because they had an addition that let them constantly piss into the pool.

"Mr. Kuester will be with you in a moment. Please make yourselves comfortable."

Roachie sat in a plush chair under an arbor. "Yep, I could sure get used to this."

"Chu min chu didn't lif ly dis when chu had a billions dollars company?" asked Chi Chi.

"Nah. I had an Airstream trailer in the office parking lot."

"Ho chi mama. No wonner chu had a wife problem."

"But I didn't have time to play house. Too much work to do. Nano research is a serious business. It's the future of the world."

"Sure is," agreed Boner. "Just ask the aliens."

"So, chu es ly one of dem computer gooks."

"Geeks," clarified Boner.

"I suppose," confessed Roachie, realizing that Chi Chi was right, that his wife, or any wife for that matter, wasn't likely to stick with a billionaire geek who lived in an Airstream trailer and thought that a romantic dinner was microwaved Hot Pockets with Muscato wine. He finally came to realize she was only interested in his money even though she pretended to be fascinated by his work and research. He should have known better the first time he met her when she glided up on roller skates to the side of his old Volvo with his order of chilly dogs, curley fries, and a strawberry shake. What was he thinking, he thought, when he gave her that hundred dollar tip and invited her to join him at the Sciences of the Future conference in Seattle? She told him she was attending night school to become a Dental Assistant. The silver stud in her tongue and the five in her left ear should have been a dead giveaway, thought Roachie.

Fruitcake immediately found and took possession of a nice cushioned lounge chair and stretched out, balls to the sun. It wasn't round like his papa-san chair but what the hell?

The others roamed a few steps as they visually explored their surroundings, taking in the meticulously cared for grounds and the grand house with the obvious feeling they were in rare circumstances far beyond anything they were used to. Boner stood in place and glanced about, remembering and smiling.

"Mr. Pearl?"

Boner turned. "Yes."

The man who spoke looked from Boner to the others and back again.

"You're not Mr. Pearl."

"Who's asking?" asked Boner.

"Samuel Kuester."

"You're not Sammy Kuester," replied Boner.

"Of course I am," said the middle aged man. "And this is my home. Always has been. I was born here. Now what's going on here? Who are you really?"

Boner studied the man closely and saw the resemblance of the Sammy Kuester he once knew though this man was taller. He began to understand.

"Arlen Pearl," said Boner, enxtending his hand in greeting. "The third."

"Oh, then that explains it," said their host. "My apologies."

"And you, I expect," said Boner. "A grandson I mean. I can see much of your grandfather Sammy in you," smiled Boner. Then the smile lessened as he inspected the face more closely. "I mean you are his grandson aren't you... of Sammy Kuester, the movie producer and director?" Boner was waiting for a wink and a smile or some form of recognition from the man but none came.

"Yes, my grandfather. The film producer who founded Westcal Studios. I run the company now. Gramps is no longer here."

"Oh," said Boner, disappointed but not surprised.

"I recognized your name from the old movie posters in our theater room. I mean your grandfather's name. And of course ol' Gramps Sammy insisted that all of us kids watch all of his favorite old movies when we were growing up. The Arlen Pearl films were among his favorites with all that action, adventure, and suspense, especially the Sea Ghost Pirate series. Your grandfather wrote those films you know, as well as starring in them. And my grandfather produced and directed. They were quite a team. He said the two of them could pull great adventures right out of the history books as though they were actually there."

"Yes, I know," said Boner, clearing his throat. "Um, well I suppose we need to move along. Sorry to have bothered you. I don't know what made me think I would find your grandfather still alive. I should have known better. It's just that I promised my folks that if I was ever in the neighborhood I would stop by."

"But he *is* still alive."

"He is?"

"Sure. It'll take more than old age to put Gramps Sammy down."

"Old? I mean…but I thought you said he isn't here any more."

"That's right. He's not here with us. He stays at the home with what's left of his old friends."

"The home?"

"The old actor's retirement home. It's a big place he bought a long time ago and set up for actors and other folks from the trade. It's not far from here actually."

"And you say he's there?"

"Sure, him and all those crazy old coots," laughed Kuester. "He brings them all here every once in a while, special occasions, and always on his birthday. They call themselves the Hollywood Hooters. You know you should pop over there and see him. I'm sure he'd get a kick out of it. Used to talk about your grandfather a lot. Said it was a sad day when the great Arlen Pearl died in that accident. 'Damndest thing,' he would always say, 'Right when we finished the last take of the last Sea Ghost film my friend Arlen got knocked overboard and disappeared into the sea.' He really missed him he did. Said they were like brothers. And I'm sure he would want to meet you. You know, you sure look a lot like him. Arlen the actor I mean. Ever think of taking a screen test? I'm head of the studio. I can set it up ya know. If you have half the talent of your namesake…

well, the possibilities are endless. Not to mention the PR angles. We could even bring back the Sea Ghost series. Wouldn't that be incredible?"

"I'll have to get back with ya on that," said Boner.

Twenty minutes later the Celestial Rocket pulled up in front of a large red brick English Tudor style estate located a mere mile from the Kuester mansion. A small unassuming sign at the entrance read, *Home of the Stars* with a graphic of the traditional smiling and frowning two faced jestor. In smaller print underneath it read *Assisted Living Center*. The younger Samuel Kuester had called ahead and the five searchers were quickly escorted to a large room where they would find the elder Sammy Kuester along with a few of his old friends, the Hollywood Hooters as they called themselves, and they were truly all *old* fiends, each in their eighties or nineties. Three of them, two men and a woman, were in wheel chairs. Another man was sunk deep in an overstuffed recliner sleeping, and another, a woman, dragged her feet in small steps as she roamed aimlessly around the room. Ocassionally she would hum and do an abbreviated soft shoe dance step.

In the corner across the room four old men sat quietly at a round table with a Parcheesi game in the center. The marbles on the game board never moved because nobody ever rolled the dice or made any moves. They would just sit and stare at the game board. Each man had a small oxygen tank sitting next to his chair and every once in a while one of them would fart. He would then chuckle and the others would immediately raise oxygen masks to their faces and shoot him a bird. They only did this on Wednesdays because Tuesday night was Mexican night in the dining room where the boys of the round table would intentionally load up on frijoles so they could play musical farts the next day. The object of the game was to see who could let the most farts between breakfeast and lunch.

In the opposite corner of the large room was a veteran actor named Cecil Berkenshire who stood on top of a coffee table and quoted lines from movies. Cecil had acted in over three hundred films and could quote every line of every part he ever played in every film, which is what he did all day long. In fact Cecil could quote lines from everyone elses movies as well. In this manner his encyclopedic mind was remarkable. The problem was most of the time Cecil couldn't remember much of anything else including who or where he was. The only time Cecil didn't quote movie lines was when he was getting his weekly enema. It was then he was very much aware of who he was and where he didn't want to be at the time. Of course, being a comrade of the business, all the other Hollywood Hooters didn't mind Cecil or his continuous dialogue at all because to them he was like a Wurlitzer jukebox. All they had to do was que Cecil up for any given movie or line and off he went... showtime. Right now Cecil was Hugh Conway in the old movie Lost Horizon. Who he would be next depended on the influence and inspiration of the conversations around him in the room that triggered his memory.

For their age, most of the residents did pretty well for themselves and maintained a fairly good awareness of everything around them because they had the best of care. Old Sammy and the Westcal Studios made sure of that. It also might have been due to the fact they had lived and worked in an industry that despite its claims to the contrary wasn't very demanding physically unless you were a dancer or a stunt person, not on a continuous basis anyway and not as far as the Hollywood Hooters were concerned. After all, how tough can it be sitting around in a climate controlled trailer for the better part of a day waiting to do a 30 second shot on camera. Half of them attributed their longevity to be a reward for living a good wholesome life and the other half claimed it was punishment for just the opposite. Both claimed the other was lying.

Their benefactor, the elder original Sammy Kuester, stood by a large window with a golf club in hand, gazing out across the lawn. When the old roaming dancing woman shuffled slowly by, Sammy turned, yelled "FOUR", and swung the club until it popped the old girl on the ass.

"Hole in one!" declared Sammy.

The wheel chair bunch all laughed until one of them began to cough and wheeze.

"What's the matter Steudy, choking on your lines again?" said Carman le Taluse from her own wheel chair.

Carman was a former director of really bad art films that always got critical acclaim but never made any money, but she continued to make them because everyone in the business was afraid of her and afraid to decline her project pitches. She once made a six hour epic about a 19th century woman who taught the Nutcracker Suite to a tribe of Indonesians. When the premier was over there were only seven people left in the theater and they were all asleep. One reason no one ever turned her down was because she was one of the first woman directors and no one wanted to be accused of gender prejudice. Another reason was Carman spoke abnormally loud which intimidated most people. This was because before she became a film director she was a school teacher known as Sally Rosalia who at one time or another taught every grade of noisy and unruly students in the New York City public school system. Before that she fought in some banana republic revolution as an artillery gun commander, which also affected her hearing. She would never tell anyone exactly which revolution it was because her side lost and she barely escaped with her life. The two professions forced her to unconsciously compensate by speaking exceptionally loud even after her hearing problem corrected itself.

"What?" said Steudy. "What did you say?"

"I said, sounds like your choking your lines again."

Steudy Carmichel was a former character actor who had the occasion to star in one of Carman's films and always flubbed his lines because Carman was always changing them without telling him. He swears she did it on purpose to make him look bad because he introduced her husband to his sister and soon after his sister and Carman's husband ran off to Tahiti together and never returned. Steudy kept trying to tell Carman that it didn't really matter because it was only an arranged marriage of convenience anyway, intended to cover up the fact that she was a lesbian, which was the thing to do back then. Plus the fact that the whole story eventually turned into a best selling book and another bad art film that generated a lot of critical acclaim and little audience interest or money.

"Hole in one!" insisted Sammy.

"Another hole in one," laughed and wheezed and coughed old Steudy.

"No, no, the bastard shanked it," said Hymie Iskowitz, the sleeping man in the recliner without opening his eyes.

"What?" said Steudy. Steudy was hard of hearing but would never admit it and refused to wear a hearing aid.

"How the hell would you know, you old fart? You didn't even have your eyes open," said Carman.

"What?" said Steudy.

"He always shanks it," said Hymie.

"Hey, that was right down the middle," Sammy argued, waving his golf club at Hymie. "I'd like to see you do better."

"What?" said Steudy. "Who's a skank?"

"Shank, shank," Carman said to Stuedy. "Open your ears you line muffer."

"Don't need a golf club for me to get a hole in one," replied Hymie with a smile and sexy waggle of his eyebrows.

searching for jimmy buffett 🌴

"Got that right," said Carman. "You'd need a penis implant you old turd."

"It was a hole in one," repeated Sammy.

"What? Another one?" said Steudy.

"One," Carman said to Steudy. "Pay attention."

"Bullshit," declared Mary Storm, as she continued to stroll around the room and dance. "Missed me by a mile."

Mary was a one time great song and dance Hollywood sex symbol and pin-up girl. At one time her legs were actually insured for a million dollars.

"Wouldn't be hard to miss that bony old ass," chimed in Daschel Hunter from his wheel chair. Daschel was once Hollywood's top western action hero star until everyone found out he still lived with his mother and his hobby was cross stitching and collecting Hummels. The news ruined his masculine image to such a degree that he was relegated to playing doctors and scientists in low budget B science fiction and monster movies.

"How the hell would you know?" replied Mary Storm. "All you ever scored was your horse."

"What?" said Steudy. "Dash scored a whore?"

"Horse," Carman said to Stuedy. "A horse. Pay attention, dammit."

"He screwed a horse?" said Stuedy. "What horse?"

"Horse. My kingdom for a horse," said Cecil atop his coffee table stage.

"I don't remember you complaining when we did the nasty in my trailer back in thirty-eight when we were filming *Song of the Prairy*. Remember, Song of the Prairy? Or was that thirty-six or maybe thirty-seven?"

"It was back in thirty-nine and that was different," said Mary.

"What was so different?" asked Daschel.

"You had hair and teeth and I was young and stupid," said Mary as she shuffled by Daschel, paused, shook her ass in his face, then continued on.

"Hey hey, Dash just got a lap dance," said Stuedy.

"Her tits were higher back then," said one of the guys in the fartathon at the round table.

"What tits," said another from the round table.

"So was her ass," said another just before he farted. BLAAAAP.

All the oxygen masks raised in unison.

"Oh listen to the dudes at the gay table," said Spanky Lane, the one time king of comedy movies who was across the room in a wheel chair. "Since when did you guys ever give a shit about tits?" He rolled his wheel chair across the room and leaned over to Daschel and asked quietly, "Hey Dash, you still tappin' that ass?"

"I'll never tell," smiled Daschel surreptitiously.

"Who's got a fat ass?" said Steudy.

"That old cowboy couldn't tap a half dead stoned pig in a rodeo pen," said Carman.

"How would you know," asked Sammy. "You ever been to a rodeo?"

"What?" said Steudy. "Did what to a pig's ass?"

"The Doc stuck his finger up my ass last month," said one of the round table farters.

"Did he find anybody we know?" asked Carman.

"Tapped a pig," corrected Mary to Steudy.

"At a rodeo," added Hymie.

"What? We going to a pig rodeo? When?" asked Stuedy.

"You'll never take me alive, copper!" declared Cecil atop his coffee table. "Not in a pigs eye! Ya hear me copper? Never in a pig's eye!"

One of the guys at the round table farted again and the other three quickly found refuge in their oxygen masks. The one that farted held up nine fingers and laughed. He was winning.

"I hope you guys are wearing your diapers," said Daschel. "Last time you had a fart festival you forgot your diapers and farted all over your pants and we all had to leave the room."

"Yep, just can't trust a fart now days," said Hymie.

"Okay now kids, time to play nice. Sammy's got some visitors," said Silvia the big nurse as she escorted their guests into the room.

Silvia was well liked by all the old timers at the Home of the Stars Assisted Living Center because she used to be in the movie business as a stunt woman. That is until she decided to become a nurse after performing a fall from a five story building and breaking both arms and a leg when she bounced off the air cushon below and landed on a moving truck. Someone forgot to open the blow out panels on the air cushion. It was then she came to realize she should try a safer profession and decided, short of becoming a librarian, nothing could be safer than nursing. They were also fond of Silvia because she kept them up to date on all the goings-on in the entertainment business as well as all the latest unreported gossip, a necessity because most of them couldn't see well enough to read the trades. And when she drove them on their weekly outing to the mall where they would sit by the cental fountain near the food court and comment on the aimlessly wandering young freaks with colored hair, baggy pants, and wires coming out of their ears, she would always stop off at the His & Hers Bar that had both male and female strippers. There the old Hollywood Hooters could enjoy an hour of martinis and sexual fantasy and talk about all the risque parties they had back in the day. And on special occasions and holidays Silvia would smuggle in marijuana and let them gather out on the grounds to take a few totes and celebrate (with her medical supervision of course). Sammy's Hollywood Hooters considered every new day to be a special occasion because it meant they didn't die in their sleep the night before, so in a like manner they thought they should celebrate with Silvia's weed every day. Silvia disagreed however, and restricted their cannibis to a limited number of special occasions such as birthdays, holidays like Christmas, Hanukkah, New Years, Independence Day, and National Kazoo Day, and of course on Grieving Day when one of their group passed on to that big silver screen in the sky. Other than that they only got the pot when their charts showed they weren't eating well enough and Silvia wanted to enhance their appetites.

"Hey Silvia, what's for lunch today?" asked Hymie.

"What the hell do you care?" said Carman. "You're always half asleep when your eating anyway. Just like this morning at breakfeast. I thought you were going to pass out in your milk toast."

"It's the pills," said Hymie. "They give me pills to go to sleep and then I can't wake up."

"What?" said Steudy. "Who made up?"

"So don't take them," said Carman. "I never take my pills. I don't even know what the hell they're for but they give me the squirts so I give them to Cecil."

"I have to or I can't fall asleep."

"But then you don't wake up until it's time to go to sleep again. And the next day you pass out in your corn flakes."

"Well, that's better than watching you drool oatmeal and prunes down your chin, you old fossel," retorted Hymie.

"I don't drool."

"That's true. She doesn't drool," defended Sammy. "Except when she forgets to put her teeth in, then sometimes, but not always."

Sammy was about to take another shot at Mary's ass with his golf club when he looked across the room at Silvia and their newly arrived guests. Seeing Boner he froze. Boner looked at Sammy, at first surprised, and then with recognition and affection a broad smile crawled across his face.

"My God," Sammy said softly to himself. "It was true. All these years it was true."

They both stood and stared at each other in silence, not believing what they saw, Boner seeing his old friend in a fragile withering old body and Sammy seeing the great Arlen Pearl just as he remembered him from 70 years ago.

One of the round table gay guys farted again, BLAAAP, and the moment was broken, prompting Boner to come across the room to embrace Sammy.

"Look at you," said Sammy. "You old pirate. All those years. I didn't believe it. I wanted to but I couldn't bring myself to believe it… that you really were dead."

"Hush," whispered Boner. "My friends don't know."

Sammy shook his head. "Yes, of course. I understand. And who are you now my old friend?"

"Boner," he said. "Boner Jones of Key West, Florida."

"Ahhh, so you went home. I should kick your ass for not keeping in touch, you know."

"You know I would have in a hundred years or so," laughed Boner. "But look at you. How… I mean, what…"

"I figured it out," said Sammy, answering the question that Boner couldn't finish. "After an eternity I finally figured it out."

"I don't understand," said Boner.

"It was simple, so simple. Isn't that always the way of things?"

"But how?"

"Love, my dear brother, love," said Sammy in a low confidential voice. "If you want to defeat the curse, all it takes is love. Simple, unequivocal, undeniable, unselfish, indestructible love."

Boner stared in amazement. Sammy's revelation had just extracted a huge burden from his very soul and the possibilities were instantly swirling around in his head.

"You see, all those years we avoided it because it was the one thing we thought we could never have because of the pain of losing it, when all that time it was the very solution. But you can't force it or search it out," explained Sammy. "You just have to be ready and open to it when it comes. It's a matter of fate."

"Was it hard?" asked Boner.

Sammy smiled, "Losing her was hard but having children and growing old together was beautiful. You'll see. Some day you'll see."

Fruitcake trotted up to the front of the recliner and stared at Hymie. *I think this one is dead,* thought Fruitcake.

Hymie snorted, his eyes still closed. "Not yet," he said. Opening his eyes but not seeing the small dog at his feet, he was surprised to find no one there. He closed his eyes and decided Fruitcakes comment was just a dream.

"What? Who died?" asked Steudy.

"You did," said Carman. "You just don't know it yet."

"Your friends, who are your friends?" asked Sammy.

"They're the reason I'm here," said Boner as he waved them over and introduced each of them.

"Glad to meet you kids," said Sammy. "You should all be my guest. What say you folks and all the Hooters here diddy up to the mansion and stay for a few days? We can have a great time. Hit the pool, watch some old movies."

"Oh, sorry," said Boner. "Don't think we'll have the time. We're trying to catch up with Beans father."

While Boner related the group's story of Bean's quest to Sammy, Fruitcake wandered around the room. When he passed the gay guys at the round table one of them let out a lengthly fart and they all raised their oxygen masks. Fruitcake quickly scooted away and joined Mary on her continuous stroll, wondering where she thought she was going. When they walked past Cecil perched atop the coffee table, Fruitcake paused and watched. Cecil looked down, his eyes grew wild as he jacked up his trousers at the belt and pointed menacingly at Fruitcake and quoted James Cagney, "You dirty rat you."

Do you know Sam Slade Ace Detective? thought Fruitcake.

"*You can't love a guy like me, sister. It's too dangerous. There's no room for love in my world. So take what heart you got left and blow this joint, see. Cause a mug like me ain't the kind for a girl like you,*" said Cecil, quoting Sam Slade.

Wow, this guy is good, thought Fruitcake.

"Well darn. Guess we gotta help this kid out then don't we?" said Sammy Kuester after hearing of Bean's mission. "Hey Silvia. What's the skinny on Jimmy Buffett being in town?"

Silvia thought a moment then said, "He played the Hollywood Bowl yesterday."

"Still in town?" asked Sammy.

"Probably not. Got a concert up in San Francisco tomorrow."

"Hmm. Guess we gotta get you folks to San Fran then don't we," said Sammy. "Can't be driving up there. You might miss him again. Tell ya what. Let me get young Samuel on the phone and see what we can do."

"Thank you, sir," said Bean. "You don't know how much I appreciate this."

"Think nothing of it, kiddo," replied old Sammy. "And you, Balios, my very old friend and brother," he said, turning to Boner. "You have to promise to stay in touch. Time is a precious thing you know. Not like before. Let's not waste it."

Boner smiled and nodded agreement, "I promise."

"What? Another one?" said Chi Chi. "Who es Balios? I thin I gonna haff to start writen all dose peoples nems down causs chu es got too many."

"What?" said Stuedy. "Did I just hear Ricky Recardo? Speak up dammit. Is Ricky here? Where's Ricky. Is Lucy with him?"

"What we have here is failure to cummunicate," quoted Cecil from the movie *Cool Hand Luke*.

BLAAAAAAP, came a champion fart from the round table.

"Damn!" said one of the round table gamers.

"Frankly my dear, I don't give a damn," came Clark Gable's famed words from *Gone With the Wind* quoted by Cecil from atop his coffee table stage.

chapter 28
Golden Gate Gamble

"What do you mean you figured it out?" said Uncle Albert.

"What I mean is I figured it out. That's why I'm in San Franscisco," said Father Sabatino as he sat on the hood of his car eating a tofu burger and talking on his cell phone. "The kid is trying to find his old man so he's following the old man's concert schedule and the next concert is tomorrow here in San Francisco."

"So the kid's in San Francisco?"

"I don't know."

"You don't know?"

"He might be or he might still be in LA."

"But you said San Francisco."

"Yeah, that's right. Yesterday his old man was in LA for a concert but he left after it was over."

"You're supposed to take care of the kid. How the hell are you takin' care of the kid if you don't know where the hell he is?"

"I tried to find them at the concert but they weren't there. I think I got ahead of them back on the interstate somehow. Might have been during that ten mile back up after that eighteen wheeler full of illegal Mexicans being chased by the cops flipped over under that overpass near El Paso. This shit ain't easy ya know. You should try it sometime; following somebody in a car all the way across the country without being noticed." Father Sabatino suddenly became aware of what he was eating, or more specifically what he wasn't eating. He wasn't eating real meat. He slid off the car and spit it out. "Shit."

"You can't take care of the kid if you don't know where the hell he is," said Uncle Albert.

"Well just how long I gotta do this crap anyway? I ain't no babysitter ya know."

"As long as it takes," said Uncle Albert.

"Well how the hell long is that?"

"Shouldn't be too long. I'm about to make the deal and once everybody signs off on it then it won't make no difference."

"Then what? Then I take care of the kid the *New Jersey* way or what?"

"No dumbass. I got power of attorney remember? That just means I got control of all the money but if the kid is dead then who the hell knows what happens after that?"

"So why don't I just take care of the kid and we go find us a new kid to pretend to be this kid and we cut the new kid in on the action? That's gotta be easier than runnin' all over the damn country."

"Not a bad idea... but... nah, too risky. You just take care of the kid the other way and be ready to stall him if he starts to come home too soon."

"This better be worth it," Father Sabatino said as he inspected the tofu burger. "You wouldn't believe the shit I'm putting up with out hear. You know these weird ass people out here don't even eat meat."

"Are you serious?"

"Damn right I'm serious. And you don't even want to know what the hell they do to pizza."

Just then a burst of thunder rumbled in the sky and Father Sabatino looked up to discover dark clouds rolling in. He tossed the tofu burger in the trash and quickly got into his red convertible Caddy to put the top up but not before the sky opened up and down came the rain. The convertible top then jammed and froze half way as it was coming down, leaving Father Sabatino sitting in his car soaking wet.

"Shit.'

🌴

The powerful California Army National Guard C-130 cargo plane banked sharply as it turned for the airport and started to lose altitude. The maneuver took the aircraft from the clear blue sky above the clouds into and through the darker rain clouds that were creeping in over San Francisco and the mid-California coast. Inside the large husky plane the well secured Celestial Rocket barely shifted its position as the aircraft banked left. Inside the Celestial Rocket Fruitcake, sleeping like a baby on his back, balls up, barely noticed as he slid across the seat. Secured on the bench at the side of the plane sat our four travelers anxiously gripping their safety belts.

"Your friends must certainly have a lot of influence to arrange this for us," Roachie said to Boner over the roar of the engines.

"Guess you can say that but it was also a matter of convenience," said Boner. "Seems the Westcal Studio is making a war movie with the cooperation of the National Guard so this here plane is sort of a movie prop. Sammy's grandson is also a General in the California Army National Guard. So it wasn't really a stretch. As long as *they* don't find out I suppose."

"They?" asked Roachie.

"Yeah, you know, them, the fourth branch with the nanobots. Don't know how they deal with misappropriation of military assets."

"What do they care, they're aliens?" said Roachie.

"Yep, they are but then that's the problem. You see, they're also control freaks. Not much goes on they don't have their long skinny fingers into."

"I sure would like to know more about their nanobot technology," said Roachie.

"Ho chi mama. Dere chu guys go again. Whack jobs. Chu es a buncha whack jobs."

Bean sat quietly, his mind elsewhere.

"Hey Bean, whassa matter witchu? Chu ain sase nothin' for dis whole plane trip," said Chi Chi. "Es chu air sick of sungthin?"

"No. Just wondering," said Bean. "Do you think we'll really find him this time?"

"Sure we'll find him. No problem. You have to think positive," said Roachie as he screwed the top off a Yoo-hoo. The aircraft banked again, dropped and lined up to land on the runway. Roachie's stomach churned and suddenly the Yoo-hoo didn't look that appealing. He screwed the top back on and clenched it tightly againt his chest next to the barf bag in his pocket.

"All I can say is we're closer now than ever, Bean. So don't be discouraged. Things could always be worse," said Boner.

"Worse? Wha chu min worse? Dat no make no sense," said Chi Chi. "Causs es no so worser now."

"Well," said Boner, "we could be abducted by aliens or swallowed by a sea monster or crushed in an earthquake or cursed by the gods or maybe even this plane could…"

"Ho chi mama. Chu no never mind. I'n no wanna hear no more of dat kina worser stuff."

"Well it's not impossible, ya know," said Boner.

There was a loud thump and bump as the plane touched down then rumbled across the tarmac to a large hanger in the private sector of the airport. When it came to a complete stop under the hanger and the engines were shut down the large ramp at the rear of the plane lowered. The entire cargo bay lit up and in came the sound of rain on the tin roof of the hanger. Near the open aft end of the plane was a waiting black limosine.

"Mr. Pearl?" inquired the driver as they exited the plane.

They all looked to Boner expecting him to respond.

"What?" said Boner, questioning their stares.

"Well, es chu him or notchu?" said Chi Chi.

Before Boner could answer Chi Chi answered for him.

"Yeah, das him," she said to the limo driver. "Bu chu better be quick causs he gonna turn into somebody else pretty soon. He es kina funny dat way."

"Um, yes ma'am," said the driver. "I'm supposed to take you folks to the hotel."

"What about my car?" asked Bean.

"Your car and the plane will be here at your disposal to take you wherever you need to go, sir. Anywhere in the country," said the pilot who had just walked up behind them.

"Anywhere?" said Bean.

"Anywhere, sir," repeated the pilot. "We are at your service as per General Kuester's instructions."

"Uh, okay," said Bean.

Can we go back to the mansion? I liked that pool and the chase lounge, thought Fruitcake. *Where's the food? Where's the mansion?*

The driver opened the limo door and they climbed in. When the driver slid in behind the wheel he discovered Fruitcake had claimed the front seat next to him, stretched out, balls up. He cleared his throat and accepted the comfortable little passenger in silence as the limo pulled off into the rain.

That's one ugly little dog, the driver thought as they cruised across the tarmac.

So's your mama, thought Fruitcake in response.

The driver looked at Fruitcake, then shook his head in disbelief, "Nah. No way," he said to himself.

A short time later the limo glided to a stop in front of the Four Seasons Hotel. When they exited the vehicle a stretched limosine pulled in behind them. Its driver got out, popped open the trunk and stood waiting until a hotel bellhop rolled out a luggage carrier full of bags, all with the monogram label JB. The two men began loading the bags into the trunk.

"I wonder who that's for," said Bean.

"At this hotel it could be for anybody," said Boner. "This is the most expensive hotel in San Francisco."

"Oh, I no thin we can stay here den, causs we no gots dat kina moneys," said Ch Chi.

"Yeah, it's not exactly the Dixie Palm," added Roachie.

"Don't worry," said Boner. "Everything's covered by Westcal Studios."

When they walked into the grand lobby their appearance drew a few quick glances but they were short lived. After all, this was San Francisco, land of the strange, domain of the weird, and the incubator of life on the far side.

"Mr. Arlan Pearl and company," Boner said approaching the woman at the registration desk.

"Yes Mr. Pearl, we've been expecting you." She set four small envelopes on the counter, each for a different suite. "Everything has been arranged and you need only call the desk to have your limo brought to the front. Your room keys, concert tickets, and backstage passes are in those envelopes. The other things you requested have already arrived and your dining reservations have been confirmed. Is there anything else you require?"

"Not just now, thank you," said Boner. He took the envelopes and passed them out as they walked to the elevators. "The concert is tomorrow at Golden Gate Park. So tonight we're going to dinner at one of the finest restaurants in town. Now get cleaned up and we'll all meet here in the lobby in one hour for dinner. Okay?"

Everyone agreed. The elevator door opened and in they went. Just as the elevator door closed, the elevator next to theirs opened and out flowed a small group of people who paraded through the lobby and out to the waiting stretch limo in front of the hotel. As the limo pulled away a newly arriving guest who just got out of a cab looked to the bellboy who was loading his luggage and asked, "Hey, wasn't that Jimmy Buffett?"

An hour later Boner and Roachie stepped out of the elevator in tuxedos, dressed to the nines as they say, each having been duded up with the assistance of an assigned personal butler. A few minutes later they were joined by an uncomfortable Bean, also sporting a tux.

"I had the clothes sent over from the wardrobe department of the studio. Hope you don't mind?" said Boner. "Looks like I sized you guys up pretty good."

Bean squirmed and twitched a bit here and there, obviously uncomfortable. The outfit was a good fit but for the boy from the beach who spent his entire life wearing nothing more than a bathing suit, T-shirt, and sometimes sandals, it was the first time he ever wore a full set of clothes and it all felt extremely confining if not completely strange, especially after being dressed by a manservant who kept smiling and looking at his crotch. The man reminded him of Uncle Joe's girlfriend and the uncomfortable Bean was so eager to leave the room that he left still wearing his Margaritaville flip flops.

"Whoa, gotta do something about those feet," said Boner, referring to Bean's flip flops. "Follow me."

He led them to a shop in the hotel where he helped Bean pick out a nice pair of alligator shoes. Bean paced around a bit, looking down at his feet, then looking up to the guys with a smile.

"How do they fit?" asked Boner.

"I don't know," said Bean. "How are they supposed to fit?"

"Do they pinch?" asked Roachie.

"Of course not, they're dead," said Bean.

They charged the shoes to Bean's room and returned to the lobby where they discovered standing all alone and waiting in the center of the lobby, a radiant princess poised in a stunning baby blue evening dress. At first they were polite and nearly dismissed the sight as a stranger until they realized it was Chi Chi. Then they each stood there in awe, speechless, until princess Chi Chi finally broke the silence.

"Ho chi mama. Dun juss stand dere like a buncha dummies. Somebody take my hand causs I dun thin I can walk in dese damn funny choos."

Bean and Roachie still could not bring themselves to move but Boner quickly stepped up to Chi Chi's side to offer assistance.

"Thang chu," she said, smiling affectionately.

Boner melted, returning the smile with his own, noting her natural beauty and how comfortable her hand felt in his.

"Wow," said Roachie as he inspected their little group. "I haven't seen anything like this since prom night in high school, minus all the zits and bad hair of course."

"Well, I guess it's time to go," said Boner, recovering a bit from his new found infatuation with Chi Chi, but certainly not dismissing it.

As they walked for the door Bean lifted his trousers and looked down at his feet. "You know, these shoes actually feel pretty good."

"They should," said Boner. "They cost eight-hundred bucks."

"Oh. Is that a lot for shoes?"

"Some folks might think so."

"It's a good thing I didn't get any socks then, huh?"

Boner laughed, "Yeah. I'm sure socks would have really jacked up the bill."

"Do you think Fruitcake will be alright?" asked Bean. "I left him with the butler and a dog groomer."

"I'm chure he's hokay," said Chi Chi. "Fruitscakes a real surfifer."

Bean looked again to his shiny new alligator shoes.

"I wonder if those shoes are related to General Jackson," said Roachie.

"Hey, chu know wha?" said Chi Chi. "Dat lady what put dis dress on me... das all she duss. She help peoples put dere clothes on. Can chu imagine dat. Wha kina peoples always need help puttin' on dere own cloths?"

"Beautiful people. Like you," said Boner.

"Ho chi mama," smiled Chi Chi as Boner helped her into the limo.

Roachie looked out to the street, "Wonder how long this rain is going to last?"

Twenty minutes later they had exited their limo, entered the restaurant and were quickly escorted to their table. Other patrons stared, wondering who they were in such formal attire and deserving such quick service without having to wait in line. Four waiters helped with their seats, another went around the table pouring water and yet another, the head waiter, after dismissing the other waiters, asked, "Would any of you care for a cocktail before dinner? Ma'am, may we offer a cocktail?"

"Chess. We would all ly a Yoo-hoo," laughed Chi Chi.

"Yes, a Yoo-hoo," echoed Roachie. "Shaken, not stirred."

"Um... Yoo-hoo?" said the waiter.

"Is that a problem," asked Boner.

"Not at all sir. I'll see if we have it in stock," replied the waiter, who then turned and walked away. He stopped another waiter nearby and asked, "Jonathan, what the hell is a Yoo-hoo?"

Jonathan laughed, "I'll take car of it, sir. There's a store just around the corner should have some."

"Good. And you can take care of that table as well. I don't have a lot of patience with spoiled rich kids doing a night out on daddy's dime," said the snobbish head waiter as he walked away.

Jonathan sent out one of the kitchen staff who returned a few minutes later with a couple six packs of Yoo-hoo. He served four of them to their guests and put the others on ice.

"Would you like to order now," he asked them. "Might I recommend the Scallops Bonne Femme and Spinach with Crispy Prosciutto as an appetizer, perhaps followed by cream asparagus soup, a Ceasar salad, and then our wonderful Chateau Briand. And for desert…"

"Do you have cheeseburgers?" interrupted Bean.

"Uh… of course," answered Jonathan the waiter. "What kind of cheeseburger would you like, sir? We have the ever popular vegetarian burger with a Sheese topping."

"Bless you," said Roachie.

"Uh… yes, um, *Sheese* is a vegetarian cheese substitute imported from Scotland and comes in various flavors. We also have an interesting *Burger le Winge* which is a combination ostrich and lamb topped with garlic basil infused goat cheese, and there's also our seafood burger consisting of…"

"Meat," interrupted Bean.

"Meat?" said the waiter.

"He means beef. Just good old fashioned cow meat," clarified Boner.

"Of course, sir. Our sirloin burger is the best in town."

"Okay then," said Boner. "We'll all have cheeseburgers… with meat."

"I like mine with lettuce and tomato," said Roachie.

"And Heinz 57," added Chi Chi.

"And French fried potatos," said Bean.

"With a big cosher pickle and a cold draft beer," added Boner. "Oh, and strawberries in champagne for the lady, please."

A smile crawled across the waiter's face as he leaned over the table and whispered, "You're all parrotheads aren't you?"

"How did you guess?" asked Roachie.

"Lets just say it takes one to know one," smiled Jonathan. "You're here for the concert tomorrow?"

"Yes," said Boner. "All the way from Florida."

"Well, welcome to Frisco fellow parrotheads, where anybody can be anything they choose, including a parrothead. That is if you ignore the government. It's margaritas all around on me, okay?"

"Thank you," said Bean. "That's very kind of you."

"Anything for fellow parrotheads," smiled Jonathan. "Cheeseburgers on the way and I'll be right back with those margaritas."

They were wined and dined as never before with special care and attention by Jonathan and a coalition of fellow parrothead waiters, during which time they laughed about all they had been through along their journey and especially when they compared their present meal with the one served up by the Jimbob Bone Boudreaux brothers back in the bayou. Bean's spirits were lifted as the evening progressed, feeling the anticipation of finally finding his father the next day. As the evening progressed the restaurant provided after-dinner entertainment in the form of an ensemble of musicians who played mellow jazz and easy dance music. Boner asked Chi Chi to dance and for the first time she offered only a shy speechless nod of yes in response.

"That's nice," said Bean as he watched his two friends embracing on the dance floor.

"Yeah, it is," agreed Roachie.

"I'm glad I met you. All of you," continued Bean. "I don't think I could have done this without you guys."

"Oh, we didn't do much except tag along," said Roachie. "So, what are you going to say tomorrow when you finally meet your dad?"

"I'm not sure. What do you think I should say?"

"I don't know. Do you think he'll believe you're his son? I mean, I imagine there are a lot of women who say…

I mean women who claim to have babies by famous people just so they can get money. I think my ex-wife did that once."

"Well, I suppose he'll remember my mom. And she's not asking for money cause she's dead. And I'm not asking for money. And everyone says I look like him."

"Don't you worry," said Roachie as a waiter set yet another desert in front of him then opened and placed another Yoo-hoo on the table. Roachie poured it into a crystal glass then began inspecting his chocolate muse for nanobots, looking closely at the little white sprinkles. "Actually, I think mothers and fathers know, they just kinda know their own kids by instinct, ya know? Like animals. It's one of those spooky human things I think. Like when animals know there's going to be an earthquake or something."

"Earthquake?"

"Well, you know. One of those sixth sense mammal things like in the movies or on the National Geographic channel."

"I've never seen a movie or the National Geographic channel," said Bean.

"Hmm, some people might say that's a good thing," said Roachie.

On the dance floor Boner's head was swimming with emotion as he somehow began to combine what both old Sammy Kuester and Odalia the gypsy told him about love and the moment at hand. Chi Chi, he thought, was like no other girl he had ever met. Aside from being naturally beautiful, she was independent, outspoken, and honest to a fault. Personal traits he was drawn to and appreciated. He wondered what she would say if and when he ever revealed his deep heavily guarded secret. She leaned back and looked at him with an easy comfortable inviting smile, the result of a safe secure warm feeling she hadn't felt since her time with her parants in Cuba when she would rest in the arms of her real father. Chi Chi wondered if this was the real Boner or just another of his many personalities because she kind of liked this one. So as not to lose the moment, she dismissed the question and there was a passing thought of a kiss but she supressed it, laid her head on his shoulder, smiled and whispered quietly under her breath, "Ho chi mama."

chapter 29
Planet Frisco?

"What's the matter with Fruitcake?" asked Boner as he joined the group for breakfast.

Fruitcake was flopped on his side under Bean's chair in the restaurant, hardly in a position to catch any food and obviously depressed.

"He thinks he's been emasculated," said Roachie. "Bean's private butler and the dog groomer gave him a bubble bath and a blow dry, cut and painted his nails, scented him with perfume, and put a bow on his collar."

"Oh wow, that's pretty harsh for a free wheeling ace detective," replied Boner as he looked down to inspect Fruitcake's pink toenails. "But then this *is* San Francisco."

"Yeah, buh dun dem guys can see dat Fruitscakes es a guy?" said Chi Chi. "Day wass sposa clean heem no makes heem a girlyman. He ain no leetle pee pee dog trophy."

Boner sat down at the table and noticed Bean playing with his food, his head hung low resting in his hand. "What's the matter with Bean? He looks as down and out as Fruitcake."

"He gots da news," said Chi Chi.

"News? What news?"

"Chu no gots da news?"

"No. What news?" repeated Boner.

"We all got it. The blinking phones when we got in last night. The message from the hotel concierge," said Roachie. "Didn't you check yours?"

"Nah. I hate telephones. Never touch 'em. You know, because *they* are always listening."

"Oh hokay, now I'n guessin' da crasy Boner es back again," said Chi Chi.

"Anyway, the message was that the Jimmy Buffett concert in Golden Gate Park was canceled because it's going to rain for the next two days. So the concierge wanted to know if we would like to have tickets for the Tony Bennett show instead," said Roachie.

"They canceled Jimmy?" asked Boner.

"I didn't even know he was still alive," said Roachie.

"You didn't know Jimmy Buffett is still alive?" asked Boner.

"No. I mean Tony Bennett," answered Roachie. "My grandmother used to listen to Tony Bennett. I mean, that guy's older than dirt isn't he?"

"Sure, but he's still alive."

"Who es Tony Bennett?" asked Chi Chi.

"He's the guy who sings about how he left his heart in San Francisco," said Boner.

"He loossess hees heart and he es still alife and singin'? Ho chi mama, dat be sungthin I ly to see. Es heem in a circus or wha?"

"No. He's a singer from the old days," said Roachie.

"An he ain gots no heart? Wha he got one'a dose paze makers or sungthin?"

Boner looked to Bean who didn't seem to be hearing anything anyone said. "Hey Bean, don't worry. We can still find him. We'll just go to his hotel."

"We already did," said Roachie.

"You found him?" said Boner.

"No," replied Roachie. "He was staying here in this hotel but apparently he left yesterday."

"You mean he left town?"

"Yep."

"Well then we'll just catch him at his next concert."

"But this was the last one on the tour and the hotel lady said she heard them talking about going to Europe," said Roachie.

"It doesn't matter anymore," Bean said quietly. "I'm just going to go home. I don't think I was ever meant to meet my dad."

"Buh Bean, we wass so close an now we gots da Sammy plane sose we can catches heem," said Chi Chi.

"Yeah, that's right. We can't give up now," added Roachie.

"No, it's all over," said Bean as he rose from the table. "I think I'll go for a walk. Come on Fruitcake."

Fruitcake rose slowly and the two depressed individuals dragged themselves out into the rain and away from the hotel.

"Hokay, now wha we gonna do?"

Both Roachie and Boner threw up their hands and shook their heads.

Bean had gotten a block away when the three caught up with him. The rain was steady but warm so they ignored it and continued walking with no particular destination in mind. Bean used to always like the rain but now thought of it, or at least thought of this rain, as the final barrier to him ever meeting his father. Fruitcake considered the rain a gift from the gods because it helped wash away and remove the scent of the *Fleur du Mâle* perfume and send it to his bad memory place along with the cold thing at the doctor's office, his brief life as a dumpster diver, the bubble bath resulting in soft and fluffy fur, and the pink bow that he chewed to pieces last night as soon as Bean removed it. Now all he had to do was figure out how to get rid of the pink toenail polish.

They walked along in silence for nearly an hour until suddenly the rain stopped and a warm bright sun separated the clouds. Soon after there wasn't a cloud in the sky and the wet world that was San Francisco began to evaporate. It wasn't hard to figure that at that rate, and with the current intensity of the sun, and given the hours until the show was scheduled to begin, that the outside Buffett concert could still have taken place. It was an ironic sign from the heavens that finally convinced Bean that coming together with his father was never meant to be. He paused at the corner of an intersection in the town, looked to the sky and continued looking to the sky as though he were waiting for someone or some thing to give him directions. Fruitcake sat and looked to Bean, waiting for the same thing. Chi Chi, Roachie, and Boner stood waiting as well, looking about the town until suddenly there came what at first sounded like music but as it grew nearer sounded more like a group of monkeys turned loose in the kitchen utensils department of a J.C. Penney department store. They turned to discover the sound was originating from a parade of what at first they thought were a bunch of clowns. Then as the parade came closer they realized it was just people, but not normal people. These people were different than any kind of people they had ever seen in any parade they had ever witnessed because all of these people were completely naked. Many of them carried various items that would make noise or carry a half-ass tune, and a great many of them were painted from head to toe with any and every kind of image that anyone could imagine you could paint on a persons body, most all of which seemed to take particular advantage of specific body parts and appendages. There were people, hundreds of them, people of all ages and physiques and of all colors. Black, white, brown, fat and skinny, short and tall, old and the very young, all bare ass naked in a celebration of apparently just... being naked.

Bean was yet to notice and continued to search the sky for some form of consolation until a nude man on a unicycle with a large feather hat and a noisy set of cymbals whizzed right past his nose. When he looked down from the sky to discover the parade and all the people strutting naked in the crosswalk his eyes grew round and his mouth fell open in disbelief. Smiling back at him was a green naked man with long bushy hair that hung down to the crack of his ass and a beard that hung all the way to his crotch. Then came a bald headed woman with a beautifully perfect body painted in eagle feathers and playing a tambourine, and another man blowing some kind of whistle who was painted to look like a woman. There was a bicycle built for three and its naked riders wore the full head masks of the Three Stooges. An extremely fat man had the entire Golden Gate Bridge painted across his belly, the Beatles crossing Abbey Road painted on his back, and part of the Grand Canyon painted on his enormous ass. The more the parade progressed the more bizarre and strange it became until as though to punctuate the spectacle with an exclamation mark, the very last of the paraders was a naked midget with a tuba who blew a hefty deep toot with each of his short steps forward. As quickly as it had arrived it was gone, leaving our five bewildered travelers standing there in the bright sunshine, still wet from the rain, trying to determine if they had really just seen what they had just seen, or if they were having some form of collective hallucination. Even Fruitcake had no comment except he did tell himself that after what he had just seen he would never again think of Sister Moonbeam-Goom-jigi as odd.

No one could speak. Not even Chi Chi could offer up one of her signature *ho chi mamas*. Finally Bean turned and slowly walked away and the others joined him. The strange sight they had just witnessed left them to move as though they were in some mollified fog of disbelief, walking through some wonderland of fantasy or twisted imagination, leaving them unable to describe there feelings until finally after a few long minutes the silence was broken.

"Wha da hell wass dat?" asked Chi Chi.

"That was embarrassing," said Roachie.

"Da wass disgussing," said Chi Chi.

"Yes," agreed Roachie. "Embarrassing and disgusting."

"That was obscene," said Boner.

"Yes," agreed Roachie. "Embarrassing, disgusting, and obscene."

It was repulsive, thought Fruitcake.

"Yes," agreed Roachie. "Embarrassing, digusting, obscene, and repulsive."

"I dun never wanna see nothin' ly dat again," said Chi Chi. "Das enough ta makes chu wanna see a shrink."

"I agree," said Roachie. "A shrink."

"Was that even legal?" asked Boner.

"Hey man, everything's legal in San Francisco," came an excited voice from behind them. "Even gettin' naked is legal in San Francisco. They call it freedom of expression. Yeah right, like those crazy bastards ever actually read the Constitution. Yep, everything's legal in Frisco… except everything that isn't legal in Frisco because of the yuppies, and that's a lot. Like that dog there. He ain't legal. Can't buy 'em, can't sell 'em. You ain't from around here are ya? Didn't think so."

They looked over their shoulder to see who was speaking.

Hey, who you callin' a dog, thought Fruitcake.

"Welcome to the ultimate liberated nanny state of San Francisco my friends. City of contradiction, where you can smoke dope but ya can't smoke tobacco. Where your kids can get sex education, free condoms, and birth control pills in school but they can't have an aspirin or a breath mint. Where teachers can put a picture of that butcher Che Guevara on the wall but your kid can't wear a T-shirt with a likeness of Jesus. Yep, welcome to Planet Frisco."

They stopped and turned to discover a very tall skinny man dressed in a red suit. He had notes written on three inch square patches of white cloth pinned all over him from his neck to his highwater pant cuffs. On each note was written the essence of a ridiculous San Francisco city law or ordinance forbidding some form of individual or God given right. His long wirey white hair bushed out from under a green plaid touring cap that was covered with Superman pins. The hat framed a lean face lined with concern and sporting a bushy mustache that extended three inches past the corners of his mouth under an exceptionally long nose and large desperate round eyes. When he spoke various parts of his body would jerk or twitch, accentuating his words. His eyes had a constant habit of darting to the left as though he was trying to look over his shoulder without moving his head.

"Did you say dogs are illegal?" asked Bean.

"Yeah, that's right. You can't buy 'em and ya can't sell 'em but ya gotta pay taxes on 'em, and if ya got one ya better stash it or leash it because those goddamn know-it-all yuppies and their PC stormtroopers will snatch it up and tell ya they saved it from a life of abuse and imprisonment and then turn it into fertilizer for their damn organic co-op vineyards."

"Who are you?" asked Bean as he picked up Fruitcake and looked around for the dog police.

"Christmas. Johnny Christmas is my name, and truth, justice, and the American way is my game. Ya know they don't even want ya to call Christmas Christmas around here anymore. That's why I changed my name. Use to be John Maynard but I changed it to Johnny Christmas. See there, I beat 'em at their own game, semantics. Christmas is what they gotta say when I'm around. *Here comes Johnny Christmas*, is what they gotta say. And they gotta say it all year round too. Christmas, Christmas, Christmas is in your face you hatched from hell evil pagan yuppies."

"What's a yuppie?" asked Bean.

"Oh you know. That's all those people who went all drug nuts and rock and roll anti-culture and earth natural freedom crazy in the sixties and seventies and then got greedy and rich and secularly sanctimonious and all environmental to mask their guilt. Too much of that LSD you ask me. First they said the earth was gonna freeze now they say it's gonna fry. Can't make up their damn minds but they think they know it all because they always followed directions and never colored outside the lines and got a sheeps skin on the wall while they were avoiding the draft and never had to work hard or get dirty and spawned all this high tech shit that's shrinkin' the planet. They wanna tell ya how to live and what to eat and what to say and want to change every other damn thing that puts a hair up their cushy asses or interfears with their squeaky clean Sesame Street concept of the world."

Wow, thought Fruitcake. *That sounds pretty bad. I wonder if they're cannibals.*

"Sure they're cannibals. They'll eat your entire soul if you let them. Hey wait a minute, who said that?"

"Yuppies eat your soul?" asked Bean.

"Sure do and they use all three of their names all the time; like anybody really gives a shit. And they say words like *multitasking* and *social interfacing* and *nesting,* and they wear bicycle helmets with little lights and fanny packs, and they childproof their homes so their kids can't learn from their own mistakes and grow up with no horse sense. And they always vote for democrats even when they know they're lyin' because some bent brain left headed subversive commie college professor told them that all republicans are evil destructive money hungry ogres who want to blow up the planet and that all conservatives are religious extremist who will eat your children. Yep, and they eat trail mix and organic weeds and quiche and drink overpriced bottled water to hydrate and flush their system after a hard day of sitting on their butts where they're jackin' up on eight dollar designer coffee full of caffeine, sugar, chocolate, and whipped cream to keep their limited misled little minds crankin'. That's what yuppies are.

They're tight-ass walkin' talkin' contradictions of their own existence, the ultimate biological dichodemy."

"Wow, really?" said Bean. "That sounds awful. What's a democrat?"

"Trust me, kid, you don't want to know. Just steer clear of 'em cause they're contagious."

"I think I used to know some of those people," said Roachie.

"Ho chi mama," Chi Chi said to Roachie. "Es no wonder chu ends up liffen under a bridge."

"I don't live under a bridge," said the strange man.

"I no mean chu. I mean dis genius guy here."

"Oh. Well, anyway, that's what yuppies are. And not only that, they make rules that offend almost everybody just so somebody else won't be offended. Does that make any sense? That's what a yuppie does. Hell, half of them won't even fly the American flag because they think it'll piss off somebody who's not even supposed to be in the country in the first place. That's right, and they want to take over and turn the whole planet into some kind of PC Barbie and Ken world." Johnny Christmas leaned over and whispered, "You know what they want to do next? They wanna ban circumcision. Say it violates our freedom of choice. Can you imagine that? They wanna tell us what we can't do with our peckers so we can choose what to do with our peckers! Duh. Tell me that ain't just postponing the pain. Does that make sense? Think about that one will ya? All those little boys in school having to line up and drop their pants for inspection so some nurse can see if they still have their freedom of choice. Tell me that won't retard your kid's self esteem. And we used to think gym class was bad. Hard to believe, huh? Yep, it's that bad. Hell, they already took over the west coast and are spreadin' across the country like poisen ivy in a nudist camp. Damn friggin' yuppies. They're in Colorado, Wisconsin, New Mexico and even Massachusetts! Well, that's no surprise I guess. After all, those folks used to burn witches and they got Harvard University."

He pulled some small flyers from inside his suit coat and handed one to each of them. On the cover of the flyer was a photo of a nuclear bomb explosion. Superimposed in bold letters it read, DIE YUPPIE DIE! Then in smaller print on the bottom asked, ARE YOU PART OF THE PC ZOMBIE RACE?

"I don't think he likes yuppies," said Boner.

"Ho chi mama, dis guy got a lots to say."

"What's wrong with following directions?" asked Roachie.

"Ain't nothin' wrong when you're just startin' out in life and trying to figure out what this world's all about and it helps you along with the basics like stayin' alive and being functional, and as long as there ain't too damn many directions to follow in the first place," replied Johnny Christmas. "Like those yuppie directions that tell little kids that their parents and grandparents are idiots. Bet that one will come back and bite those yuppie bastards on the ass. The only directions most folks need are the ones that tell other folks to mind their own damn business and leave 'em alone. A little benevolent neglect can go a long way for most folks, ya know. Folks gotta have some breathin' room. Freedom, that's what it's all about. Freedom to make it on your own without some damn know-it-all deciding how you should live or what you should eat. Know what I mean? Not freedom to dance naked in the streets and make everybody puke like all those fruitcakes in that parade but the other kind of freedom like that freedom that let all those damn yuppies turn into yuppies in the first place."

Hey pal, watch who you're calling fruitcakes, thought Fruitcake.

Chi Chi whispered to Bean, "I dun know if dis guy es ever gonna stop talkin'. Wha chu thin? Es he ever gonna stop talkin'? Chu thin maybe he go away if we gives him a quarter?"

"It's time to revolt. Stand up and be counted. Take back the country! Damn yuppies are ruining the country, cut its balls right off they did, and now they're turning it over to the wimps and goths and gamers and tech-heads and socialists commies who don't even have a clue. What kind of generation is that to run a country? They don't know where we been so how the hell they gonna figure out where we're goin'. It's a sad day, a sad day indeed. And it started right here on Planet Frisco with all those damn hippies that morphed into yuppies that morphed into greedy snobs. But I'm gonna stop 'em. You wait and see, I'll stop 'em. Damn yuppies."

"Um... what do you do?" asked Roachie.

"Who me? Oh... well I used to be a nuclear physicist until I heard my calling. That was right after they took my dog, shut down my mother's church bizarre for selling cupcakes, and then arrested me for smokin' in a bistro."

"Um... we're going to go now," said Bean who didn't have the slightest idea what this guy was babbling about. "Best of luck, sir, with... um... all that stuff."

They turned and walked away but the strange tall talkative man followed.

"You have to rise up and take a stand!" he continued. "Oh, I know. You think I'm crazy. Well that's okay but I know you folks aren't from around here. So that's okay. But don't you linger here too long or the next thing you know these damn yuppies are gonna drive you nuts just like me and get your brain and values so twisted that you'll end up marchin' in one of those crazy damn nudy parades like all those other people whose brains are all askew. Yep, you folks run along home and you be strong and stay the course. It's up to you now. Watch out for those damn yuppies. You see any of those damn yuppies you tell 'em Johnny

Christmas is comin'. You tell 'em that! Tell 'em Johnny Christmas is comin' and he's bringin' hell along with him!"

They continued walking and Johnny Christmas continued talking about the impending national doom due to the influence of the over educated left headed yuppie race. Then at first opportunity he latched onto a couple of Japanese tourists passing in the opposite direction and began to unload his social grievances on them. He was a man with a mission, dedicated to a cause and asking nothing but a sympathetic ear so he could hand out his flyers and spread his Planet Frisco counter revolution to save the world. The couple snapped his picture and quickly trotted away. The odd determined man followed.

"Somebody chould sends dat guy to Kooba and let heem walk around Habana," said Chi Chi. "Buh he no would lass so long causs Fidel he would choots heem."

"You really think so?" asked Roachie.

"Chure, causs Fidel he es a equal opportunity killer. He dun care where chu es from. If he no likes chu den chu es history."

"Takes all kinds to make a world," said Boner as he looked over his shoulder at Johnny Christmas raining his grievances down upon the visiting Japanese couple.

"I thinin dis peoples in dis town efen makes *chu* look kina normals," Chi Chi told Boner.

Boner smiled and laughed. She melted, smiled in return and affectionately nudged him with her elbow.

Wow, dogs are illegal. Can you imagine that, thought Fruitcake as he rested securely in Bean's arms. *Good thing we don't have any dogs with us. Hey Bean, what's for breakfeast?*

Bean hadn't taken into account where they had been, where they now were, where they were going, or where they would end up, and so they began to wander aimlessly about the town in hopes of finding their way back to the hotel. Eventually their wandering landed them on a back street that obviously was not a path to the Four Seasons. What they discovered instead was a small community of homeless people living under makeshift plastic covers and in cardboard boxes, their entire lives stored in plastic garbage bags or shopping carts.

"Oh, that brings back a few memories," said Roachie.

"I don't think this is the Four Seasons," said Boner.

A dirty ragged woman who sat huddled in a nearby cardboard box spotted the group. "There you are!" she yelled as she crawled out of the box and jumped to her feet. "Where have you been? I thought you'd never get here. Did you bring food and warm clothing? We had to eat the horses you know. We've been waiting so long you see, so long, and some of our party has died. Frozen and starving in the snow. It was horrible. And that man over there; I think he ate somebody. I saw him. I saw the whole thing. It was horrible. Have you seen Mr. Donner? I can't find him anywhere. He went to find help but I think he might have froze to death and they ate him."

"Really?" said Roachie. "That's horrible?"

"Worse than horrible!"

"Worse?" said Roachie. "How could it be worse?"

"Much much worse, more worse than you can imagine."

"Worse than I can imagine," said Roachie.

"Yes. Worse even than a History Channel dramatization," said the strange woman.

"Oh wow, that's pretty bad," agreed Roachie.

"You bet it is," said the woman. She appeared to be in her fifties, had dirty red hair, was dressed in an old 49ers football jersey over a dirty yellow baggy pair of double knit pants that stretched down over her bare feet. Her eyes were round and desperate as she approached them dragging a dingy stuffed dog on a leash that was tied to her wrist. Both arms and hands clutched a very large well worn library volume of Websters Dictionary close to her chest. She walked right up to Bean and stared desperately into his eyes until suddenly she reached out and tweaked his nose, then poked him on the forehead with a firm forefinger.

"Hey, that hurt," said a surprised Bean.

"You better pay attention young man. I'll not have any slackers in my classroom. Now quickly, tell me who wrote the Magna Carta?"

"Um…the what?" asked Bean.

"Wrong wrong wrong. And I bet you don't even know where to find the peanut butter in Wal-Mart do you? Do you? I didn't think so. Pay attention! Pay attention! You'll never pass my class unless you pay attention. Now tell me, tell me, in what country is the Panama Canal located? Well, speak up. And who killed Cock Robin, huh? Can ya tell me that, can ya? Do you know what the Fourth Branch of government is? Do you? Of course not, because you don't pay attention."

Bean knew all the answers except for the one about Cock Robin, but had no idea what to make of the weird woman so he simply offered only a blank stare in response.

"Hey she knows about the fourth branch," said Boner.

"Of course I know about the fourth branch of government because I pay attention," she said as she backed away and looked down at her dingy stuffed dog, "No Cleveland, you can't piss on the man's leg. It's not polite." She leaned toward Boner and whispered, "They took me, they did. And they put nanobots in my ass."

"Ho chi mama," said Chi Chi. "Dis woman done losses her mind."

"Mine? Mine? What's mine is yours. What's yours is mine. Share the wealth. Share the wealth. Democracy? Democracy? We don't need no stinkin' democracy, we got Nancy Pelosi from the Fourth Branch." She again addressed her stuffed dog, "I said no Cleveland. You can't piss on the man's leg."

Damn, thought Fruitcake. *No wonder the dogs around here are illegal. They're really stupid.*

The crazy lady locked her eyes on Roachie, snapped to attention and saluted, "Mr. President, it is my duty to report that the state of the union is in a terrible state indeed because, well, it just sucks, and we need more egg rolls and fewer Berkeley Scholars or else we won't have enough hydrocarbons and stuff."

"Whoa," said Roachie. "This woman is freaky."

"I thin es tine to go," said Chi Chi. She pointed behind the crazy woman and yelled, "Oh lookit! Dere goes Christopher Columbus!"

"Oh my. Oh dear. Come on class, let's all go meet Christopher Columbus. Maybe he's seen Mr. Donner," said the woman as she turned away and began walking down the back street. "No Cleveland, you can't shit on the man's leg either. You're so rude. I can't take you anywhere."

"Wow," said Roachie. "I wonder if all these folks are as nuts as she is."

"Yeah, and I thought Key West was a freak factory," said Boner.

"They look hungry," said Bean. "Maybe I should…"

"Oh no chu dunt," said Chi Chi as she snatched Bean's arm and pulled him away. "Chu no gonna adopt no more peoples. We gonna get outta dis crazy town and take chu home."

Bean acquiesced and they departed the scene but when they turned the corner onto a main street a man dressed in a woman's ballerina tutu and tights danced up to them and handed them each a flower. "I love you, man," he said. "I love all of you."

"How chi mama," said Chi Chi.

"There certainly are some very strange people in this city," said Bean as he was being pulled away by Chi Chi.

Eventually they found their way back to the hotel, checked out, and returned to their waiting plane. Just seeing the Celestial Rocket again seemed to afford Bean a little comfort, but not much because after traveling across the entire country, he had failed to connect with his father and as far as he knew he probably never would. In his mind his quest had ended. To rid himself of this heavy emotional funk Bean began thinking about the future, but not his future because Bean was not a self-centered selfish boy. It was his friends he was concerned about now. What would become of his newfound friends now that his quest was ending and he was going home? What would become of his newly adopted family?

chapter 30
Sacred Stones

They had been airborne for nearly thirty minutes when Roachie developed a thirst for a Yoo-hoo so he detatched his safety belt and made for the rear of the Celestial Rocket.

"Anybody want a drink?" he asked as he popped open the trunk and bent to open the cooler.

Just then the pilot made an announcement, "Hang on back there folks. We're coming into some turbulence but we should be through it in just a few minutes."

No sooner had the pilot made his announcement than the plane hit a rough patch of air that buckled the smooth ride and brought the top of the trunk down on Roachie's head, sending him back to plop down on his ass on the deck. The turbulence also tossed bottles of Yoo-hoos out of the cooler and all over the trunk.

"OW!"

"Hey Roachie, es chu hokay?"

"What?"

"Hees hokay," said Chi Chi.

Roachie rubbed his head then got up and rubbed his ass as he inspected the trunk. "Oh wow, that was lucky. Not one bottle broken." He was retrieving and returning his precious chocolate drinks when he noticed an old leather bag that had spilled out from behind the cooler. It was with the stuff Yoyo had placed there after he had done his custom work. Spilling out of the bag was what looked like a bunch of old rocks. Roachie shoved them back in, took the bag and one of the drinks, closed the trunk and returned to his seat. "Hey Bean, why you keeping this bag of old rocks in your car?" asked Roachie as he held up the bag for Bean to see.

"What?" replied Bean, still preoccupied by his disappointment of not connecting with his father.

"Rocks," said Roachie, pulling a few samples from the bag to show him. "I found a bag of rocks in the trunk of the car."

"Oh, those were my mom's," said Bean.

"Rocks?" said Boner. "Let me see."

Roachie handed a couple of the stones to Boner who inspected them carefully then took the bag and looked inside at the rest of its contents. "Yeah, they're rocks okay but you won't believe what kind of rocks. Holy smokes, Bean, these are diamonds!"

"Diamonds. Are you sure? How do you know?" asked Roachie.

"Trust me. I've seen a lot of jewels in my time, both rough and refined, and these are fantastic high grade diamonds in the rough."

"Oh um…yeah those things. Mom brought those back from Africa I think. Souvenirs I guess. She collected all kinds of stuff; seashells and beach glass and stuff. She always forgot where she put them though and would say, 'Well, if I can't find them neither can anybody else.' She was like that. Would always forget where she put stuff."

Yeah, like sometimes she would forget to make the Creola, thought Fruitcake. *But she always had the cookie thing going on. Where's the house? Where's the food? Creeeooolaaa.*

"Creola? Whas dat?" asked Chi Chi.

"But Bean, don't you realize what these are?"

"Yeah. They're rocks."

"No, not just rocks. These are diamonds. And damn big ones at that. Dozens of them. Bean, this means you're rich. No, actually, it means you're richer than rich."

"Chu min our Bean es a rich guy? Like dat micro gook Bill Gates?" said Chi Chi.

"Geek," corrected Roachie.

What's a geek? thought Fruitcake.

"Well, maybe not that rich, but rich enough not to have to work anymore," confirmed Boner.

"I already don't work," said Bean.

That's right. We already don't work, thought Fruitcake.

"Well, now you can really not work for the rest of your life and get away with it like me," said Boner.

"I dun know wha dat mins," said Chi Chi. "How chu gets away wit it when chu no gots no furniture an es beggin' for bucks at dat sunset freak cho? An how comes chu always gots some credit cards and moneys?"

Boner just smiled.

"I was rich once," said Roachie. "I bought a really nice Airstream trailer and went to Disney World twice a year. Even had an American Express Card. But I worked a lot."

"Diamonds are valuable?" asked Bean.

"Very," replied Boner.

"That must be why Uncle Albert was looking for them. The rocks, I mean," said Bean.

"Who es Uncle Alberts?" asked Chi Chi.

Bean explained how Uncle Albert came into his life immediately after Sister Moonbeam-Goom-jigi fell victim to the waterspout and how Uncle Albert sent him on his quest to find his father after taking over his legal matters. Boner was quick to recognise Albert's scam and explained it to Bean. Albert, he told him, was after his valuable beachfront property and the more valuable stones as well. Bean was hard pressed to believe that a family member could be so malicious or sneaky but he finally came around to accepting the truth. All this now presented the traveling foursome with a new mission. They would go from trying to find Bean's father to foiling the plans of Uncle Albert to save Bean's legacy. Fruitcake's mission, however, stayed the same.

Where's the food? Where's the house? What the hell are diamonds? Can we eat 'em?

Boner got out of his seat and started for the cockpit. "Where are you going?" asked Bean.

"To tell the pilot we need to change course for Key West."

"But I thought we were going to St. Augustine."

"We are. But first we have to see a man about some stones," smiled Boner. "Then we see about a lawyer."

"Chu min dat lawyer whas gonna sue dem tax peoples in Key Wess?" said Chi Chi.

"Oh no. That guy's actually a quack, a freshwater conch from Chicago who lost his law license when he got caught changing wills for married women he was having affairs with after their husbands had died. I'm only using him to buy time. As long as he keeps threatening them with law suits and doing his thing they don't try to collect their unjust taxes. He's not a very good lawyer but he's a nice guy and he needs the work to supplement his income from his job as a breakfast cook at the Holiday Inn. No not him. We need a good serious lawyer."

"Wha for es chu buyin' tine. Wha chu gonna due wit all dat tine. I thin chu gots too much tine already an maybes dat makin' chu a leetle whacko," said Chi Chi. "We ain gonna see no alien lawyer I hope causs I dun thin I wanna meet no aliens."

"Oh hey, that would be really neat," said Roachie as he finished off his Yoo-hoo. "Meeting an alien I mean, and a lawyer at that. Is he one of those little guys with a big head and big eyeballs or one of those long stringy looking dudes? Does he have five fingers? Does he know anything about nanobots? I'd sure like to ask him some questions about nano science."

Boner just smiled, turned and headed for the cockpit. "No, he's just a normal human lawyer. I think you'll like him."

The expansive Mojave Desert seemed to move in the distance, a visual deception caused by the extreme heat radiating off the surface of the road and the baked dry dirt surrounding it. On the side of this long lonely stretch of road there sat baking in the sun a dusty classic red 1958 Caddy convertible, the hood raised and steam pouring out from its engine. On the other side of the road paced a hot, miserable, sweating, angry Father Alphonso Sabatino in his Hawaiian shirt, cargo shorts and sandles, with a hanky tied over his head to block the sun. In hand was his cell phone. Father Sabatino had found the hotel where Bean and company were staying and subsequently discovered their departure via the C-130 and its destination. Now he was trying to make calls for roadside assistance and to warn Albert that the kid was on his way home but there was no signal on his cell phone. He moved about trying different spots but again there was no signal on the phone. He turned the phone from one side to the other, held it high then low and wandered around on the dry sand in the drastic desert heat as he tried again and again and again, but still there was no signal. Once again he put the phone to his head but this time it burned his ear having heated up from its exposure to the desert sun. "Shit!" He yelled, looking out to the desert, frustrated. Turning around he realized he was now a hundred yards away from his car and standing next to a ten foot cactus. "What the hell you lookin' at?" he said to the cactus, then pulled out his magnum automatic and shot the large desert plant three times. Upon impact the meaty insides of the cactus blew back into his face. "SHIT!" exclaimed Father Sabatino as he turned and stomped back toward his car. "That's it. That's it. I quit. I SAID I QUIT!

YA HEAR ME ALBERT?" he shouted across the vast empty desert. "I AIN'T DOIN THIS SHIT NO MORE! I'M COMIN' HOME AND GETTING' MY MONEY AND... and... and then I'm goin' someplace where there's lots of women and water. And then I ain't never leaven'. Ya hear that Albert. Ya wanna know why? I'll tell ya why. Cause I'm a Jersey guy and Jersey guys ain't no damn babysitters." He hurled his cell phone into the side of the car and it shattered.

In the back of the Mel Fisher Maritime Heritage Museum building on Greene Street in Key West was a small office where a frail, short, round, balding man in his late sixties plied his trade as an assessor of fine antique jewelry and precious stones. He went by the name of Franco Gonzales, claiming to be a Cuban refugee, but in truth his real name was Adolf Hermann Goering Kaiser. He was born in Berlin, Germany in 1942, where his parents had relocated from Frankfurt in the late 30s. Adolf was a confused man for most of his life when it came to his personal heritage because his parents, jewelers by trade, were die-hard card-carrying Nazis during the time of Hitler's rein over Germany and the Third Reich's attempt to conquer the world. When young Adolf's parents finally saw the writing on the wall as the wall was being blown to hell by the Russians they decided it was time to get the hell out of town as well as out of the country. They were also motivated by the fact that the Nazi Gestapo was about to dicover their real name was actually Reizenstein and that they were Jewish, and being Jews who were also card-carrying Nazis wasn't likely to be received well in anybody's camp, not the Germans, Russians, or even the Americans, so they escaped to Argentina.

Speaking only German, their exodus to Argentina brought them to settle in a community of other expatriate

Nazis, many of them German SS and former Gestapo types. Their friends and neighbors instincts eventually led them to suspect and eventually determine the Kaiser family secret when they were accidently discovered celebrating Hanukkah. Fast becoming a family without a country, the Kaisers fled to a small village in Cuba where after his parents' death during the Cuban revolution, young Adolf, who had come to be known as Franco Gonzales, made his way to Key West with the assistance of a Haitian smuggler known as the Voodoo King. It was in Key West that Adolf Hermann Goering Kaiser, whose Nazi appeasing name given at birth was supposed to insure a safe, secure, and prosperous future in the new Germany, came to spend the bulk of his adult years, untethered by his past and his religion simply because everyone assumed he was just another illegal Cuban. Only one person in all of Key West knew his secret and that person along with his companions had just walked through Franco's door.

"Wie sind Sie mein feiner alter Freund?" said Boner with a wide smile.

"Ah, wie nett, Sie wieder zu sehen, Jean Claude," returned Franco.

"Ho chi mama. I dun know wha all dat foreign stuff min buh I thin Boner juss turn into a nudder guy," Chi Chi whispered to Roachie.

"Um… I think they just exchanged greetings and that man called him Jean Claude," said Roachie.

"I never hear no Kooban soun ly dat before."

"So what precious airloom have you brought for me to see today my good friend? And of course, I'll not bother to ask from what ancient sunken vessel it came." said Franco as he sat up in his seat behind a desk cluttered with books and photos of old relics recently taken from the bottom of the sea. "A fine old ruby set in a gold necklace perhaps? Or maybe a Spanish cross made of Inca gold encrusted with emeralds? You never dissapoint me and somehow always produce the most fascinating and beautiful treasures." The old man laughed with enthusiasm as he pushed aside everything from the center of his desk and adjusted his lighted magnifiying glass in anticipation of exploring Jean Claude's (Boner's) latest find.

To Franco, Jean Claude was his oldest and most valued customer, another down island treasure hunter who occasionally came up with some of the most incredible items he ever had the pleasure to inspect and appraise. In that way Franco was a connoisseur, always content and excited by being the first to appreciate the fine art and quality of precious pieces that had not been seen by schooled human eyes for centuries.

Boner set a single diamond on the desk in front of him, stepped back and smiled. Franco at first looked puzzled because this wasn't in character with the usual items presented by his friend Jean Claude the wreck diver. He suddenly became aware of the others in the room, looked at them, then looked again at the stone on his desk. He handled the stone carefully between his fingers and brought it up behind the magnifier to study it more closely. "Oh mein Gott!" exclaimed Franco, looking to Boner and back to the diamond. "What a specimen! My old friend, I'm thinking this did not come from the sea as most of your other treasures."

"You're right, Franco. It belongs to my young friend here. Can you tell us its value?"

Franco examined the stone again. I see no obvious flaws. With no flaws and depending on the cut, I would say it is worth somewhere between three million four to three million six, U.S. currency, wholesale of course and providing you can skirt the usual red tape as you always do. Undocumented I assume?" asked Franco.

Boner nodded a yes, "But come by honestly many years ago in Ghana by the young man's mother."

"The current legal beauocracy of the diamond trade is enough to choke a Maultier, much less erect suspicious barriers in the face of a good honest man such as you. Barriers created by the world's dominant diamond suppliers who don't care for competition of course. You could die of old age by the time this is cleared for sale."

"Oh, I don't think that's likely," chuckled Boner.

"Ah, but that is of no concern. I can introduce you to one of the finest cutters as well as a good honest buyer in Mexico City if you like. There you can get its full value without complications."

"Ho chi mama," said Chi Chi. "Das lotsa moneys."

"That's good to know," Boner replied and then reached out and dumped the entire contents of the old leather bag on Franco's desk. "And these?" he said with a wide grin.

"Oh mein Gott!" said Franco as he looked down at nearly two dozen similar primo stones, some even larger than the one he just examined.

According to Franco Gonzales's rough estimates, Bean's old African rocks were now worth in the neighborhood of $97,000,000. And Boner, judging from what Bean told him about his beach front property added another $3,000,000 to increase Bean's total worth to about a nice round figure of $100,000,000. Providing Bean cashed everything in at once, of course. More if he saved some for the future. Bean's only response after being told he was now a very wealthy individual was, "Well, I guess that's good. Now I can buy a new used surfboard. I lost mine in the waterspout." Of course Fruitcake grasped the concept of wealth right away and immediately had visions of laying about, balls to the sun, in a brand new papa-san chair and possibly even hiring someone who knows how to make Creola. Things were looking up.

chapter 31
Applegate, Applegate & Applegate?

Roachie opened his eyes the next morning at the crack of dawn to the sound of a cat crowing like a rooster in Boner's back yard. His first realization was the discomfort of the hard floor beneath the blankets on which he layed in one of Boner's empty bedrooms. "Ouch. This sure isn't the Four Seasons," he mumbled to himself. *But it's better than living under an overpass,* he thought.

You should try living under a dumpster, thought Fruitcake as he trotted into the room.

"No thanks," replied Roachie.

Come on, wake everybody up. I'm hungry, thought Fruitcake. *And I can't find Boner.*

"You can't?"

No, but he left a note. I'd tell you what it says except I can't read, thought Fruitcake.

"Oh, that's too bad. Would you like me to teach you."

No, not really, thought Fruitcake. *If I learn how to read then I won't be able to go past the no dogs allowed sign on the beach. I have to maintain plausible deniability in case I get arrested. You know, like a politician.*

Fruitcake zipped out of the room and quickly returned with the note in his mouth. Roachie took it, wiped off the saliva then read it. It was from Boner, telling them that breakfeast was in the kitchen and giving them instructions to meet him at 9:00am at the offices of the law firm of Applegate, Applegate, & Applegate on Whitehead Street. Roachie woke the others and informed them of the planned meeting.

A few hours later the group walked through the door of the attorney's office where they were greeted by a pleasant chunky little round woman receptionist by the name of Mrs. Pinthrow.

"Hello," said Bean. "We're supposed to meet Mr. Jones here at nine."

"Are you Mr. Buffett?" she asked.

"Yes ma'am."

"Right this way Mr. Buffett," she said as she led them to the rear of the building.

The building's small façade on Whitehead Street was deceptive; giving the impression this was a small town law office when in fact the structure grew much larger in the rear where it took a turn behind other buildings. Mrs. Pinthrow escorted them through the workspace of a number of employees and other lawyers and around to where she eventually opened two large double doors that led into a large opulent wood paneled office. It was full of extremely high quality hand-crafted furnishings including a large mahogany desk with hand carvings depicting various scenes of tall ships at sea, a large collection of law books, and assorted valuable nautical antiques. She motioned for them to have a seat at the conference table then pointed out a refreshment center in the corner of the room. "Please help yourselves to any refreshments. Mr. Applegate will be with you in just a moment," she said, then departed, closing the doors behinds her.

Bean and Chi Chi sat at the conference table. Roachie wandered about, inspecting some of the many certificates on the wall including the law degree of one Thermon Harcore Applegate.

"Hey, this guy went to Harvard," said Roachie.

"Es dat a good thin?" asked Chi Chi.

"I don't know. My wife's lawyer boyfriend went to Harvard and he helped her steal my company."

"Den maybes all dem Harvard guys no can be trusted," said Chi Chi. "Maybes dis guy he gonna take all Bean's moneys ly dat guy what tooks chur stuff."

"Oh, I wouldn't worry about that," came the voice of a man who just entered the office.

They turned to discover a very well dressed individual in an expensive tailored pin striped suit and a very confident smile.

"Allow me to introduce myself. Thermon Harcore Applegate, atourney at law of the law firm Applegate, Applegate, and Applegate."

"Ho chi mama," said Chi Chi.

"Why am I not surprised," said Roachie.

"Boner?" said Bean.

Here we go again, thought Fruitcake.

"Oh no. Now he thin he es a lawyer. How dat gonna be any good for Bean? Chu can no be no pretend lawyer or we all gonna go to jail."

"Who's pretending," said Attorney Thermon (Boner) Applegate.

Roachie looked again at the Harvard Law degree on the wall. "It sure looks real to me."

"It is," said Boner.

What Roachie didn't notice on the degree was the date.

"Oh well. If Obama can pretend to be a lawyer den I'n guessin' our Boner he can be one too," observed Chi Chi.

"So lawyer Applegate is going to stop Uncle Albert from taking my land?" asked Bean.

"Yes," said Boner as he crossed the room to the refreshment center. He opened a small refrigerator under the bar, withdrew some cold Yoo-hoos and passed them around, then joined them at the table. "But not right away. First we have to stop off in Miami."

"Me'ahmi! Oh, I no so chure I'n wanna go back dere too soon righ now."

"Don't worry, Chi Chi. You're going as my secretary, Miss Rosa Vasquez, who is not likely to draw any attention to anyone working for Castro. And Bean is going to be my Junior Intern from, um... the Florida State University College of Law."

"I am?"

"Sure. Don't worry, it will be fun."

"Buh how all dis pretendin' stuff gonna help Bean make dat Uncle go away?" asked Chi Chi.

"Yeah, and what am I going to pretend to be?" asked Roachie.

"Nobody," Boner told Roachie. "Because you're going to be yourself, *Rochier Rogers,* the rightful CEO and Chairman of the Rochier Rogers Research Corporation."

"But why would I want to do that?"

"Because before we go to St. Augustine to take care of Uncle Albert we're going to Miami to take your company back."

"Really!" asked Roachie.

"Really," said Boner.

"I think that's a great idea, Roachie," said Bean. "Then you can get your Airstream back and you won't have to sleep under the overpass."

"Buh I no know wha a lawyer secretary sposa do," said Chi Chi.

"Just look pretty and sexy and hand me papers when I ask for them."

"Chu really thin I can do dat?" asked Chi Chi.

"You mean look pretty and sexy. No problem," smiled Boner.

Chi Chi smiled back, seeing some of that other character of Boner's that she met and liked in San Francisco. "But I'n dun know nothin' abou no papers."

"We'll work on it," said Boner.

She perked up and smiled. "Chu know, I'n thin dis whacko stuff es maybe gonna be fun."

Roachie opened the Yoo-hoo then held it up to make a toast. "Here's to... here's to, um..."

"Here's to justice and struttin' naked in the cross walk," said Boner."

🌴

The home of the Rochier Rogers Research Corporation complex in Miami was an new expansive and impressive structure with wings that spread out like a horseshoe from a modern central multi-level administration building. To the rear of the large building inside the large horseshoe was a large park-like courtyard with a jogging trail, tropical gardens, fish ponds, flamingos, a tropical bird atrium, and even a pair of free-wandering peacocks. Inside the all glass front of the building could be seen a large atrium where gentle music played and a two story waterfall surrounded by exotic tropical plants flowed down to a pond filled with beautiful Japanese coy fish. Glass elevators to the right and left quietly rose and descended carrying studious looking passengers in white lab coats. Others chose to use the grand stairway that led to the second level. All this impressed Roachie greatly as he and the legal team from Applegate, Applegate, & Applegate glided to a hault at the entrance in the Celestial Rocket.

"Wow," said Roachie. "It looks like they've done pretty well without me."

The four of them exited the car, stood and looked at the new facilities.

"Looks can be deceiving," said Boner. "I did a little research and from what I can tell, your ex-wife and her boyfriend have done very well selling the company on the stock market, but I have a hunch all that stock was backed with false hopes and deception. In other words, they've been selling a pig in a poke."

"You mean this place is just a house of cards?" asked Roachie. "But they must be doing some research."

"Sure, some, but nothing like when you were running the show. You were the heart and soul and direction of the company and all its research. For the most part the company's basic operation is still in tact and still functions but without you it's just floundering. The company's real value however is in the many patents you secured before your departure, but its financial foundation is a little shaky. So the trick will be to patch the money leak before the ship sinks."

"Ship? Wha ship? Roachie gots a boat?" asked Chi Chi as she squirmed uncomfortably in her new sexy business suit.

"A figure of speech," said Boner.

"Oh," said Chi Chi.

Bean looked around in all directions as he adjusted the tie that wrapped around the uncomfortable stiff collar that went with the light grey business suit he was wearing, then said quietly to Roachie, "I wonder what they did with your Airstream?"

"Don't know," replied Roachie.

Then Bean looked down at the alligator shoes he had gotten in San Francisco, rocked back and forth so he could feel their comfort and smiled. "Shoes aren't too bad," he said. "But I like them better without the socks."

"You better stay here Fruitcake," Boner said looking back to the car where Fruitcake was poised to jump out and join them.

What, and miss all the fun, thought their one-eared companion.

"I'm pretty sure they have a fat man with a gun in there," lied Boner. He didn't want Fruitcake tagging along for fear his presence might bring their credibility into question. "Besides, you need to guard the Rocket... and the diamonds."

Fat guy with... Hey, good idea. I'll just stay here and guard the getaway car, agreed Fruitcake.

On the top floor overlooking the building's central park and gardens was the large modern office of Lolita Rogers, Roachie's ex-wife, with an adjoining office for her legal council and lover, Benjamin Hillery. Into her office, against the continuous objections of the executive secretary, crashed Roachie and his intrepid legal team. The secretary then scurried into the adjoining office to get assistance.

"Rochier?" said the very surprised Lolita looking up from her desk where she was perusing a fashion magazine. Her eyes showed her surprise and not really knowing what to do she began to stand, then sat, then again stand.

"Hi," said Roachie. "Miss me?"

Through the door of the adjoining office came Benjamin Hillery and the secretary. He was a tall young handsome man with slick dark hair and a confident way. "What's going on here? Mrs. Rogers doesn't see anyone without an appointment and no one gets an appointment without going through me. Just who the hell do you people think you are?"

"Hello Benjamin," said Roachie.

"Rochier," responded a surprised Ben Hillery.

"My name is Thermon Applegate, Mr. Rochier Rogers' attorney," said Boner. "And you are?"

Benjamin Hillery, Mrs. Lolita Rogers' attorney and the head of all legal affairs for this corporation as well as the Chief Operating Officer. And I must insist that you people leave immediately or I'll call our security and have you escorted from the premises."

"Oh chure, ly chu sung kina tough guy," said Chi Chi.

Boner quickly held up a single finger in Chi Chi's direction and she quickly remembered her role.

"Oops. Sorry," said Chi Chi, stepping back.

"Speaking of leaving the premises," said Boner. "That's precisely why we are here. To inform you and the former Mrs. Rogers that it would be wise and prudent for you to leave the premises immediately… before it's too late."

"What? What the hell are you talking about?

"You see, Mr. Hillery, you may have duped Rochier here but not me. And to be honest, in a way I suppose Mr. Rogers shares some of the blame because he made the mistake of trusting you just as he does most other people he meets. He is at heart after all a good natured and trusting individual. A personal attribute of which you and Lotlita here took full advantage, and in fact had planned to take advantage of before they were even married."

"Bitch," mumbled Chi Chi.

"Unfortunately your efforts have done nothing but reveal what complete incompetent asses you are."

"That's it, we've heard enough. Get the hell out of here," said an angry Benjamin Hillery as he went for the phone on the desk.

"Oh, you haven't heard anything yet," continued Boner. "It's like this; through your incompetence as a fraudulent lawyer you placed all the company patents in Rochier's name, which means he still possesses the essential worth of the company and in fact, as such, he is owed a great deal of money." Boner held out his hand to Chi Chi which was the sign for her to hand him the file with the patent registration papers in question. She fumbled through her document case until she found and handed him a file. Boner opened and glanced inside where he saw the menu from Harry's Crab Shack instead of the copies of Roachie's patents.

"Oops," said Chi Chi as she handed him the correct folder.

"And yes, we know you're not really a Harvard lawyer or any other kind of lawyer, Benjamin," said Boner as he slammed the copies of the patents down on Lolita's big glass desk. "In fact, you're not even a Benjamin, Benjamin. I had you checked out. You are actually Ronald MacNeary and you've only had one incomplete semester of higher education and that was at the… what was it? Oh yes, the Rocky Mountain Junior College. But I believe you did gain further education at a well known state institution where you served three years for identity theft and grand larceny. By the way, you still owe on your student loan."

Ronald MacNeary, alias Benjamin Hillery, was at a loss for words. He looked at Lolita who only shrugged and offered a blank look in return then got angry.

"We're not going anywhere," stated an angry Lolita. "You think you can come in here and just take away this company like a bunch of pirates or something? This is my company now and there's nothing you can do about it."

Boner laughed. "A very good analogy my dear. If you only knew. But not a very wise decision," countered Boner. "You see, at any moment now a representative from the U.S. Attorney's office and the FBI along with a few Federal Marshals are going to arrive and arrest you and charge you with a number of crimes. Not the least of which is impersonating an agent of the court, inside trading, falsifying financial statements, embezzling, and… oh, lets just say it's a long bothersome list. So I would suggest that you make a very hasty exit. As a good friend of mine, Captain Purdey Boon, would say, 'there's a serious storm on the horizon and you're floatin' in a dingy'."

Suddenly the sound of sirens could be heard followed by a disturbance in the atrium that sounded like shouting. It grew closer as a platoon of law enforcement officers spread throughout the building to secure all the facility's records.

I knew it. I knew it. That fat guy with a gun must have shot somebody, thought Fruitcake as he watched the vehicles slide to a halt all around him and the federal officers rush into the building.

"Hey, did you see that ugly dog in that car," asked one of the U.S. Marshals. "He only had one ear."

"Yeah," said another. "And I think he had pink tonails. Now who the hell would do that to a dog? Even an ugly dog."

"Oops, too late," Boner said to the criminal couple.

Lolita and Benjamin looked at each other then hastily scooted through the door into the adjoining office. A minute later FBI agents and a U.S. Attorney walked in.

"They went thataway," said Rochie with a big smile.

The Marshals rushed into Ben Hillery's office where they found the two of them pulling packets of money from a large safe and shoving it into a bag.

"Wow, that was pretty neat," said Bean. "Looks like you got your company back, Roachie."

"Dat will teach dat bitch to mess wit our Roachie," said Chi Chi. "How wass my secretaries job?"

"I think you better stick to the movie thing," replied Boner.

"Oh, hokay. Buh I thin I ly dis suit. Do chu really thin dat es sexy?"

"Very," said Boner.

Chi Chi blushed.

"Yeah," agreed Roachie. "Don't you think so too?" he asked of Bean.

"Um…" Bean blushed. "Uh huh."

"Do chu thin maybes I can be a secretary in da moofies?"

They all nodded their heads, demonstrating unanimous agreement that she could, but each politely harboring the knowledge she would first have to work on her accent.

"Well, Roachie, looks like you have a lot of work to do," said Boner.

"Yep, looks like," said Roachie. "Thanks."

"No problem. It was my civic duty to help preserve the security of our nation. But you've got a little time because there's some legalities to be completed before you can take over again.

"What did you say? Preserve the nation?"

"Your nano science research. You might be our only hope to defeat the aliens and the Fourth Branch."

"Ho chi mama. Now he es da whacko Boner again."

"But not now," said Roachie. "First we gotta go take care of Uncle Albert before he takes Bean's land."

"I agree," said Boner. "But before that I think we should go to Harry's Crab Shack to celebrate your victory and have some lunch."

"Why not," said Bean. "I have the diamonds and my land isn't going anywhere."

🌴

Just outside of Tallahassee in the Florida pan handle Father Sabatino finally got through to Albert on a pay phone. He had been stopping and trying to call every few hours all the way across the country but he kept getting switched over to Albert's voicemail. Father Sabatino never left messages. He didn't like talking to machines. It made him feel stupid.

"Well it's about damn time you answered your damn phone," said Father Sabatino.

"What you talkin' about? I always answer my phone," said Ablert.

"The hell you do. I been calling you for two days. You ain't been answering your phone."

"Okay, so I met this girl and I forgot to turn it on a couple times. She keeps callin' and callin', like I give a damn. So what? Who gives a damn?"

"What ya mean who gives a damn? How the hell am I supposed to tell ya anything if you got your damn phone turned off? Like how am I gonna tell ya that I quit. Cause I quit. I ain't doin' this crap no more."

"What? You can't quit now," said an excited Albert. "I'm about to close the deal and then we'll be in the money."

"Oh yeah, just watch me. Are you watchin'? Here goes. I quit. Did ya catch that? I said I quit."

"No you don't."

"Yes I do."

"You can't."

"I can't? What the hell ya mean, I can't?"

"You can't because the kid's on his way home," Albert informed Father Sabatino.

"I know the kid's on his way home. Why the hell ya think I been tryin' to call you," said Father Sabatino.

"The kid called me. Called me from Miami. Said he was on his way back. Ya gotta stop him. Ya hear? If he shows up today he could kill the deal."

"He called. How the hell did he call? You had your damn phone turned off."

"I got voicemail."

"I don't give a shit about your mail. I'm talkin' about phones."

"Shut up and listen. You gotta stop this kid."

"So what ya expect me to do. I'm in Tallahassee," replied Father Sabatino.

"If you hurry and shoot across the state you can catch him. Cut him off on the beach road down south someplace, dammit. Do whatever you gotta do but don't let him show up here. Not now. Not till I cash the check and get our money."

"How much money?"

"A lot."

"How much is a lot?

"A bunch."

"So how much is a bunch. This better be worth it." said Father Sabatino.

"Uh… a million…," lied Albert, "…and a half."

"I want a bigger cut," said Father Sabatino.

"Sure, sure, whatever. Just get down there and stop that kid before he screws everything up. He said they're driving the coast road so you should be able to catch 'em. Do somethin'. Stop 'em."

"A bigger cut. I want a bigger cut."

"Yeah, yeah, okay. You got it."

"Got what?"

"A bigger cut."

"How big is bigger?"

"Um… 20 percent."

"30."

"Okay, 30. But get your ass on the road and stop that kid. Do whatever it takes. Just stop that kid," concluded Albert.

Tired, thirsty, and frustrated, Father Sabatino decided he could drive no further without a serious steak and a drink. His sweet red '58 Caddy was now covered with over 6000 miles of dirty brown road crud and even the bobbing head Jesus on the dashboard had stopped bobbing after it nearly melted under the desert sun. The good ol' boy road house he decided to pull into wasn't particularly crowded, showing only a few pickup trucks, a beer delivery truck, and a half size yellow school bus with special doors. The food smelled more than appetizing however, as did the beer when he slid into a corner booth near the window.

"How ya'll doin' today?" asked a pleasant middle-aged bleach blonde waitress.

"*We*… are damn hungry… *ya'll*," replied Father Sabatino. "You got a decent steak in this roadside dump?"

The waitress took pause before she decided to answer and a few nearby patrons turned to see what man had decided to insult their favorite dining establishment and watering hole and their southern heritage.

"Would you like to see a menu?" asked the irritated waitress.

"Save the menu and the nicities for the dumbass that's drivin' that retard special bus outside, lady, and just bring me the biggest steak in the kitchen and a cold beer in a longneck bottle. You cornballs down here do eat steak down here don't you?"

"How would you like that steak done, sir?"

"Make sure it's dead then just walk it across the grill."

"You like a baked tater to go with that steak?" asked the waitress as she turned and looked at a very large woman sitting at a nearby table to see if she had heard what Father Sabatino had said. The woman had indeed heard and she wasn't very pleased.

"No, don't want no damn spud. Just a big-ass steak is all."

"Hey mister, don't be callin' my bus kids retards. They ain't retards, they is challenged."

"Yeah lady, I guess they'd have to be challenged to get around your fat ass on that bus every day," said Father Sabatino.

"Hey mister, ain't no call to be rude to the lady like that," said one of the good ol' boys who owned one of the pickups.

"Lady, what lady?" laughed Father Sabatino.

"Sure ain't no way for a priest to talk," said the waitress. "You are a priest ain't ya. Don't know bout them clothes but you got a priest collar."

"What I am, lady, is hungry. So how bout you get crackin' on that steak."

"You're a very rude man," said the special bus driver.

All the boys who drove the pickup trucks nodded their heads in agreement. An old farmer sitting alone with his coffee and pie and a newspaper blew his nose so hard it echoed off the ceiling. "Yep, rude," said the old man as he wiped his nose clean and shoved his hanky back in his pocket. "Ain't no call for it."

"Now that's what ya call rude," mumbled Father Sabatino. "Snot nosed old pecker. All the damn places to eat and I gotta pick some damn *Do Drop In* full of rednecks. I said *rednecks*," he repeated so it could be heard.

"We ain't rednecks and my little angels ain't retards. And you're an asshole," said the angry bus driver as she rose and strutted from the establishment.

The waitress set a cold beer on the table and Father Sabatino waisted no time snatching it up and downing half the bottle. "Bring me another one, honey," he said.

She returned with the second beer and when he was about to finish off the first and start on the second he heard the crash and crunch of metal outside in the parking lot. He looked out to see the special bus pull away and roll from the parking lot onto the highway. The woman's fat arm came out of the side window and shot a bird. When Father Sabatino looked at his '58 Caddy he discovered the entire passenger side had been swiped and dented and left with the tell-tale marks of school buss yellow paint.

"Looks like you had a bit of an accident," said the waitress.

The old man blew his nose again then snickered, "Don't think that lady liked you much."

"Shit," said Father Sabatino.

chapter 32
The Homecoming

Sammy Kuester's courtesy C-130 was on its way back to California and Bean and his friends were on their way to St. Augustine in the Celestial Rocket. All seemed well with the world as our travelers anticipated yet another legal victory to thwart the intentions of the devious Uncle Albert, bringing a conclusion to Bean's exciting but ultimately disappointing long journey. Though Bean tried his best to hide his disappointment in not connecting with his father, he was saddened none the less. Only the presense of his friends and again cruising the open road in his late mother's car kept his chin up for now.

They were stopped at the Flagler Beach pier on the coast road A1A about 40 minutes south of St. Augustine to stretch their legs and buy themselves an ice cream when along came Father Sabatino in his dirty, dusty, dented 1958 Caddy convertible that now looked as though it had barely survived the last apocalypse. He had pushed his patience and his car to the limit to shoot across Florida and would have missed them entirely had they not decided to take a break. Just as his Caddy passed the pier Father Sabatino caught a glimpse of the parked Celestial Rocket. He slammed on the brakes but unfortunately the quick stop resulted in a rear end collision by a rusty old Ford Explorer SUV sporting a load of surfboards on the top and a load of six stoned members of the University of Florida girl's field hockey team inside. The collision lurched the Caddy forward along with Father Sabatino's head, bashing his nose and right eye into the steering wheel. The impact set off the horn on the girl's SUV and it stuck, drawing attention and a fast growing crowd. Bean and company promptly decided there wasn't much to see so they mounted the Celestial Rocket and continued on their way.

"You Goddamn idiot! Where the hell'd you learn to drive!" yelled the stoned girl driver above the sound of the irritating horn as she exited the SUV. When she slammed the door shut the horn ceased.

Father Sabatino got out of his Caddy and went back to inspect the damage. The impact had dented the trunk, crushed one of the Caddy's trademark raised tail wings and light, and loosened the bumper. Not bad considering the entire front end of the SUV was smashed inward.

Another girl jumped out from the other side of the SUV and when she slammed her door the horn came back on. "Yeah, you stupid bastard! Why don't you... Oh, uh... shit. Sorry Father."

As the other girls pored out of the vehicle the horn would stop and start respectively with each door action until finally it just fizzled out like a dying donkey. One of the girls joined their driver who was cursing and beginning to dial 911 on her cell phone. "Hey man, that dude's a priest... I think."

"So what, he's still an idiot," said the driver.

"Uh... I don't think that's a good idea," said her friend.

"What's not a good idea?"

"Calling the cops."

"Why, just because he's a priest?"

"No, cause we're all stoned and we got a car full of weed, stupid."

"Oh. OH SHIT! You're right. Oh shit, we gotta get outta here." She looked to Father Sabatino, "Oh hey man, like, uh... sorry. Listen can we do this really fast cause we gotta go."

"Your friend is right," said Father Sabatino as he tenderly played his fingers over his bruised and fast swelling right eye, then wiped the blood running down the bridge of his nose. With his other hand he abruptly reached out and snatched the girl's cell phone. Just then the dented trunk on the Caddy popped open exposing a large assortment of deadly weapons and fire arms. Father Sabatino quickly slammed it shut. "Now get lost kid or I'll turn you in."

The girls just looked at each other, ran back to their vehicle and began trying to maneuver it through the crowd and other cars but the damage was too severe and they had no steering control. The horn started blaring again, the irritating sound mixing with the sound of a police siren as it pulled up behind them. Six girls immediately began eating their stash of marijuana.

When Father Sabatino started back to get in his car the trunk popped up again. "Shit," he said, as he went to close it, then as a second thought removed one of his assault rifles and slammed the trunk shut. This time it stayed closed. He looked to the parking area where he had seen the Celestial Rocket and saw it was gone, tossed the weapon in the front seat, then looked down the long straight road ahead but Bean and the Celestial Rocket had already driven far out of sight. He hopped in, started the engine, leaned on the horn to clear the crowd away, threw the car in gear and slammed his foot down on the gas, speeding away in a cloud of hot burning rubber.

A mile ahead of him he spied two Flagler County Sheriff's cars with sirens blaring and lights flashing, speeding towards the scene of the accident where they had a report of a major drug bust with heavy weapons. Father Sabatino quickly turned left onto the first available road, a dusty dirt and shell road that eventually wound through the palmettos and scrub oaks and back around to end at an old abandoned restaurant gift shop on A1A. He slammed on the brakes, backed in behind the building, cut the egine, and pulled out the cell phone he had taken from the girl. In the heat of the moment he forgot that he had someone elses phone and so he hit the speed dial thinking he was calling Albert. A man answered.

"Hey baby, now I know you ain't already smoked all dat good damn weed I sold you, so dat muss mean you be lookin' fo some dat really good shit and you know dat yo sugar daddy always got what you need long as you got what I need. Are you feelin' me baby?"

Father Sabatino rolled his eyes, realizing he had just connected with the girl's drug dealer. He then smiled and said into the phone with great authority, "This is the FBI. We have you surrounded. Take off all of your clothes and exit the building with your hands up immediately or I will send in my agents with orders to shoot to kill. You have one minute. Are you feelin' *me* baby?"

The drug dealer on the other end of the line immediately took him seriously because he could hear the sirens of the two County Sheriff's cars in the background on the phone as they flew by the old abandoned restaurant where Father Sabatino was hiding. Father Sabatino snickered as he discontinued the call and dialed Albert's number. The phone on the other end seemed to ring forever until it finally switched over to voicemail.

"This is Albert Freewater. If I don't owe you money leave a message." Beeeep.

"Shit," said Father Sabatino as he cut off the call. He didn't leave messages. He hated leaving messages but then he decided this was important and this time he would leave a message. He re-dialed and at the beep said, "Hey Albert, listen up dammit. The kid's headin' your way but I'm gonna try and cut him off. Then I'm gonna take care of this shit my way. You hear me Albert. My way, the *Jersey* way. Not your way. My way. Cause I'm tired of all this shit and I'm a Jersey guy and Jersey guys ain't no damn babysitters. So you better have my money ready. You don't have my money ready then I'm gonna take care of you too, the *Jersey* way, cause I'm tired of this sh…"

Beeeep.

"Shit!" He cranked the Caddy up and pulled out onto the coast road A1A. On his left were low brush and palmetto plants with an occasional secluded house or store. On his right was the beach with white breakers and a horizon that went on forever. In front of him was a long straight empty two lane road. He floored it, determined to catch Bean and the Celestial Rocket before they reached St. Augustine. "Babysitter my ass," mumbled a very, very angry Father Sabatino.

Albert Freewater was feeling pretty satisfied with himself, partly because he was working on his fifth beer and third shot of Crown Royal and partly because he was about to clinch a deal for the sale of his late sister's ten acres of beachfront property. The sale will not only net him a few million bucks but also an interest in the condominium project slated to be built there; a lush luxury development of over 200 units selling for nearly a half million dollars each. Today is the day that Albert and the buyers, along with their architect and a few of the project's investors, will meet at the site in question and close the deal.

As he sat in the Tropical Trade Winds Lounge waiting for the clock to tick away the nearly full hour left until the meeting, he hummed along with the old Jimmy Buffett classic song, *Come Monday*, that was playing over the sound system. He forgot he had turned the ringer off on his cell phone again. He had turned it off while watching some movie about penguins on a display flat screen at Wal-Mart and didn't want to be disturbed. That's how Albert often watched movies because he was too cheap to buy a ticket at a regular movie theater. The only time he paid for tickets was at multi-cinemas where he could sneak from one movie to another, seeing sometimes as many as four films in a day.

"Hey," Albert called to the bartender. "This ain't such a bad old place. Could use a little work though. You want to sell it?"

"Not mine to sell," said the bartender. "Don't think the owner would sell, anyway. Makes too much on the day trade from the tourist and packs 'em in at night. Been that way for years."

"Yeah, know what ya mean. Got a place like this myself up north."

"You want another beer?"

"No. Just one more Crown Royal and I'm outta here. Gotta meet some folks out at the beach."

Little did Albert know that he was downing his Crown Royal in the very same place where his sister had spent a great many evenings for the last four decades of her life. So many evenings, for so long, hoping and waiting for her Jimmy to return.

"Say, didn't I see you at Sister Moonbeam's funeral?" asked the bartender.

"Yeah, that's right," said Albert after downing the shot in a single gulp. "She was my sister."

"Real nice lady," said the bartender. "Made me a blue banana pie once. Didn't look like much but it sure as hell tasted good. I think it was laced. Just got to know her the last few years when I took over for Joe. Boones Farm apple wine – with a twist. Nice lady. Always paid her bill in advance though. Even the tips. I never could figure that out."

"Oh really? You didn't think she was a little... uh... you know, like a little off plum?"

"Hey man, in my world from behind the bar everybody's a little off plum. Know what I mean?"

Albert nodded agreement. "Yep, know what ya mean. By the way, she ever mention anything about an African rock collection?" asked Albert.

At the small airport just north of town a private jet landed, rolled across the tarmac and came to a halt where its passengers and their entourages disembarked and slid into three waiting limousines. The passengers included a wheeler dealer realestate tycoon and financier from Miami named Lance Parks and a young Saudi Arabian Prince in flowing white silk attire and turban with a gold braided head hoop. The Saudi Prince's name was too difficult for Lance to pronounce so he simply called him Prince which sometimes displeased the Prince. But money and deals were money and deals and since the Prince was making the most money on the deal he decided to overlook Lance's lack of etiquette. The money and deal that had brought them to St. Augustine was the condo development on Bean's ten acres of beachfront.

"I hope this gathering will not be as eventful as the one in Miami," said the Saudi Prince. "Police officers, guns, and crashing blimps tend to make doing business a little difficult you know."

"Oh don't worry Prince. Nothing exciting ever happens around here. It's just a quiet little tourist town. Why I intend to buy one of these condos myself just so I'll have a nice quiet place to get away and relax."

"Good. Good. This is good to know because that disruptive exhibition in Miami was like a night in Beirut and my father the King was so displeased that he raised the price of oil by twenty dollars a barrel."

"Not to worry Prince Your Highness. Not to worry."

As they cruised north on the coast road Bean noticed a darkened sky over the ocean out on the horizon. In a way it reminded him of that fateful day when he lost everything he knew. But he didn't let the memory get him down. He was too busy singing *Ninety-nine Bottles of Yoo-hoo on the Wall* and lost in the high spirits of the moment with his friends. Nor did he notice the grungy '58 convertible Caddy gaining on them in the far distance. They sang their way through Marineland and Summer Island, across the Matanzaz Inlet Bridge and on up through the small communities of Crescent Beach, then Treasure Beach and Butler Beach where Father Sabaitino was about to overtake them and open up with his assault rifle when an old couple in an RV pulled out in front of him and got him caught in traffic.

Finally Bean was on his home turf of Anastasia Island and St. Augustine Beach and just breathing the familiar air was enough to lighten his spirits. He smiled as they came to the intersection of A1A and Route 3 where hung Sister Moonbeam-Goom-jigi's triumphant traffic light just as it turned red.

Coming out of a nearby convenience store with a two-for-one hot dog and a large cherry slushy was a St. Johns County Shariff's deputy by the name of Cory Singletary. Cory was one of those local cops who spent a few years in the Marine Corps tromping around in 120 degree desert heat in Iraq courtesy of Judge Weingarberger. The judge determined his enlistment was necessary because Cory got caught committing the high crime of pouring a half gallon of dishwashing detergent into a town fountain which subsequently caused a massive sudsy traffic gridlock. When Corey finally returned home after his hitch with the Marines he discovered his girlfriend had joined the Southern Society of Unwed Nuns of the Universal Church of Maternity. Needless to say, Deputy Corey Singletary didn't like Judge Weingarberger very much. It was also a given that like most of the other deputies in the county he was protective of Sister Moonbeam-Goom-jigi's young son Bean, so when he spotted the new and improved Celestial Rocket sitting at the intersection with Bean at the wheel he immediately got on the horn to Sheriff Bubba Boyd.

"Hey boss, the kid is back," reported Deputy Singletary. "What? Yeah I'm sure it's him."

Sheriff Bubba Boyd instructed Deputy Singletary to follow Bean and make sure he didn't get in any kind of trouble that would bring him to face the judge, but before the deputy could confirm the order a shot rang out from a dirty, dented, grungy Cadillac convertible that screeched and bumped into the back of the Celestial Rocket. The sudden stop along with his right eye now nearly swollen shut caused Father Sabatino's shot to go wild and pierce the deputy's patrol car windshield. It also caused him to once again crash his nose into the sterring wheel after the recoil of his big Coonan 357 Magnum Automatic hit him in the other eye. "Shit!"

"Shots fired! Shots fired!" yelled Deputy Singletary into his radio as he tossed the hot dog to the floor and the cherry slushy out the window.

A second shot was fired and passed between Bean and Chi Chi to shatter the rear view mirror.

"Ho chi mama!" cried Chi Chi. "Dat crasee guy tryin to choot us!"

Bean hit the gas, flew through the red light and turned right following A1A toward the beach. He was quickly followed by Father Sabatino who in turn was followed by Deputy Singletary who was reporting the situation and the tag number of the shooters vehicle.

"Hey, this guy's shootin' at the kid!" said Deputy Singletary.

"Be advised," came back a call on his radio. "Suspect vehichle was involved in a drug bust and hit and run at Flagler Beach one hour ago and was also indentified at the scene of a homocide in Citrus County six days ago. Flagler Sheriff's office says witnesses report the driver is heavily armed and may be extremely dangerous."

Sheriff Bubba Boyd wasted no time putting out a call mobilizing his entire on-duty force to converge on the small community of St. Augustine Beach. Then he quickly called for his chopper. His forces were joined by the local police as well. There was hardly a uniformed law enforcement officer within 50 miles who didn't dislike Judge Weingarberger and most all considered Sister Moonbeam-Goom-jigi their hero. And so their motivation to save Bean Buffett was tantamount to that by the British in the Charge of the Light Brigade.

Sheriff Bubba's chopper thundered low over the beach road. The city of St. Augustine and the entire island screamed with squad car sirens sending the entire population into a near panic thinking they were being attacked by terrorists. People grabbed their pets and children and scurried inside and locked their doors. Fire department sirens sounded and their trucks flew out onto the road not even knowing where they were going. People on the beaches grabbed their things and took shelter in the nearest building they could find. The spread of panic was quick and thorough throughout the community. That is everywhere except the Beachcomber.

"What's all the fuss?" asked the chunky creamy cottage cheese fluorescent bikini lady.

"They're rounding up all the Canadians," said Porky Fister. "You better run."

The sounds and the desperate panic did not go unnoticed by the Saudi Arabian Prince and the investment group who had just stepped out of their limousines by the road in front of Bean's ten acre beachfront lot. About that same time Uncle Albert arrived, too drunk to even notice all the commotion but no one noticed. They didn't notice because everyone there was immediately distracted by Sheriff Bubba Boyd's chopper that came to hover low just above them. The chopper's rotary wash blew sand and dust everywhere and the Saudi Prince's pretty white silk garb flew up over his head exposing his red spedo and a Lady Gaga T-shirt. Sheriff Bubba didn't even notice the group below them. He and his pilot had their eyes on the Celestial Rocket speeding down the road in their direction. It's desperate and frightened driver, Bean Buffett, gripping the wheel with Chi Chi bouncing around in the seat next to him while covering her head to avoid the shots. In the rear Boner and Roachie were curled up trying to become as small as possible and between the seats only Fruitcake's ass and tail were visible.

Bean saw the Sheriff's department helicopter, then saw Uncle Albert and the investment group, then the approaching law enforcement vehicles with their flashing lights and sirens and he slammed on the brakes and slid to a halt. When he looked across his ten acres to the beach his eyes grew round with fear. "HO CHI MAMA!" he cried, then jammed the gas peddle to the floor. The beefed up powerful custom engine installed by their friends the Los Hermanos Cubanos Para La Libertad in Miami took charge of the Celestial Rocket and blasted it forward like it had never moved before. Another shot rang out from behind, fired by Father Sabatino who now could barely see out of either of his eyes. He was swerving all over the road. When his pistol went empty he reached to the seat and picked up the assault rifle.

Uncle Albert looked to the road and couldn't believe what he saw. "Sabatino! You damn idiot! You stupid damn…"

Father Sabatino fired a burst of shots that barely missed Albert and shattered the side windows of two of the limos. Albert ducked, then looked up just in time to jump out of the way as Father Sabatino's Caddy crashed into Albert's old Buick. Albert stood, relieved he hadn't been hit by either the bullets or the car. He turned just in time to let out a loud desperate but brief scream. Brief because he was immediately hit by – a waterspout.

chapter 33

Am I Dead Yet?

"Some may say it was a freak of nature. Yet others may claim it was divine intervention when a second waterspout, an ocean born tornado, struck the very same spot in this picturesque community of St. Augustine Beach. Yes, the very same spot in less than only a few weeks," said Jane Smith, the hot blonde TV reporter from CNN News who went by the more memorable and impressive name of Di'Ahna Parnella St. James. She stood near the pile of twisted metal that was once three limousines, a Buick, a '58 Caddy, two patrol cars, a helicopter and who knows what else? "The odds of this happening are mindboggling to say the least," she continued while taking a few steps and nodding her head to dramatize her poetic delivery. "The first took a woman's life and the second took lives and wreaked havoc in the midst of a wild police chase and shoot out. What an unimaginable series of events. What drama. What a story. All the characters of this phenomenal tale are yet to be defined. Why was an entire police force mobilized? Who was the terrorist they were after and most importantly, what... and I repeat, what is his connection with Saudi Arabia and the recent murder of a suspected former government operative which led to the apprehension of the head of a Pakastani terrorist cell by the name of Abdul-hafeez? A complicated story indeed, and as it unravels is creating ripple affects that are being felt all the way to Washington where there are now more questions than answers."

Satisfied with her dramatic story intro, she turned and took a few steps to the side where two other people came into camera view. She continued, "I have with me now two of the heroes of this incredible event that took place right here at… if you will… *ground zero*, to share with us their exclusive testimony as to what took place. Paramedics Zippy DeMonza and Herbert Johnson. So gentlemen, you were the first to arrive at the scene where you were faced with this incredible sight of twisted metal and desperate victims," she said extending the microphone to the two men.

The two paramedics looked at the mike, smiled and shook their heads in agreement, thinking the obvious, that there was no question in her statement meaning they didn't have to answer, so they didn't answer.

"So tell us in your own words how you were the first to arrive at this horrible scene and faced with this incredible sight of twisted metal and desperate victims," said the reporter who again stretched the microphone out to the two interviewees.

Herbert leaned toward the mike, "Well, we were the first to arrive at this horrible scene and were faced with this incredible sight of twisted metal and desperate victims." He said, then stood back and smiled.

"And…" said the reporter.

"And what?" said Herbert.

She quickly went to Zippy. "Paramedic DeMonza can you tell us what happened here?"

"Sure," said Zippy, who then stood silent and smiled.

"And…" said the reporter.

"And what?" said Zippy.

"In your own words. What incredible events took place here?"

"It was a waterspout," said Zippy.

"Yes. And then what?" asked the reporter.

"Oh. Yeah, well, Herbert and I were just cruisin' down the road eatin' some Krystal burgers… You know those little square burgers? They're really bodacious ya know? Especially that yummy gooey stuff inside. Yeah well, we're cruisin' down the road with the burgers and playin' with some bandaids. You know those pink and blue ones with the Little Mermaid on 'em. Stickin' 'em on the dashboard and our ears and nose and stuff, you know, for fun and stuff. We got kind of a heavy job so we gotta lighten up once in a while, ya know. Anyway, then we heard all this stuff goin' on and the next thing you know here we are lookin' at all this shit. That desert monkey in the white sheets looked like he wasn't hurt too bad but he kept yellin' a lot like a girl and we didn't understand because it was in Arabic or Hodgie or somethin'. Turns out he only had two broken legs. But some of those other guys were messed up pretty bad."

"Yeah, pretty bad," said Herbert. "That guy we pulled out of that Cadillac was all messed up and that guy underneath it was pretty bad too."

"Yeah, those guys were all broken and bleedin' and messed up inside just like that lady in that other twister. Except these guys screamed and cussed a lot when we moved 'em. That other lady in the other twister was cool. She didn't complain a bit. But she died. These guys all screamed like little girls."

"Tell us about the helicopter," said the reporter.

"It's right there," said Zippy.

"Right there?" said the reporter directing the camera man to shoot where she was pointing.

"No, right there," said Zippy. "All mangled between those crunched up limos and that cop car. See there?"

The camera panned to the pile of destruction. None of which could be recognized as what it actually was.

"You mean there?" asked the reporter.

"Uh no. I think that was a Cosco truck. Boy was it hard gettin' that big guy out of there. But he walked away. Said somethin' about goin' back on the Miami route, whatever that means."

"Yeah, and then there was that fat guy. He got messed up pretty bad. The one that fell asleep on the beach and got picked up by the twister and ended up in a tree on the other side of the Intracoastal Waterway," said Herbert.

"Oh, that sounds horrible," said the reporter.

"Well, maybe. He was broken up pretty bad. Bad I guess but not if you ask me cause it was the Judge," said Zippy. "Nobody likes that asshole. That fat bastard made me join the Army."

"Yeah, me to."

"Um… yes, well, um… can you give us an idea of the human toll of this incredible disaster?" asked the reporter.

"You mean like just whole people or whole people and body parts," replied Zippy.

Herbert leaned to Zippy and whispered, "Hey man, she's got a nice ass. Reminds me of Mrs. Gorby."

In the hospital lying dormant in intensive care bed number 1 was Sheriff Bubba Boyd Trumain. In intensive care bed number 2 was Judge Weingarberger. In number 3 lay the Saudi Prince, in bed 4 lay Uncle Albert and in 5 was Father Sabatino. With the exception of the Saudi Prince who only sported a cast from the waist down because he only had two broken legs, the rest were all completely wrapped in a plaster cast from their toes to the top of their heads with all four limbs extended and hanging up in the air from straps and lines that ran through pulleys that were attached to stainless steel frames and connected to counter weights. There was a small opening where their mouth was supposed to be and another slit of an opening that ran across from one eye to the other revealing part of the bridge of their noses. The scene was like some factory assembly line that cranked out people by pouring them into plaster molds. The only stand out was the fat Judge whose body cast bulged profusely around the torso and spread over the entire bed like a big wad of rising bread dough.

Through various outlets in the massive cast the hospital staff and doctors had managed to fit all the essential life support connections such as plumbing lines, oxygen tube, heart monitor, pulse monitor, and IVs. Around each bed was a collection of high tech monitoring machines that beeped, clicked, sucked, gurgled, and oozed in a symphony of sounds and critical care drama. Suddenly amid the music of desperate biological monitoring came desperate and demanding foreign voices. They were demanding the release of their Saudi Arabian Prince and inspite of all the objections and all that was said by the nurses and doctors, the Saudis rolled their Prince right out of the hospital and into a waiting medical transport helicopter complete with armed guards. When a hospital administrator questioned where he was to send the bill he was handed a one pound bar of gold without comment.

"I'm not sure this will cover it," he said, stepping forward and getting blown about by the strong rotor wash of the helicopter. One of the Saudi Prince's security men quickly cocked and pointed an AK47 assault rifle. "Oh, well..., um okay. We'll just send the bill to Medicaid then."

The commotion of the Prince's abduction stirred the senses of the four plastered survivors who as they became conscious were both surprised and confused at their condition. This of course sent the array of monitoring devices into emergency overload and in rushed the entire emergency room staff, hovering over each patient, adjusting their medications, checking their heartbeats and pulse, increasing their oxygen.

"Ohmmmg?" moaned Sheriff Bubba.

"Ohmmmg?" demanded Judge Weingarberger.

"Ohmmmg?" complained Father Sabatino.

"Ohmmmg?" cried Uncle Albert.

The doctor quickly decided the patients were too talkative and consequently too excited and in pain and so immediately increased their morphine intake.

"Mmmmm," said Sheriff Bubba as he mellowed out.

"Mmmmm," said the fat Judge, meaning more, more.

"Ommmmg," objected Father Sabatino, who's only thoughts were of escape and why he couldn't open his eyes.

"Ommmmg!" said Uncle Albert, meaning he desperately had to take a piss but didn't realize he had a tube up his penis for just that purpose.

Later that evening as things calmed down, the lights were dimmed, the hospital night staff was settled in, and the hospital became quiet - that is except for the 90 year old woman in room 107 who kept yelling for the nurse and asking if she was dead yet. That was when Deputy Cory Singletary stopped by to check on Sheriff Bubba Boyd. Deputy Cory was mainly there because he was feeling a little guilty. He couldn't quite understand how he had been so close to the twister yet wasn't affected in the least and didn't suffer a single scratch. He was also there at the request of his mother who was Sheriff Bubba Boyd's sister.

"Hey there Uncle Boyd, how ya doin'," asked Deputy Cory.

"Ohmmm," moaned Sheriff Bubba.

"Mom says to say hi. She said she'd have come to see ya but tonight is ladies night at the Trade Winds and, well, you know mom."

"Ohmmm," moaned Sheriff Bubba, rolling his eyes in the direction of Judge Weingarberger in the bed next to him.

"What?" said Deputy Cory. "I don't understand."

"Ohmmm!" moaned Sheriff Bubba, again angrily rolling his eyes in the fat Judge's direction.

Deputy Cory looked at the Sheriff then looked over at the Judge. It took a slow minute but he finally figured out what the Sheriff wanted him to do and nodded agreement.

"Well, guess it's time for me to go. I'll tell mom that you're going to be just fine... uh, some day."

Deputy Cory looked around. The only other non-patient he saw was the duty nurse sitting at her station.

"Am I dead yet!" yelled the 90 year old woman in room 107.

The duty nurse rose and went to assure the old woman that she wasn't dead. When she did, Deputy Cory slid cautiously over to the side of Judge Weingarberger, inspected all the beeping, clicking, sucking, gurgling, and oozing instruments and determined which one was most critical. He then sort of accidently on purpose slid his foot across the cord connected to the plug that fed the juice to the machine that kept the Judge breathing. The plug slipped out of the socket and Deputy Cory slipped away and headed for the back door.

"See ya later Uncle Boyd," he said as he quickly and quietly exited the building.

"Ohmmmg," smiled Sheriff Bubba Boyd.

There were only three plastered victims left in the critical care unit of the hospital the next night when the Southern Society of Unwed Nuns of the Universal Church of Maternity were making their rounds. They gathered around the bed of Sheriff Bubba and prayed then gathered around the bed of Albert Freewater and prayed.

"Am I dead yet!" cried the 90 year old woman in room 107, prompting the duty nurse to leave her station and go assure her she wasn't dead. As the nurse tended to the old woman the sisters gathered around Father Sabatino and prayed. When they finished their prayers and departed the intensive care ward, Father Sabatino was flying high and about to overdose on morphine.

"Am I dead yet!" cried out the 90 year old woman in room 107 again.

"Not yet," mumbled the nurse as she was just about to sit. She once again left her station to attend to the old woman. "But I'm seriously considereing it."

The next night Bean came in to visit his Uncle, surprised to find a scene very similar to that of his late mother, Sister Moonbeam-Goom-jigi.

"Hello Uncle Albert. Um… how do you feel?" asked Bean.

"Ohmmmg," moaned Albert through the little hole in the plaster.

"I wanted to see how you were and let you know I was okay because I drove out of the way of the waterspout just in time, and also to tell you that you don't have to bother about my legal affairs anymore because I have a really good Harvard lawyer now."

"Ohmmmg?" moaned Albert.

"He's a really good lawyer and he found another buyer for the beach place. Five million dollars he got for it. I really didn't want it anymore anyhow, too many waterspouts. I'm going to give the money from the sale to the sisters so they can build an orphanage for kids like me. You know, the sisters at the Southern Society of Unwed Nuns of the Universal Church of Maternity. Mom liked them a lot."

"Ohmmmg!" moaned Albert. His heart monitor machine started beeping faster as the his heart accelerated.

"Oh, and also you don't have to worry about taking care of me anymore. I found mom's diamonds and they're worth more than ninety-million dollars. So I think I'll be okay for a while. And I don't want you to worry about your hospital bills either because I've already paid them in advance."

"OHMMMMG! OHMMMMG!" The heart monitor kicked into high gear as though Albert were running a cross country marathon. His eyes grew wide and desperate. Fifteen seconds later he flatlined, never to recover.

"Uncle Albert? Uncle Albert? Are you okay?"

"Am I dead yet," cried out the 90 year old woman in room 107.

chapter 34

Adieu Mes Amis

It was a few hours before dawn and one of those rare times when the tide and the ocean were dead calm and the surface was like glass, a special time that usually only coast dwellers and sailors get to experience. The small fire near the dunes on the beach crackled and snapped, a warm red glow barely lighting the faces of those who sat on the cool sand surrounding it. Bean lay stretched out, searching the sky, remembering the many times in the past he looked up at this same starry sky from his hammock on the porch of Sister Moonbeam-Goom-jigi's little cottage. Roachie sat staring into the fire, fascinated by the dancing flames, and Chi Chi sat leaning comfortably in Boner's arms. Fruitcake lay as Fruitcake always does, on his back, balls to the night sky.

"I guess we'll all be saying goodbye tomorrow," said Roachie. "Time for me to get back to work I suppose."

"Yep, and I have some serious business to take care of that I've been putting off for a very long time," said Boner.

"Es chu gonna need a personal secretary?" asked Chi Chi.

"That might not be a bad idea," replied Boner.

"Maybes es not a bad idea buh den maybes es a bad idea," said Chi Chi, sitting up and tossing another piece of wood in the fire. "Maybes before I works for chu I'n gonna wanna know who chu really es, maybes. Causs I thin I forgots causs chu gots too many peoples inside chu. Sungtines I no so chure who you es and sungtines maybe I not chure I wanna know who chu es."

Boner laughed and looked around at each of them, then grew serious. "You're my very good friends so I'm going to trust you with my secret," he said. "A secret I have trusted to very few people over the years."

Bean sat up to listen more closely.

All they had to do was ask me, thought Fruitcake. *The guy is an open book.*

"It muss be a long secret causs dere es lots of chu peoples inside dere somewheres," said Chi Chi.

"Okay, so I'll give you the short version." Boner paused, thinking where to begin, then continued. "You see it all started a few thousand years ago when I pissed off a few Greek gods."

"Ho chi mama. Thousands years. Dat dun soun so chort to me."

"We Greeks were at war with the Romans and my brother and I... You met him in LA, Sammy Kuester, the older Sammy Kuester. His Greek name is Xanthos and mine is Balios. Our father named us after the two immortal horses that pulled the chariot of Achilles."

"Chur papa nemmed chu after a horse? I thin maybes chur papa hees no like chu too much."

"Actually it was quite an honor," replied Boner.

"I dun thin so. Es chu ever smell a horse?"

"Well anyway, my brother and I were Greek sailors and were responsible to guide a great warship in a great sea battle. In the midst of battle I was ordered to steer and ram our ship into the command vessel of the Romans which would have sunk her and given us a sure victory, but as we bore down on the Roman ship my brother was shot by an arrow and fell overboard. I love my brother and couldn't let him die so I jumped off the ship and saved him but my abandonment of our ship's rudder caused it to turn and run aground and so we lost the battle."

"Hokay, I'n no makin' no connections here. So es all dis stuff when chu was taken by dem aliens?" asked Chi Chi.

"Oh no," said Boner. "That was a couple thousand years later. That's another story altogether."

"Oh," said Chi Chi. "Hokay."

"Well, to make this long but short story even shorter, the Greek Gods were pretty pissed off and blamed my brother and I for losing the war and so they banished us from Greece forever and cursed us to a thousand year sleep followed by eternal life."

"Hey, that doesn't sound so bad," said Roachie.

"Well, actually it is, especially after the first couple hundred years of eternal life when you outlive all your friends and lovers and children. After a while you just sort of... well, I guess you turn into me and become whoever you want to be whenever you want. When you've been everywhere and seen it all and done it all and material things just don't mean much any longer you sort of turn life into a kind of game just to keep your sanity, all the while trying not to get too close to anyone because you know that you'll lose them. That's the real curse. It gets complicated. Centuries of life can be cruel. Sometimes I'm not sure who I am anymore."

"Wow, that's sad," said Bean.

"So all those family pirates and Arlen the movie star and other people over the years were you?" asked Roachie, "Even all three Applegates?"

"So many I can't even remember them all."

"Holy cow, talk about a generation gap," said Roachie.

"An dass why dat leetle tiny witchy woman calls chu da *ancient mariner?*"

"Yep, sailed all around the world. But now there's hope. My brother found out how to beat the curse which is why he was so old, and I think I might be close to doing the same thing," said Boner, putting his arm around Chi Chi.

"Dat all soun pretty whacko to me," said Chi Chi. "Buh I thin I ly chu anyways."

Bean looked at the cozy couple, drawing the obvious conclusion. "I guess you two will be heading back to Key West?" he said, sounding a little sad with the idea of losing his friends.

They smiled and nodded a yes. "But don't worry. We'll keep in touch," said Boner. "Besides I'm your lawyer now."

"And mine," added Roachie.

"An me too," said Chi Chi. "Buh I dun know wha for yet."

They had been there for most of the night and the fire was burning dim. It was the darkest part of the night just before the dawn and soon the sun would be pushing up over the far horizon and would wake the sea, bringing it back to life along with everything that lived near.

"How ya'll doin?" came the friendly voice of a man strolling along alone in the darkness. He was an older man, with a well worn and faded tan cap over a balding head showing gray hair on the sides, a blue T-shirt, tan shorts, and sandals. Aviator glasses hung comfortably around his neck. "Nice night isn't it?"

"Yes sir. Very nice," said Bean, squinting into the darkness. He couldn't see the stranger's face but judged by the sound of him that he was a nice man.

"Mind if I join ya?"

"No sir," replied Bean.

"I used to do this a lot, all-nighters on the beach with a fire and good friends, I mean. Nothing like spending time with good friends," he said as he sat on the sand next to Bean who sat staring into the dull nearly defunct embers. "A wise little lady back home once told me that and she was right. Yep, me and a few good friends had us some all-nighters right here on this very same beach as a matter of fact, back when I used to live around here. Say didn't there used to be a little cottage right there with some hippie girl living in it?"

"Yes sir," said Bean.

"Yeah, I remember her. Pretty little thing. Used to dance in the surf and talk to the seagulls," said the man as he looked around then looked to the sea. "Sun's gonna come up soon. Always catch the sunrise on the beach when I visit. Nice."

"Yes it is," agreed Bean.

"But some folks say sunset on the beach is the best time," said Boner.

"Maybe," said Bean. "Sun sets are nice but I think sunrise is the best time. Sunset is when this old world and everything in it quits because it's all tired and worn out and needs to rest, but the sunrise is special. It comes up slowly on the horizon and everything gets bright and warm and renewed with energy. That's when everything starts all over, fresh and clean and new. If you listen real close it's like a symphony is what my mom said once. I think it's like music of the soul. It's magic and there's nothing like surfing at dawn."

" Ya know, I think you're right, son. Of course ya gotta be straight and sober to enjoy it, and some of those all-nighters we had... well...," he laughed, "I won't mention those times."

"I can see it now," said Bean. "The sun I mean. See out there, out there on the horizon. See that dim red glow. It'll grow soon, slow at first and then spread and then get orange then yellow until it's above the sea where it will turn bright and light the sky. Like a good friend who's always there each day, keeping us safe and warm."

"You sound like a true sailor poet my friend. You should put those words to music some day," said the stranger as he rose to take his leave. "Well, guess I better be goin'. Got a plane to catch. Just came to town to visit some old friends who are waitin' for me up the beach there. Always like to visit my old beach when I'm here. Good to remember where you've been, good for the soul if ya know what I mean."

"Nothing like good friends," said Bean with a smile as he looked to his friends next to him.

"Yep, looks like you've got a few right here. You folks have a good day now, ya hear?" said the stranger as he walked away into the darkness.

"Nice guy," said Roachie, staring into the fire.

"Yeah," agreed Boner. "What'd he say his name was?"

"Oh, I forgot to ask. Too tired to think right, I guess," said Bean. "Sorry."

Sometimes I think you guys just don't have a clue, thought Fruitcake as he rolled over just long enough to scratch behind his missing ear, then rolled back on his back, balls to the stars.

A short time later when the embers were burned down into dull coals and the light from was stretching across the horrizon, Bean and his friends had their attention drawn to the sea beyond the mild surf that came with a beautiful sunrise. They first heard the rumble of the engines then saw the white chubby Grumman HU-16 Albatross sea plane lift off and take to the sky. When it cleared the water, gained a few hundred feet of altitude and came parallel to where they were sitting on the beach the pilot saluted them by rocking the seaplane's wings.

"What was that for?" asked the man in the co-pilot's seat."

"Oh, I'm just sayin' goodbye to some friends I met down on the beach there," said the pilot as he slipped on his aviator shades and smiled, "Now what ya say we fly this big bird on home?"

"Sounds good to me, JB."

The plane banked and turned away from the coast toward the rising sun. As it did the morning light shimmered along the sleek aerodynamic lines of the aircraft to finally catch and illuminate the big round Margaritaville logo on its tail.

Epilogue

Boner (Balios) Jones retrieved the documents of ownership of Key West island from a secret vault in the basement under his old house where they had been safely hidden along side his massive centuries- old pirate's treasure. The law firm of Applegate, Applegate, & Applegate represented Boner and argued the case of ownership of Key West against the State of Florida and the United States, taking the challenge all the way to the U. S. Supreme Court and winning. Rather than take possession of the island Boner instead agreed to accept compensation in the form of one-billion tax free dollars and exemption from paying taxes for the rest of his life. He then used the money and prominence gained from the court action to launch a successful political career as a Tea Party Independent in the United States Senate where he initiated numerous investigations to expose and make known the existence of a secret Alien *Fourth Branch* of government.

Rochier (Roachie) Rogers salvaged his research and development corporation and filed more than 12,000 new patents, becoming a very, very... very rich man. In partnership with Boner Jones and Bean Buffett they formed the *Roadtrip Investments Corporation* and due to Boner's excellent thousand-year experienced eye for good investments, had become exceptionally wealthier than they already were. With the assistance of the law firm of Applegate, Applegate, & Applegate they became the major stockholders of a number of large corporations such as Microsoft, Google, and Facebook. Rochier Rogers was also credited with developing the technology used to expose members of the mysterious Alien Fourth Branch, which included among many other prominent government figures: Representative Nancy Pelosi, Senator Harry Reid, former Vice President Al Gore, Secretary of State Hillary Clinton, and President Barack Obama. Roachie also purchased a new custom luxury Airstream trailer where he often withdraws to listen to Jimmy Buffett music and enjoy the product of his latest acquisition, the company that produces Yoo-hoo. On the wall in his impressive executive office is a framed cardboard sign that reads, "WILL WERK 4 FUDE", a reminder of what once was and never again should be.

Corena Maria Christina Gertudis de Avellaneda (Chi Chi) received an offer to sign a three movie deal with Universal Studios after they saw and read about her in Surfer Magazine. However, with the assistance and management of the law firm of Applegate, Applegate, & Applegate as her agent she instead did a screen test and signed an extremely lucrative deal with Sammy Kuester's Westcal Studio, becoming a major *moofy* star. (after extensive speech lessons of course) She is known best for her Oscar winning role as the beautiful, sexy, sharp-witted, and sophisticated lawyer in the movie *Maria for the Defense*, and as the swashbuckling Spanish diva pirate adventurer in Boner Jones' *Cayo Hueso Productions* of the feature film series *Daughter of the Ghost Pirate*. She and Boner married, had four children and live in Key West.

James William (Bean) Buffett Jr. purchased an island in the South Pacific where he currently resides with Fruitcake in a small purple, green, and yellow cottage, which includes a hammock and a papa-san chair. He surfs nearly every day and cooks his own Creola. Once each year Bean hosts his own three day Parrothead Festival with the furtive hope that someday his father will attend. Each year in attendance are

433

many of his good friends and their guests, including: the Dawn Patrol Surf Natives of Sebastion Inlet, the 3Js and the Los Hermanos Cubanos Para La Libertad, what's left of Sammy Kuester's Hollywood Hooters, Uncle Joe the bartender, Roachie with his security detail and senior staff, and of course Boner and Chi Chi Jones. On karaoke day when Bean sings the entire litany of Jimmy Buffett songs he is always backed up by the good Sisters of the Southern Society of Unwed Nuns of the Universal Church of Maternity. And though he doesn't know it, Bean has in fact achieved Sister Moonbeam-Goom-jigi's final wish.

Fruitcake never learned how to read but did discover audio books. When he isn't surfing with Bean he spends much of his time lying on his back in his new papa-san chair, balls to the sun, listening to cheesy novels about cannibals and detectives.

On the island is a large sign that was placed there at Fruitcake's insistence. It reads,

WARNING!
NO FAT MEN, PIRATES, OR PRIESTS
WITH GUNS PERMITTED

Oh yeah, as for the *Celestial Rockit*? Well, it's now one of the most visited displays of all time where it sits in the Smithsonian Institution Museum of Modern History after becoming a national icon while appearing in a movie called *Searching for Jimmy Buffett*.

AND THAT'S THE END
"DUDES"

about the author

Frank Mosco began collecting awards for writing while still in high school, then again as a journalist in college where he majored in Broadcast Management & Media. He went on to produce material for all forms of media as a reporter, columnist, producer, director, and photographer as well as media and communications work for the Federal Government. His writing coupled with his business management and retail experience led him to form his own advertising & promotions agency where his work netted two Addy Award nominations for overall multimedia campaigns and another for print media. Preferring the life of an independent however, he eventually returned to freelance writing and photography.

Frank is a native of Annapolis, Maryland, and after many years on the beaches of Florida which has influenced a number of his books, he now resides and writes near the waters of the Chesapeake Bay in Virginia where he produces mostly fictional novels of which he says, "...*can be just as strange as reality but far more convenient and definitely more fun.*" "*And,*" says the author, "*I've always lived with one foot in the ocean and one in the clouds, all the while hoping like hell that the pelicans in between have good vision.*"

www.ingramcontent.com/pod-product-compliance
Lightning Source LLC
Chambersburg PA
CBHW071143020726
47502CB00002B/242